A MOTHER'S SACRIFICE

Kitty Neale was raised in South London and this working class area became the inspiration for her novels. In the 1980s she moved to Surrey with her husband and two children, but in 1998 there was a catalyst in her life when her son died, aged just 27. After joining other bereaved parents in a support group, Kitty was inspired to take up writing and her books have been *Sunday Times* best-sellers. Kitty now lives in Spain with her husband.

To find out more about Kitty go to www.kittyneale.co.uk.

By the same author:

Nobody's Girl
Sins of the Father
Family Betrayal
Desperate Measures
Lost and Found
Forgotten Child
Lost Angel
Mother's Ruin
A Father's Revenge
A Broken Family
Abandoned Child
A Daughter's Disgrace
A Family Scandal

KITTY NEALE

A Mother's Sacrifice

Avon
A division of HarperCollins*Publishers*
1 London Bridge Street,
London SE1 9GF

www.harpercollins.co.uk

This Paperback Edition 2017
1

Copyright © Kitty Neale 2017

Kitty Neale asserts the moral right to
be identified as the author of this work

A catalogue record for this book is
available from the British Library

ISBN-13: 978-0-00-819167-2

Typeset in Minion by Palimpsest Book Production Ltd, Falkirk, Stirlingshire

Printed and bound in Great Britain by
Clays Ltd, St Ives plc

MIX
Paper from
responsible sources
FSC™   FSC™ C007454
www.fsc.org

For my Mum.

To the most amazing and inspirational woman I have ever known. You have always been there for me to share my tears and my joys and have offered unconditional love and support throughout, without which I may have floundered. You have my greatest admiration and respect, and leave me in awe of your strength. You have given me life and opportunity, and I thank you for everything. I love you xxx

Part 1, 1947

Chapter 1

Battersea, London, 1947

'Glenda!' The front door flew open and Glenda Jenkins tensed as she heard her husband shout.

'Get your glad rags on, we're going down the Castle. Alfie Ledger's missus had a boy last night. We're gonna wet the baby's head.'

Glenda pulled the covers over Johnnie, tucking him into his crib. At seven months old, he was teething and it made him tetchy, so she didn't want to wake him and drag him out in the damp evening air to Harry's parents' house. She hated going to the pub too, but knew it would be useless to protest. Anyway, it sounded like Harry was in a good mood and she dared not rile him.

She took a deep breath and moved her slim frame to the top of the stairs as she called down, 'All right, love, just give me a few minutes. Have you checked with your mum that it's OK to drop Johnnie in?'

'No, but you know she loves having the little munchkin. Just get a move on, will you? We're missing valuable drinking time.'

Glenda sighed heavily again. It was Thursday, Maude's

Tombola night at the Catholic church, so she might not want to look after her grandson. But Glenda was used to Harry barking his orders, and when Harry said jump, she knew better than to argue. She would take Johnnie's bottles and formula for Maude to make up. Once again, she felt a familiar surge of guilt that she'd been unable to breast-feed.

Quickly slipping off her housecoat and smoothing down her drab dark-green dress, Glenda checked her reflection in the bedroom mirror. She was twenty-four and her long legs would have looked good in one of those fashionable new knee-length skirts, but Harry wouldn't let her have one as he said only tarts and whores wore them. She would have loved a smart jacket with shoulder pads too, but Harry said that big shoulders were for men, not for decent wives and mothers. Anyway, with clothes still being rationed, and only stuff made of cheap, scratchy material available, she'd have to make do with what she had.

Content with her dress, she patted her brown hair, wrapped a scarf over her waves and tied it under her chin before leaning in closer to the mirror to apply a touch of lipstick. Damn it, she thought as she noticed the yellowing mark still visible on her jaw. Harry rarely hit her on her face but his violence seemed to be escalating and last week, after a skinful of beer, he had come home the worse for wear and woken her, dragging her out of bed to warm up his dinner. She had thrown it away earlier, thinking he wouldn't want it, but that had been the wrong thing to do. She had paid for her mistake with several blows to the head.

* * *

When they entered the smoky pub, Harry steered Glenda towards the saloon bar where several of his mates' wives were already sat. Before the war women weren't seen in London pubs, but things were changing and, as long as you were escorted, it was now acceptable to be in the saloon bar. A cheer went up from the group of men. 'Look, Harry's here!'

'All right, lads, where's the proud new father?' Harry said, smiling as he greeted his mates. 'There he is. Alfie, my old mucker, let me get you a drink.'

Glenda stood back shyly, her head lowered as Harry summoned the barman and ordered a round of drinks for everyone. His generosity and popularity had once been attractive to her, but now she worried as she saw the rent money going over the bar.

'Glenda, hello, love. How are you? I ain't seen you in ages!'

Glenda looked up and inwardly cringed. It was Betty Howard, the last person she wanted to be seen with and the biggest gossip in Battersea. If you wanted something known locally, Betty was the person to tell. She was also the most gossiped about and had worked in the local greengrocer's since she was fifteen. Though she was nice looking and had dated most of the men in the area, Betty was still single and known to be flighty. Harry had come home only yesterday and said that Betty had her eye on Billy Myers now. Apparently she had turned up at the old bombsite on Lavender Hill which was now a building site and brought sandwiches for Billy. All the workmen had had a right laugh about that.

'Oh, hello, Betty,' she said. It wasn't in her nature to snub anyone. 'Yeah, I'm fine, thanks. I've been busy with little Johnnie lately. He's teething at the moment; you know how it is.'

'Well, not really,' Betty answered as she drank her gin and tonic. 'I've not had much experience with babies but you never know . . . I'm hoping Billy Myers will be coming in later. You know him, don't you? He works as a labourer on that site where your Harry is. He's a bit of all right, I must say! Tell you what, your Harry reminds me a bit of Billy, both with their dark hair and stocky build. I do like a muscly man, what about you? Here . . . have you tried gin with this Schweppes stuff? It's ever so ladylike, don't you think?'

Glenda looked at Betty, rather bemused. Blimey, she thought as the woman jabbered on, but thankfully, before she had a chance to engage in too much conversation, the pub door opened again and Billy Myers walked in, bringing with him a blast of chilly autumn air.

Betty spotted her target instantly and sashayed towards the door, wiggling her hips in her satin skirt. Glenda admired Betty's outfit and wondered how she had come to own such a garment, what with the shortage of clothing. Betty was brave to wear it in here, she thought.

Harry appeared at Glenda's side and handed her a small sherry. 'Look at that bloody tart,' he said, nodding towards Betty and Billy.

'Yeah, she came in on her own and it's disgusting,' said one of the wives who was just passing them and had overheard Harry's remark. 'I wouldn't walk into a pub, saloon bar or not, without my husband.'

'You never know,' Glenda said with a smile, 'Betty might have one soon. They might find true love together.'

'Don't be daft, woman! She'd eat Billy alive. I've never

seen him with a girlfriend. I doubt he would know what to do with one.' Harry laughed and went back to join his mates.

Glenda sipped her drink. She hated the taste of alcohol but Harry would insist she drank with him when they were out. She glanced around the crowded bar, but her eyes were soon drawn back to Betty who was now draped over Billy, crooning something in his ear. Billy looked up and his eyes met Glenda's. He held her gaze and she shifted uncomfortably, quickly averting her eyes back to the floor. There was something about him that she really didn't like.

Billy Myers had been disappointed when he walked into the Castle and saw that Betty was there. He'd known she would make a beeline for him, and he would have to suffer the mocking and jibes of his mates at work tomorrow. But his disappointment had been short-lived when he had set eyes on Glenda Jenkins.

He wondered what Glenda saw in Harry, thinking what a lucky bugger the man was. Yes, Harry was flash with his cash and always held centre stage in a crowd, but Billy had seen the darker side of him. He knew that Harry could pack a punch and had no qualms about hitting a woman. Before Harry had married Glenda, Billy had witnessed Ruby Edwards take a beating when she had thrown his engagement ring back at him, yet somehow the woman had remained silent and Harry had got away with it. And Glenda's so quiet, Billy thought. I bet she never complains if he does knock her about.

As Betty rubbed her hand up his back, Billy caught sight of Glenda looking at him with her dark eyes. He quickly took Betty's arm and thrust it to one side in the hope that Glenda didn't think he was interested in the old trollop. How could he be attracted to someone like Betty? She couldn't hold a candle to Glenda. Glenda was a proper lady, she had class and she'd even kept her lovely figure after having the baby.

'What's the matter, Billy, don't you wanna buy me a drink?' Betty whispered. 'I'm terrible when I'm tipsy, you know. I just can't control my urges . . . and another drink might make me a bit tipsy.'

'Yeah, all right, I suppose. Later though,' Billy abruptly answered as he stared at Glenda. The last thing he wanted was to get lumbered with Betty and her 'urges'.

Glenda was looking at the floor again. Probably embarrassed that I caught her checking me out, thought Billy. He wanted to approach her, offer to buy her a drink, but Harry was close by and always kept an eye on his wife. It wasn't worth the risk, but he would bide his time. He knew Glenda would be going down the high street then up to the Latchmere baths on Wednesday morning. She always did, like clockwork. He could throw a sickie and accidentally bump into her. Could he get away with yet another sickie, though? He'd taken quite a few in the last couple of months but it'd been worth it; it had given him the opportunity to follow Glenda around and work out her routines. Now all he had to do was get her alone.

'Oi, Billy,' Harry shouted across the bar. 'Come and toast Alfie's little 'un . . . if you ain't too busy with Betty!'

'Leave it out, will you,' Billy replied, laughing as he sauntered over to his friends, not looking back to give

Betty a second glance. 'To Alfie –' he raised his pint of beer '– and whatever he calls his new nipper.'

It was almost closing time and Glenda was pleased when the bell rang out for last orders. She stifled a yawn, not wanting to appear bored whilst sat in the company of two of Harry's friends' wives. They were nice enough women, but all they talked about was the continuing food rations and the war years. Glenda would have loved to chat about the new Gracie Fields song she had heard on the radio, or ask them whether they preferred Frank Sinatra to Bing Crosby.

An old boy in a flat cap with a pipe hanging from the side of his mouth was tinkling away on the piano in the corner. Glenda closed her eyes, lost in her own world as she listened to the tune of 'If You Were the Only Girl in the World'. Suddenly she was brought back to reality by rough hands pulling at her arms and the tempo of the piano changed to a more upbeat 'My Old Man Said, "Follow the Van"'.

'Come on, darling. Have a spin with your old man.'

Harry was tugging at her, trying to get her up to dance with him.

'No, Harry. Stop it. I don't want to dance,' Glenda tried to whisper to him, but it was no use. She was on her feet now, with Harry clumsily whisking her around the floor. 'Harry, please stop. You're showing me up.'

'All right, all right,' said Harry, finally letting her go. 'If you don't wanna dance with your old man, that's fine by me.' Harry looked at his mates and laughed as he walked back to the bar. 'Bloody woman's got two left feet anyway and I ain't got me work boots on.'

Glenda was left standing in the middle of the room, all eyes on her. She felt her cheeks flame as Harry's friends joined him in laughter, except Billy, who was leaning against the bar, staring intently at her again.

She ran to pick up her coat and dashed to the exit, glad to feel the breeze outside cooling her cheeks. She took a cigarette from her small, round clasp handbag, lit it and drew in a long, grateful breath. Harry didn't like her to smoke, especially in public, but he was drunk again and she reckoned he wouldn't notice.

But just then the door swung open and she looked up to see her husband walking towards her.

'What have I told you about smoking?' He glared at her, snatched the cigarette from her mouth and angrily threw it to the floor. Then he grabbed her arm and marched her off down the road towards home, her chunky sensible heels furiously snapping on the pavement.

'But what about Johnnie?' Glenda asked as they crossed the top of the street where Maude and Bob lived. She was anxious to collect her son from Harry's parents, even though it was late.

'Don't worry about him. Me mum would have put him in bed with her by now so you can pick him up in the morning,' Harry growled. Glenda swallowed; she feared she was about to feel the brunt of his anger yet again that night.

Bloody woman showing me up, thought Harry as he slammed the front door of their two-up, two-down terraced house. How dare she walk off like that and have the audacity to say *I* was showing her up! He stormed into the small living room, throwing his ex-army overcoat over the back of their threadbare winged armchair whilst Glenda went through to the kitchen.

'Glenda! Where are you?'

Glenda appeared in the doorway. 'I'm just about to put the kettle on. Do you want a cup of cocoa?'

'No, I don't! I want to know what your bloody game is.'

'Game . . . I–I don't know what you mean,' Glenda answered, her voice sounding shaky.

Harry took three swift steps forward until he was face to face with his wife. She's not fucking stupid, he thought.

'You know exactly what I mean,' he said as he grabbed her around her neck with one of his large, calloused hands. The force he used caused Glenda to stagger backwards but still Harry held on, pushing her up against the wooden door of the under-stairs hallway cupboard. 'Don't you ever leave the pub like that again.' He squeezed her neck tighter. 'And showing you up, eh. Me showing you up! It was the other way round, woman, and I ain't standing for it!'

He lifted his other hand, slapped her hard across her cheek and for a moment she closed her eyes, but when she opened them again to look back at him Harry could see there were no tears, just a look of defiance which he took as a challenge.

'You fucking bitch,' he spat, remembering how he had noticed her looking at Billy Myers. 'Fancy that Billy, do you?'

'No . . . Harry, please. Don't be silly. Of course I don't.'

'Silly . . . So I'm *silly* now, am I?' Without further thought Harry released her neck to punch her in the stomach, and Glenda fell to the floor. 'Now who's silly, eh?' Harry snarled as he kicked her in the ribs. 'Get up and get up them stairs. I'm telling you, woman, you had better behave yourself in future. You're my wife! Mrs Harry Jenkins, and don't you bloody forget it!'

Harry stood back as Glenda scrambled to her feet and ran for the stairs, clutching her belly. The hallway was normally dark, but now it was well illuminated by the lights from the kitchen and living room. Huh, Harry thought, I bet she turns the tears on now.

He held on to the wall as he swayed behind her, slowly stumbling up the stairs. When they were in bed he would have his husband's rights. Harry grinned to himself as he made his way into the bedroom; at least he never suffered from brewer's droop.

The alarm clock rang out at six o'clock in the morning. Glenda was already awake, her back to her husband and the covers pulled up tight under her chin. Her side hurt so she tried not to move too much, but she knew she'd have to get up to make Harry his morning cup of tea and pack some Spam sandwiches for his lunch. She felt a moment of resentment at the thought of having to do anything for him after what he had inflicted on her last night.

Oh, he would be sorry today, probably bringing her some cheap flowers and promising her he would never hurt her again, yet it was always the same – good behaviour for a week or two until he'd have a drink and she would become his punchbag.

Last night he had gone too far. The kick to her ribs had damaged her, possibly cracking a bone or two, and, as she had laid in bed sobbing with the pain, Harry had forced himself on her, disregarding her discomfort and ignoring her pleas to stop.

'Argh,' Harry grunted now as he slammed his hand down on the alarm clock. 'My head's banging and I think the tooth fairy shat in my mouth in the night.'

Glenda remained motionless, waiting for Harry to go to the bathroom before she would get out of the bed.

'Sod these mornings,' he moaned, throwing his legs over the side of the bed, 'it's freezing and more like winter than autumn.' He turned and shook Glenda's hip. 'You awake?'

'Yes,' she answered through gritted teeth.

'You gonna get up and put the kettle on then?'

Without answering, Glenda winced as she slowly climbed out of the bed and made her way downstairs to the kitchen. As she stood on the cold linoleum, staring at the kettle waiting for it to boil, she gently rubbed her aching ribs and wondered what had happened to the charming man she had married three years earlier. The one who had lavished gifts on her and made her feel so safe and secure in his muscular arms. Harry used to make her laugh so much that her sides hurt. Yet now her sides hurt for a very different reason.

She had loved Harry so much when they'd first met, but now, instead of adoration, Glenda found herself contemplating how she could ever get out of this situation. It was impossible of course. She had little Johnnie to think about and nowhere to go. Her parents couldn't help, and even if she left, Harry would easily track her down to drag her back home. He would never let her go, and, with no other choice but to stay with him, she felt trapped – trapped with a man who was growing more and more violent.

The kettle whistled on the gas stove as Glenda feared that one day Harry would send her to an early grave.

Glenda turned the corner onto the street where her in-laws Maude and Bob lived. As she looked down the row of little terraced houses, she thought how all the streets around here looked the same, apart from the Latchmere estate with its impressive five-storey tenement blocks. Maude had said she wouldn't mind living in one as the views would be spectacular, and they would have an indoor lavvy. But the idea of living up high didn't appeal to Glenda, and she was lucky as her street was more up to date so they all had bathrooms inside, with electric geysers for hot water.

As was usual at this time of the morning, housewives in their housecoats, cardigans, curlers and scarves were busy outside, cleaning their doorsteps and enjoying neighbourly natters. A few younger children were kicking balls across the street, wearing short trousers even though it was a nippy day. Glenda put her head down and paced towards Maude's house, hoping that none of the middle-aged busybodies would stop her for a chat. Her cheek was still puffy and she was running out of excuses to cover for Harry's violence. The women around here must think I'm so clumsy, she thought, hoping the embarrassing truth would never come out.

The worst thing was that everyone in these streets who knew her also knew her mother Elsie. She was a frail woman who had had Glenda late in life. The pregnancy and a traumatic childbirth had left her weak and sickly. In fact, Ted, her father, had said Elsie had never properly got over it. Her father was getting on in years too, so the last thing that Glenda wanted was to worry them both with her marital problems.

'Wotcha, Glenda,' Mrs Williams called from over the other side of the street, 'you look like you're in a hurry, love.'

'Oh, hello, Mrs Williams. Yes, just off to pick up little Johnnie. I can't stop, he's teething so I don't want to lumber Maude for much longer.' Glenda was pleased the woman was far away enough not to notice her swollen face.

'All right, dear. Give Maude my regards and say hello to your mum.'

Glenda hurried on, glad when she finally reached number 127 and could retreat inside, away from the prying eyes of the neighbours. She still had Maude to face, though. The woman was a godsend when it came to babysitting Johnnie, but Glenda had never really liked her.

Maude's door was painted red, a colour she must have got from someone doing a bit of black-market dealing, and it stood out from the others on the street which were mainly black or dark blue. The knocker and letterbox were both shiny brass and there was a white wire milk-bottle holder next to the pristine doorstep. The windows were always gleaming and Maude's net curtains were crisp white. Glenda inwardly smiled as she pictured what lay behind the ostentatious front door. The house was over-filled with crystal ornaments and carnival glass bowls, remnants of the Romany heritage that Maude strongly denied. But all the family had dark hair and swarthy skin and, although Maude tried to pass them off as Spanish, Harry had confided in Glenda about their real roots.

Maude greeted Glenda with a warm smile and ushered her up the hallway towards the small kitchen at the back of the house.

'Here's your little mite,' Maude said, beaming, 'snug as a bug in a rug. I put him in here next to the stove 'cos it's warmer. He's been as good as gold for his old Nan. He was a bit whiney this morning, but I rubbed a drop of whisky on his gums and he's been as happy as a sandboy.'

Glenda silently seethed. She hated that Maude would use her old-wives'-tale remedies on Johnnie and had asked Harry on many occasions to have a word with her. But Harry's response was always the same: it never did him any harm when he was growing up.

'Thanks, Maude,' Glenda answered, hoping she sounded sincere. 'You're so good with him. I don't know what I'd do without you.'

'It's just experience, my girl. When you've had four of your own, you know a thing or two about rearing the little sods! Cor, my Harry was a little tyke! He used to run rings round me. And you'd have thought that with him being the last born I would've known better. Anyway, sit yourself down. I'll make us a cuppa.'

Glenda was desperate to pick Johnnie up from his pram and hold his soft body to hers but she resisted, knowing that Maude would berate her for disturbing the child whilst he slept. Instead, she took her coat off and slowly eased herself onto one of the four wooden chairs.

'You all right there?' asked Maude, frowning as she looked at Glenda's discomfort.

'Yes, I'm fine, thanks, Maude. I just slipped getting out of the bath last night. Caught my side on the edge.'

Glenda could see Maude's disbelieving expression and knew she was going to get some motherly advice.

'If you say so –' Maude shook her head '– but I know that boy of mine has been at it again. I'm right, ain't I?'

'No, Maude, honest. He's been really good lately. He's hardly raised a hand to me since Johnnie's been born.'

'I don't believe you. Sorry, gal, but your puffed cheek tells me a different story. So come on, what happened this time?'

Glenda's heart sank. There was no hiding anything from this woman, but she would never give Glenda any sympathy. In fact, it was almost as if she blamed Glenda for Harry's outbursts.

'It was the usual thing, Maude, too much alcohol. It's always when Harry's had a drink, you know that. The rest of the time he's lovely, and he's so good with little Johnnie. I just don't know what to do.' A tear slipped down her cheek which she quickly wiped away, hoping that Maude hadn't noticed.

'Well, firstly, you can stop that snivelling. That won't do any good,' said Maude firmly as she stirred the tea cups. 'I've told you before, Harry's just like his father. My Bob tried putting me in my place, more than once in fact. But I showed him, waited for the bugger to fall asleep then hit him square in the face with me frying pan. Broke his nose, I did. And of course he couldn't tell his mates at the wood yard that it was a *woman* that did it to him. He made out he got jumped in the back alley by two big blokes. I told him, if he ever laid a hand on me again, I would cut his bloody knackers off.'

Maude paused for a moment, took a slurp of tea and said, 'You've gotta stand up to Harry. Show him you ain't no pushover. I know he can be a handful, he always has been, but I used to get the broomstick out to him when he was a nipper. I bet he would still bloody run now if he saw me with it.'

Maude began to chuckle, but Glenda couldn't find it in herself to laugh. Harry was nothing like his father as Maude had suggested. Bob was a quiet, gentle man whose only vice was his Saturday-morning flutter on the horses. Maude was a strong woman who ruled over him. Some would call him henpecked, but Glenda thought he seemed happy enough to do as he was told. Maybe because he liked a quiet life, one in which he didn't have to think for himself.

If anything, Glenda thought, Harry was more like his mother. Maude had raised her four boys in fear of the strap and had taught them to hit first and ask questions later. Out of all of Harry's siblings, Glenda had only met the eldest brother, Len, and his wife Connie. The other two brothers always seemed to be on the road somewhere or another. She had heard they were both prize bare-knuckle fighters, which unnerved her a little. Len seemed nice enough, though, albeit a know-it-all. She wasn't too sure about Connie. The woman came across as cold and stuck-up but apart from Christmas Glenda didn't have to socialise with them much.

Maude's family were tough and had a bit of a reputation. In fact, most of the women on the street only spoke to Maude out of fear and politeness rather than chatted because they liked her. She had caused many a fight in her younger days, slapping down any woman who even so much as looked at her the wrong way. And even now, in her later years, Maude was still a powerful force to be reckoned with, and her large frame meant she certainly had the strength to back up her fierce mouth.

'It's not as easy as that, Maude. He's too strong for me to fight back and I'm sure if I did I would end up twice as bad.'

'Well, if you ain't prepared to fight him, you've gotta stop giving him cause to hit you. What set him off last night? Something happen down the Castle, did it?'

Glenda paused to sip her hot tea. Was it her fault again? She had been a bit of a killjoy when Harry had wanted to dance. *And* she had run out on him. But all that about Billy Myers? Yes, she had looked over at him, not in that way of course, but Harry wasn't to know that. Maybe it *was* down to her. Harry always said she pressed the wrong buttons, just like last week with his dinner. Throwing good food in the bin, wasting his hard-earned cash. She hadn't wanted to make love last night either, but she knew it was her duty as his wife. Not that what Harry had done to her could be described as anything like making love, she thought, wincing at the memory.

'Maybe,' Glenda answered as she realised that by now she should know what her husband was like. She should be able to please him instead of continually making him angry. 'Now I think about it, Maude, maybe I was a bit moody last night. He was still out of order for hitting me, but I suppose I asked for it really.'

'There you are. You know what starts him off so make sure you don't do it again. Harry's a good man, Glenda. You could have done a lot worse. Blimey, when I think of all the girls that used to come sniffing round my doorstep for him. He was a bit of a catch, you know. And now look at him – working hard for you and Johnnie, doing that bricklaying in all weathers, and, like you said, he's a proper good dad. All right, so he likes a pint after work, but he bloody well deserves it after grafting all day. He doesn't smoke, he doesn't gamble and I know he wouldn't go chasing after any skirt. You've got a good 'un there, my girl. You've just gotta learn not to wind him up.'

'Thanks, Maude, I appreciate your advice, but please don't say anything to him about this. Like you say, I don't want to wind him up again.'

'Mum's the word!' Maude answered as she pursed her lips and pretended to zip them.

As she drained the last of her tea, Glenda thought about getting home and making sure the house was spotless for when Harry finished work, with fresh sheets on the bed, dinner on the table and her looking ravishing. She couldn't fight her husband, but she could make sure that she didn't give him a reason to knock her about again.

Chapter 2

Billy Myers pulled up the collar of his long trenchcoat, shielding his face from the chilly wind. He had been hanging around on the high street for nearly an hour, dodging anyone who might recognise him. After all, he couldn't risk it getting back to his foreman that he was well enough to go shopping but was too sick to work.

As he stamped his feet to relieve the numbness, he saw Glenda Jenkins standing at the crossing with her navy-blue pram loaded with bags. At last, he thought, pleased that his efforts hadn't been in vain. He had been looking forward to this moment since he'd seen her in the Castle a week before. He quickly darted into the ironmonger's shop and sneaked a look through the window, waiting for her to approach. Her head was lowered against the inclement weather and her shoulders hunched as she hurried over the crossing, but Billy's heartbeat quickened as he admired her long hair whipping at her face in the wind.

Just as she was about to pass the shop, he made a dash for the door. 'Hello, Glenda,' he said with a smile, trying to appear casual.

'Oh, hello, Billy.'

Billy noticed she didn't smile back at him but supposed it was because she was obviously in a hurry.

'You look a bit overloaded there,' he said as he pointed at the bags on the pram. 'Let me give you a hand. Where you off to? Washday at the baths?'

'Er, yes, I am, though I'm going to the butcher's first before the queue gets too long. Thanks, Billy, but I can manage.'

'Nah, come on, I'll take these for you.' Before Glenda could object further, he had grabbed the two large bags and was walking along beside her. 'It's a cold one today,' said Billy, furiously trying to find conversation. 'Winter will be here before we know it.' He had planned this moment all week since seeing Glenda in the pub, but hadn't thought about what he would say.

Glenda didn't answer. She just nodded as she looked ahead.

'How's the boy?' Billy asked, nodding towards Johnnie, who was sleeping soundly in the warmth and shelter of his pram.

'He's fine, thanks, Billy.' A few moments' silence fell as they arrived outside the butcher's to see that they'd made it ahead of the queue. 'Thanks for your help,' Glenda said, 'I can take it from here.'

'It's all right. I could do with getting out of this wind for a bit anyway.'

'There's no need, really. I don't wanna hold you up.'

She's always so polite, thought Billy before answering, 'You won't be holding me up. I've got plenty of time to kill this morning so don't worry about me. You just get what shopping you need and I'll carry these washbags for you.'

Billy smiled as Glenda sighed but entered the butcher's,

where a gust of wind was blowing sawdust around the floor. He stood awkwardly as she handed over her ration book and ordered her small piece of meat, then held the door open for her to leave. I'll show her I've got good manners too, he thought, doubting that Harry ever treated her like a proper lady. Judging by the remnants of a bruise on her cheek, it looked like he'd been knocking her about again.

As they headed up towards the public washhouse, the chilly breeze made Billy's eyes water. He would be glad to get to the baths and retreat from the horrid weather. His nerves were getting the better of him and he was finding conversation difficult to come by.

Finally they reached the Latchmere, and once inside Glenda removed her coat to drape it over the pram before donning a floral apron. She then took a stall and began to unload her sheets. Billy sat on a long wooden bench that ran down the length of the rear wall, enjoying the warmth of the steamy hall. He pulled his flat cap lower over his face and, as Glenda bent over to take washing from the bags, he watched and admired her pert backside. What I wouldn't do to get my hands on that, he thought, instantly feeling hot.

Johnnie stirred in his pram, letting out a small cry. Glenda abandoned her washing to see to her child. As she stood with Johnnie in her arms and her back turned, Billy carefully ambled towards her washbags, stealthily popped his hand in and quickly removed a pair of Glenda's knickers, which he stuffed into his coat pocket. As he felt the silky material in his hand, Billy found himself aroused at the fantasy that one day he would have his hands on Glenda's knickers while she was still wearing them.

Johnnie settled down and Glenda placed him back in his pram. 'Shouldn't you be at work, Billy?'

'It's me mum's legs, Glenda. They're up like balloons! She asked me to run a few errands for her so I've taken the morning off. Only thing is, I had to tell a bit of a porky to my gaffer. I couldn't tell him I was looking after Mum, so can you do me a favour and not mention to Harry that you've seen me today? Only him and my gaffer are pretty tight and I don't wanna get my cards.'

'Yeah, sure. I won't say anything. But shouldn't you be getting back to your mum?'

'Nah, she's all right for a bit. She was dozing off in her chair when I left so I don't really wanna go back now and disturb her. Tell you what, once you've done your washing, do you fancy a cuppa and a bun at them swanky tearooms up the Junction? My treat.' Billy salivated at the thought of a big, sweet cake, and who better to share it with than Glenda Jenkins! He hadn't planned on asking her out, but it had just sort of slipped out and now the idea was very appealing. And, he thought to himself, I bet Harry never takes her anywhere nice.

'Er . . . no, thanks, Billy. I've still got to go to the greengrocer's and then get home to sort Harry's tea out.'

Billy was disappointed, sure that she would have accepted his generous offer. 'Never mind,' he said, smiling at her. 'It was just a thought. Warm your cockles and all that. I'll tell you what then, I'll walk up to the shop with you and pick up the bits my mum wants.' Billy raised his eyebrows at Glenda expectantly, then instantly regretted his suggestion when he remembered that Betty Howard would be working in the shop.

'If you want,' Glenda replied, though Billy noticed that

she didn't seem very keen. Maybe she too was worried about Betty seeing them together.

Glenda walked as fast as she could along the bustling street, wishing to spend as little time as possible with Billy Myers. She felt uncomfortable with him at her side and wished he hadn't accompanied her to the shop, but she couldn't think of a way to get rid of him. It had been embarrassing in the baths with him hanging around. After all, it's not the sort of place you would expect to see a man. She had noticed some of the other washer-women whispering and tittering and had seen the disapproving looks, but what could she do? She didn't want to appear rude to one of Harry's mates.

Billy had taken her by surprise; she hadn't expected him to suggest they go for tea. She did love a nice pastry and the ever-so-posh tearooms served up the best cakes in the area, far better than the rock cakes she baked every Sunday morning (if she could get hold of the ingredients). Harry liked the tearooms too and once a month they would visit them together on a Saturday afternoon, Harry's way of spoiling her. Of course, Harry knew the girls who worked as waitresses and thanks to his cheeky grin and flirty banter he always got an extra slice of Victoria sponge on his plate. She could just imagine his reaction if he heard that she was in there with Billy Myers. And the girls in the shop would definitely tell him, that she was sure of.

The conversation with Billy felt fraught and though Glenda didn't like the man, he seemed lonely and she couldn't help but feel sorry for him. It was also good of him to take time off work to look after his mother, but

Billy obviously didn't know Harry very well. If he did, he would never have invited her to afternoon tea.

Once they got to the greengrocer's, Billy stopped in his tracks and rummaged through his pockets. 'I've only gone and left the list indoors,' he said, 'I'll have to pop home and get it.'

'OK, Billy. Thanks for your help. I hope your mum feels better soon,' Glenda replied as relief washed over her. Thank goodness he's finally going, she thought, but before he turned to walk away, Betty Howard pranced around the corner and glared accusingly at her.

'Fancy seeing you two here . . . together,' Betty sneered as she eyed Glenda up and down. 'There's me just finishing my fag break and look what I find.'

'Billy's mum is poorly,' Glenda explained, suddenly feeling guilty but not knowing why. 'He was on his way to get her some shopping and I bumped into him.'

'Oh, yeah,' said Betty, 'so how come she was in here early this morning, buying spuds for your dinner tonight, Billy?'

Glenda was taken aback. She couldn't think why Billy had lied to her. Unless of course, he was just skiving off work for no good reason. Now both women glared at Billy, waiting for him to answer.

'I . . . I . . . I dunno what you're on about. She must have felt better and popped out when I went to the post office for her.'

Billy didn't sound very convincing but Glenda found she didn't care. She didn't want to stand around in the cold wind to question him any further.

'Funny,' said Betty, 'she didn't mention anything.'

'What is this, the Spanish inquisition? What's it got to

do with you anyhow? Bugger this, I'm off!' said Billy as he turned on his heels and marched down the street.

'Wait, Billy,' called Betty as she rushed after him.

Glenda glanced back at the two of them as she entered the shop, and just caught sight of Betty tugging at Billy's arm. Good luck to them, she thought, then focused on what was needed for the larder at home.

It was half past seven that night when Glenda finally heard Harry's key in the front door. She rushed to the kitchen and, using a tea towel, took his plate from the oven which she'd set on low to keep his dinner warm. As she placed it on the kitchen table, Harry leaned against the door frame and she could tell from the smell of stale cigarettes and alcohol that he had been in the pub for a good few hours. Her heart sank. It had been such a good week together; the atmosphere had been light and cheery. Harry had even run her a hot bath before bed on two occasions, but as he walked towards the kitchen table with a scowl on his face, she dreaded his blackened mood.

'Hello, love. I've done you a nice bit of belly of pork, here you go,' said Glenda nervously. If he had knocked off work early and had a few, she didn't want to do or say anything to start him off.

'Where's my boy?' Harry asked as he sat at the table.

'He's tucked up in bed, fast asleep.'

'Put him to bed early, did you? Wanted him out of the way?' Harry was growling and Glenda felt her stomach tie in knots.

'What do you mean, Harry? He goes down at seven every night, you know that.' She tried to make her voice sound light, hoping it would placate him.

Suddenly Glenda heard the chair scrape back as Harry jumped to his feet. She watched in frozen horror as he lifted the dinner plate and threw it across the room, the china smashing against the wall just to the side of her head.

'Don't take me for a bloody fool, woman!'

Glenda could see gravy dripping down the wall, but was rooted to the spot as Harry upturned the kitchen table – the only thing standing between him and her getting another beating. There was no way she would be able to pass him to get to the kitchen door and, before she had a chance to dodge his grasp, Glenda felt her head tug back as Harry grabbed a handful of her hair.

'I know you've been with that Billy Myers today,' he hissed in her face. 'Betty couldn't wait to tell me!'

'I . . . he . . . I just bumped into him down the high street. That's all. He spoke to me and I couldn't just ignore him.' The pain in her scalp intensified as Harry clenched her hair tighter.

'What a load of crap! I've seen you looking at him. Off shopping together, were you? Has he been round here, in my house? IN MY BED? Is that why you've got Johnnie out of the way, so you can be with your fancy man?'

'No, Harry! I swear. There's nothing going on. I don't even like the man,' Glenda was squealing but, as she pleaded for Harry to believe her, he brought his fist down hard on her face. She felt her head swim then warm blood trickle down her cheek. She tried to focus but her right eye wouldn't open. Then she saw his fist coming towards her again and suddenly her legs went wobbly as the world faded out around her.

*   *   *

Glenda's head was throbbing as she tried to open her eyes. She could feel someone patting the back of her hand as a woman's voice slowly drifted into her consciousness.

'That's it, my dear, open your eyes. You're all right now. You're in hospital.'

Who was that talking to her? What did she say? I'm in *hospital*? Glenda's thoughts were confused. Bright lights blurred her vision as she lifted her other hand to her painful head and felt something wrapped around it. Bandages . . . Hospital . . .

'You took a nasty fall down your stairs. Don't worry, though. A few days' rest will sort out that bump and those bruises.'

'Johnnie . . . where's Johnnie?' Glenda managed to whisper. Her throat felt so dry and coarse.

'Is Johnnie your husband, dear? Don't worry, he'll be back later when it's visiting time. Lucky for you that he found you when he did. Now just you rest. I'll be back to check on you later.'

Glenda saw the figure of a nurse in a blue dress and white starched apron and hat get up from her bedside. She turned her head to the side and could see another bed a few feet away from her and one on the other side too. The nurse had said she had fallen down the stairs but although Glenda had taken a bash to the head, there was nothing wrong with her memory.

As she lay in the hospital ward, she recalled the moment when her husband had knocked her out cold. This time, his fists had finally knocked the love out of her too.

Chapter 3

Friends and relatives of the other patients buzzed around the ward as visiting time commenced. Some carried bags of fruit, probably late apples, and others had newspapers and magazines ready to greet their poorly loved ones with.

As Glenda lay in bed with the pillows plumped up behind her a little girl tiptoed past, holding her mother's hand. Glenda tried to raise a smile at the young child but found her face was too tender as a sharp pain shot through her jaw. She winced and noticed the little girl looking back at her with a look of dismay.

'Mummy, Mummy,' the girl cried loudly so that all in the ward could hear, 'look at that lady. Why does she look like a monster?'

Glenda was horrified. She hadn't seen her reflection in a mirror and had no idea what she looked like – did she look grotesque? Ashamed, she quickly pulled the bed covers high and painfully rolled to her side, trying to hide from prying eyes.

'Glenda, Glenda, love. It's me.'

Glenda recognised Harry's voice behind her at her bedside but was reluctant to turn over and face him.

'Look, I've brought you a lovely bunch of flowers. Chrysanthemums, your favourite.'

No, they're not, thought Glenda bitterly, daffodils or white lilies are my favourites.

'Here, love, I've got you a packet of Jaffa Cakes too. Don't ask me how I got hold of them,' he said, 'but I'd do anything for you, love.'

Who are you trying to kid? she thought, still unwilling to speak. It's him that loves them and I bet Maude got them from one of her many cronies. Oh, how bloody thoughtful! She wanted to tell him where to stick his flowers and Jaffa Cakes, but instead she reluctantly eased herself round to face him, desperate to know of Johnnie's well-being.

She heard Harry gasp as he saw the state of her face and the bandage wrapped around her head. From what the little girl had said, she knew it was bad. Her lips felt twice their normal size and she had felt with her tongue that two of her side teeth were missing. That's it, she thought, take a good look. You did this.

'Glenda, oh, baby, I'm so sorry. I can't believe I've put you in here,' Harry whispered. 'I bloody hate hospitals, the smell and all that. This place gives me the heebie jeebies so I won't stay long, but my mum will be up to see you later and I've had a word with the doc. He says you'll be out in a day or two. I promise you, I'll make it up to you then.'

He leaned in to kiss her cheek but Glenda turned her face away.

'Come on, girl, don't be like that. You know I didn't mean it. Look, I admit I went a bit too far, but you've gotta learn that you can't go running around the streets with a low-life like Billy bloody Myers! What do you reckon all the lads down the Castle think, eh? They've all heard about you and Billy, Betty made sure of that, and I can't have them thinking I can't control my own wife, now, can I? Come on, give your old man a kiss . . .'

Glenda could feel her temperature rising along with her anger. The selfish bastard, she thought, wanting to spit in his face rather than kiss him, but she forced herself to keep calm, still desperate to know about her baby.

'Where's Johnnie?' she asked curtly.

'With my mum, of course. I could hardly leave him with yours. The poor old girl can hardly put the kettle on by herself, let alone see to the boy.'

'And is he all right?'

'Course he is, but he'll be glad to get his mum home.'

'Can you ask your mum to bring him to see me?'

'Nah, she said it's best not to. There might be all sorts of germs and things in this place and we don't want him catching anything nasty. Now, how about that kiss?'

'Harry, can't you see it's painful for me to talk, let alone give you a kiss? Anyhow, I really don't feel like kissing you right now!' Glenda answered huffily through gritted teeth.

Lips tightening, Harry whispered menacingly, 'Stop being so bloody daft and just be grateful that I didn't leave you at the bottom of those stairs.'

'Stairs!' Glenda exclaimed, her voice getting louder. 'You and me both know that I didn't fall down any stairs!'

There was a bit of a scuffling noise behind Harry and he turned to see what was going on. Glenda noticed a hospital porter in a dark grey coat helping a woman in the next bed into a wheelchair.

'Keep your bloody voice down, will you!' Harry hissed

into Glenda's ear. 'If you say one word to any of this lot about how you came to be in here, I promise you, you'll regret it.'

Glenda held her breath, terrified by Harry's threat. She knew exactly what he was capable of now, and she had to stay strong for little Johnnie. 'OK, I promise. I won't say a word,' she said, her heart sinking. This was a fight she was never going to win.

Harry hadn't stayed long, much to Glenda's relief, and just as the final visitors were leaving the ward the woman who had been in the next bed returned with the same hospital porter wheeling her chair. As two nurses helped the woman back into bed, Glenda winced as she turned on her side again, not wanting to engage in conversation with anyone. Thankfully, whoever was in the bed to this side of her had their curtain pulled round, so at least Glenda felt she had a little privacy to cry in peace.

'Excuse me, Miss.'

Glenda turned to see who was addressing her now, assuming it must be a doctor, but was surprised to see the porter hovering close to her bedside.

'I just wondered if you'd like me to find a vase and some water for your flowers,' he said, indicating the chrysanthemums on her bedside cupboard.

'Oh, thank you. That's very kind of you,' answered Glenda, but in reality she didn't care if the flowers wilted and died.

'Back in a jiffy then,' said the man with a smile.

A few minutes later, true to his word, the porter was back at her bedside and was placing her flowers in the vase he had found.

'There you go, pretty as a picture.' He smiled at Glenda again.

She immediately noticed his piercing blue eyes that were emphasised by jet-black hair which he wore greased back.

'The flowers, I meant, not you . . . pretty as a picture. Oh, no, I mean . . . you are pretty as a picture, but I didn't mean that when I said pretty as a picture . . . but you are. I wouldn't want you to think I was being forward. I didn't mean . . .'

Glenda hid a smile. He was so nervous, but he was kind too, so she assured him, 'It's all right. I know what you meant, and thanks.'

'Sorry, I'll start again. Your flowers look as pretty as a picture. Did your husband bring them in for you?'

Glenda's momentary light mood rapidly darkened again at the thought of Harry. 'Yes, he did,' she answered, avoiding the porter's kind blue eyes.

'I thought he had. My name's Frank, by the way. I work here, across this and three other wards on this floor. Amongst other things I take patients to departments for X-rays and tests. I hope you don't mind me saying, but you looked a bit upset earlier when your husband was here.'

Glenda would have loved to tell Frank that her husband was a selfish, violent man and it was because of him that she was in this hospital bed, but with Harry's threat still ringing clearly in her ears she thought better of it. 'I'm just missing my little boy, that's all,' she lied instead.

'Only, from where I was standing, I was pretty sure he was warning you off about something.'

'No, not at all. Look, I don't mean to be rude, Frank,

but it's really none of your business,' Glenda answered, surprised that Frank had heard the conversation with Harry.

'Yeah, you're right. Sorry for sticking my nose in. I just don't like to see women getting knocked about. I saw my dad lay into my mum enough times when I was a kid and wished I had been older and big enough to stand up for her. But I wasn't. Thank God the old git is dead now, killed when a bomb landed on our house, but all the same I wouldn't want to see a bully like Harry Jenkins hitting a defenceless woman like yourself.'

'So you know my Harry, do you?' Glenda asked in surprise.

'Not as such, but I know of him. He was a few years above me in school, but even back then he was known for being a bit handy with his fists. I've got a list of all the patients on the ward and when I saw you was a Glenda Jenkins, I put two and two together.'

Glenda had always known that Harry had a reputation for being tough, but when she met him she hadn't known he was a bully. She used to like the way he would warn off other men that looked at her; it made her feel special. Unfortunately, she knew differently now.

'Frank,' she said, 'you seem like a nice man and thanks for your concern, but honestly you'd be well advised to keep out of Harry's business, especially where I'm involved.'

'You don't have to suffer in silence, Glenda. I'm just saying, if he's done this to you and threatened you to keep your mouth shut, you don't have to. I know what blokes like him are like and if you wanna talk, I'm happy to listen.'

But before Glenda could answer, a rotund woman

called out to Frank, 'Mr Myers, if you have quite finished with Mrs Jenkins, please make your way to ward seven.'

'Gotta dash.' Frank winked. 'Sister will have my guts for garters if I stand around here chatting much longer. See you later.' And with that he was gone.

Glenda lay gobsmacked. Sister had called him Mr Myers, but surely he couldn't be related to Billy Myers? She didn't know anything about Billy's family, and he had only ever mentioned his mother, but both he and Frank had black hair so maybe they *were* related in some way. Glenda closed her eyes, thinking that if Frank had anything at all to do with Billy, it was all the more reason why he should stay well clear of her.

The next morning, Glenda awoke early as nurses hustled back and forth medicating patients, and tea trolleys clattered up the stark ward. She longed to get home and see Johnnie, especially as Harry had said that Maude didn't think the baby should be brought to the hospital. She could understand why, and, not only that, but the state of her face would probably frighten the life out of him. Nonetheless, she missed her baby desperately and was eager to get out of there.

Visiting time seemed hours away, which was a relief to Glenda. She was worried that Maude might find someone to keep an eye on Johnnie and come visit her alone, and she wasn't up to facing the woman. It would mean yet another lecture about how wonderful her son was and how she should be grateful that he'd picked her to marry. And though she appreciated the fact that Maude was looking after Johnnie, she worried about the sort of food he would be given. Despite the shortages, Maude was fond of feeding him bread and butter dipped in sugar, insisting it was good for him, but Glenda feared that all that sugar would rot his new teeth that were just breaking through his gums. And the whisky, well, surely that wasn't healthy!

Frank's cheery voice suddenly snapped her out of her worrying thoughts. 'Good morning, Mrs Jenkins! I must say, you're looking a lot perkier today.'

'Hello, Frank. Thanks, yes, I'm feeling much better than I did yesterday. Obviously the bed rest and hospital food agree with me.'

'Glad to hear it, as I have a little treat for some of you lovely ladies today,' said Frank, smiling at several of the women in the surrounding beds.

'And what's that then, Frank?' a middle-aged woman called from across the ward.

'Well,' Frank answered, looking rather pleased with himself, 'Sister has agreed that as the weather has changed, an Indian summer making it warm for October, those that are feeling up to it can come on my voyage surprise. How about that then, ladies!'

'What the blinking 'eck is a voyage surprise?' asked the same woman.

'It's a film, a French one which I have on good authority was very funny when it was shown in Paris. Now in the meantime, my voyage surprise means I get to wheel you lovelies outside to the gardens for an hour. And look, I've got some old crusts for the birds.'

Glenda watched, amused, as a quiet cheer went around the small ward. Frank was certainly popular with the patients and had an ease about him that made you feel instantly comfortable.

'And what about you, Mrs Jenkins? Will you be joining us today?' he asked.

'Oh, I don't know, Frank. I don't think that will be such a good idea. What with Harry, you know,' Glenda whispered.

Frank stepped closer to her bed. 'Don't you worry about him,' he said with a grin. 'What he don't know won't hurt. Anyhow, it's Sister's orders so let Harry have it out with her if he dares!'

For the first time since being in hospital, Glenda laughed. Sister was quite a forbidding woman and Glenda couldn't see Harry arguing with her. In fact, she reminded Glenda a little of Maude.

'I'll take that giggle as a yes then,' said Frank and he turned, clicked his heels in the air and bid a 'see you all later' to the rest of the ladies on the ward.

Helen Atkins looked at the small bag of fruit in her hand. It wasn't much, but her part-time cleaning job didn't pay very well and the two apples were all she could stretch to. Still, she reasoned, Glenda had never really been one for fruit. She knew her friend well. They had grown up living next door to each other and had formed a very close bond.

The red double-decker tram left Battersea Junction and headed along Falcon Road towards the park. From there, Helen would walk to the Free Hospital and, although she was familiar with the area, she still loved to look out at the views from the top deck.

As the tram rumbled along the track, Helen rolled the paper ticket in her hand and remembered the last time she had been to this hospital. It had been when her father had had a funny turn, which turned out to be a stroke. He had been left disabled, and Helen now had to care for him as well as her mum, who sadly had a touch of dementia.

Helen didn't mind, though; she understood that it was difficult for her two elder sisters to help out much. After all, they were busy with their own families, and, although Helen doubted she would ever have children of her own, she did enjoy being her nieces' and nephews' favourite aunty.

The tram conductor called out the name of the next stop, jolting Helen out of her thoughts. She patted her mousy brown hair, which she wore in a very out-of-date bun, and checked her reflection in the tram window. A few years ago, she probably would have liked to be taller, slimmer and more glamorous, but, to be honest, she thought, what would be the point now? She was content with her short, round stature; it just made her more of a cuddly aunt. And at least she avoided the attentions of the local men, especially the likes of Harry Jenkins and his mates.

Helen shook her head at the thought of Harry Jenkins. If only Glenda had listened and not married the man. Helen had begged her not to but Glenda was blinded by love, and look where that had got her: in a hospital bed.

As she made her way through the hospital corridors to find the ward where Glenda's bed would be, her heart sank, dreading what sort of state she would find her best friend in. Maude had said that Glenda had fallen down the stairs and was apparently black and blue, but Helen knew the story was yet another cover-up for Harry's violence.

Helen turned the corner into Glenda's ward but immediately stopped in her tracks, recognising her friend despite her battered face. Although she'd been expecting a few marks, she was shocked by what she saw. The rotten bastard, she thought, seething. Harry was probably the only person in the world whom Helen truly hated.

'Helen . . .' Glenda sat upright in her bed as she called and waved across the ward.

'Hello, Glenda,' said Helen, her voice full of pity.

'Oh, Hel, take that look off your face, it's not as bad as it looks.'

It's worse, thought Helen, feeling at a loss for words. She had always believed the adage that if you can't say anything nice, then don't say anything at all. 'How are you?' she asked Glenda, thinking that was probably the stupidest question ever.

'I'm all right, thanks. I just wanna get home, I'm missing Johnnie so much. But what are you doing here? I didn't expect to see you! How did you know I was in here?'

'Slow down, love. I bumped into Maude and she told me about your "accident".'

'Oh, Helen, you didn't say anything to my parents, did you?'

'No, I guessed that as usual you wouldn't want them to know.'

'With my mum the way she is, my dad has got enough on his plate. Anyway, shouldn't you be at work?'

'I would normally be, but I took the morning off. You know Mrs Cooper who lives up the road from me? She always sits with Mum and Dad when I'm at work, but I told her I was popping up to see you and she was happy to stay at mine and keep an eye on them. Now, enough about me. What really happened, Glenda? You know I don't believe any of that codswallop about you falling down the stairs,' Helen said, her heart going out to her friend as tears welled in Glenda's eyes. Perhaps she shouldn't have been so direct with her, but it was time Glenda faced up to the truth once and for all.

'You know what Harry's like,' Glenda said as she wiped her eyes. 'He just went berserk. But he's gone too far this time and I've had enough! I just don't know what to do . . .'

At last, thought Helen, the woman has finally come to her senses and realised what a disgusting pig she's married to. 'You know exactly what you've got to do, Glenda. You have to leave him!'

'But it's not as simple as that. Think about it. Where can I go and what about Johnnie? You know if I stay in Battersea Harry will find me and my life won't be worth living. My only choice is to get well away from him, his family and the area. But how? I don't know anyone outside of London and I haven't got any money, Harry sees to that. I'm stuck, Helen, stuck with a man I don't love and don't feel safe with.' Glenda cried softly, big, fat tears rolling down her face and onto the crisp white bed sheets.

Helen rubbed her friend's arm. 'Don't worry,' she said soothingly, 'I'll help you think of something.' The two women sat in silence for a minute. In reality, Helen couldn't see a way out for Glenda either.

Once the morning visiting hour was over and lunch was out of the way, Frank returned to the ward, eager to take the patients out for their little treat. But really he wanted to spend a little more time with Glenda Jenkins. Her face was so swollen and one of her eyes almost completely closed, the skin around it black and purple, yet despite her awful wounds Frank felt drawn to her. He found her attractive and wanted to know more about her and her life. Why did she stay married to a man who could inflict such horrendous injuries on her? Surely it was out of fear, not love.

As he entered the ward, those that were able were sat on the edge of their beds, wrapped up in warm dressing gowns and ready for the off. But Frank immediately noticed that Glenda's bed had the curtain pulled around it. He panicked slightly, concerned that she had taken a turn for the worse, and hurried to speak to Mrs Fowler in the neighbouring bed.

'What's going on with Mrs Jenkins?' he quietly asked Mrs Fowler, not wanting to show the other patients that he had a special interest in Glenda.

'Well, the doctor has spoken to her and now I'm pretty sure the nurse is changing her bandages. They're giving her a bit of privacy on account of how she looks because she's asked to see in a mirror,' Mrs Fowler whispered back.

'That's going to be a bit of a shock for her,' Frank replied.

'From what I heard it seems she had a straight nose before she took the tumble. Shame, 'cos I think she's probably a very pretty girl under all them bruises, but she'll never have a smashing smile again, not with those couple of teeth gone!'

Frank was so shocked at the reality of Glenda's injuries

40

that he felt bile rise in his throat. It wasn't the broken nose or knocked-out teeth that sickened him. It was the fact that the man who was supposed to love Glenda and look after her could actually do such a heinous thing to her. He wondered what sort of monster this Harry Jenkins really was.

Suddenly, the curtain around Glenda's bed was pulled back and two nurses walked away into the ward. Glenda had obviously been crying but appeared to be composed at the moment, though she looked pale and wan. Probably from the shock, thought Frank.

He cautiously approached her side and saw the fresh bandages around her head. 'I'm sorry, Glenda. I can't believe he did that to you. It's a stupid question, but are you all right?'

Glenda's eyes were watery but at least her swollen one was beginning to open.

'He's mad, Frank. That's the only explanation I can think of. He's out of his mind. He must be or else how could he have been so brutal? But you know the funny thing?'

'No,' answered Frank, 'I can't think of anything funny at the moment.'

'The funny thing is, all I can think about is where the bloody hell has he put my teeth!' Glenda said and for a brief moment a small smile crossed her face.

Frank couldn't believe how resilient this woman could be. 'Well, it ain't all bad,' he said, trying to make light of the situation. 'You've got plenty of others in your mouth!'

But Frank's joke suddenly seemed in bad taste when Glenda's face fell and she burst out crying.

'I'm gonna look terrible, Frank. He's damaged me good

and proper this time. Look at my crooked nose! Oh, blimey, what if it scares my Johnnie?'

Frank wanted to take her in his arms, soothe her pain and tell her it would all be okay, but he knew he would be sacked for doing that. Instead, he looked her straight in the eyes.

'Look at me,' he said, pan-faced and very serious. 'No matter what that evil bastard has done to you, take it from me, Glenda Jenkins, you are still and always will be a beautiful woman. So what, you've got a bit of a bumpy nose and a couple of missing teeth. It ain't the end of the world. You still look like you. Of course you ain't gonna scare your little boy. But you've gotta get away from his father, Glenda. He's dangerous and you and Johnnie deserve better.'

Glenda had regained her composure and Frank hoped that what he'd said had made her feel a little better. He handed her a hanky from his trouser pocket. 'Dry your eyes, love, and let's get you out for some fresh air.'

Once outside in the hospital gardens, Frank handed out some stale bread from the hospital kitchens to a few of the women and soon a flock of sparrows were bobbing around the small group, along with a couple of pigeons.

Glenda was pleased to feel the warm sun on her face and thought how Johnnie would have enjoyed seeing all the chirping birds fluttering around.

Frank sat on a park bench beside her wheelchair.

'Penny for them,' he said gently.

'I was just thinking about my Johnnie. He always chuckles when he sees birds,' Glenda answered.

'Does he?' asked Frank. 'Well, then, once you get home,

I know a lovely little place we should take him to. You get all sorts of birds and wildlife there, lovely countryside, clean air, not like the dirty town pigeons and rotten air here.'

It sounded very inviting. Glenda would love to take Johnnie out to the country, but it was impossible with Harry the way he was. 'Frank, you know I couldn't, even if I wanted to.'

'I've told you, Glenda, you can't go back to living with that animal of a man. Look what he's already done to you, and what if it's worse next time? He could kill you and what about Johnnie then? Have you thought about that?'

'Of course I have,' Glenda answered, almost angrily, 'but I don't have any choice. I had this very same conversation with my friend Helen just this morning. Where would I go? What would I live on? Not only that, if I tried to leave Harry he would find me and then he'd definitely kill me.'

It felt hopeless to Glenda. She didn't want to go back home to a man she no longer loved, a man who now terrified her, but she'd thought about leaving him before and had come to the same conclusion. With no other choice she would have to stick it out – to placate Harry by being the perfect wife so he didn't lose his temper again. As Maude had said, sometimes it's better the devil you know – yet that thought didn't stop Glenda's shiver of fear at what the future might hold.

Frank had always enjoyed his job, and for the last week the thought of seeing Glenda had made it even more of a pleasure to go to work. He had been leaving home early and coming home late, just so that he could spend some extra time with her. But this morning he felt glum as he sat at the kitchen table and drained the dregs of his tea. Glenda was due to be discharged from hospital and he couldn't stand the thought of never seeing her again.

His brother Billy ambled into the kitchen and lifted the lid off the teapot.

'Huh,' he grumbled, 'you didn't bother saving me a cuppa.'

'Sorry, Billy, I didn't know you was up, and good morning to you too!' answered Frank.

'Good? What's bloody good about it? It's all right for you, drinking the last cup of tea and working in a warm hospital. What about me, eh, shovelling shit out there in the freezing cold? Still, least I've got a *real* job, not some poncy job like you.'

Frank rolled his eyes and ignored his brother's quips. He was used to hearing Billy dig at him whenever the opportunity arose and had learned a long time ago to turn the other cheek. It was much easier that way and saved their mother any upset. Frank could never understand why Billy seemed to resent him so much. It had been frosty between them for years and had started when they were kids, with Billy moaning about having to have Frank's hand-me-downs. It wasn't as if the boy never got anything new for himself, but he was always jealous of anything Frank had.

Frank left Billy to sulk at the kitchen table and made his way to the hospital. He had arranged to meet Glenda for the last time in the canteen before his shift started. He hoped he would have the courage to ask her out but was worried about what her reaction would be.

As he walked into the canteen, Glenda was already seated and greeted him with a beaming smile. The swelling on her lip hadn't quite subsided, which almost hid the gap where her teeth were missing, but Frank still thought she looked beautiful.

'Good morning. You don't 'alf brighten up a miserable day,' said Frank with a wink and he noticed that Glenda blushed.

'Morning, Frank. Is it miserable outside then?'

'It's a bit nippy but you'll find out for yourself soon enough. What time are you off?'

'Harry's coming for me at ten-thirty. I can't wait to see my Johnnie!'

'I bet you can't, and I bet he's missed his mum too. I got to say it, Glenda – I hope I never see you in here again.' He wanted to add that he would love to see her again somewhere other than the hospital, but the words stuck in his throat and he couldn't get them out. He could have kicked himself.

'I hope so too, Frank. This is the last place I ever want to be again, but thank you so much for being my friend in here. It's been good to have someone to talk to. I've never really told anyone about what Harry does to me. I suppose I've been too ashamed. You've been such a good listener and I've really come to trust you. I'll miss you.'

Frank reached across the table and took Glenda's hand. 'I'll miss you too,' he said. More than she would ever know.

Chapter 4

Harry shifted impatiently in the entrance of the hospital ward. Get a move on, he thought, as he waited for Glenda to gather her belongings.

Harry was pleased that his wife was finally coming home after nine days in the ward. He had missed her home cooking. He'd been at Maude's every night for his tea, but his mother wasn't nearly as good a cook as Glenda. And he missed her warm body in their bed at night. But right now he felt peeved that the hospital wouldn't release her without someone coming to collect her. It meant he had had to take the morning off work, which would give him a lighter pay packet at the end of the week, and he could really have done without that, especially as he had good reason to go out and celebrate tonight now that his wife was home.

'OK, Harry, I'm ready now,' Glenda said.

She does look a bloody sight, thought Harry, what with that thick lip and her purple eye. Gawd knows what people are gonna think when I get on the tram with her looking like that. Maybe I should have forked out for a taxi after all.

'Ain't you got no dark glasses or a big hat or something?

You look bloody horrible!' Harry barked at her, but as soon as the words were out of his mouth he reprimanded himself, remembering what his mother had said. Maude had sat him down last night and given him a right good talking-to. She'd said that he was lucky Glenda was coming home to him after what he'd done, and made him promise to be nicer to her. Harry felt guilty, knowing Maude was right in everything she said – but if only Glenda would do as she was told! He couldn't stand the way other men looked at her and, even worse, he felt sure she flirted with that Billy Myers. But, like Maude had told him, he had to leave the past where it belonged and concentrate on the future. Glenda might be a lot of things he didn't like, but at the end of the day she was the mother of his child and as such deserved respect.

'No, I haven't got glasses or a hat,' Glenda said, looking close to tears.

'Sorry, love,' Harry said as he put his arm around Glenda's shoulders, 'take no notice of me. It's just this bloody place, you know I hate it.'

Glenda didn't answer but Harry thought he felt her flinch when he put his arm over her. They walked along the stark corridor and turned towards the main exit just as Frank Myers walked around the corner and came face to face with them.

'So you're off then, Mrs Jenkins?' asked Frank.

Harry could feel Glenda's body stiffen and his blood boiled as he looked at the skinny hospital porter who dared to have the nerve to talk to *his* wife.

'Yes, Frank,' Glenda answered nervously, her eyes darting around the corridor, 'but we've gotta dash. We don't wanna miss our tram.'

Glenda put her arm through Harry's and pulled him towards the doorway, but before they went through Harry looked over his shoulder and saw Frank staring at his wife. His fists clenched and his jaw tightened, but then they were through the door and Harry felt himself being pulled along again.

'So who the hell was he?' he asked.

'Nobody, just the porter from my ward.'

'A nobody who seems to know you pretty well,' said Harry with a distinct note of sarcasm.

'Harry, please, just leave it, will you. I just wanna get home to see my Johnnie.'

Harry looked down into Glenda's bruised but still sexy eyes. His suspicions subsided and he pulled his wife towards him and gently kissed the top of her head. 'Blimey, we ain't even out the door and I'm off again. You're right, let's get you home. Johnnie's gonna be chuffed to bits to see you. And I've got a little surprise waiting for you too.'

Maude couldn't help but keep dashing to the front window of Harry and Glenda's house and twitching the net curtain. She was really looking forward to Glenda coming home from hospital. 'Don't get me wrong,' she had told Bob the night before, 'I love having little Johnnie here with us, but I ain't as young as I used to be and I don't mind admitting that the little bleeder is wearing me out!'

Maude glanced around and noted that Harry had bought a lovely yellow chrysanthemum in a pot, which brightened up their rather drab living room. And he had repainted the kitchen in green. Maude hadn't thought the kitchen needed doing up, but had soon worked out that he was probably covering up Glenda's splattered blood that had stained the walls. Oh, that boy of mine, she thought, he'll be the death of me.

For the umpteenth time that morning Maude looked out of the window. She was pleased to see her son and Glenda walking down the street at last. She rushed to the kitchen and put the kettle on to boil. She thought about opening the window to let out the toxic smell of the newly painted walls, but then decided against it as it was far too chilly outside.

As the front door opened, Maude was waiting in the living room with Johnnie in her arms, ready to welcome Glenda home.

'Hello, love,' she said, beaming as Glenda walked into the room, but unable to help noticing how her lip was swollen. Her nose looked a funny shape too. 'Get your coat off and sit yourself down. I've got some hot water in the kettle for a cuppa and a little bundle of joy here who's been waiting to see his mum.'

'Johnnie!' Glenda squealed as she took her child from Maude's arms. 'Mummy's missed you so much.'

Maude watched Glenda hold her baby close to her and instinctively rock him from side to side. Bless her, she thought, she may not be the best woman in the world for my Harry but she's a good mum. I just hope she doesn't turn the kid soft with all that soppiness. Boys don't need hugs, they need discipline and a good hiding from time to time. Never mind, she'll learn. As soon as the little blighter is up and running around, she'll realise the need for the strap!

* * *

49

Glenda sat back on the lumpy brown sofa, relieved to finally have her son in her arms.

'Here, love, look what I got for you,' said Harry as he pointed to the bright yellow flowers on the old oak side-board.

'That's nice,' said Glenda but she didn't care about anything at this moment except holding Johnnie.

'And you know that surprise I told you about?' Harry said excitedly. 'Well, look behind you. Can you see, through the door? I've done up the kitchen for you.'

Glenda had noticed as soon as she had walked through the living-room door and there was no mistaking the strong fumes of the paint. 'Yes, it looks lovely. Thanks, Harry.'

'You don't sound too enthusiastic,' Harry snarled. 'Put the boy down and come and have a proper look.'

Just then Maude walked back into the room with a tray of three cups of tea and a plate of sandwiches. 'Now then, son.' She raised her eyebrows at Harry. 'Glenda has only just got through the door. Leave her be and let her rest. Come on, take this tray.'

For once, Glenda was grateful for Maude's interference. She felt quite tired after their journey back from the hospital and just wanted to spend some time with her baby.

'And, Glenda, I managed to buy a bit of something from a mate so I've put a nice mutton stew in the oven. When you're ready for your dinner later, all you have to do is warm it through. My stew will help build your strength back up far better than that 'orrible hospital food!'

I doubt it, thought Glenda, but she pasted a grateful

smile on her face and looked at Harry, who had wrinkled his nose in mock disgust at the thought of his mother's stew. The meat was probably stolen from some poor farmer, butchered and then sold on. Still, she knew better than to say anything, having learned the hard way to keep her mouth shut about any extras that Maude and Harry got hold of.

'Thanks, Maude,' she said. 'I must admit, I do feel a bit tired so I'm glad I won't have to cook tonight.'

'Well, then, it's nearly time for the boy's nap so why don't you finish that cuppa and go and have a lie down with him. I've gotta get back to get Bob's lunch ready. It's Wednesday so he'll be home early today.'

'Yes, I'll do that,' Glenda agreed.

'Thanks, Mum. We're good here so you get yourself off home now,' said Harry as he collected Maude's coat from over the banister.

This isn't good, thought Glenda, dreading being left alone with Harry. As her body tensed, Johnnie seemed to sense her fear and squirmed in her arms. 'It's all right,' she pacified him, pulling him closer to her.

Once Harry had packed Maude off through the front door, he walked back into the living room, putting on his heavy overcoat.

'Right then,' he said with a smile, 'you're all settled so I'm gonna pop down the Castle for a couple of pints and then I'd best get to work. I've lost enough pay having the morning off, so I'll see you later.'

Glenda listened for the front door to close then breathed a heavy sigh of relief. Thank God, she thought as she got up, placed Johnnie in his pram and hurried into the hallway. She grabbed her bag from the hospital and frantically pulled through the clothes inside. When she had been on the ward packing her stuff to leave, she had seen a note inside her bag, which at a quick glance she could see was signed by Frank. But with Harry loitering in the entrance she hadn't dared to read it properly so had bided her time. Now, though, with Harry out of the way, she sat on the third step of the hallway stairs and savoured Frank's written words.

Chapter 5

The Indian summer had been short lived and it was beginning to rain quite heavily, which made Frank further doubt that Glenda would turn up to see him. At least he had suggested a place to meet where he could shelter from the downpour. He patiently waited under the bandstand for her.

He had swapped some shifts around at the hospital, which enabled him to be in the park on a Friday morning, but it meant he would have to work tomorrow and he detested working over the weekend. But Glenda Jenkins was worth it. He wouldn't have minded waiting all day for her or getting soaked through to the skin. It would be nice to spend some time with her outside the hospital, but, more importantly, he wanted to know that she was well and safe. Leaving the note in Glenda's bag had been a risk, more so for Glenda than for himself, and he just hoped that Harry hadn't found it and attacked her again. The thought of that man laying a hand on Glenda turned his stomach. But as worries for her safety began to stab at his mind, he spotted a woman running towards the bandstand, pushing a navy-blue pram. Even from this distance, Frank could tell it was Glenda. The closer she got, the more the butterflies in his stomach fluttered – for, though he had hoped, he hadn't really believed she would risk secretly meeting him.

Frank removed his oversized long grey mac, ran towards Glenda and held the garment over her head in a bid to protect her from the torrential rain. Between them, they quickly lifted the pram up the steps of the bandstand and once sheltered they both spoke at once.

'You first,' said Glenda with a smile.

Frank noticed the swelling around her eye had almost disappeared and she looked even more beautiful than he'd remembered. She wore a scarf around her head, but her marcel waves were wet at the back, making her look windswept and interesting.

'Hello, Glenda,' Frank said, laughing. 'I didn't think you'd come, especially in this weather.'

'I can't stop for long,' Glenda said, shaking the rain-water from her black woollen coat. 'Harry likes to have an account of what I've been doing and I don't think he'd believe that I was out for a walk in Battersea Park in this weather.'

'Not to worry. I'm just glad you're here now, if only for a little while. How have you been keeping?'

'Not bad, thanks, Frank. It's nice to be back at home with Johnnie, and Harry is actually making an effort, though I don't know how long it will last. Still, I'm thankful for small mercies.'

'I haven't had the pleasure of meeting Johnnie yet. Do you mind if I stick my ugly bonce in his pram and say hello?'

Glenda laughed. 'Of course you can,' she said, 'but don't expect much conversation. He's out for the count.'

'It's a good job he can't talk. We wouldn't want him telling tales on us to his daddy now, would we?'

'Oh, Frank. Please, don't even joke about it! Harry would kill me if he knew I was here and probably you too! I couldn't believe it when I found that note in my bag! What were you thinking, Frank Myers?'

'I was thinking about you, Glenda. You're pretty much all I think about these days.'

'You mustn't talk like that, Frank. I'm a married woman and it isn't right.'

'And it isn't right that your old man knocks you from here to kingdom come!'

'I know, sorry, Frank. But can we please not talk about him any more?'

'Yeah, good idea. Least said about him the better. Look, I've brought some cheese sandwiches, though I'm afraid there's only a smidgeon of cheese in them, and a bottle of lemonade. I know it ain't much, but I thought it would be nice to have a bit of a picnic. It's a shame about the rain, though.'

Glenda smiled, a smile so warm that Frank immediately forgot about his cold hands. He laid his mac on the concrete floor for Glenda to sit on and shared out the sandwiches, which they eagerly ate.

'Frank, I don't care about the weather, and I've got to say, nobody has ever done anything like this for me before. It's so lovely. Thank you.' She leaned over to tenderly kiss Frank on the cheek.

Frank knew he had turned red but he didn't care. Everything felt so relaxed and carefree with Glenda and for a moment he was tempted to return her kiss, only this time passionately on her lips. Instead, he took her hand and said, 'I'm enjoying this. It's been great spending time with you and I hope you'll agree to see me again.'

'I shouldn't, Frank. You know this is dangerous, but even so I would like to, very much. I know we're only friends, but if we meet up we'll still have to be careful and discreet.'

From there in the small, elegantly designed bandstand, Frank could have sung out across Battersea Park. Glenda hadn't said so out loud, but he could tell she liked him. If he could just persuade her to leave her brutish husband, then life would be pretty damned good . . .

The rain had almost stopped as Glenda walked back through the park on her way home. A small glimmer of sunlight was breaking through the clouds and a large rainbow arched across the sky. For a short while she felt as if she was walking on air through a paradise.

What a wonderful couple of hours, she thought, picturing Frank's kind smile and remembering his cheery voice. It was wrong, she knew it was, yet even so Glenda couldn't wait to see him again. We're just friends, she told herself as if to ease her guilty conscience, while smiling like a village idiot as she recalled the kiss she had planted on his cheek.

It had been a bold move to go and meet Frank and several times she had nearly backed out. She was glad that she hadn't. Spending time with Frank was like a breath of fresh air. He was so easy to talk to, unlike her husband, whom she tiptoed around as if walking on eggshells. It was very different with Frank and she found it refreshing to be herself – the happy and carefree woman she had been before Harry had destroyed her.

She passed through the wrought-iron black gates of the park but the closer she got to home, the more her heart sank and paranoid fears of Harry knowing who she had been with began to set in. Don't be daft, she told herself. No one could have seen her; it had been tipping it down, so it was unlikely that anyone she knew would have been out in the park. Even if they had spotted her, she was absolutely entitled to take her child for a walk, wasn't she? But could she really use Johnnie as a cover for her secret tryst? Yes, she thought to herself, she could – she had no other option if she was to see Frank again. They had arranged to meet the following week, which seemed like such a long time to wait, but in the meantime at least she could hold on to the memory of one of the best days of her life.

As Glenda turned a corner she sneaked a glance behind her, knowing that Frank wouldn't be too far behind, on his way home to the prefab down Sheepcote Lane that he shared with his mum and his brother. His brother, Billy Myers! Glenda hadn't mentioned that she knew Billy when Frank had talked about how lucky they were to be alive after a doodlebug bomb had flattened their house during the war. His father hadn't survived but Frank hadn't sounded too bothered by that. It seemed there was no love lost between them. She hadn't wanted Frank to know that it was partly because of his brother she had ended up in hospital. The whole time she had shared with Frank had been so magical; she didn't want to spoil it by bringing up horrible things about Harry.

When Glenda thought of Harry her stomach knotted again and, though there was still a bitter chill in the wind, small beads of nervous sweat broke out on her forehead.

Harry wasn't due home from work for a few hours, but she just couldn't face going home yet. She wanted the feeling of euphoria never to end, so instead she decided to pop in to see Helen. As her parents lived next door to Helen, she could visit them too, but though her bruises had faded she wouldn't be able to hide her missing teeth and broken nose from her father.

Mrs Merton lived a few doors up from Helen's house and sold homemade toffee apples. Glenda decided to purchase one for her mother as a little treat. She tapped three times on Mrs Merton's front window, the signal for her to come and sell her apples. They were very popular with the locals and though everyone knew that Mrs Merton must have managed to acquire extra sugar on the black market, nobody minded as she sold her wares at a fair price and they were a rare treat for those who could spare the tuppence.

Glenda thanked Mrs Merton, tucked her toffee apple away in her handbag and first visited her best friend. She knocked on Helen's door, smiling as she desperately tried to force Frank from her mind.

Helen seemed genuinely pleased and surprised to find Glenda standing on her doorstep.

'Glenda!' she exclaimed. 'I wasn't expecting to see you today. Come in out of the cold, love.'

'Thanks, Helen. I was just taking Johnnie for a stroll – a bit of fresh air is good for him. Not that the air round here is all that fresh. That blinking stench from Garton's glucose factory and the fumes from the brewery . . . I swear it's getting worse!'

'I know, and so many people complain about it,' said Helen as she helped Glenda in through the door with the pram. 'I'm sure there's sticky stuff on my windows from that factory. Come through to the kitchen, Dad is in his bed in the front room and Mum is upstairs having a nap.'

Glenda sat at the table in the cramped kitchen and stretched her neck to look out of the back door at the apple tree Helen had planted during the war, which sadly still wasn't producing any fruit.

'Sorry about the state of the tea,' said Helen, 'these leaves must have been brewed four times over and we haven't got any sugar. This rationing is getting really tiresome now. I queued for over two hours yesterday afternoon just for a loaf of bread. It wouldn't be so bad, but you know it's hard for me to leave Mum and Dad by themselves.'

'You should have said. I could have got you a loaf when I got mine,' Glenda offered. 'Talking of parents, I want to pop round to see mine, but does my face look all right?'

'There's still a faint bruise, but a bit more foundation and powder should cover it up. I'm afraid there's not much else we can do about your wonky nose or gappy grin,' Helen said lightheartedly, continuing to look at her. She paused. 'There's something else. You look different, Glenda. I can't put my finger on it but there's definitely something. You ain't pregnant again, are you?'

'No, don't be daft,' Glenda said, laughing. She could feel her cheeks begin to flush as she thought of Frank, and her friend quizzed her further.

'So what is it, Glenda Jenkins? And don't you go saying nothing 'cos I know there's something! You can't keep secrets from me, you know. I've been your best mate all your life and I know when you're up to something. Look at you, smiling like the cat that's got the cream.'

'Oh, Helen,' Glenda gushed, 'you know me too well. You're right, I can't keep things from you, but if I tell you, you have to promise to keep it a secret.'

'Of course I will, Glenda, you know that!'

'Well,' Glenda paused, 'it's this bloke I met called Frank . . .'

Ted was pleasantly surprised to find his only daughter standing in the front-room doorway, gently rocking his first grandson on her hip.

'Glenda,' he fussed, rushing over to take Johnnie from her arms, 'leave the pram there, it'll be fine. How lovely to see you, my gal. It's been weeks. Come in, come in and sit yourself down. Look, Elsie, look who's come to visit. It's our Glenda and don't she look a sight for sore eyes!'

Elsie raised a bit of a smile, but soon closed her eyes again as she drifted off to sleep on the small couch in the corner of the room.

'Your mother's a bit tired, love. It's this weather. It's turned cold again and it keeps her up at night when the wind blows down the chimney.'

'The sun's come out now and I've got her a little pressie from old Mrs Merton. Here you are.' Glenda handed the toffee apple to Ted.

Such a thoughtful girl, he thought, but as a ray of sun shone through the window and illuminated her face, Ted caught sight of Glenda's bruised eye. He could tell she'd tried to cover it with make-up and, as he studied her more closely, he noticed her nose looked misshapen too.

He inwardly seethed, instantly knowing that her thug of a husband had been bashing her again. He wanted to question her about it but knew from experience that his daughter would always lie to cover for Harry, and he hated it when she did that. He took a deep breath and tried to carry on as normal.

'And how have you both been? We ain't seen you in a while.'

'Yes, I know, Dad, and I'm sorry. It's just that Johnnie's been teething and I've been busy. You know how it is.'

Oh, yes, thought Ted, he knew exactly how it was. More like she's been too injured and ashamed to show us her face. Though he expected to get the same old fairy story, Ted found he couldn't help but have it out with her.

'Look, love,' he began, 'we've been through this before and I don't expect you'll tell me anything different from last time, but if that old man of yours has been hitting you again, you don't have to stay with him. You'll always have a roof over your head here, and Johnnie too.'

Ted held his breath and stared intently at his beloved daughter. She had come late to them, when Elsie had been over forty. He himself was now nearly sixty-two years old, with gnarled hands from arthritis, but if he had been a younger and fitter man he would have marched straight round to Harry Jenkins and punched him on the nose.

'I know you'll always take me in, Dad, and thanks. I ain't gonna lie to you again, so yes, Harry has been hitting me, pretty badly this time. But how can I leave him? He knows this is the first place I'd run to and he'd soon come round here to kick up a stink. He'd drag me back home and I'd suffer for daring to walk out on him. Not

61

only that, I couldn't divorce him. Oh, Dad, just think of it, the shame. Women round these parts don't leave their husbands. It's unheard of!'

Ted's heart nearly crumbled as he saw the anguish in Glenda's eyes. For her to finally admit that Harry had been hitting her . . . he must have really hurt her badly this time.

'Sod what other people think. I couldn't give a damn about all the gossips. If you want a divorce, my gal, then you bloody well get one! You've always been too good for the likes of that Jenkins lot. Rough they are, the whole lot of 'em. And I'll tell you something else – there wouldn't be a single person in these streets who would blame you for leaving that man. He's got no right to hit you! Gawd rest his soul, if your brother was still here, I'd send him round there right now. See how brave that Harry is if a real man stood in front of him.'

Ted could feel the pain again like a stab to the heart when he thought of his son Philip, who had been killed in action during the D-Day landings. He'd been eight years older than Glenda and twice as big a man as that Harry Jenkins. He would have gone mad at the knowledge of anyone beating up his little sister and would have sorted the bully out.

'I know what you're saying, Dad, but that still doesn't help if Harry comes round here to get me. What about Mum? You know how easily she gets upset. All the commotion would be too much for her.'

Ted noticed the tender look in Glenda's eyes as she glanced over at her mother who was lying peacefully on the sofa, quietly snoring with her mouth slightly agape. He was thankful that Elsie seemed oblivious to the conversation between him and Glenda. It would have broken the woman's heart had she known that their daughter was being beaten by Harry.

'I'll worry about your mother. You just go home now, get whatever stuff you need for you and the boy, then get yourself back round here sharpish. I'll have your room ready and we'll deal with whatever happens. If push comes to shove, I'll call the Old Bill. Not only that, my mate Mick has a boy at Battersea Park station and I can have a word with him.'

'Dad, you know the police aren't interested in husband-and-wife stuff. They wouldn't get involved even if Harry came round here to drag me home. They'd probably be on his side and tell me to go back to my husband where I belong. No, it's best I just get on with things. I made my bed so I'll have to lie in it. Anyhow, little Johnnie here needs his dad. I couldn't take him away from his father.'

Ted bounced his grandson on his knee, his heart melting as the baby gave him a toothless grin. 'Oh, Glenda. I wish there was something I could do. Maybe if I have a quiet word in Harry's ear he might listen?'

'I know you mean well, Dad, but please don't. It'll only make things worse. Harry doesn't like me talking about our married life so it's best if we keep this little chat between ourselves.'

Ted sighed. 'All right, my gal, you're a grown woman, so it's your choice at the end of the day. I ain't happy about it, though, so if you change your mind don't you hesitate to get yourself home here.'

Ted tickled Johnnie's tummy, making the child coo in delight, and as Glenda watched the two of them play,

Ted could see there was something else behind the little smile that kept breaking out on his daughter's face. The woman had been abused and battered, so why was she looking so happy?

'Anything else been going on in the world of Glenda Jenkins?' Ted teased. 'Only you look like Churchill did on VE Day!'

'Course not, Dad, just the usual stuff. I called in on Helen next door before I came round here. Seems her mum is getting more and more forgetful. She was asleep upstairs, but when she woke up and came down, she called me Elsie! Helen tried to tell her I was Elsie's daughter but she wouldn't have it. She even tried to drag me out while going on about the "protest" and how we would be able to vote soon. She started getting quite excited and poor Helen had a job calming her down!'

Ted chuckled and sat back in his chair, remembering the feisty little thing Elsie had been years earlier when they had first met. 'Cor, that takes me back.' He smiled at Glenda. 'Your mother and her next door were a formidable twosome in their day. They kicked up quite a stink round here, banging on about the right of the ordinary woman to vote. Must have been about twenty-odd years ago when they finally won and huh, the jollies them two had that night. Course you won't remember, you was just a nipper then yourself, not much older than Johnnie boy now.'

'What? Mum was a Suffragette?'

'Well, not as such, but she had a right gob on her and stood up for what she believed to be right. She went on quite a few marches and protests up in London town, swinging her banner and shouting her mouth off. Blimey,

64

the temper on her too. I used to call her "Frowny Crowny" on account of her name being Elsie Crown.'

'I never knew Mum was like that! She's always been so . . . so quiet.'

'She changed when you were born, but she was one helluva woman when we first met.' Ted looked across to his wife. He would never cry in front of his daughter, but his eyes glistened. It had been love at first sight when he'd met Elsie and she had proved to be the love of his life.

'I remember the first time I saw her. She was coming out of a big house over Chelsea way. She was in service there, see. Anyhow, right haughty she looked, nose in the air, marching down the Embankment in her shiny black boots, ankle-length dress with a nipped-in waist, pretty as a picture she was, just like you now. I remember catching sight of her and thinking how I wished I was brave enough to make her acquaintance.'

'Well, you must have managed it,' Glenda pointed out, smiling.

'Yeah, well, as luck would 'ave it for me, this old horse and cart went rushing past her, almost galloping it was. It nearly knocked her off her feet and as it sped through a dirty old puddle, a big splash of mucky water went all over your mother's dress. Cor blimey, she shouted out some obscenities, words I had never heard a woman use before, but it did make me laugh! Course, she caught me laughing, didn't she, and that was that, she turned her anger to me then. I did my best to calm her and eventually she let me introduce meself. Funny little thing she was, and when she told me her name was Elsie Crown, she added, "Crown, like what the Queen wears." It still tickles me all these years later.'

Ted stood up and placed Johnnie back in his pram then walked over to his wife and gently pulled a blanket over her legs.

'Oh, Dad, that's a lovely story,' Glenda said as she rose to her feet. 'I know the sun's shining, but it's a bit nippy for Mum in here. I'll go out to the shed and bring some coal in. You could do with lighting that fire.'

'No point, love,' said Ted glumly, 'you won't find no coal in the shed.'

'I know there's shortages, Dad, but the coal cart was round the streets last week. Didn't you get any?'

Ted was a proud man, but after Glenda's openness earlier he felt she deserved the same honesty in return. 'He would have stopped if I could have paid him. Thing is, love, I'm a bit strapped at the moment. Your mother needed some tonics from the doctor and he ain't cheap, but not to worry. There's an old railway sleeper out in the back yard. I'll chop that up and use it but I'm waiting 'til it gets a bit colder yet. And if need be, Philip's old wardrobe is sitting empty now so that'll make a good bit of firewood.'

'Oh, Dad, why didn't you say?'

'And what would be the point of that, eh? I won't take no handouts from my own daughter! Don't worry, love, we've been through tougher times than this. Us Webbers are made of stern stuff, ya know!'

'I'm not.'

'Of course you are. You've just had a bit of your courage knocked out of you, but one day, like a worm, you'll turn. I know you will.' It was then that Ted noticed a silly smile again on Glenda's face and a bit of a twinkle in her eye. 'You still haven't told me what's making them cheeks of yours nice and rosy, and don't tell me it's the wind!'

Glenda blushed again and went over to the window to look out onto the street, moving from one foot to the other and obviously excited about something. It was nice to see her looking so happy, thought Ted, but he knew it was not of Harry's doing.

'It's nothing really, Dad. I've just got a new friend, that's all.'

'Oh,' said Ted, raising his chin in the air, 'and this new *friend*, does he have a name?'

Glenda spun round to look at her dad, her expression one of shock, but she nodded. 'Yes, his name is Frank. He's such a nice bloke, Dad, a proper gentleman. Of course Harry mustn't find out, but we're only friends. It's just nice to have someone to talk to who is kind and caring. I dunno, maybe I'm being silly, but I just like spending time with him, that's all.'

Ted nodded his head. He recognised that look when his daughter spoke of Frank. It was the same way Elsie used to look when they had first gotten together. Glenda never had that look when she talked about Harry. Oh, well, if this Frank made his daughter happy, who was he to question it? The girl deserved at least a small bit of joy so good luck to her. He only hoped that awful Harry never found out . . .

Chapter 6

It was a sunny but chilly Friday morning as Glenda pushed her pram over Battersea Bridge, excited about meeting Frank on the other side. She was glad of the good weather, but if she was honest even a hurricane wouldn't put a dampener on her spirits today. This was the second time she was meeting Frank in secret and though she hadn't known him long, she felt she knew him well. It was odd, she thought, that Frank was so different from his brother Billy. Not just in appearance but in personality too. Frank was warm and funny; he had a confident air about him but his light spirit made her feel instantly relaxed. On the other hand, his brother gave her the creeps. She shuddered as she dismissed any further thoughts of Billy.

The week had dragged by so slowly, but she had managed to tolerate Harry and his demands by creating her own little daydream world with Frank as the focus of her thoughts. Oh, why couldn't Harry be more like Frank? she mused as she glanced at the dirty-looking River Thames flowing under the bridge below her. There had been a time a short while ago when she'd felt like throwing herself off this bridge, but something was different now. Something was bringing light into her life, just like the sunshine that was warming her face. That something was Frank and she quickened her pace, eager to get to the other side.

Soon enough, Glenda spotted a man in a long grey mac and trilby hat whom she instantly recognised as Frank. He was holding a carpet bag and waving furiously at her. Oh, good, she thought, he looks just as keen to see me as I am to see him! She almost ran, and was slightly breathless as she reached Frank, who dropped his bag and swept her up into his arms, lifting her feet from the ground and squeezing her tightly.

Glenda was taken aback by such an enthusiastic greeting and slightly embarrassed by a public show of emotion, but, as soon as Frank spoke, her embarrassment faded and her heart melted.

'I've missed you, Glenda Jenkins!' Frank crooned as he stared intently into Glenda's dark eyes. 'I couldn't wait to see you.'

'You too, Frank,' whispered Glenda, nervous but excited at the same time. Oh, dear, she thought, is he going to kiss me? Her body tensed. She wasn't sure if Frank felt her stiffen but he released her from his fervent hug and she found her feet back on the ground.

'I'm sorry, Glenda, that was a bit much. It's just that I've been thinking about you all week and it's been driving me crazy not seeing you. I got a bit over-excited.'

Glenda smiled as Frank winked at her and flashed her one of his cheeky grins. She knew how he felt; it had been the same for her too.

'I've done us a bite to eat for lunch. How about we take a stroll down Cheyne Walk first?' Frank asked.

'Sounds lovely. I must admit, I've never been over this side of the water. It's a bit different from Battersea!' Glenda suddenly felt very scruffy and out of date in her black wool coat, which was bobbled with age, and her headscarf looked so old fashioned compared to the fancy hats the women here were wearing.

'This is where the rich and famous live. Do you know Turner lived down this road?' said Frank, gesturing with his hand.

'I hope you don't think I'm an idiot, but I have no idea who you're talking about, Frank.'

'Turner – he was a famous artist. And for the record, no, I don't think you're an idiot. Well, apart from staying with that husband of yours!'

'I can't say you're wrong on that point, Frank,' Glenda said, nodding, 'but this Turner bloke can't be that famous. I mean, I've never heard of him!'

They both laughed and Glenda looked around her: at the Thames to her right, glistening as the sunlight caught the tops of the ripples, and the tall, gated mansion houses to her left, which held so much wealth and luxury for their lucky residents. This was such a perfect day and she didn't want it ever to end.

Frank stopped at a vacant black iron bench that faced the river. Perfect, he thought, as he beckoned Glenda to sit down.

'Well, I don't know about you, but that walk has given me a bit of an appetite. Fancy a bite to eat?' He rummaged in his carpet bag and pulled out two sandwiches, along with a bag of chewy bonbons. 'I hope you like egg sandwiches.'

'Egg! Real egg?' Glenda exclaimed as she parked the pram.

'Yeah.'

'Oh, Frank, I hate powdered egg so this is a real treat, and sweets too!'

'Well, I had a bit of luck with the sweets. An old dear on the hospital ward had a visit from her granddaughter who used her sweet rations to buy her the bonbons. She didn't like to tell her that with no teeth she couldn't eat them. The eggs came from my mate down the street where I used to live before our house was bombed. He's turned the old bomb shelter in his garden into a chicken house.'

Glenda took the proffered sandwich, relishing the taste as she bit into it, and for a few minutes a comfortable silence fell between them as they ate. Frank poured two cups of dandelion and burdock and handed one to Glenda, and the pair of them clinked their tin cups, both announcing 'Cheers'.

Frank felt the urge to lean across and kiss Glenda but refrained from doing so, reminding himself that they were just friends. Although he wanted far more than that, he didn't want to frighten Glenda off and he knew she was far too loyal to be unfaithful to Harry. In spite of this, he couldn't stop himself taking her hand in his. Her skin felt beautifully soft.

'Glenda,' he began, 'I understand that this is difficult, but you must know how I feel about you.'

'I think I do, Frank,' she answered, lowering her eyes to the pavement. 'I'm falling for you too and I know I shouldn't. I just can't help myself. And having you in my life somehow makes things at home more bearable.'

Frank's heart was breaking for the poor woman. She

was stuck in a loveless marriage with a man she feared and, as much as he wanted to take her away and save her, he had nothing to offer.

'I love you, Glenda. There's no mistaking it. I want you to leave your husband and be with me, but I know how hard that would be for you. So if once a week is all I get of you, then that will have to do. I can't say I'm happy about it, but I would rather have something than nothing. I can't let you go, not now I've found you.'

'I'm so sorry, Frank. I never expected this to happen, but it has and I'm the same – I have to see you, even though I know it's wrong. I . . . I can't give you anything more than friendship, it just wouldn't be right, so are you sure that's enough for you?'

Although Frank knew Glenda would never be his, it still felt like a blow to the stomach. Hearing her say that they could only be friends hurt him physically, yet still he had to be with her, had to see her on any terms. He managed to raise a smile.

'Friends it is then. I tell you what, I've got Wednesday off work, some sort of mix-up with my shifts. How about we go for a walk in Battersea Park?'

'Yes, I'd like that.'

'The nipper can feed the ducks,' Frank said, leaning forward to look in the pram.

'Don't be daft. He's only a baby,' said Glenda with a smile.

Daft, yes, I'm certainly daft about you, Frank mused, but refrained from voicing those words. He didn't want to upset Glenda, and a walk in Battersea Park was better than nothing.

*　.　*　　*

On Wednesday Billy Myers had bunked a day off work in the hope of seeing Glenda out and about doing her shopping and washing. Trouble is, he had to think of yet another excuse to be in the high street instead of at the building site. He'd nearly got caught out last time, when he lied about his mum being ill, and he didn't want Glenda thinking badly of him. I'll fake a limp, he thought, and pretend I've hurt my ankle or something.

His brother Frank had been up early that morning, and his chirpy whistling woke Billy, so, although he didn't expect to see Glenda for at least an hour, he set out eagerly, deciding to 'accidentally' bump into her at the shop on the corner of her street. This would give him the opportunity to spend a little more time with her as well.

Billy reached the corner of Inworth Street and went into the shop. He picked up a magazine and paid for it, but then pretended to be flicking through it whilst watching out for Glenda. Shortly after, her front door opened and the familiar sight of Johnnie's pram emerged. Billy was perplexed to see that there were no laundry bags balancing on top, and when Glenda came into view he saw that she wasn't wearing her usual headscarf. Instead her hair was pinned in neat waves close to her head. She looked a knockout.

He left the shop, ready to bump into her, but when Glenda reached the corner of the street, instead of turning right and towards him, she turned left. Puzzled, Billy frowned. This wasn't Glenda's usual routine. Her pace was brisk as she marched along the road, while Billy followed discreetly, keen to find out where she was going. Though it had been dry when Glenda left her house, drizzle began to fall and as she stopped for a moment to tie a headscarf over her hair, Billy stopped too.

Twenty minutes later, Billy watched as Glenda entered Battersea Park. With the rain becoming heavier, he thought it a bit odd to go out for a walk, and he couldn't go limping up to her pretending to be out for a walk himself, not with a twisted ankle. So instead he remained a short distance behind her whilst he re-thought his plan.

Suddenly, Glenda was waving and to Billy's horror he saw his brother running up to her. Frank kissed her affectionately on the cheek then embraced her in a way that looked far too friendly. The cheeky swine, Billy thought, no wonder he'd been acting so cagey lately. He was secretly meeting Glenda! Jealousy coursed through Billy's veins and an angry knot grew in his stomach. It was bad enough that he had Harry to contend with when it came to Glenda's affections, but now there was Frank too. What was wrong with Glenda that she could see anything in his skinny runt of a brother? Hatred for Frank surged through him and he ground his teeth. Billy pictured Harry kicking Frank's head in. He wanted his brother to suffer big time.

Billy hated seeing them together, yet something kept him following the couple, unable to take his eyes off Glenda as she headed towards the park café, happily nattering away to Frank.

'No, this won't do. I ain't having it,' Billy muttered over and over, 'I'll put a stop to this! Just you wait and see, Frank. Yeah, you're gonna pay for taking my girl!'

He took Glenda's stolen knickers from his pocket, twisted the material tightly and watched as his knuckles went white, imagining that those knickers were around Frank's neck.

Frank's mother, Joyce, was draining some boiled cabbage as he came through the front door of the prefab, whistling the same happy tune as he had that morning. Even his mum's stinking veg couldn't ruin his mood, Frank thought, clicking his heels as he skipped up the hallway to his bedroom.

Then Frank heard his mother call out.

'Where 'ave you been, Frank? I thought you had the day off and you was gonna clean me windows?'

Bugger, he'd forgotten. He walked back to the kitchen, taking his braces from his shoulders and letting them fall to his sides.

'Yeah, sorry, Mum. The window cleaning went clean out me head, ha ha, get it, clean out me head? Never mind,' he said, looking at his mother's blank expression. 'I went up Charing Cross way. I fancied a mooch around them old bookshops.'

'Charing Cross! Books? You ain't blinkin' normal, Frank. Do you think any blokes around here ever got anywhere on books! Your father would be turning in his grave . . . bloody books my arse! Typical of you though. You've always thought you're a cut above the rest of us, but just remember, son, you ain't! You're just like the rest of us, so forget those fanciful ideas of yours and worry about how we're gonna get a proper house. Your brother never seems to bring home a full pay packet and you, pushing them invalids around, well, you should be out there looking for a real man's job!'

'Leave it out, will ya, Mum? I've got a "proper" job.

Just 'cos I don't come home every night covered in muck doesn't mean I'm not working. And as for my books, I enjoy reading them!'

'The only thing those bloody books are good for is fuel for the fire! Now cut out the backchat and get washed up for your tea. Where's that brother of yours? The lazy sod didn't go to work again today so he should be home by now. He thinks I'm stupid and didn't suss it out, but as he was dressed up in his best white shirt it was a bit of a giveaway. I dunno what he's been up to, but you can bet your life it involves a woman.'

It was gone ten that night when the front door opened and Billy staggered in, the smell of beer billowing from him.

'About time too. Where the hell 'ave you been? Spending my house money down the Castle again, no doubt?' Joyce spat.

'Don't bloody start, woman,' Billy slurred as he bounced off the kitchen door frame, 'I've had it up to here today.'

'Who do you think you're talking to?' Joyce snarled at her younger son. 'I'm your bleedin' mother so show me some respect. Don't take me for a fool neither. I know you haven't been to work.'

'No, I ain't, and so what! Shall I tell you where I went earlier today?' Billy glared at Frank. 'I went to Battersea Park, and do you know what I saw? Eh? I'll tell you, shall I, Mum? I saw our Frank with a woman, but you'll never guess who she is. No, of course you won't so I'll tell you –'

'Billy!' Frank yelled, panicked. 'Shut your mouth! Come on, let's go outside for a little chat.'

'I don't think so, Frank. I reckon Mum should know what's been going on. After all, we both know there's gonna be trouble, and trouble that will end up on her doorstep.'

Joyce was suddenly standing between the two men, her eyes dark with anger as she pushed the sleeves of her cardigan up to her elbows, which was a sure sign she meant business.

'Billy! Frank! The pair of you, sit at that table, and you had better tell me what's going on!'

Frank went to speak but Billy got in first.

'Frank has been seeing that Glenda Jenkins – you know, the one who is *married* to Harry.'

'It's not what you think, Mum, honest. We're just friends,' Frank quickly protested. He wasn't prepared for this. Apart from Harry, the last people he wanted to know about him and Glenda were his mother or his brother. He knew his mother would give him an ear bashing about having anything to do with a married woman and as for Billy, well, it was none of his business.

'From what I saw, it looked like more than that,' said Billy sarcastically.

'I don't know what you think you clocked, Billy, but I'm telling you, there's nothing more to me and Glenda than friendship.'

'So you're saying that you have a "friendship" with Glenda Jenkins, one that I don't suppose her old man knows anything about. Is that right?' asked Joyce.

'Yeah, but that's all there is to it, Mum. Like I said, we're just mates.'

'Not any more you ain't! I know all about them Jenkinses, bloody gyppos, the lot of them. He's a nutter, that Harry. If he finds that you're seeing his missus he'll be straight round here and he'll have your guts for garters! You've got to stop seeing her,' Joyce warned.

Frank looked at his younger brother, who was smiling slyly, before turning to his mother again. 'I don't see why. We're doing nothing wrong. We just talk, that's all.'

'In that case, if it's so innocent, how come her old man knows nothing about it?'

Frank sighed and said heavily, 'Because, like Billy, he might get the wrong idea.'

'Anyone would. She's a married woman and you're meeting behind her husband's back. You've got to knock it on the head, Frank. If you don't and Harry Jenkins gets wind of it, as I said, he'll be round here to give you a kicking. From what I've heard about him he might give me a slap too, so stop seeing her, Frank. She ain't worth it.'

Frank saw that his mother was wringing her hands in fear and knew that she was right. If Harry found out, he would go berserk and he'd be vying for Frank's blood. However, his mum was wrong about one thing. Glenda Jenkins *was* worth it.

Billy woke up the next morning with a thumping headache. He'd drunk far too much beer the day before, but had felt the need to drown his sorrows after the shock of finding his brother with Glenda. Though his memory was a bit fuzzy, Billy recalled the conversation at the kitchen table with Frank and his mum. He knew that Frank wasn't prepared to stop seeing Glenda. Nothing his mother had said would change Frank's mind, so if she couldn't make him stop, Billy was left with no option other than go to the one person who could – Harry.

He really didn't feel like going to work today, not with this stinking hangover, and the cold October morning wasn't doing anything to encourage him out of the warmth of his bed, but he suddenly felt invigorated and spurred on at the thought of grassing Frank up to Harry.

The builders were in full swing when he arrived, already fifteen minutes late for work. His foreman had seen him and was shaking his head disapprovingly, but Billy took up his shovel and got stuck in to mixing mortar for the wall that Harry was bricklaying.

'All right, Bill,' called Harry. 'You were a bit worse for wear when you left the pub last night. You don't look much better this morning. I reckon you're a bloody lightweight who can't keep up with us men.' Harry laughed and several of the men around him joined in.

Yeah, you can laugh now, thought Billy, but you'll be laughing on the other side of your face soon. He just had to pick the right time to tell him, and by half past twelve that afternoon, much to Billy's relief, the rain was falling so hard that work was stopped. They headed for the nearest pub, Billy rehearsing his words in his head as they hurried through the downpour. He was nervous about broaching the subject with Harry, worried that the man would lash out at him in anger, but a few pints of stout gave him the Dutch courage that he needed.

'Harry, can I have a word, mate?' he asked, drawing the man to one side.

'Yeah, go on, Billy, what's up?' Harry was in a cheerful mood but Billy knew that what he was about to tell him would change all that.

'Look, I dunno how to say this, but it's about your Glenda.'

'What about my Glenda?' asked Harry, his smile suddenly diminishing.

'It's just that with you being a mate and all, I don't really wanna have to tell you this, but I wouldn't be much of a friend if I didn't.'

'Billy, what are you on about? Just spit it out, will you?' Harry's tone of voice revealed his loss of patience.

'I've seen her, Harry. Seen Glenda out and about with another bloke.'

Before Billy could say another word, Harry had slammed down his pint glass and had him by the throat up against the pub wall, snarling, 'What you on about, Billy? What are you trying to say about my Glenda, eh? Reckon she's a slag, do you?'

This wasn't how Billy wanted the conversation to go and he could feel his legs weaken with dread, his voice becoming high-pitched with fear. 'No, Harry. I ain't saying that, mate. I'm just saying that I've seen her, and the thing is, I know the bloke.'

The pub had gone quiet, all eyes on them, and then the landlord spoke. 'Any trouble, take it outside, lads.'

Harry dropped Billy and yanked on his arm. 'Outside, now,' he growled in his ear.

Billy was almost shoved out of the door and stood with his back against a brick wall as Harry paced in front of him. 'Harry –' he began nervously.

'Right then, you'd better tell me what's going on,' Harry interrupted, and to Billy's relief he seemed to have calmed down a bit.

'It's my brother, Frank. I saw him and Glenda in

Battersea Park yesterday. I had a word with him about it and he says they're just friends, but if you don't know about it, I think it's a bit suss.'

Billy saw the colour drain from Harry's face and his fists clench at his side.

'Are you sure about this, Billy? My Glenda's a good woman and, let's face it, you've always had your eye on her. You sure you ain't a bit jealous and out to cause a bit of bother?'

Billy had feared that Harry might not believe him so had come prepared. 'Harry, I wouldn't lie to you. And the thing is, I found these in Frank's bedroom. Do you recognise them?' He took the stolen knickers belonging to Glenda and held them out to Harry.

Harry grabbed them, crushing the fabric in his hands before he spoke.

'Friends, eh? This brother of yours has obviously been seeing my wife behind my back and he reckons they're just friends? So what the fuck is he doing with these? Where is he? Where will I find him?'

'Harry, come on mate, he's my brother. You ain't gonna hurt him, are you?' Billy asked, but in truth, he guessed that Harry would knock the living daylights out of Frank. Billy didn't care much for his brother, and if that's what it would take to put a stop to Frank and Glenda, then so be it, he thought to himself.

'Nah, nah, I won't hurt him, Bill. What makes you think that?' Harry asked sarcastically. 'I just want a quiet word in his ear, so come on, are you gonna tell me where he is or am I gonna have to knock it out of you?'

These were the words that Billy wanted to hear. Harry had threatened him, which left him with no choice but to tell the man what he wanted to know. 'He'll be at work. He's a porter at the Free Hospital.'

Harry spun on his heel and with head and shoulders bent against the beating rain steamed off down the street towards the hospital.

Billy smiled with satisfaction. After what Frank had coming, he doubted his brother would be seeing Glenda Jenkins ever again.

Chapter 7

Harry's mind was racing as he approached the hospital. All sorts of sordid images flashed through his mind of his wife with Frank Myers. The dirty tart had left her knickers behind! Had they only been at it in Frank's house or were they together in *his* bed?

It all makes sense now, he thought, remembering how Glenda had acted so nervously when he had collected her from the hospital. Frank Myers must be the bloke who had been hanging around when he went to pick Glenda up, and yes, come to think of it, he remembered her calling him Frank. He scowled. This meant she'd seen him at least once since then, and maybe even before.

His jaw clenched as he thought about his wife. The bitch. He'd fucking kill her! And of all the people to find out from, it had to be that tosser Billy Myers! He was sure that Billy had enjoyed telling him. Well, he hadn't heard the last of this yet. He'd kick Billy's fucking head in too once he'd finished with his brother.

Harry yanked hard at the wooden entrance door and walked in, shaking the rain from his dripping black hair. He looked up the corridors, left and right, wondering where he would find the man who had been screwing his wife behind his back. A nurse walked towards him and somehow Harry managed to plaster a big fake smile on his face. If he wanted to find Frank, he knew he would have to turn on the charm.

'Excuse me, Miss, but would you be so kind as to tell me where I might find Frank Myers? He's a porter here, a good mate of mine.'

The nurse thought for a moment then replied, 'Frank's gone home for the day, I believe. I'm quite sure I saw him leaving about an hour ago. He must have been on an early shift.'

Without bothering to thank the nurse, Harry rushed back out of the door, then stopped in his tracks halfway down the path. He suddenly realised he had no idea where Frank lived, so he began to retrace the route he had just taken and headed back to the pub to find Billy.

Helen was so grateful to Glenda for 'babysitting' her parents. It was always a worry to her when she popped to the shops, never quite sure what she would come home to. The larder at home was looking like Mother Hubbard's so Helen had jumped at the offer when Glenda said she would stay there for a while so that Helen could go shopping. She didn't plan on being out for long, especially in this horrendous rain.

Glenda had called around that morning, eager to tell her all about the wonderful hours she had spent with Frank the previous day. It was so lovely to see her best friend happy again, and though Helen was worried about the consequences of Harry finding out, she felt confident that Glenda wouldn't do anything silly to give the game away. Frank sounds like such a nice man, thought Helen, as she recalled the tales Glenda had told her. Who would have thought that anyone related to Billy Myers would be nice!

Helen was soon outside the greengrocer's but hesitated to go in, knowing that Betty Howard would be ready to pounce, keen to get any gossip she could. Prepare yourself, she thought, and just at that moment she heard a man's voice shouting her name.

Helen turned to look and was taken aback to see Harry storming towards her. Her heart rate quickened and her mouth went dry. She could see from the look on his face that he wasn't happy.

'Have you seen Glenda lately?' Harry barked.

'Er, no, I haven't,' Helen lied. She was panicking inside, thinking it was strange for Harry to stop to talk to her. Normally, if she saw him in the street, he would just about manage to acknowledge her with a bit of a grunt.

'I bet you're fucking lying. All of you, you're all as bad as each other! Glenda's a lying bitch and a two-timing slag. I ain't no fool!' he yelled. 'I know what she's been up to and she's gonna fucking well regret it! And so will that Frank Myers when I get my hands on him. You will too if I find out you knew anything about it.'

Betty Howard was standing in the shop doorway with wide eyes, listening to the threatening exchange. Helen wanted to run and hide behind Betty, but somehow she gathered the strength to stand there and answer Harry back. 'I don't know what you're talking about, and quite frankly I don't want to know. This has nothing do with me, so please don't try to involve me in anything to do with your marriage,' she said, pretending to be affronted. 'Now if you'll excuse me . . .'

Helen walked around Harry in the most dignified manner she could muster and headed back towards home. Her chest was hammering and tears welled up in her eyes. She could hear Harry shouting from behind her, his words terrifying her.

'I'm telling you, Helen, I'll find the pair of them, and I'll knock down every fucking door in Battersea until I do. If you see her, tell her I'm coming for her and don't think she can hide out at Ted's house either!'

A feeling of foreboding came over her. Obviously Harry had somehow found out about Glenda and Frank.

After a few minutes, Helen looked back over her shoulder to see that Harry was nowhere in sight. With the view clear, she ran as fast as her chubby little legs would carry her, adrenalin speeding her along. Breathless and close to vomiting, she fumbled with the key in the door, desperate to warn her friend about Harry's discovery.

'GLENDA, GLENDA!' Helen ran through to the kitchen to find Glenda gently rocking Johnnie on her lap. 'I've just seen Harry and he's on the warpath. He knows about you and Frank!'

Glenda turned as white as a sheet and her bottom lip started to quiver as she placed Johnnie back in his pram. 'How does he know? Oh, God, he's gonna kill us! What can I do? Helen, I . . . I . . .'

'You've got to get away. It's the only thing you can do. Harry's out for blood, Glenda.'

'Oh, God, Frank! I've got to warn him. I've got to get to him before Harry does! Where was Harry going when you saw him?' Glenda was shaking and pulling at her hair.

'I don't know, but how are you going to warn Frank? Do you know where he lives? And even if you do, it ain't safe for you, Glenda. Think about it. What if you find out Frank's address and go there, only for Harry to turn up too? It'll make things worse.'

'It can't get any worse than this,' wailed Glenda, 'and I *have* to let Frank know. I love him, Hel, and I can't let Harry hurt him. I know he lives in one of those prefabs down Sheepcote Lane so I'll take my chances and make a dash for it.'

'I still think it's too dangerous, but if you insist on going I think you should leave Johnnie here. You'll be faster without him, and just in case you do see Harry and he kicks off, it'll be better if Johnnie's safely here with me.'

Glenda looked thoughtfully at the pram for a moment. 'Yes, you're right. Thanks, Helen. I'll be back as soon as I can.'

'Just keep safe and be careful, and watch out for him when you come back here. He thinks you might try and hide from him at your mum and dad's,' said Helen as she anxiously ushered her friend out of the door.

The wind was behind Glenda as she raced through the streets of Battersea, thankful that she knew the short cuts and back alleys. It was a fair jaunt to Sheepcote Lane but the terror of Harry getting to Frank before she did kept her going fast.

The prefabricated single-storey homes were packed in quite tightly in the lane and Glenda had no idea which one Frank lived in. Most windows and doors were firmly closed to keep out the bad weather but there was nothing Glenda could do other than shout out Frank's name in the hope that someone would hear her and direct her to where she could find him. She was taking a big risk as Harry could walk around the corner at any second and hear her shouting, but in her desperation she wasn't thinking clearly.

'FRANK . . . FRANK MYERS . . .' Glenda had stopped running and was walking at a fast pace with her hands to her mouth like a loudspeaker, repeatedly calling his name.

A stout old woman in a grubby white apron opened her front door and poured out a tin bucket of dirty water next to her step.

'Can you tell me where Frank Myers lives, please?' Glenda asked.

'I can, love, it's the second one in on the right, over there, see . . .'

Glenda thanked the old woman and dashed off. She furiously rapped on the front door, still shouting out Frank's name. Nearby curtains were twitching and a few nosy neighbours had appeared on their steps to see what all the commotion was.

The front door of the house opened and a concerned-looking Frank stood there.

'Frank, thank goodness I've found you. You've gotta get out of here, now, quick. He's coming. He knows about us.'

'Whoa, girl, slow down. What's happened?'

Glenda didn't think there was enough time to explain; she just wanted Frank to get to somewhere safe, any place where her husband couldn't find him. 'It's Harry, he knows about us,' she repeated, 'and he's looking for you. It won't take him –'

Glenda was interrupted by Joyce, who suddenly appeared in the doorway and pushed Frank to one side. 'What's going on? What's all this noise about and who the hell are you?' she asked as she eyed Glenda up and down.

'It's all right, Mum. Leave it, will you? Go back inside,' said Frank, trying to push back past his mother.

'I'll do no such thing, and I'll thank you not to give me orders in my own home. Now, tell me what's going on!' Joyce demanded, hands on hips, and judging by the look on her face Glenda reckoned Frank had better do some explaining – and fast.

'Just tell her, Frank,' Glenda pleaded, nervously looking over her shoulder, 'and quickly. We haven't got much time!'

'Come on, get inside. You too, Mother,' Frank said as he looked up the lane.

Glenda glanced around the kitchen, but hardly took anything in. All she could think of was what would happen when Harry came knocking on the door. 'Mrs Myers, I'm so sorry, but I've become friends with Frank and my husband has found out about it. He's none too happy about it and he's on the rampage. If he finds Frank I dread to think what he'll do to him. He's out looking for him now and it won't take him long to find out where you live. We've got to get out of here. Once he's finished with Frank, it'll be me next.'

Joyce's eyes widened with horror. 'What did I tell you, eh? I knew this would happen,' she said, shaking her finger at Frank.

'I know that, Mum,' said Frank as he put his arms around Glenda, who almost collapsed into them, 'but we've got to do something. We can't just sit here and wait for him to come knocking.'

'Please, Frank, please, you've got to get out of here,' Glenda pleaded.

'No, I'm not leaving you to face this alone. We know what Harry is capable of and he's already put you in hospital. '

'Frank, please, he . . . he'll kill you. You've got to make a run for it.'

'It's nice to see that your main concern is for my son,' Joyce said, her tone softer, 'and it seems to me that there's only one thing for it. You'll both have to disappear down to my sister's place in Margate. Your aunty Anne will put you both up, Frank, and Harry won't find you there.'

'But what about you, Mum?'

'Don't worry about me. I'll pretend I know nothing about the pair of you seeing each other, and if he dares raise a hand to me I'll threaten him with the police.'

'I still don't like the idea of leaving you,' Frank said worriedly.

'Look, I'll be fine, and as it sounds like there isn't much time to spare, I think you should go now. Go on, get a move on!'

'Thanks, Mrs Myers,' Glenda said gratefully.

'We'll have to go to Clapham Junction to catch a train, but I don't get paid until tomorrow, I'm almost skint.'

'I – I've only got about a shilling,' Glenda said, feeling as though they'd lost any chance of escape.

Joyce reached for an old biscuit tin on top of her kitchen unit. 'Here you go,' she said, tipping out a pile of coins. 'It's my savings, a bit of money I've been putting away for my house. There's a good few bob there.'

'No, Mum, I can't take it.'

'Don't be daft. It's only a loan and you can pay me back when this all blows over. When Harry turns up I'll do my best to put him off your scent, but please, now just go!'

'I've got to fetch Johnnie before we go to the station! He's at my friend Helen's house.'

'From what you've said, I don't think we can risk going to get him. What if we run into Harry?'

'But Frank, I can't leave him!'

'It won't be for ever, just for now. Once we know it's safe, we can come back for him.'

'Frank's right,' Joyce added. 'You can't take a baby on the run with you.'

Glenda couldn't bear the thought of leaving her son behind. It was her job to protect him, and though she knew that Harry would never hurt Johnnie, she didn't believe anyone would be capable of looking after him and loving him as she did. Tears filled her eyes. She knew that Frank and his mother were right; that until she could provide a home for Johnnie she would have to go without him, but she felt as though her heart was breaking. She hated Harry for forcing her to leave her child – and not only that, she wouldn't be able to see her parents either. She was sobbing now, barely aware of Frank saying goodbye to his mother before he took her arm to lead her outside.

Hoping to avoid Harry, they took the back streets to the station, Glenda still in a daze of pain and anguish at the thought of leaving her son. She couldn't speak, didn't want to speak, time passing in a haze until they were on a train, heading out of the station.

She howled then, while Frank held her close, but she found no comfort in his arms. She couldn't be happy without her baby.

Harry tried the pub near the building site, but Billy had left. With a good idea of where he might be, Harry next pushed open the door of the Castle and was unsurprised to see Billy Myers leaning up against the bar having a laugh and a joke with the landlord. Billy's face changed when he set eyes on Harry, his smile quickly fading as he nervously said, 'Harry, hello, mate. Did you find my brother?'

The slimy bastard, thought Harry. 'No, he'd finished work by the time I got there, so you'd better tell me where you live.'

'But you can't go round my house, Harry. You'll upset my mum.'

'I couldn't give a flying fuck about your mum. Just tell me where you live, Billy . . . or else,' Harry said, not sure if he could hold back much longer from smashing Billy's face.

'Tell you what, Harry. I'll come with you to show you the way,' offered Billy.

'Nah, just tell me, Billy, or I swear I'll rip your fucking head off!'

That was all it took for Harry to find out Billy's address, and as he walked out of the pub he sneered, thinking what a little squirt of a coward the man was. He relished the thought of giving him a good pasting too . . . and soon. His pace quickened and his jaw was tight with anger as he reached Sheepcote Lane. Fists clenched, he hammered on the front door, and shortly after it opened. 'You must be Mrs Myers,' he snapped.

'Yes, that's right, and I don't take kindly to anyone pounding on my door. Who are you? And what do you want?'

'I want a word with your son Frank, and now!'

'He ain't here and I'll ask you again, who are you?'

'I'll tell you who I am. I'm the husband of the woman your son has been seeing behind my back. Get him out here now, or do I have to come in there and drag him out myself?'

'How bloody dare you come round here throwing your weight about! My son wouldn't get involved with a married woman, never in a month of Sundays. You wanna get your facts straight before you go threatening me. And anyway, I told you, he isn't here! Feel free to come inside and take a look if you don't believe me, but you'll be wasting your time. Frank's gone off; said he wants to do a bit of travelling and I don't know when he'll be back.'

Harry wasn't stupid. He knew the woman was spinning him a yarn, no doubt trying to protect her precious son. He barged past her and checked every room, scowling with disappointment not to find the man he wanted to turn into pulp. 'He can't have got far,' he spat in Joyce Myers's face. 'I'll find him, and when I do he'll be coming home in a box!'

'Get out! Get out of my house!'

'Don't worry, I'm going,' Harry snapped, and, as he stormed out, his thoughts suddenly turned to Glenda. He wanted to get home now to make sure that she hadn't been stupid enough to run off with Frank Myers. Fury consumed him. If she had, he'd catch up with her. No woman was going to make a monkey out of him and he'd make sure Glenda suffered – suffered badly before he killed her too.

It was gone six in the evening and the sun had set when Maude heard someone thumping on her brass door knocker. When she went to answer the door, Maude was astonished to find Helen standing on her step with Johnnie in his pram.

'Hello, Mrs Jenkins. Sorry to bother you, but I didn't know what else to do,' Helen said through snotty tears.

'That's all right, love. Come inside in the warm. Now, stop your bawling and explain to me why you're here with Johnnie.'

Bob sat bolt upright in his armchair and folded away his newspaper, looking just as surprised as Maude to find Helen in his front room with baby Johnnie.

'Evening, Mr Jenkins,' Helen managed to gasp as she wiped her nose. 'I – I'm sorry about this.'

'Sit down, Helen,' Bob offered, his brow furrowing.

'I don't suppose you know what's been going on with Harry and Glenda?' Helen asked nervously.

'No, love. We ain't seen them this week,' Maude answered, but then felt a surge of anxiety. 'Why are you asking? Has something happened to them and that's why you've got Johnnie? Have they had an accident or something?'

'No, no, it's nothing like that, but, oh dear, this is so difficult,' Helen cried.

'For goodness sake, just spit it out,' Maude urged.

'It . . . it's Harry. I saw him down the high street earlier on today and he's got it into his head that Glenda has been having an affair with a bloke called Frank Myers.

She hasn't been, they're just friends, but Harry will never believe that. Anyway, she left Johnnie with me while she went to Frank's house to warn him that Harry was on the rampage and looking for him. But that was hours ago and she hasn't come back. I'm really worried, Mrs Jenkins. If Harry found Glenda with Frank, I dread to think what he'd do to them.'

Maude slumped back on the couch, trying to digest the information Helen had just bombarded her with. So Glenda was seeing another man. Just friends, my arse, thought Maude. If Harry had found out about it, there was no doubt in her mind that blood would be spilt. This Frank bloke, whoever he was, he wouldn't stand a chance against Harry. Serves him right, thought Maude, he should never have messed about with a woman married to a Jenkins. But she didn't want Harry getting into bother with the law and going down for a crime of passion.

'Bob, get yourself round to Harry's house and see if he's there,' Maude ordered her husband. 'Find out what's going on and why Glenda hasn't been to pick up Johnnie.'

'What if he isn't there?'

'Then try the pub. And you, Helen, I know your mum shouldn't be left alone, so leave Johnnie here and get yourself home.'

'OK, but I'm going to be worried sick until I know that Glenda is all right. As soon as you know, will . . . will you get word to me?'

'Yes, of course I will,' Maude assured her as she ushered her to the door.

'And, Mrs Jenkins, please don't let Harry know that it was me who told you about what's been going on.'

'No, I won't bring your name into anything. Now, off you go.'

Bob put on his flat cap and followed her out into the cold evening, closing the door behind them both. Maude returned to the front room, still reeling from what she had just been told. If it hadn't come from Helen's mouth, she would never have believed that Glenda would have an affair. Her daughter-in-law was so quiet and timid, like a mouse; she just didn't seem the type. Then again, it's the quiet ones you've got to watch out for, thought Maude.

As the shock began to wear off, anger set in. Maude wondered what on earth Glenda was thinking of; after all, she knew full well what Harry was like and she must have known how he would react to her being unfaithful. He would go berserk and by the sound of it he had. Maude twisted her hands with worry. Glenda was a sly bitch and deserved whatever she had coming to her but Harry wasn't good at controlling his temper and she fretted that he would go too far. Wait 'til I get my hands on that girl, she thought. If my son don't give you a good bloody hiding, Glenda Jenkins, then I will!

Johnnie began to cry loudly, obviously hungry. As Maude picked him up, she whispered in his ear, 'There, there, it'll all be all right,' though in her heart of hearts she didn't believe her own words.

She still had a bottle and some formula, but as she made up the baby milk Maude had a deep feeling of dread, her intuition telling her that nothing was ever going to be 'all right' again.

Chapter 8

It was almost half past nine at night when Glenda and Frank disembarked from the steam train at Margate station. Frank had been here to see his aunty Anne a few times before, but only as a child. He felt he recognised the station, but was unsure of the way to his aunt's house.

It was cold and Frank pulled his collar up around his neck, then took Glenda by the arm, gently leading her towards a taxi sitting just outside the station. He took in a long breath of the fresh air, thinking that in different circumstances it would have been nice to be away from the dirty stench of Battersea.

Frank tapped on the driver's window and the driver wound it down, offering Frank a big, toothless grin.

'Evening. Could you tell me how to get to Tivoli Road, please, mate?' Frank asked.

'Course I can. Jump in, boss, and I'll run you up there,' the driver offered.

'Thanks, but I can't afford it. If you could just give me the directions, I'm sure I'll find it.'

'No bother,' the driver said with a smile, 'I won't be getting any more fares tonight so get in and I'll drop you there on my way home.'

Frank was slightly taken aback by the kind offer, but grateful, especially as Glenda looked completely washed out. It wasn't any wonder, he thought, considering how devastated she was at having to leave her baby. He'd thought she would never stop crying, but eventually her tears had dried and she'd dozed off for a while, no doubt mentally exhausted.

They climbed into the back of the taxi, glad of the warmth, but less than five minutes later Frank was thanking the driver as he bade him goodbye. With Glenda behind him he walked up the short path to tap on his aunt's front door, thinking as he walked that turning up out of the blue like this was going to take some explaining.

His aunt Anne answered the door in her slippers and dressing gown. Her grey hair was tucked into a hairnet and a cigarette dangled from the corner of her mouth. She was a round woman, just as Frank remembered her, and though she could look as fierce as his mother, Frank knew she was a jolly old soul. He recalled how she used to bounce him up and down on her big belly and sing a little ditty to him, 'Diddily diddily, diddily dum, he's got a dirty bum.' The memory brought a warm smile to his face but he wondered if his aunt would recognise him now.

'Hello, young man, can I help you?' she asked as ash dropped from the end of her cigarette onto the tiled hallway floor.

'Aunty Anne, it's me, Frank Myers. Joyce's boy,' Frank answered, holding out his arms for the huge hug he expected to greet him.

'Frank? Well, I never! What on earth are you doing

here?' she asked as she scooped him into her flabby arms.

Frank chuckled. 'If you let me breathe for a minute, I'll tell you.'

'Sorry, love,' Anne guffawed. 'Come in, son, and your pretty lady friend there too. Blimey, you look like you could both do with a good hot drink inside you.'

Frank was pleased to be so warmly welcomed. It would make it easier to explain the reason they were there. He looked over his shoulder at Glenda, who was silently following him up the hallway, her face pale and her expression glum. All he wanted was to hold her, to protect her and make her happy, but he knew that, until she held her son in her arms again, that was unlikely to happen.

Anne made them tea and then bustled off again, before long returning with two large bowls of vegetable broth and a lump of bread which Frank gratefully accepted on behalf of them both. The large front room was lit by two art deco style wall lamps and a roaring fire positioned in the centre of the back wall, with a long wooden table and six chairs in a bay window on the opposite side. There were two large, comfortable sofas and an armchair close to the fire.

'So then, son, what brings you to my door at this time of night?' asked Anne.

'It's a long story, Aunty, but the long and short of it is that Glenda and me need a place to stay for a while. We've come as you see us, just in the clothes we're standing in. We've hardly any money to spare, but I'm willing to do any handy jobs round the house, and Glenda can cook and clean. We ain't asking for charity, but we do need your help.'

'No problem! I've got plenty of jobs that need doing and the house isn't as clean as I'd like it due to these old bones of mine. Now, tell me why you're here. Are you in some sort of trouble?'

'Well, you could say that,' Frank said.

'I hope you haven't been breaking the law. I don't mind you staying here, but I don't want the police on my doorstep.'

Frank slurped his broth and enjoyed the warm liquid as it passed down his throat. If only it *was* the police that they had to be afraid of, he mused, rather than Harry Jenkins! 'No, don't worry, Aunty. The police aren't looking for us. It's Glenda's husband and he's a nasty piece of work. He doesn't like it that we're friends. In fact, he hates it so much that if he finds us he'll probably kill us. We've come here to hide away from him.'

'Oh, I say, I've only just noticed your wedding ring. So you're a married woman then, Glenda?' Anne looked shocked to say the least.

'Er, yes,' Glenda replied meekly. 'But it's not what you think. Frank and I are just friends, but my husband is a very jealous man.'

'It's none of my business what you two have been up to, though I will say that whilst you're under my roof I won't have any shenanigans going on. I keep a respectable house, so you, Glenda, can have the spare room, and Frank, you'll be down here on that couch. You'll find it comfy enough. And one more thing – this lot down my street love a bit of scandal so make sure you keep your business to yourself.'

'Yes, all right, Aunty,' Frank agreed.

'I expect with you wearing a wedding ring people will

take you for a married couple. If you don't want that, Glenda, I suggest you take it off,' Anne said.

Glenda didn't answer and when Frank looked at her he saw that her eyes were vacant again, as though nothing had really registered with her. She seemed to be in a fragile state of mind and it worried him.

Bob could see the lights on at Harry's house, but no one was answering the door even though he'd repeatedly hammered on it. He tried calling through the letterbox and tapping on the front-room window, but still nothing.

He was about to give up when through a chink in the curtains he spotted that someone was sitting in the front-room armchair. It looked like Harry so Bob tapped harder on the window. Eventually, he saw Harry rise to his feet and at last he came to the door.

'Dad, what do you want?'

'Your mother sent me round,' said Bob as he entered the house and wrinkled his nose at the smell of strong alcohol. 'Where's Glenda?' he added casually, though inwardly he was frantic with worry.

Harry threw himself back down into the armchair, picked up what was left of a bottle of cheap whisky and downed the remainder of the contents before he answered, 'I don't know where she is. I can't find her and it looks like she's fucked off with my boy.'

'Johnnie's round at ours,' Bob said, confused. 'He ain't with Glenda.'

That information made Harry more alert. 'Johnnie's at yours? That doesn't make sense. Glenda wouldn't leave without him, I'm sure of that.'

'Look, I don't know what's going on, but I'm telling

you that the boy is safe and sound with your mother. Now you'd better tell me what's going on 'cos your mother will skin me alive if I don't go home with the full story.'

'I heard that my slag of a wife has been seeing another bloke so I went to sort him out, only to find that he's done a runner. As Glenda ain't here, I assumed she'd gone with him, but, as I said, I ain't so sure now.'

'But you haven't seen her?'

'No, I've already told you that,' Harry snapped. 'Now you tell me how Johnnie ended up at your house.'

Bob was calmer now he knew that Harry hadn't hurt Glenda. He hadn't heard Helen's request to Maude on the doorstep and was oblivious to keeping her name out of anything. 'Helen dropped him off a little while ago. From what I can make out, Glenda was at Helen's when she found out you were looking for this bloke. She went to warn him, and no doubt that's why he's done a runner.'

'I'll find him and when I do . . .' Harry growled.

'Forget about him for now. Johnnie needs his mother and I can't believe that Glenda would run off without him. She must be hiding somewhere locally, probably until she thinks you've calmed down.'

'She'd better not show her face!' Harry screeched. 'I'll kill her if she has the audacity to set foot in here. And I'm telling you, she's never going to see Johnnie again! The dirty fucking bitch ain't fit to be a mother. Nah, that's it, she's fucked up and when I get my hands on her I'll make sure she knows it!'

The room smelled musty, and a thick layer of dust had settled on the small oak dressing table under the window, but Glenda was glad of the time alone in Anne's spare room. It gave her the chance to clear her head and to plan what she was going to do next.

She climbed under the candlewick bedspread in an old flannelette nightie that Anne had found for her to wear. It was huge and swamped her small frame, but she was glad of its warmth. It was very kind of Frank's aunt to put them up, but Glenda could think of nothing but Johnnie. She wondered who was looking after him, and if he was crying for his mummy. She felt deep pangs of guilt and questioned how she could have left him, but everything had happened in a frantic haste, leaving her little time to think. That was no excuse, though. She had still abandoned her son. What sort of awful mother was she?

And what about her parents? No doubt Harry would be on the rampage so she daren't get in touch with them. She knew what Harry was capable of – knew he'd try to intimidate her parents into telling him where she was. The only way to keep them safe was to give them no clue as to her whereabouts.

Glenda sobbed into her lumpy feather pillow. She had to find a way to get her son back, but to do that she would have to get past Harry. Oh, Johnnie, my baby, she gasped as she curled into a ball of pain.

Eventually Glenda fell into a light sleep, which was broken throughout the night with images of a distressed Johnnie needing his mum.

As the weak morning sun broke through the thin curtains, Glenda rubbed her sore eyes and slowly managed to drag herself from the bed. She could hear light chatter between

Frank and his aunt drifting up the stairs along with the smell of toast which, despite her unhappiness, made her tummy rumble.

The toilet was outside in the small back yard, which meant she would have to brace herself to face the cold and to greet Anne and Frank, so she did her best to plaster a smile on her face as she entered the back kitchen.

'Good morning, love,' Frank chirped, 'did you sleep all right?'

'Yes, thanks, but I need to pop outside. Please excuse me for a minute.'

Glenda closed the door behind her, but not before she heard Anne's loud whisper. 'She's telling fibs, Frank. These walls are paper thin, and with my room being next door I could hear her breaking her heart half the night.'

When she returned to the kitchen, Glenda found that Anne had made her a cup of tea, along with some hot buttered toast. 'It's much easier to get the likes of bread and butter down here compared to the queues in London,' said Anne. 'Get stuck in, girl, there's plenty more where that came from.'

'Thanks, and I'm sorry if I disturbed you with my crying last night. It's just that I'm upset about leaving my baby behind.'

'Yes, Frank told me this morning, and no wonder you're upset. You'll get him back, but in the meantime you've got to keep your strength up, so tuck into your breakfast.'

Glenda felt a little heartened by Anne's reassurance and bit into her toast. 'Thank you,' she said quietly.

'Good girl, and don't you go worrying yourself about having a bit of a cry.'

'I–I miss Johnnie so much.'

'Right then,' said Anne brusquely, 'we'll just have to get our heads together and work out how you're going to get him back. What do you think, Frank, any ideas?'

Frank looked thoughtful. 'I know you won't want to hear this, Glenda, but I don't think we can rush it. Harry won't have calmed down overnight. In fact, I bet he's even more worked up now he has realised you've left him. I think we should leave it be for a couple of weeks at least. Let him think you're never going home, lead him into a false sense of security, and then . . .'

'A couple of weeks! I can't wait that long, Frank! Johnnie will forget who I am.'

'No, he won't,' Anne insisted. 'Your baby won't forget his mum, and, to be honest, Frank's right. Your husband will be on his guard. In fact, even if he lowers it, I think you should both stay away from Battersea. You could get someone in your family to bring Johnnie to you, somewhere well away from London.'

'I can't get my parents involved. My mum has been poorly for years and I dread to think what Harry would do to them if he found out.'

'A friend then?'

'No, I can't put a friend at risk for the same reason,' Glenda said, close to tears again at the hopelessness of the situation.

'Look, love, don't get upset,' said Frank. 'We'll find a way, but as I said, I think we'll have to bide our time for a while before we make our move.'

Glenda nodded sadly. She couldn't bear the thought of being away from Johnnie for so long, but what Frank suggested made sense. She could hardly just waltz through

Harry's front door and take Johnnie. Anyway, chances were Johnnie would be with Maude and there was no way her mother-in-law would simply hand him over. 'I think you're right, Frank. As much as it breaks my heart to admit it, I'm going to have to bide my time.'

Chapter 9

Maude warmed up a small pot of stewed apples and called through to Bob, 'Fetch Johnnie in here. I've done him a bit of breakfast.'

It was a Saturday morning and although she was more than happy to look after her grandson, Maude thought that Johnnie should be with his father on weekends. However, there was no sign of him; no doubt Harry had been down the Castle last night and was probably nursing a hangover this morning.

'There you go, love. There's a good boy,' Maude cooed as she spooned mouthfuls of the stewed apples into Johnnie's mouth. The poor love, she thought, he misses his mum and Glenda is missing out on her son growing up. It's been over three weeks since she's seen him and look at Johnnie now, eating solids like a big boy. Still, she had never really liked Glenda, and as it had turned out Johnnie would probably be better off without her. After all, Maude reasoned, what sort of woman could run off with another man and not even think twice about leaving her own flesh and blood behind?

'Bob,' Maude said as she put Johnnie back into his

pram, 'get round to Harry's and get him up. He should be here with his son, not feeling sorry for himself.'

'Leave the poor bloke be. He's getting over his wife doing a bunk, and he's entitled to a bit of self-pity.'

'Enough is enough and it's time he pulled himself together,' Maude argued. 'This baby needs his father and I'll thank you, Bob Jenkins, to do as I bloody well ask!'

Maude didn't see Bob roll his eyes, but she knew it was exactly what he'd be doing. However, no matter what her husband said, she wasn't prepared to let her son wallow in self-pity for a moment longer. He needed to step up now, and, so help her, she'd make sure that he did.

Harry could hear the front door banging, but really didn't want to get out of the warmth of his bed. Whoever was knocking could bugger off!

'HARRY . . . HARRY . . .' Bob was shouting through the letterbox.

For God's sake, thought Harry, can't a man get any peace round here? He had a thumping headache. Feeling agitated, he reluctantly got out of bed and made his way to the front door. 'What are you playing at, Dad? It's only ten in the morning.'

'Your mother wants you up and round at ours. She reckons Johnnie needs to spend some time with you.'

Harry could see his father looking at the mess in the front room as he followed him inside: dirty clothes strewn around, plates scattered about with half-eaten meals left on them, and several empty spirit bottles. The kitchen didn't look any better; the sink was overflowing with washing-up.

'This won't do, son,' Bob shook his head. 'You've got to pull yourself together. Look at the state of this place, it's filthy and you don't look much better yourself.'

'Yeah, well, housework is a woman's job and I ain't got a woman now, have I? As for me, I just need a good soak and a bit of breakfast. Tell you what, give me half an hour to spruce myself up and then I'll come round to yours and Mum can make me something to eat.'

'All right, son. I'll see you soon,' said his father, adding sternly, 'but don't you go taking advantage of your mother! She's already run ragged looking after that boy of yours so I don't want to find that she's been round here cleaning up your mess too!'

Harry could do without his father giving him an ear-bashing, but he had a point and his mother did too. He hadn't seen his son all week and with his sober head on he did miss the little lad. As he closed the door behind his father, Harry ran his fingers through his greasy hair. He'd been so consumed with fury towards Glenda, and so frustrated at being unable to find any trace of her, that he'd been drowning his sorrows night after night.

He looked into the mirror over the hearth, appalled at how bad he looked. Though he hated to admit it, he was missing his wife. But, he thought to himself, even if Glenda showed her face again and begged him to take her back, he'd refuse out of pride. She had turned him into a local laughing stock and to spite her he would never let her set eyes on their son again. Feeling indignant, Harry turned away from the mirror, avoiding his own eyes. Despite everything, he knew in his heart that he still loved Glenda, and probably always would.

* * *

Glenda looked out across the bleak, shingled landscape towards the grey sea. It was blowing a gale; huge waves crashed on the shore. Frank had managed to find work with a local fishing family and, although the pay was low, he brought home enough to cover the small amount of rent on the converted railway carriage that they called home. She smiled ruefully at the thought of him coming home later, smelling like a battered cod.

Despite the sometimes wild weather, Glenda quite liked living in Dungeness; she enjoyed the quiet, and it felt like a lifetime away from Battersea. But mostly she felt safe. Harry would never find them here. Anne had friends in Margate who rarely used their holiday home, especially in winter, and they had been happy for them to rent it for a six-month period. Thankfully they hadn't minded that Frank couldn't pay up front, and when Glenda had first seen the old sleeper carriage she could see why. She hadn't thought it possible that anyone could actually live in such a confined space, but she'd got used to it in the last couple of weeks and now found it quite cosy. There was an outside toilet, but that didn't bother her. It was all she had known as a child growing up in her parents' house in Battersea, and with the carriage there was the bonus of a bath in a small inset.

Their first night in the carriage had been a bit awkward to begin with. There was only one bedroom and Frank had uncomfortably raised the subject of them sharing it. He had said he didn't want to push Glenda into anything she didn't feel ready for. She loved how he was always so thoughtful about everything and considered her feelings, something that Harry never did.

There hadn't been any need for the awkwardness, as once Frank had held Glenda in his arms, she had melted into his body and relished their gentle lovemaking. It had felt so natural and had cemented their love for each other.

There were only three things Glenda felt unhappy about: the first was missing Johnnie, the second that she was worried about her parents, and the last problem was boredom. There wasn't much she could do about Johnnie and her parents until she received news of them from Helen, but she could do something about the boredom and had taken to crocheting woollen blankets. So far she had made two from the large bag of wool remnants that Anne had given her, and she'd been successful in selling them both to the vicar at St Mary's Bay church. He had told her how draughty the old vicarage could be and hoped to see her in a few weeks' time for the Christmas service.

The thought of Christmas felt like a stab in the heart to Glenda. She couldn't bear to be away from her baby, especially as it was his first one. Her crochet needle became blurred as her eyes filled with tears and she gave way to the emotions that she had kept bottled up for weeks.

Glenda threw her head back and wept heavy, racking sobs as she held her half-made blanket to her chest. 'I miss you so much, Johnnie,' she cried loudly, but no one would hear her wailing in the small railway carriage on the shingle of Dungeness. As her body shook and she howled, so did the wind as if echoing her grief.

* * *

It was rare for Helen to receive letters, but she instantly recognised the handwriting on the envelope that had just dropped through the letterbox as Glenda's. She ran up the stairs to her room and, sitting on the edge of her thin mattress, she eagerly ripped open the envelope, overjoyed to finally hear something from her best friend.

My dearest Helen,

I'm so sorry that it's taken a while to write to you, but me and Frank have been busy trying to sort things out. And I'm ever so sorry about abandoning Johnnie with you the way I did. I didn't have a choice when it dawned on me that with Harry baying for blood there was no time to do anything other than to get on a train and go. I hope it didn't cause you any trouble with Harry.

We've found somewhere really nice to stay for a good few months. To prevent any gossip we are posing as a married couple and I'm using Frank's surname. He's got a job packing and selling fish. We're living right next to the sea which is wonderful, albeit bitterly cold at the moment. Despite that, Johnnie would just love it here! I'm guessing he's at Maude's most of the time and I know it's hard for you, but please, I'm desperate for news of him. I don't want to put you in a difficult position, but I would be ever so grateful if you would write back to me and let me know how he is. And my mum and dad, I know they'll be worried about me, so can you tell them that I'm fine, though please don't tell them where I am in case Harry tries to force it out of them.

To protect you as much as I can too, I've given you the address of a little church. The vicar said it's all right for me to have letters delivered there. I told him it's because the post doesn't come out to where me and Frank are living, and anyway, it's best this way. Like my parents, if you don't know where I am then Harry can't bully you into telling him.

I haven't worked out how I'm going to get Johnnie, but somehow, one way or another I'm going to. In the meantime, I shall really look forward to hearing from you.

I want you to know that I'm fine, Helen, and other than pining for my son, I'm happy. Frank is a good man and takes good care of me. Once I get Johnnie back, I know my life will be perfect.

I hope you are well. I miss you. Please don't say a word to anyone about me contacting you, not even my mum and dad.

Thanks Helen, thank you for everything.

Your best friend, Glenda xxx

Tears dropped onto the thin white paper and smudged the black ink. Helen rubbed her eyes and forgot for a moment that her left one was still painful from where Harry had unceremoniously punched her.

Glenda was right to be cautious, and Helen shuddered as she recalled her encounter with Harry. Quite a crowd had gathered around them as he'd drawn attention by shouting obscenities at the top of his voice, and when Helen had fallen to the wet pavement, not one man had stepped in to help. They were all too scared of him and his reputation. When Harry had raised his booted foot to kick her in the stomach, it was Betty Howard who had screamed out for him to stop. He did, and though

Helen didn't like Betty, she would be forever indebted to her for her bravery in saving her from a savage beating.

Her dad had been furious and urged her to get Harry arrested for assault, but she doubted anyone would own up to witnessing what had happened. Not only that, she was scared of Harry and how he'd react if she put the police onto him. In the end, she just nursed her wound and said nothing.

Harry was a nasty piece of work, and after that he'd tried to intimidate Glenda's dad into telling him where she was too, but thankfully, though he'd yelled and expostulated, he hadn't actually laid a hand on Ted. How Glenda had put up with such a nasty, violent man for so long was beyond Helen, and after having read the letter she was over the moon for her friend and pleased to know she was safely out of Harry's wicked reach.

She would happily write back with news of Johnnie and keep her up to date with the health of Elsie and Ted, but she would have to warn Glenda about writing too often as she was sure the postman had been nobbled by Harry. The postie hadn't said anything, but there was something about the way he'd looked at her when he handed her the letter. It had roused her suspicions and she didn't want another run-in with Harry.

Helen was keen to get news back to Glenda, yet realised she knew nothing of Johnnie. She hadn't seen him since she'd dropped him at Maude's on the night that Glenda had run away. She'd wait until Monday, and while Harry was at work she'd pop over to Maude's. Hopefully Maude would let her have him for an hour or two, and then she could take him to see Ted and Elsie as they must miss seeing their grandson.

Helen carefully dried her eyes and then smoothed down her dress. It wouldn't be long before her sister arrived with her toddler niece and nephew for their monthly visit. She would have to get a move on and get their favourite gingerbread men baked or all hell would break loose in the Atkins house!

Chapter 10

It was Christmas Eve and though Glenda wasn't full of Christmas spirit she was determined to make an effort for Frank's sake. She had found two similar-looking pebbles in the shingle that both had a hole through them. She thought they would make quaint matching keyrings, one for Frank and one for her. It wasn't much of a gift for the man she loved but she did think it was quite romantic. The pebbles were wrapped in a pair of crocheted socks that Glenda had fashioned into the shape of fish. She thought the socks were practical but would also make Frank laugh, and she did love to hear him chuckle.

Frank had found a pine branch to use as a Christmas tree and, as she knelt down and placed her gifts underneath, she noticed a small wooden box balanced in the foliage. It must be a present for her and though she was curious she resisted the temptation to sneak a peek inside.

The carriage door opened as Frank walked in. The wind from outside caused the paper chains suspended from the ceiling to flap in a frenzy.

'Quickly, Frank, close the door, the decorations will break,' called Glenda.

Frank had been working overtime most nights and the

long hours meant much of their time was spent apart. She missed him terribly when he was at work and jumped up from her knees to rush and greet him.

'Hello, my sexy lady. I hope you haven't been snooping around that Christmas tree?' Frank teased as he wrapped his arms around Glenda.

'I was tempted,' she answered, 'as I did notice there's something in the tree. Is it for me?'

'Of course it is, but only if you've been a very good girl,' said Frank, and he playfully slapped her behind.

'Oh Frank, you know me – I'm always a good girl . . . and when I'm bad, I'm even better!' Glenda flashed him a saucy smile and ran giggling as Frank chased her through the carriage.

He caught up with her and embraced her tightly, lifting her off her feet. 'I love you, Glenda . . . you naughty little minx.'

Glenda smiled, 'I love you too, Frank Myers. Now put me down and jump into that nice hot bath I've run for you, you bloody reek of fish. I'll stick your dinner on to warm and you never know, if you're lucky, I might come and wash your back.'

Frank didn't need telling twice and stripped down to get in the bath. As Glenda went to the kitchen, she glanced at her naked lover. She couldn't wait to be snuggled up in bed with him later. It was going to be a Christmas tinged with sadness for her, but she was looking forward to waking up in the morning with Frank by her side. It would be one of the best Christmas Days she had ever had, and one thing was for sure: she would not be missing Maude's limp vegetables or Harry's unreasonable demands. Of course, she missed Johnnie, but in spite of that, for the first time in a very long while, Glenda felt a true sense of happiness and contentment.

Billy Myers woke up on Christmas morning to the sound of his mother loudly humming 'The Harry Lime Theme'. Bloody hell, he thought, she's in a good mood considering her precious son isn't here today. He climbed out of bed and drew back the curtains to reveal a blanket of white snow covering Sheepcote Lane. It didn't look like it was going to thaw any time soon.

In the warmth of the small kitchen, Billy offered up a kiss on the cheek to Joyce, who quickly dismissed him. 'Pack it in, you silly sod!' she chortled, ruffling his hair. 'Sit yourself down and I'll knock you up some powdered eggs for your breakfast. Shame our Frank ain't here. He was always like a big kid at Christmas and didn't half used to make me laugh.'

Billy hung his head in shame as he tried to hide his guilt from his mother. He liked the fact that Frank wasn't around but wished it hadn't been his doing. His stupid jealousy over that Glenda Jenkins had driven him close to madness. How could he have grassed up his own brother to Harry? And by doing that he had put his mum at risk too. He had known that Harry would do his nut, and he had expected Frank to get a bit of a pasting, but it had never crossed his mind that Harry would have killed Frank if he had found him.

And where had it got him? Nowhere, that's where. Harry had still come after him and given him such a beating that he'd been off work for a week. He didn't really understand what he'd done to deserve it as he thought he was doing the bloke a favour. When he had been on the receiving end of the punches, in between the blows, Harry had spluttered that Billy had enjoyed telling him about Glenda, something Billy would've denied had he only had a chance to answer.

When he'd returned to the site he'd been given the sack. The foreman said it was because of all the sick leave, but Billy guessed that it was more likely to be Harry's doing, what with him and the foreman being good mates. And Glenda had gone too. Who would have thought that she would have run off with Frank?

'Oh, don't look so downcast, Billy. I guess you're missing your brother too, eh?' said Joyce, her large hips rolling from side to side as she walked across the kitchen.

'Yeah, I miss him' – like a hole in the head, he added to himself. 'Like you said, Mum, Christmas ain't the same without Frank here, winding me up along with his laughing and joking.' More like getting on my nerves, thought Billy, glad that his goody-two-shoes brother wasn't there soaking up all the attention. Joyce had never said so, but Billy felt that Frank had always been his mother's favourite. He surmised it was on account of Frank being the eldest, Joyce's first born, but it wasn't fair that Billy had to play second fiddle just because he was the younger brother.

'I just hope he's happy, wherever he is and whatever he's doing. I wouldn't have minded a Christmas card from him though, but there you go, that's sons for you!'

Billy inwardly cringed. Joyce was obviously missing Frank and though it suited him that his brother wasn't there, his secret was eating him up inside. He wondered if he should tell her that it was his fault that Frank was forced to do a runner. He thought she might hate him for it and favour Frank even more than she already did, but Joyce had always told them that honesty was the best policy. Maybe if he was honest with her she might have more respect for him, and it would go a long way to easing his conscience.

His mother sat down as Billy tucked into his eggs, and she slurped her hot tea. 'There's a little something for you on top of the mantel,' Billy told her. 'It isn't much, what with me being out of work at the moment, but go and get it, Mum, and happy Christmas.'

She scraped her chair back and did a little jig, bosoms bouncing. 'Oh, son, you shouldn't have, but I do love a surprise,' she said, rushing to the front room. She soon returned, clutching a small package wrapped in brown paper. She untied the string and slowly peeled back the paper to reveal a long red wool scarf with matching gloves. 'Billy, they're lovely! Thank you. I'll need these in this bloody weather!'

'I'm glad you like them, Mum.'

'Now, this is for you,' she said, taking a box from the kitchen unit and placing it on the table in front of him. 'Go on, open it.'

Billy looked at the box and felt awful. His mother was being so good to him. She had nursed him back to health after the beating he'd taken from Harry, yet she had no idea that it was because of him that Frank had disappeared. He found he couldn't live with the guilt any longer and said, 'Mum, I think there's something you should know. All that business with Frank and Glenda Jenkins. It was me that told Harry.' He immediately felt better having confessed, but squeezed his eyes shut and waited for the onslaught from his mother.

'What, did you think I didn't already know that? Don't be daft. It's been the subject of gossip around here for weeks. I'm sure you meant no harm by it, and whether you let it slip to Harry by accident or because you thought you was doing the right thing, it's done now.'

'I still feel rotten about it.'

'Let's get one thing straight. Frank shouldn't have been messing about with a married woman, but he was and now he's paying for it. It'll never be safe for him to come back to these parts, not while that Harry Jenkins has got breath in him. I just wish I knew where he was, and that he's all right.'

Billy couldn't believe that his mum already knew and hadn't blamed him for Frank's departure. It was a massive weight off his mind, but he still felt a pang of jealousy when he thought of Frank with Glenda Jenkins.

Later that afternoon, whilst his mother busied herself in the kitchen preparing Christmas dinner for the two of them, Billy looked through the half a dozen cards on the mantelpiece. There was one with a picture of a Scottie dog on the front and a tartan border, which he guessed would be from his uncle Joe who had moved to Scotland twenty years ago, and another with children carolling which had been signed inside from Maurice and Lilly. Maurice was his dad's brother whom Billy had never liked. The others were from neighbours, but then he spotted something just poking out behind the clock. Billy pulled it out to find it was another card, one with a funny seaside cartoon scene that had probably been sent by his aunty Anne in Margate. He hadn't seen her in years, but held fond childhood memories of holidays splashing in the cold sea and donkey rides along the beach. He wondered why his mother had stuffed this card out of sight behind the clock.

Puzzled, Billy opened the card to read inside, and suddenly his blood ran cold. There was a little note attached, which referred to the 'happy couple' having settled in well and the young man finding work. In an instant Billy knew who Anne was talking about. Frank and Glenda were in Margate and his mother must have known about it for all these weeks. Nearly two months and the sly old cow had kept it quiet! Billy fumed. He'd bet she'd bloody helped them get away too.

And there was me, he thought, feeling guilty! All the warmth he'd been feeling towards his mother went up in a puff of smoke as he wondered what Harry would think if he told him that he knew where the lovebirds were shacking up. That sort of information had to be worth something!

Even with the stove lit and wearing two pairs of socks, Frank's feet were still numb from the cold. He guessed that Glenda wouldn't feel much like celebrating today so he had politely declined the offer from his aunt Anne to share her Christmas lunch. Anne had said she was secretly pleased as she really would rather go down to the village hall where a good crowd of old folk were going to have a bit of a knees-up.

Frank had gathered enough driftwood for the burner to keep them warm all day, and his boss had given him two nice pieces of plaice, which he planned to gently fry for himself and Glenda later. He couldn't wait to gather around their pine branch and watch Glenda's face as she opened her gift. They couldn't be married as it would be impossible for Glenda to get a divorce, but they were living as husband and wife so Frank had decided he should make it more official. The small wooden box in the pine branch contained a gold ring. It was second-hand and hadn't cost Frank much but the extra hours he had been working just about covered the price. He was sure Glenda would love it and hoped it fitted her.

Frank climbed out of the bed, being careful not to disturb Glenda who was still sleeping. He shivered with the cold as he made a pot of tea, arranged a plate of toast and went to gently wake Glenda.

'Good morning, my lovely,' he said as he placed the tray down and gently kissed her on the cheek. 'Happy Christmas, darling, and can I just add that you look absolutely radiant this morning!'

'Oh, Frank, stop it. I must look a right sight!'

Her dark hair was tousled, and overnight a big red spot had sprouted on her chin, but as Frank looked at Glenda he thought as always that he had never seen a sight so beautiful. However, before he could tell her so, Glenda flew out of bed and made a barefoot dash for the outside lavvy.

'Are you all right?' Frank called after Glenda, but she hadn't made it to the toilet and was vomiting just outside the door on the icy shingle.

'I'm fine, Frank,' said Glenda lifting her head and wiping her mouth, 'I don't know what came over me . . . it must be all this Christmas excitement.'

'Come on, love, get back inside in the warm. I'll get you a glass of water.'

'Thanks, Frank,' she answered but he noticed she appeared a bit distant and wondered if she felt giddy.

'Do you need a hand? You ain't going to faint or nothing, are you?' he asked, genuinely concerned by her pale complexion.

'No . . . no . . . I think I'm OK,' she said but her face was creased into a frown and Frank wasn't convinced.

'Let's get you back into bed for a bit. It's warmer in there and I've made you some tea and toast. It might settle your belly a bit.'

Frank tucked Glenda under the covers and plumped up the pillows behind her before handing her a cup of tea. 'How are you feeling now, love?' he asked.

She looked like she had seen a ghost. Frank began to worry what he would do if she was taken ill on Christmas Day as he wouldn't be able to call a doctor out to her.

'I'm feeling better now, thanks, but I'm not sure I can get this toast down me. I should try, though, Frank . . . especially as I think I'm eating for two.'

It took a while for the penny to drop, then Frank suddenly felt like the wind had been knocked out of him and he jumped to his feet only to grab hold of the door frame to steady himself. 'You're p–p–pregnant?' he stuttered.

'Yes, Frank – I think I am.' Glenda smiled and her cheeks finally filled with colour again.

'I'm gonna be a father? Oh, Glenda, that's the best Christmas present ever!'

For a brief moment Glenda looked truly happy, but all too soon the sadness that Frank was so used to seeing in her eyes reappeared and he knew that she was thinking about Johnnie. 'Come here, love,' he said, his arms outstretched. 'We'll get your boy back soon, I promise you. We can all be a family together.'

The stocking for Johnnie hanging on the front-room mantelpiece was filled with mostly homemade presents for his first Christmas. Maude had knitted him a teddy bear and a dog and Bob had carved him a toy car, which made Maude smile as Johnnie was still a bit too young to play with it. He was growing fast, though, and held under the arms he would balance on his chubby little legs, but Maude felt it would be some time yet before he was walking. Crawling wasn't far off, though, and then she'd need eyes in the back of her head to keep a watch on him.

She'd roasted a chicken that she had managed to buy under the counter and she was now awaiting the arrival of Harry, his elder brother Len and Len's wife Connie.

Harry arrived first, looking dishevelled, but with his arms loaded with gifts. 'Merry Christmas, Mum. Where's that boy of mine?'

Maude led Harry through to the front room where Bob was happily bouncing a contented-looking Johnnie up and down on his knee.

'Look who's here, Johnnie, it's your daddy,' said Bob.

Johnnie chuckled in recognition. 'Da, da, da,' he squealed in delight.

'Mum, did you hear that?' Harry said excitedly. 'Johnnie just said his first words, he called me Dad!'

'He certainly did. Who's a clever boy then?' Maude said with a smile. 'Shame his mother isn't here to witness it,' she added through gritted teeth.

'Look, I ain't being funny, but it's Christmas Day and

I don't want that woman's name mentioned. She's out of our lives now and good riddance to her,' Harry growled.

'That's fine by me, son,' said Maude. 'Now, get your coat off and I'll put the kettle on. Len and Connie will be here soon.'

Maude could feel the tension emanating from Harry. Sure, he was putting on a cheery face, but he'd snapped far too quickly when she had mentioned Glenda, and it didn't look as if he'd seen a bathtub for at least a week. Still, she reasoned, it's still raw for him. It's only been a couple of months but at least he gets up and goes to work every day. It was a shame he didn't come round more often for his tea; no doubt he was spending all his nights down that bloody pub.

A knock on the door stopped Maude from her worrying thoughts and she went to greet her eldest son and his wife. Connie had never fallen pregnant, but they seemed happy enough without kids and lived a good life in Clapham. Len had worked for the same timber merchant for years and had worked his way up to general manager. He earned a good wage, and although he wasn't a violent man like his younger brothers, he was seen as just as arrogant and known to be a bit of a showoff.

Maude opened the door to see a large shiny car in the road behind Len and Connie.

'Hello, Mother,' Len greeted her. 'Yes, take a good look. That's my new car. What do you reckon? Go and get Dad, will you?'

Len looked smart in his grey suit and fresh white shirt, with a smart black overcoat and glossy shoes. Blimey, thought Maude proudly, this will be one in the eye for the neighbours. There weren't many cars that drove down this street, or many men that turned up looking like they had just walked out of a fine West End department-store window.

'Oh, look at you,' Maude shrieked, hoping to see curtains twitching. 'Don't you look a picture, and fancy that, having your very own car. BOB! Bob, come 'ere and take a look at this.'

Bob came to the front door and looked just as impressed as Maude at the sight of his son and his new car.

'Fancy a quick ride in it?' Len asked.

'I don't know about that. I've never been in a car before, but I would like to sit in it,' Maude said as she climbed in to admire the leather upholstery and polished wooden dashboard. She held the steering wheel and looked around at her family's happy faces. Happy, that was, except for Harry, who had pulled back the net curtains and was scowling through the window.

As she got out of the car, Maude could see a few curtains moving and was glad that the neighbours had noticed. She deliberately took her time as she sauntered back to her front door. Huh, she thought, that'll give them all something to talk about. My boy's got a car.

Harry greeted his brother with a nod and grunted an abrupt 'Hello' to Connie, and though Maude thought it was a bit rude she held her tongue. Truth be told, none of the family had ever thought much of Connie with her haughty accent and her finicky manner. She hadn't come from anything special, but she liked to think of herself as something other than working class.

Maude noticed her looking down her nose at the

slightly tatty furniture, but chose to ignore the silent insult. Yes, her stuff might have seen better years, but it was all clean and well cared for, unlike Connie's house, where Len had hired a cleaner as Connie couldn't keep on top of the housework. Too busy out spending my son's hard-earned cash, Maude decided, noticing the expensive jacket and skirt that Connie was wearing and the string of pearls around her slender neck.

It was only mid-morning, but Maude was concerned about Harry, who was now sitting silently in the corner of the room and knocking back a bottle of beer. He didn't seem to want to interact with his brother, and Maude thought maybe there was a bit of jealousy there. She was relieved to see that he was pretty much ignoring Johnnie too. He had had quite a few beers, and Maude wasn't sure if he was still in a fit state to hold the child. When lunchtime arrived, Bob handed Johnnie over to Connie while he and Len brought in the kitchen table for them all to sit round. The atmosphere was light and Harry seemed to have cheered up a bit, but he was still drinking heavily. Maude laid the table and put out the chicken, vegetables and potatoes, pleased with her efforts and looking forward to toasting lunch with a large sherry.

However, just as Maude put the gravy boat on the table, Connie squeaked and held Johnnie out at arm's length. 'Oh, goodness me,' she complained. 'This child absolutely stinks and I do believe his nappy needs to be changed. Get him off me! Someone – anyone – please take him!'

Maude saw Connie's look of disgust, and that Johnnie was wriggling and crying in her bony hands. She also noticed the flash of anger on Harry's face, he too annoyed at Connie's reaction to his son.

'Give him here,' said Maude quickly, taking Johnnie into her arms. 'There's no need for that, Connie. He's just a baby and can't help soiling his nappy.'

'Well, he should have his mother here to look after him. It's a disgrace, it really is. And we can all guess why she took it upon herself to leave with another man,' Connie said accusingly as she looked at Harry then back at her long red nails.

Before Maude could react Harry leaped from his seat and upturned the table laden with lunch. 'You bitch!' he screamed at Connie, who now sat pale-faced and frozen in her chair. 'I know what you're saying, you fucking stuck-up mare. You reckon it's my fault that the slag ran off.'

'I–I'm just saying she must have had good reason,' Connie answered, her voice faltering as she struggled to maintain her composure.

Harry's fists clenched. 'Len, I'm telling you, get her out of my sight before I do something we'll both regret!'

Johnnie was screaming, Bob looked dumbfounded, Maude was surveying the upturned table and Len was making a hasty retreat down the hallway, pushing Connie out of the front door in front of him. 'You'll never change, Harry. You ruin everything, always have and always will,' Len shouted at his brother as he slammed shut the front door.

Maude rocked Johnnie and looked down at her lovely Christmas lunch, which was now just a mess strewn over the floor. Harry had sat back down and was swigging from another bottle of beer, his head hung low.

'Well, don't just stand there gawping,' said Maude to Bob. 'Go and get a mop and bucket. You can clear this lot up while I make us some spam sandwiches. Harry, what have you got to say for yourself?'

'Sorry' was all Harry answered but Maude doubted that he truly was. His outburst had been ugly to witness and over the top, yet there were no real signs of remorse. He had just flown off the handle and, she had to admit, it hadn't taken much to get him started.

For the first time, Maude could understand why Glenda had been so frightened of her husband – scared to the point of abandoning her child.

Chapter 11

It was a bitterly cold January, yet Glenda was pleased to see in the New Year and put 1947 behind her. The royal wedding of Princess Elizabeth to Philip Mountbatten had pretty much passed her by, but now with this new life growing inside her she had actually felt like celebrating. It was only overshadowed by guilt and the ache in her heart of missing Johnnie.

Glenda snuggled close to the stove and pulled a blanket over her legs as she took from its envelope the letter that Helen had sent. This must have been at least the twelfth time she had read it since the vicar had passed it to her at the Christmas Nativity play.

Dear Glenda,

I had been worried sick so it was so lovely to hear from you.

I'm so pleased to hear you and Frank have settled in well. The address you gave me for the church is in Kent, so I know you must be living somewhere there. I hear it's a beautiful part of the country. Dad calls it the garden of England, though I did read somewhere that large areas of Kent had suffered with bomb damage. Still, it can't be half as bad as here.

I called round to see Maude, she's been looking after Johnnie and honestly Glenda, she's doing a wonderful job. He looked really well and happy. She's agreed that I can take him for a few hours once a fortnight. It gives her a break and I thought it would be nice for your mum and dad to see him. By the way, they are both well too, though your dad is worried for you. I told him that you're fine and with Frank which has eased his mind, but you know what dads are like.

I talked to Johnnie a lot about you. I'm not sure how much he understood, bless him, but I won't let him forget you. He's grown quite a bit, I think he must have had a bit of a growing spurt but Maude has bought him lots of clothes from the second-hand shop, all washed, and she even got him a special little coat from Arding and Hobbs.

The rest of the letter contained general chitchat and a warning about the postman, so Glenda read the first bit over again. Helen said that Johnnie had grown and she tried to picture him in her mind. Oh, how she longed to hold her child in her arms again, to smell his soft skin and stroke his fluffy hair. The familiar feelings of despondency and guilt overwhelmed her, and she gave in to the tears and heartbreak again.

When she was able to pull herself together, Glenda went to the small cold bathroom to splash some icy water on her face in the hope that her eyes wouldn't look puffy when Frank got home from work. He had gently told her off about getting so upset, saying it wasn't good for the new baby, but nearly three months had passed since she had last seen her son and she was beginning to despair of ever seeing him again.

In desperation, and against Helen's warning about writing too frequently, Glenda took out her pad and scribbled a fraught letter to her friend. She begged Helen to meet her somewhere outside Battersea, if only for just an hour or so. She *had* to see her son.

Glenda hoped against hope that Helen would be brave enough to come, and willing to risk it. She knew it would be painful to have to say goodbye to Johnnie again, but she couldn't put Helen in the dangerous situation of returning to Maude's without him. There was no doubt in her mind that Harry had it in him to seriously hurt Helen. But just to see her child for even the briefest of moments, to cuddle him and love him – it would be better than nothing, which was all she had now.

Frank couldn't wait to get home to see Glenda and sing a song to her belly. She wasn't showing yet, but nonetheless he couldn't resist talking to her stomach. He was so excited about his firstborn child.

He shoved his chilblained hands into his thin mac pockets and walked briskly against the wind. As much as he loved living in this part of Kent with the sea views and the salty fresh air, he couldn't wait for the summer to arrive. Never had he known a wind so cold that it actually caused pain as it lashed his face. He was sure that, if he stopped for just a second, icicles would form in his hair.

Pleased to be in the warmth of their railway-carriage home, Frank went to greet Glenda with a kiss, but just one look at her swollen eyes and he could tell she'd been crying again.

'Yuk, Frank! Please go and wash before you try to kiss me. I'm not being funny but you stink of fish and it's making me feel quite queasy,' she said.

'Sorry, love, of course I will. I didn't think. It never used to bother you, but with the baby and all now I suppose there's gonna be quite a few changes.'

'Yes, I suppose there will be. When I was pregnant with Johnnie I craved coal. Can you believe that? Coal of all things! Harry said it was dirty, bad for me, and he locked the coal shed up. I got so desperate that I had a secret stick which I used to literally drag bits out from under the door.'

Frank laughed, and then went to the bathroom to wash. He could just picture his pretty girl sitting there in the back yard, legs akimbo and her mouth blackened as she chewed on lumps of coal. When he returned, smelling fresher, he bent to kiss Glenda again and this time she didn't protest, though her conversation returned to her son.

'Talking of Johnnie,' she said quietly, 'I've written a letter to Helen asking her to bring him to meet me.'

'Glenda, we've talked about this. It ain't fair on Helen. Harry will go mental if she gives Johnnie to you!'

'No, listen, Frank. I don't intend to take him. I just want to see him – I *have* to see him, if only for a little while.'

'But are you sure you can handle letting him go again, Glenda? It will be like mental torture, and you're bound to get overly upset, which won't be good for our little one,' said Frank as he gently patted Glenda's tummy.

'I know what you're saying, Frank, but *not* seeing him

is causing me more anguish. It's more than I can bear. I don't even know if Helen will agree to meet me, but I have to try.'

Frank wasn't convinced that this was a good idea, but he had so far failed to come up with a way of getting Johnnie home with Glenda on a permanent basis. He'd considered going back to Battersea to snatch the boy, but that would fuel Harry's anger and he'd go all out to find them. Not only that, Frank's wages only just covered the rent and groceries so he had no idea how they'd manage financially. They'd need things for the baby when it arrived: a cot, a pram, clothes and who knew what else. He felt helpless and was desperate to complete Glenda's happiness, especially with her being pregnant, but at the moment he just didn't see how he could support Johnnie too.

He sighed heavily. They were both so full of joy and excitement about the forthcoming baby, but a dark cloud always loomed, and Frank knew Glenda would only be truly content when Johnnie was back in her arms for good. He looked at her, her eyes pooling with tears, and decided that if just seeing Johnnie for a short time would help, it was better than nothing.

'All right, love,' he said at last. 'I ain't the sort of man to stand in the way of a mother seeing her child and if you're positive that you can cope then so be it. Give me the letter and I'll post it in the morning.'

Glenda at last smiled, while Frank worried about how he was going to find the train fare for her to travel to London. He offered up a small prayer. 'Please God, I've never asked you for anything in my life before, but please, Glenda needs this and I want to give her a bit of the happiness she deserves.'

Chapter 12

Maude was looking worn out and old, Bob decided as he tucked into his breakfast while surreptitiously studying his wife. Taking on Johnnie was too much for her, but he knew better than to voice his thoughts. She adored the boy, they both did, but Johnnie was more of a handful now that he could crawl and was running Maude ragged. He would have to get the playpen he was making finished, but he needed a bit more wood to complete the job. Once made it would at least confine Johnnie to one place for a while.

Maude strapped Johnnie into his pram and gave him a finger of bread, butter and sugar to chew on, something that never failed to quieten him. She then flopped onto a chair, her legs spread wide, and said, 'I'm glad Helen will be here to pick him up later. I could do with a break.'

Bob wasn't sure that it was a good idea to let Helen take the boy out again, but as usual he kept his thoughts to himself. Instead he said, 'Where's she taking him?'

'To see Glenda's parents again.'

He picked up his cup and gulped the last of his tea while thinking that if Harry found out all hell would break loose.

As though reading his mind, Maude said, 'Don't say anything to Harry. What he doesn't know can't hurt him.'

'I ain't stupid.'

Maude's eyes narrowed. Bob stood up quickly and grabbed his coat. 'I'd best be off or I'll be late for work.'

'Don't forget to bring the wood home for the playpen. If you weren't so bloody useless you'd have finished making it weeks ago.'

'I'm doing it as fast as I can. Every part of it needs sanding to make sure that Johnnie doesn't get any splinters from the wood, and then it will need a good few coats of varnish.'

'Don't stand there making excuses. Just get it done. Now go on, bugger off to work. I'm sick of the sight of you.'

Bob wished he had the nerve to tell his wife that he was sick of the sight of her too. He also wished he had the courage of Glenda, his daughter-in-law. If he had, he'd have walked out on Maude years ago.

The steam train rumbled along the tracks, and the noise seemed to beat in time with Helen's pounding heart. She amazed herself at how brave and defiant she was being, but Glenda was her lifelong best friend and she would do anything she could to help her out.

When the letter from Glenda had arrived, the postman had given her that look again, but Helen had just ignored him and snatched the letter from his hand. It didn't come as any great surprise that Glenda had asked to secretly meet with her and Johnnie, because the same idea had crossed her own mind. But she had been surprised to read that Glenda was in the family way. It was quite sudden, but Helen was pleased for her friend, though she knew the new baby could never replace Johnnie.

Now they had actually put their plan into action, Helen found herself shaking with nerves. That confrontation with Harry had scared her more than she cared to admit, and Helen really didn't want to be faced with his temper ever again.

The train pulled into Bromley station, where Helen spotted a very excited-looking Glenda waiting on the platform. Johnnie had been asleep for most of the journey but suddenly woke up. It was almost as if he could sense Helen's excitement and anticipation as he gurgled in glee.

As Helen got off the train Glenda ran towards her through the steam, her arms waving frantically and tears streaking her face. Her sweater was pulling tightly across her swollen stomach but it wasn't obvious that she was pregnant.

'Helen, I can't believe you're here, that you did this for me! Oh, look at my gorgeous baby,' Glenda exclaimed as she eagerly took Johnnie from Helen's arms.

Helen grabbed the folded-up pushchair then watched in fascination as Johnnie traced his fat little hand over his mother's face, beaming with delight.

'I've missed you so much, my beautiful baby boy. Mummy loves you and oh, you're just so gorgeous.' Glenda pulled Johnnie close to her and looked over his shoulder. 'Thank you, Helen, thank you so much.'

They walked to a local park and played together for just over an hour. Glenda's eyes filled with tears when she saw that Johnnie could crawl. 'I'm missing so much,' she said sadly. 'I think he'll be taking his first steps soon but I won't be there to see them.'

Helen didn't know what to say to comfort her friend, but Glenda was so thrilled to see her son that the moment of sadness soon passed. 'How are my parents?' she asked, though her eyes were still on Johnnie.

'They're about the same and, as I said in my letter, relieved to know that you're OK. It's good of Maude to let me take Johnnie to see them and though your mum is like mine and distant a lot of the time, your dad is really chuffed when I turn up with him.'

Glenda turned. 'It's so good of you to take him to see them, and to do this, to bring him to me, I . . . I can't thank you enough.'

'You've already thanked me.'

'I worry that I'm putting you at risk with Harry. It's enough of a risk when I write to you.'

'If our roles were reversed, you'd do the same for me, so stop worrying and just enjoy your time with Johnnie.'

'You're such a good friend,' Glenda said. She leaned forward and began to play with Johnnie again. She looked so happy that Helen didn't want to interrupt, but after a while she couldn't help but become aware of the time. She daren't be late getting Johnnie back to Maude. She'd be faced with a barrage of awkward questions. She hesitated, unsure of what to do. How could she tell Glenda it was time to go? It was just so heartbreaking.

'It's all right, Hel, I know what you're thinking,' Glenda reassured her friend. 'I know it's time for me to say goodbye. I knew this wasn't going to be easy and I've prepared myself. I won't be able to afford the train fare to do this very often, especially when this little one pops out –' Glenda patted her stomach '– but I can't wait 'til next time. Here, Helen, this should cover the cost of your ticket.'

'No, no, there's no need for that. I'm just sorry I can't do more to help,' said Helen glumly.

Glenda pressed the money into Helen's hand. 'Frank did a bit of overtime to cover the fares and as you've done me a massive favour you shouldn't have to be out of pocket. If you don't take it, I won't feel that I can ask you to do this again.'

'All right, if you insist. I just wish I could leave Johnnie with you, but I'm too scared of what Harry would do to me,' she said, deciding to keep to herself the fact that she'd already been attacked by Harry. It would only upset Glenda if she knew, and telling her served no purpose.

'I know what he's like and I wouldn't let you put yourself at risk. The only way would be to snatch him from Maude, and that way you wouldn't be involved.'

'Glenda, I'm not sure if Harry is still looking for you or not, but if you took Johnnie he wouldn't rest until he found you.'

'I know, but this is so hard, Helen,' she said, hugging Johnnie. 'I know he's heavy now, but I want to hold him for as long as I can. Do you mind pushing the pram again?'

'No, of course I don't,' Helen said as they set out for the station.

They showed their tickets and checked the train arrival times.

'Your train leaves first,' Glenda said, 'so I'll come to your platform to see you off.'

Helen nodded, but she could see tears gathering in

Glenda's eyes. She knew it was going to be really hard for Glenda to part with Johnnie again, so when the train came into view she reluctantly folded the pram then held out her arms to take him. 'Oh, love,' she said softly, 'don't cry, it'll upset him, and you'll see him again soon. Take care of yourself, won't you, especially now you're in the family way again.'

Fighting back tears, Glenda fiercely kissed Johnnie, and as though aware of her distress, he began to cry. 'Shush, darling, shush,' Glenda soothed, her voice cracking.

Helen opened a carriage door and shoved the pram in, then once again held out her arms, but Johnnie was clinging to his mother. The guard called for passengers to board and, reluctantly prying him loose, Glenda at last handed him over.

Helen quickly climbed into the carriage and sat down, soothing Johnnie as the guard blew his whistle and the train pulled away. It was heartbreaking to see Glenda running alongside the train to get a last glimpse of her son, tears streaming down her cheeks, but then the train gathered speed and Glenda disappeared out of sight.

Betty Howard hadn't got anywhere with using her feminine charms on Billy Myers. She had the distinct impression that he wasn't interested in her and the thought crossed her mind that maybe he had an eye for the fellas. It wasn't legal, but what else could explain his ability to resist her? After all, as lots of men had told her, she was one of the best-dressed and best-looking young women in Battersea.

Her boss had let her off work early today as there was a lack of deliveries. Stock was pretty low so he'd gone off to source some new suppliers. Betty had wanted to take full advantage of having the afternoon free and had decided on a little shopping spree up the Junction. She had spent the afternoon going in and out of shops, but there wasn't anything that took her fancy. It was all so drab, utility stuff mostly, and she was sick and tired of the military cut. She longed for colour, flamboyance, and so finally settled on a bit of blue material that she could turn into a half-decent skirt using her trusty sewing machine.

Betty's feet were aching and she decided to make her way home, but as she passed opposite the train station she spotted Helen on the other side of the road. It was a surprise to see her pushing a pram, one of those folding ones, which she recognised as Glenda's. Helen wouldn't have Glenda's pram unless Johnnie was in it, would she? Something didn't add up in her mind. Betty was about to call out to Helen, but paused in thought. What was Helen doing with Johnnie at the train station, and did Harry know about it? She smiled to herself, thinking this would give her the perfect opportunity to have a quiet word with him. She had always thought Harry was a bit of a looker and though he had a vile temper on him, she was convinced that the love of a good woman could tame him. And now, with Glenda out of the picture, the man was fair game.

Betty grinned to herself. She knew that Harry always went for a drink after work. She would need to hang around for a while, so she turned on her heels and headed for a little café. She'd bide her time in there; rest her feet, have a cuppa, and then in an hour she'd contrive to bump into Harry.

After taking her time over two cups of tea and several cigarettes, Betty set out on her mission. Her luck was in. She was only halfway along Falcon Road when she saw Harry coming out of the Queen Victoria.

'Wotcha, Harry. I haven't seen you in a while. How are you?' she asked as she fell into step alongside him.

'Betty, yeah, I'm all right,' he answered, but he didn't look at her properly and Betty felt as though her sexy stride and fluttering eyelashes were going to waste.

'Are you on your way to the Castle?'

Harry grunted, which she took as a yes.

'Mind if I accompany you? Only if you want to buy me a drink or two, I've just seen something that you'll find very interesting,' she said, and Harry stopped walking to look at her. Good, she thought, she'd got his attention. She quickly licked her lips to add a bit of shine.

'I doubt it, Betty. Unless you've seen that slag of a wife of mine or her fancy man, I ain't interested.'

'No, I haven't, but I've seen something else that you should know about. As I said, it's something I'm sure you'll find interesting, so why not buy me a drink and I'll tell you all about it?'

'This had better be good,' Harry growled as he began to walk again.

Betty tottered along, trying to keep up and smiling to herself. She was finally going to get Harry's undivided attention.

Maude had to admit that she'd enjoyed an afternoon off from Johnnie while he was with Helen, but now she was starting to get a bit anxious. For the first time, Helen was late. She should have been back an hour ago. Maude paced the floor nervously, and then looked out of the window again, hoping to see Helen pushing the pram down the street.

She hadn't mentioned anything to Harry about Helen taking Johnnie out because she knew he'd disapprove. Harry didn't want Johnnie to have anything to do with the Webbers, but they hadn't done anything wrong and she felt it was cruel to stop them seeing their grandson. However, despite Helen's reassurances, there was always that constant worry, a niggling fear that Helen would be daft enough to give Johnnie to Glenda.

At last there was a knock on the door and Maude's concern was replaced with anger.

'You silly girl,' she snapped as she opened the door to Helen, 'what time do you call this? You should have had Johnnie back here over an hour ago!'

'I . . . I'm so sorry, Mrs Jenkins,' Helen stuttered. 'I took Johnnie to the park and lost track of time. It won't happen again.'

'Too right it won't,' Maude screeched, 'I don't think this is going to work out. It might be best if you just stay away from the boy. You know my Harry would go mad if he knew about you taking him out and now you turn up late, worrying the life out of me. It just won't do!'

Helen paled. 'Please, Mrs Jenkins, I love having him and Elsie and Ted love to see him. It would really upset them if you put a stop to it, what with Glenda being away.'

'Well, it ain't my fault their daughter's a tart!' Maude yelled, shaking her fist, and seeing Helen flinch she remembered hearing gossip that Harry had once gone for her, knocking her to the floor. She had chosen not to believe it at the time, but seeing Helen's fear softened her anger. 'All right. I'll give you one more chance, but if you're ever late back again, that'll be it!'

'Oh, thank you, Mrs Jenkins. I promise not to do it again.'

Maude took Johnnie indoors and lifted him out of his pushchair. That's blinking strange, she thought as she noticed bits of black grit on his blankets. It looks like he's been near the railway but Helen said she took him over to the park. Very peculiar indeed!

Bloody Betty Howard and her gossiping. Harry wasn't really in the mood for her tittle-tattle, and didn't want to fork out to buy her one of her fancy drinks, yet maybe, just maybe, if she did have something useful to tell him it might be worth it. And let's face it, he thought, if anyone is going to know anything about what goes on around here, it'll be Betty Howard.

Harry paid the landlord for the drinks and joined Betty in a dim booth where he found her moving up very close to him.

'Thanks, Harry,' she purred and looked over the top of her glass as she sipped her drink.

Though Harry hadn't been bothered about seeing women since Glenda had left, he could still read the signs and got the distinct impression that Betty wanted a little more than to just impart a bit of gossip. The trouble was, Betty was known to be the local bike and he cringed at the thought of who might have been there before him. Still, even so, if she was willing . . . Harry felt a stirring in his groin. He did still have his needs, after all.

'So come on then, Betty, what's this all about?' he asked,

dropping the aggression and smiling as he placed his hand on her knee.

'Well, you know me, I ain't one for telling tales, but you'll never guess who I saw leaving the train station.'

'I've no idea, Betty, who?'

'Helen, that's who,' Betty answered as she pushed her thigh up against Harry's.

'So what? What makes you think I'd find that interesting?' Harry asked, wondering where this conversation was going.

'As I said, she was leaving the station, Harry, and she was pushing your son in a pram. Now I don't know about you, but I found myself wondering where she'd been with him.'

Harry quickly removed his hand from Betty's knee and knocked back his pint. Johnnie was supposed to be with his mother, so what on earth was Helen doing with him? A thought occurred to him. Could she have been to meet Glenda? What was his mother playing at? Questions whizzed through his mind and he stood up angrily. Without saying goodbye to Betty, Harry left the booth and rushed out the door, keen to get to his mum's house for some urgently needed answers.

He let himself in and found his parents in the front room, with Johnnie quietly playing on a blanket in front of the fire.

'Hello, son,' said Maude. She looked up, apparently pleased to see him.

He could feel his patience teetering and didn't bother to greet his parents properly, choosing instead to get straight to the point.

'What's all this I've been hearing about Helen taking

my boy out? Somewhere on a train, too? I want to know everything, now!'

Maude looked flabbergasted. 'I don't know what you mean, son,' she answered.

'Don't try to deny it. Betty Howard said she saw Helen coming out the station with Johnnie in his pram. Is she lying to me then?'

'I don't know about her lying, but I think she must have been mistaken. Johnnie's been here with me all day.'

'So Helen hasn't been here?'

'Of course not. Do you think I'd be stupid enough to let her have Johnnie? I mean, given the chance she could hand him over to Glenda – I wouldn't risk that.'

Harry took a seat in the armchair and sighed deeply. He could feel the anger ebbing away from him. 'That Betty Howard's a stupid bitch. This is typical of her, though, thinks she sees something then can't wait to spread it about. For a while there, Mum, I've got to be honest, until you put me straight I thought you'd gone soft in the head or something.'

Maude laughed, 'I'll be a long time dead and buried before my head goes soft, son, don't you worry about that.'

Harry leaned down and picked up Johnnie. That wife of his still had the power to evoke such strong emotions in him. He stroked his son's back, allowing his thoughts to move back to Betty Howard. He thought of her thigh pressing up against his in the pub. Daft bitch or not, he found he couldn't help wondering what it would be like to have her in his bed.

Chapter 13

Maude had sighed with relief when Harry had left last night to go back to the Castle. She hated having to lie to her son, and tossed and turned half the night, angry with Helen. The grit she had found in Johnnie's pram now made sense – Helen had been on a train with him. Why had she lied about it, and, more importantly, where had she been and who had she seen?

She had her suspicions, but surely if Helen had taken Johnnie to see his mother, Glenda would have kept him. It didn't make sense and she was determined to get to the bottom of it, one way or another. As Helen worked in the mornings, Maude waited until after lunch to go see her.

It had been a long time since she had been down this street, but not much had changed. The houses looked a little scruffier and the steps and windows weren't as clean as they used to be, but it was little wonder, thought Maude, considering the austere times people were having. With a stern face, she knocked on Helen's door and was glad to see the girl looked scared stiff when she saw her.

'Mrs Jenkins, I wasn't expecting you. What can I do for you?' Helen asked, her face ashen.

'You, my girl, have got some explaining to do!'

148

Helen, with obvious reluctance, opened the door wider. 'You'd better come in,' she said nervously. Maude took Johnnie out of his pram to carry him inside, and Helen pointed to a chair for her to sit on. 'My parents are upstairs having a nap, so please, would you mind keeping your voice down?'

'That depends on you,' Maude said as she sat down, Johnnie perched on her lap. 'Now then, my girl, I ain't here for niceties so I'll get straight to the point. I know you've been up to something with Johnnie. So come on, spit it out and don't bother spinning me a yarn.'

Helen's eyes widened and her jaw dropped. Her mouth opened and closed, but no sound emerged.

'It's no good looking like a fish out of bleedin' water. Just tell me what you've been up to.'

'I—I don't know what you mean,' Helen gasped at last, looking close to tears.

'Look, I know you lied about taking Johnnie to the park yesterday. You took him on a train, and I think I can guess why.'

'I—I can't tell you.'

'Yes, you can. I want the truth, though if my suspicions are right, I certainly won't be telling Harry about it.'

Helen looked somewhat relieved, but she was still biting her bottom lip. 'I'm so sorry, Mrs Jenkins, but you're right, I did lie to you. I think you've guessed that I took Johnnie to see his mum, but it was for the first time. I should have told you, but I didn't think you'd allow it so I had to do it behind your back.'

'You know where Glenda is then?' asked Maude.

'No, she won't say. We met at a train station in the country and she travelled there by train too.'

'Did she try to take the boy from you?' Maude questioned.

'No, no, she didn't. She just wanted to see him and made it quite clear she had no intention of taking him. She gave me her word and she kept it.'

Maude sat quietly for a moment as another lightbulb seemed to flick on inside her head. 'So this meeting at this train station wasn't a coincidence, it was well thought out and planned. How did you arrange it? Has she written to you?'

Helen's bottom lip started quivering again and Maude could see that Helen knew exactly where this line of questioning was leading.

'Yes, she has sent me a few letters,' Helen answered uneasily.

'So you must have a return address for her then?'

'No, Maude – sorry, I mean Mrs Jenkins! I don't write back. Glenda said in her last letter that she would be at the station and would wait to see if I turned up.'

'Don't take me for a fool,' Maude raised her voice, 'she knew exactly what day you had Johnnie and the only way she could have known that is if you told her! You've been straight with me so far; don't ruin it with more lies now.'

Helen hung her head. 'OK, yes, I have written back to her, but I don't know her address. I send the letters to a church and she collects them from there. Please, please don't make me say any more. Glenda is my best friend and I'm not prepared to give you the information for Harry to find her and hurt her.'

Maude had known that Helen would protect her friend from Harry, but what Helen didn't know was that Maude would do the same. She had seen the rage in Harry on

Christmas Day and how easily he could flip. Maude was convinced that no good would come of Harry finding his wife. He had made it quite clear what he would do to her if he did, and Maude knew they weren't empty threats. As much as she hated what Glenda had done to her son, she had to protect him from going to jail. Harry was out of control and if he found out where Glenda and Frank were, Maude was convinced it would result in Harry doing time for murder.

'Look, love,' Maude said calmly, 'I don't want my Harry finding out where they are any more than you do. I just hope that Glenda doesn't think she can take Johnnie. Harry's bad enough now, but if that happened it would send him over the edge and somehow he'd find them.'

'Glenda knows that. As much as it's breaking her heart, she doesn't hope to get Johnnie back. She just wants to see him, but from what she's told me money is tight and she'll find it hard to afford the train fare. She's asked me if we can just meet occasionally, perhaps every few months.'

Maude couldn't believe the audacity of the girl.

'I'm not having that, Helen. It's too risky. Harry was round last night asking about you having Johnnie and taking him on a train.'

'No, oh, no,' Helen gasped, her eyes rounding in fear.

'That bloody gossiping bitch Betty Howard saw you and told him, but you can calm down. I denied it all and he believed me.'

Helen visibly slumped with relief. 'Thank goodness.'

'We were lucky this time, but Helen, I don't trust you now. I can't let you have Johnnie again.'

'Mrs Jenkins,' Helen begged, 'Glenda is his mother and

you should have seen them together. It isn't right to stop her seeing him. Not only that, if you don't agree to it she might get desperate and try to snatch him back.'

Maude's first reaction was to say no, but then she paused in thought. What Helen said made sense. If Glenda had access to Johnnie, if only three or four times a year, she might be happy to leave him with Harry. Whereas to deny her access might well push her into coming back for the child. She sighed.

'You might have a point, though I ain't happy about it. Still, I suppose at the end of the day, like you say, she *is* his mother and I know what that feels like. I couldn't begin to imagine the pain it would have caused me if I couldn't have seen my boys growing up. But then –' she paused, her face hardening again '– I wouldn't have left their father and run off with another man – not without taking my kids with me.'

Helen was quick to respond. 'I don't think Glenda thought she had any other option. She had to run for her life. She thought Harry was out to kill her.'

Maude said nothing. She knew Helen was right in what she had said. If Glenda had stayed for the sake of Johnnie, the child would have been motherless now. Harry would have seen to that.

Chapter 14

It was a sunny July day, but Glenda wasn't interested in the weather as she screamed in agony.

'ARRRGGGHHH! I can't take this any more!'

'Come on, Glenda, there's not much more to do now, the baby's head is crowning,' the stand-in midwife Flo reassured her as she looked between Glenda's spread legs.

Glenda didn't know the woman very well but was grateful for her coming so quickly. When her labour had started earlier than expected, Frank had gone into a blind panic. To calm him, Glenda had sent him to fetch Flo to help. She was Frank's boss's wife and had always been so accommodating and friendly to her and Frank, but she hoped that this wasn't asking too much of the woman.

'Where's Frank? I need Frank,' Glenda cried, sweat dripping from her brow.

'He's outside, looking like he's having kittens himself, pacing up and down on that shingle. All your blinking screaming is probably frightening the life out of the poor fella. Now stop worrying about where Frank is and concentrate on your breathing!' Flo ordered. She wasn't a midwife but had delivered plenty of babies, her daughter's too, so her confident manner calmed Glenda.

'Thank you for coming round, Flo. I don't think I would have managed on my own,' said Glenda, panting the words in between contractions.

'You would have. We women have been giving birth since the beginning of time and as long as everything is straightforward, there's nothing to it. And anyhow, the way Frank was hammering and shouting at my door, I thought someone was dying!'

'He panicked.'

'It was a relief to find out it's just another baby on the way.' Flo smiled warmly at Glenda. 'Now come on, one more push. That's it, go on, nearly there.'

Glenda felt like her insides were being ripped out of her. Even though she'd done this before, she had forgotten how excruciating it was. She sat up on her haunches and looked down to where her baby's head had just come into the world, but panic suddenly gripped her. 'NO,' she bawled, 'my baby, my baby, it's not breathing!'

'And neither would you if you had that gripped round your neck.' Flo almost laughed. 'So stop being silly and get on with it, one more push and . . . there you go!'

There was a moment of silence as both women waited for the first cry of the newborn baby girl, then with gusto she howled and waved her tiny arms, her little legs kicking.

The door of the carriage flew open and Frank rushed in, almost falling over himself in his haste.

'Frank Myers, you shouldn't be in here yet!' Flo said as she busied herself with the baby.

Frank didn't reply but stared wide eyed as Flo finished what she was doing and wrapped the baby in a blanket and handed her to Glenda. She gazed at her newborn daughter, tears of emotion filling her eyes before she looked up at Frank.

'It's a girl,' she said. 'Say hello to your daughter.'

Glenda held the baby towards Frank and watched as the sweetest smile spread across his face. 'You clever girl,' he whispered to Glenda as he gently kissed her wet forehead.

Flo was busy cleaning up, but Glenda saw a tear trickle down the woman's face. She's got a bigger heart than she lets on, thought Glenda, and she thanked her again for her help.

'Make sure you get plenty of rest now, and Frank, don't worry about coming into work for a couple of days. Stay here and look after these two,' said Flo. 'Don't worry, you won't lose any pay. I'll square it with my Tommy. We'll call it a little welcome present from us for the new baby.'

'I don't know what to say. Thank you, Flo, that's really good of you, and be sure to pass on my gratitude to Tommy too. You're smashing bosses, you really are!'

Flo looked a bit embarrassed, and blustered, 'Yeah, well, have you thought of a name for the baby yet?'

Glenda squeezed Frank's hand. She could hear his voice breaking and knew he was becoming emotional. 'We agreed that if I had a boy, Frank would choose the name, but as she's a girl, it's down to me.' Glenda looked down at her precious baby. 'I think Polly really suits her. My little Polly perfect!'

'Polly . . .' Frank stroked his daughter's cheek. 'Hello, my gorgeous girl. I'm your daddy.'

Glenda closed her eyes for a moment, exhausted, her emotions a mixture of sadness and exhilaration. She almost had the perfect little family; the man she loved and her baby girl, but her happiness wouldn't be complete until she was reunited with her son.

'Get off me, woman,' Harry groaned at Betty as he turned away from her in his bed.

'But it's Sunday morning, we ain't got work today, so how about we spend the day in bed and have a little fun?' Betty hummed as she stroked her finger up and down Harry's arm.

'I can't, I've got things to do. I'm going to my mum's place for dinner and I want to spend some time with Johnnie.'

'It's not fair,' Betty sulked, 'you hardly spend any time with me at the weekends, and I had a special surprise lined up for you today.'

Harry shifted his naked body from the bed and quickly dressed in a vest and pants. 'Shut up moaning and go put the kettle on. I'm parched,' he snapped as he headed for the bathroom.

'But, Harry,' Betty shouted, 'it's such a lovely summer's day. Surely you don't have to rush round to your mum's straightaway. If you don't want to come back to bed, how about a walk in the park?'

Harry stormed back into the bedroom where Betty was sitting up in the bed, grabbed her clothes from the floor and threw them at her, saying harshly, 'If you're gonna keep on at me, then you can bloody well sod off!'

'There's no need to be so moody, Harry,' said Betty indignantly. 'It's just that I'm supposed to be your girl-friend, but come the weekends you don't seem to want my company.'

Harry ground his teeth for a moment before answering, 'You ain't my bloody girlfriend!'

'What do you mean?' Betty asked. 'We've been seeing each other for months now. In fact, I've been hoping you might be thinking about giving me a ring soon.'

'Leave it out,' Harry laughed mockingly. 'Marry you? Are you having a laugh? Anyway, I'm still married to Glenda, or had you forgotten about my wife?'

'You . . . you could get a divorce.'

'No! No way, and even if I did, do you really think I'd marry someone like you? You've got to be kidding me!'

Betty paled. 'But . . . but I've got something to tell you. I'm –'

'I ain't interested,' Harry interrupted impatiently. 'Now get up, get your clothes on and bugger off.'

'But –'

Harry didn't wait to hear any more. He turned on his heels and headed again for the bathroom.

Twenty minutes later, Harry was sitting at the kitchen table enjoying a cup of hot tea when Betty appeared in the doorway, her face slick with perspiration.

'I've been a bit sick, do you mind if I sit down for a minute?' she asked.

'Suit yourself,' said Harry, but he just wanted her to go.

Betty took a seat and folded her arms on the table. 'I'm guessing you've got a bit of a hangover and that's why you're being so nasty, but that thing I wanted to tell you, I was on about it earlier . . . well, I didn't want to say it like this, but . . . I'm pregnant.'

Harry sat in stunned silence for a moment before blurting the first thing that came into his mind. 'Is it mine?'

'Of course it's bloody yours,' Betty said indignantly.

'So you say, but I'd never be sure,' he said harshly.

'You can be. I'm telling you the truth.'

'Nah, I ain't having it. You were seeing Billy Myers before me. It could be his kid.'

'I didn't sleep with Billy.'

'You've slept with half of Battersea, but I'm supposed to believe that you didn't give it out to Billy?'

'Honest, Harry, I didn't!'

'You're a lying tart and I don't believe you. All that talk about getting you a ring – you must think I'm a right mug, but you ain't trapping me into marrying you,' Harry shouted as he scraped back his chair and rose to his feet. He pulled his wallet out of his back pocket, took out a few pound notes and threw them onto the table.

'What . . . what's this?' Betty asked, looking bewildered.

'Take that money and get rid of it. I don't care how you do it, just make sure that you do, and Betty –' he leaned forward so his face was up against hers, their noses almost touching '– don't tell anyone about this or you'll live to regret it. That isn't an idle threat. I'll kill you if you open your mouth.'

'K–kill me!' cried Betty, the colour draining from her face.

'Yeah, that's right. Now get out of my sight, and don't try to see me again.'

Betty at last stood up, but she didn't pick up the money. Harry pushed the notes towards her, but she only cried out, 'Harry, please, it really is your baby.'

Harry banged his fist hard on the table, so hard that Betty jumped in fear. 'Get out!' he yelled.

Her hands shaking now, Betty quickly grabbed the notes before making a dash for the door. As soon as he heard it slam behind her, Harry flopped onto his chair with relief.

'Fucking women!' he mumbled to himself. 'That's it, I'm staying well clear of 'em all!'

Chapter 15

Billy Myers sat back in his chair, watching as his mother bustled around the kitchen. It was August and since Frank had done a runner things had changed. He was the only son at home now, and, as though worried that he might leave too, his mum was making sure that he was well looked after, with decent food put in front of him as soon as he came home from work, and his clothes always freshly washed and ironed. Of course, he knew why. His mother enjoyed the money he provided, and as he was on better wages now, he'd increased her share.

He had something else to smile about nowadays too. Harry Jenkins was no longer the big man. He had blotted his copybook big time with that Betty Howard situation, and most people avoided him now. Billy had never forgotten the pasting Harry had given him and was glad to see the man brought low.

Billy's thoughts turned back to his brother. 'Mum, have you heard from Frank?'

'No, son, not a word.'

'I'm surprised he hasn't been in touch, if only to let you know that he's all right.'

'Well, love, as the saying goes: no news is good news.'

Billy hid a smirk of derision. His mother was a lying bitch. She knew Frank was in Margate and probably had regular updates from her sister. Of course, after finding Anne's note Billy also knew where his brother was, but so far he'd kept that bit of knowledge to himself. 'Do you think Frank's still with Glenda?' he asked his mother.

'I don't know, but as she hasn't come back to these parts, I should think so.'

The thought of them together still sickened Billy, and unbidden images plagued his mind. It'd been a long time since he'd had a woman, but his brother had the one he'd fancied next to him in bed every night. He groaned in frustration. He needed to find a woman, but it was rare that they'd give it out before marriage. There were tarts, of course, but the thought of all the men who had been there before him made him feel sick to his stomach. He'd heard of the things you could catch from them and it made him fussy. He wanted a decent woman, he thought to himself, but as he was so desperate perhaps he wouldn't worry too much about her looks. It was then that the perfect solution came into his mind. He could have a woman, one on tap, available whenever he wanted her, and, though she wasn't an oil painting, she had nice big assets that he wouldn't mind getting his hands on. She wasn't Glenda but she was friends with her and at least she didn't sleep around. In fact, Billy thought she was probably still a virgin.

He stood up, smiling, knowing where he'd be able to find her. Hopefully he'd manage to grab her before his shift at work even started too . . .

*   *   *

Maude pinned her black hat to her head and checked her reflection in her bedroom mirror. The last time she had worn this hat was at Mr Taylor's funeral over a year ago, but he had died an old man who had lived a long and full life. It didn't seem right today, burying such a young and vibrant woman. She knew that tongues would be wagging, people talking about her today, yet even though she dreaded it she had to go to the church. It would look even worse if she didn't.

When she went downstairs, Bob was reading his newspaper and Johnnie was crawling around on the front-room floor. Maude looked at the time on the wooden-cased clock on the mantel. It was half past eleven; she had expected Harry to be here by now. I bet he's hiding in the bloody Castle, she thought, too ashamed to show his face.

'Bob, get round the Castle and see if Harry's in there, will you? If not, go and drag him from home. He may not want to face this today, but tough bloody luck. Like it or not, he'll have to. It's the least he can do,' Maude ordered.

'Come on, love,' Bob pleaded, 'you can't blame him for not wanting to show his face. He really does feel bad about what happened and he's unlikely to be in the Castle, or any other local pub. He's probably keeping his head down.'

'Bob, the same as most of the folk round here, I blame Harry. I'm having to face the shame of it, and he should too. Now, like it or not, I won't have him hiding away from his responsibilities; that's how he got himself in this mess in the first place. Now do as I say. Wherever he is, go and find him and get him here sharpish. We

162

can't be late for the funeral and, as hard as it will be, I want him there.'

Bob grudgingly followed Maude's instructions and trudged out of the front door. She sat down on the sofa, still unable to come to terms with what had happened. She was aware that her son could be cold and heartless, especially when it came to women, but never would she have believed that he had it in him to force a young woman to abort his own child . . . her grandchild.

Johnnie was heading for the hearth so she quickly rose to pick him up before placing him in the playpen. He started to protest so she hastily gave him his favourite toy animal to stem his tantrum. As she watched Johnnie, her mind returned to Harry. He was such a loving father to his son, so how could he be so cruel? He must have known that back-street abortions were illegal, and been aware of the risk he was forcing poor Betty to take. Mind you, she thought, I don't suppose he expected Betty to die from the procedure.

Of course it was only gossip, but Maude knew that what everyone was saying was true. It couldn't be proved so Harry was in the clear with the law, but their family name was dirt around here now. Harry Jenkins, once well respected, was now considered low life.

Johnnie was becoming a bit fretful again so Maude went to the kitchen to get him a biscuit. He gurgled with delight when she gave it to him. Maude's mind returned to Harry. He couldn't have married Betty Howard as he was still married to Glenda, but he could have looked after her, seen that she was all right. But no, he had turned his back on her, forced her to see a back-street abortionist, which had left her with a fatal infection, and today half of Battersea would be packed into the small church to see the poor young woman laid to rest.

Twenty minutes later and Bob returned with Harry in tow.

'Mum, I don't think this is a good idea,' said Harry, pacing the front-room floor with his hands in his pockets.

'I don't suppose you do, but did you think it was a good idea when you made that poor girl seek the help of that butcher? No, but you still made her do it so you can at least show her the respect of saying your last goodbyes to her. For Christ's sake, son, she was your girlfriend! How do you think it would look if you don't show up today?'

'She was *not* my girlfriend! And do you really think her family will want me there today? They all blame me and I hear what everyone's saying – Harry Jenkins this and Harry Jenkins that – but I do feel bad about it, really I do. I didn't want Betty to die.'

Maude watched as Harry flopped onto the sofa. He looked exhausted. Maude softened a bit.

'I know, son,' she said. 'Of course you didn't want the poor girl dead, but she is and now you've got to face up to it. Drowning your sorrows and staying away from the funeral isn't going to give the right impression.'

'I don't think I can face it.'

'Now look, we all know what Betty Howard was like. She was hardly a woman of virtue and should never have been putting it about with a married man so you're not entirely to blame. Come and show your respects. At the end of the day, that butcher of a back-street abortionist is the one who killed her.'

'But, Mum, I–I'm so ashamed. I feel bloody rotten.

164

The more I think about it, the worse I feel. I'm even having nightmares about it. How could I have been so hard on her? She may have been a bit of a tart, but she was really giving and caring. She put up with my moods and tried to make me happy, but look what I did to her. She was carrying my baby and I made her kill it. Mum, am I some sort of monster?'

Maude walked over to her son and placed her hand on his shoulder. She had never seen him so vulnerable, and never before had he been so open about his feelings. This business of Betty's death had hit him hard and left him looking almost broken.

'No, Harry, you are *not* a monster,' she said. 'You just made a very rash and bad decision, one with terrible consequences that I'm afraid you'll have to live with for the rest of your life.'

'It's no more than I deserve.'

Maude glanced at the clock worriedly. 'Maybe going to Betty's funeral is your chance to show a bit of remorse and to pray for penance. Now come on, here's your dad's black tie. You can wear it today while he stays here to look after Johnnie.'

By the time Maude and Harry arrived at the church the service was about to start, but as they entered people began to nudge each other and a silence fell across the congregation, a hush that was quickly followed by whispers. Maude could see heads turning to look at the man whom everyone held responsible for Betty Howard's death. Betty's mother kept her eyes to the front, firmly focused on the cheap wooden coffin in which her daughter's lifeless body lay.

They found room in a pew towards the back. Helen was seated in the one in front of them. She quickly turned to offer them a curt but polite greeting. That's when the thought struck Maude – she would have a quiet word with Helen as soon as the service was finished.

After prayers, a few hymns and a eulogy read by Betty's cousin, the service came to an end and people gathered in the churchyard in small groups, some looking at the flowers, others thanking the vicar, whilst a few offered comforting words to Betty's mother, who was being supported by her two sisters. And though many people glanced sideways at Maude and Harry, no one came and spoke to them.

'Let's get out of here, Mum,' Harry whispered. He was obviously uncomfortable in the situation and shifted from one foot to the other.

'Yeah, come on, then,' said Maude, 'but I just have to say a quick goodbye to someone. You wait just outside for me, love. I won't be long.'

With Harry out of the way, Maude approached Helen. She took the girl by her arm and gently led her away from the crowd. 'Helen, I've had an idea but I've got to be quick. Listen, Harry has taken Betty's death really badly, and I think it's made him realise a few home truths about himself. I don't know, he's different, softer somehow. Anyway, I think it might be a good idea if you go up to him now and ask if it's all right for you to take Johnnie out to see Ted and Elsie. I reckon he'll go for it and then we ain't got to keep sneaking about. Mind you, don't say anything about Glenda. That would be taking it a step too far.'

Helen didn't look too pleased at the idea of talking to

Harry and, as if reading her mind, Maude added, 'He's just outside the gates. Go on, he won't bite your head off, and I'll be there with you.'

'All right, Mrs Jenkins, as long as you come with me.'

'Helen would like a quick word with you,' Maude said to Harry, who didn't look overly pleased to see her walking through the church gates with his mother. 'Go on, gal, speak up.'

'Er,' Helen began nervously, 'I wondered if you'd allow me to take Johnnie to see Ted and Elsie. They really miss him.'

'Well, they are his grandparents and it seems only right,' Maude chirped. 'What do you think, Harry? It would give me a bit of time off too. I could get my washing or a bit of housework done in peace.'

'Yeah, whatever you like,' Harry answered, looking distracted and anxious to be away as more people left the church.

Maude was relieved. It had played on her nerves every time Helen had taken Johnnie out without Harry knowing. At least this way it was all out in the open, except of course neither woman would ever let on that he was also being taken to see his mother every few months. Yet Maude knew that it would have to stop soon. Johnnie was talking a little now, just odd words, but soon he'd be stringing them together. Though Helen might not have considered it, she had. It might only be baby talk, but when that happened he might say that he'd been on a train, or, worse, he might talk about his mother.

No, it was definitely getting too risky, and though Maude worried about the consequences of Johnnie being cut out of Glenda's life, she worried more about what would happen if Harry found out that he was being taken to see her.

Helen was glad that was over. She hadn't wanted to be seen talking to Harry, but at least he'd agreed to let Johnnie see his grandparents. Poor Betty Howard, thought Helen. She had never really liked her much, yet remembered how Betty had stepped in once to stop Harry from kicking her in the stomach. She might have been a gossip, but she was a brave girl to face up to Harry like that. She wondered why Betty hadn't been equally brave when it came to her pregnancy. If she'd refused to have an abortion, maybe she would be alive now. What an awful way to go.

It was said that after Betty had visited Mrs Burton – the back-street butcher, as she was known – the girl had been seen walking down Elsey Road, clutching her stomach and sweating profusely. Mrs Appleton, who saw her, had stopped to ask her if she was all right but Betty mumbled something about her monthlies and carried on.

When Betty didn't arrive home that day, her mother wasn't worried. She was used to her daughter staying out all night, ashamed of her and aware of her reputation. However, when another two days passed, she began to worry. She asked around, but, other than Mrs Appleton, nobody had seen Betty.

Becoming increasingly worried, Betty's mother went to the police station to report her daughter missing, but their position was that as Betty was a grown woman, they didn't take her concern seriously.

It was six days later when a couple of young lads playing on a bombsite made the gruesome discovery of Betty Howard's body curled up in the remnants of an old bricked chimney breast. A post mortem revealed that she must have lain dying for days, her body ravaged with septicaemia, and the thought of how she must have suffered and died alone brought tears to Helen's eyes.

Helen dashed her hands over her cheeks as she turned the corner of her street, and was still thinking about Betty when she heard a voice calling out her name. She turned and had a sinking feeling when she saw Billy Myers walking towards her. He must have followed me, she thought, recalling how she'd spotted him half an hour earlier at the church.

'Hi, Helen,' Billy said as he quickened his pace to catch up with her.

'Hello, Billy. What you doing here? Ain't you going to Betty's wake?'

'Nah, I've got to go to work for the afternoon shift. I've got a job at Price's Candle Factory now and I'm on most Saturdays, but it's good money so I don't mind.'

'Good for you,' Helen said sincerely. 'Sorry, but I've got to dash. I don't like to leave my parents for too long. See you, Billy.'

Billy grabbed her arm as she made to dash off. 'Hang on a minute, Helen. I want a word with you.'

Helen didn't like his tight grip and there was something threatening in the way he was looking at her. 'Let me go, Billy. I'm in a rush,' she said as she tried to yank her arm away.

'It's about your mate Glenda and my brother. See . . . I've known something for quite some time now, but so far I've kept it to myself. I know where they are, so what do you think about that?'

All thoughts of her parents at home by themselves suddenly diminished as she realised that Billy Myers had information that could lead to Harry finding Glenda and Frank. Helen stared at him. Why was he telling her? She would have to tread carefully, but she had to find out what he was up to.

'Well,' she answered slowly, 'I assume you're keeping that knowledge to yourself to protect your brother. After that pasting Harry gave you, we all know what he's capable of and you certainly don't owe him any favours.'

'That pasting Harry gave me was nothing compared to what he would do to my brother and Glenda if he got hold of them, and, well, Frank and me have never been close so I can't say I miss having him around. But Glenda's your best friend, ain't she? I bet you miss her. You wouldn't want anything bad to happen to her, would you?'

Helen didn't like the tone of Billy's voice but did her best to remain calm. 'Of course I miss her and no, I wouldn't want to see her come to any harm. Is there a point to all this, Billy?'

'That depends on you,' he answered with a sly grin.

'What do you mean?'

'If you want me to keep my mouth shut about their whereabouts, you're going to have to be really nice to me.'

Billy licked his lips and Helen frowned. Her mirror told her that she was no oil painting. She was short and dumpy and men didn't pay her any attention, so what could Billy possibly want from her? He licked his lips again, lasciviously, and she felt sick. Surely Billy wasn't suggesting that!

'I–I–I don't understand,' Helen stuttered. 'What do you mean, be nice to you?'

Billy ran his hand up Helen's arm and then briefly brushed it against her breast. 'I think you know, Helen. We'll have to come to some sort of arrangement.'

His meaning was clear enough now and Helen wanted to spit in his face, to run home, but she was frozen to the spot, aghast at his suggestion. 'What . . . what sort of arrangement?' she gasped.

'Come on, Helen, you're a big girl now, you know what I'm getting at. Let's say you meet me by your back gate on Friday night at eight o'clock. There's an alley opposite that nobody uses and it'll be nice and private. You can show me those lovely big tits of yours and if you're really good I just might keep my mouth shut about Margate.'

Billy didn't wait for Helen to answer; he gave her a wink and sauntered off, casually throwing back, 'See you on Friday.'

Helen felt her legs begin to shake. Although she would do anything to protect Glenda from Harry's wrath, the thought of Billy Myers touching her, of having to touch him, made her feel sick to her stomach.

Shakily she hurried home and, seeing her parents dozing in fireside chairs, she ran to her room, shut the door behind her and sank onto her mattress. Her stomach was still churning as she wondered how she could get out of this sickening situation. She couldn't tell her parents, they were too fragile, yet there was nobody else – nobody she could turn to. She threw herself across the bed in despair. If only there was someone she could go to for help! It was then that a name popped into her mind. Maude!

Maude didn't want Harry to find Glenda and Frank either, so surely she would help. She might be middle-aged, but she was tough; someone you wouldn't want to mess with. The idea brought Helen some relief. Her parents would probably wake up soon so she knew she couldn't go to see Maude now, and it was doubtful that she'd be able to catch the woman alone tomorrow as it was a Sunday. No, it would have to wait until Monday, and then as soon as she could get away she'd go to her for advice and, hopefully, help.

Helen rose to her feet to go back downstairs, feeling comforted by the thought that she might find an ally in Maude. Surely between them they could find a way to sort Billy Myers out, without her having to go along with his disgusting demands.

Chapter 16

On Monday afternoon, Maude was enjoying a cup of tea in a quiet moment whilst Johnnie had his after-lunch nap. She hadn't been home from the shops long. There was a knock on the door. She tutted impatiently before opening it to find Helen on the doorstep, the young woman looking pasty and worried.

'I'm sorry to bother you, Mrs Jenkins, but I need to talk to you.'

Maude invited Helen in and poured the girl a cup of tea from the fresh pot, thinking that she looked like she needed one. 'What's troubling you, gal?'

Helen's eyes filled with tears. 'I've got a problem with Billy Myers and I don't think I can handle it by myself.'

'Billy Myers? Him that told my Harry about Glenda and his brother?'

'Yes.'

'He's a dirty scumbag.'

'I know, but he said he knows where Glenda and Frank are. He . . . he's blackmailing me to keep quiet about it.'

'Blackmailing you? What does he want? Money, I suppose?'

Helen looked awkward before answering, 'No, not money, Mrs Jenkins. He wants . . . you know . . . favours.'

'Favours? What sort of favours?'

'Sexual ones,' blurted Helen, her face reddening with embarrassment.

'Oh, does he indeed? The filthy pervert. But are you sure he knows where Glenda and Frank are?'

'I'm sure,' said Helen and the tears overflowed. 'If I don't agree to meet him, he'll tell Harry where to find them. I'm sorry, Mrs Jenkins, I just didn't know who else to turn to. What can I do?'

Maude slurped her tea and handed Helen a hanky that she had stuffed up the arm of her sleeve. 'Stop that bawling malarkey for a start,' she answered firmly, 'and tell me more. When are you planning on meeting the dirty swine?'

'Friday at eight, but I can't do it, I just can't. I love Glenda, but –'

'Shut up, girl, you haven't got anything to worry about. You won't be meeting him,' Maude interrupted with a wicked smile, 'I will be.'

In Dungeness, Glenda was hot and it was no wonder that Polly was fretful; the carriage on the beach was stifling. She carried her outside, and sat on the wooden bench that Frank had knocked up. She'd made a couple of cushions for it and it was a lovely place to perch and look out to sea. Polly was mostly a good baby, and this time she was able to breast feed, but every time she fed her, Glenda found tears welling up. She had felt guilty that she hadn't been able to breastfeed Johnnie, because her milk was insufficient, but that was nothing compared to the guilt she felt at leaving him. She longed to see him again and had written to Helen a few weeks ago, but so far she was still awaiting a reply.

There were quite a few people scattered about. Glenda gazed at an old man sitting on a small seat by the sea, fishing. The nearest person to him was a woman sitting on a blanket wearing a floppy sun hat, two children frolicking next to her at the edge of the sea. They were shrieking with glee as the waves came in, soaking their legs up to their knees before washing out again. Glenda saw the old man turn to look at them, and suspected he was none too happy that the noise was probably scaring off any fish that might venture close to shore. He stood and reeled his line in, picked up a canvas bag and, carrying his rod, moved further down the beach. Glenda doubted he'd catch any fish, but maybe he just enjoyed trying.

The summer weather had brought more visitors, along with a few people staying in other redundant railway carriages. Glenda had feared that she and Frank would be asked to leave, but her fears were unfounded as they'd been given another six-month lease. She tried to avoid the other carriage dwellers as much as possible. If they were Londoners using their holiday homes, there was always the possibility that one of them came from Battersea. Of course the chance of that was probably remote, but Glenda didn't want to take any risks. Harry might not be looking so hard for her now, but if someone reported seeing her he'd be down here like a shot and she shuddered at the thought of what he might do to them.

She heard the sound of someone walking on shingle and tensed up. Then a familiar voice said, 'Hello, love. It's a proper scorcher.'

Glenda sighed with relief when she looked up. It was Frank's aunt Anne, wearing a billowing sundress with crooked seams. It looked homemade. 'Hello, Anne, it's lovely to see you, and yes, it's really hot. It's worse in the carriage, but out here there's a bit of a sea breeze.'

Anne flopped down beside her. 'It's a bit of a trek to get here, a train then a bus.'

'Can I get you a drink? Tea or, as it's hot, squash?'

'Squash, please,' Anne said, and took Polly into her arms while Glenda went inside to fetch the drinks.

When she returned, they were quiet for a moment as both sipped their orange squash. After a moment or two, Anne said, 'I've heard from my sister and she's asked me for a photograph of Polly.'

Glenda frowned. 'I . . . I don't think –'

'Now listen,' Anne interrupted. 'Joyce is Polly's grand-mother, and it's only natural that she wants to see her first grandchild.'

'I know you write to her occasionally to let her know how we're getting on, and that she destroys your letters as soon as she's read them, but I doubt she'd destroy a photograph, Anne. It's dangerous for me.'

'Glenda, love, I think you're being overly paranoid. I'm sure she'll keep it hidden. She hasn't told Billy or anyone else where you are, or that she's a grandmother now, so you have nothing to worry about.'

Maybe Anne's right, Glenda thought, maybe I am being over-cautious. The thought of Harry finding them still gave her nightmares. She took a deep breath. 'All right, you can take a photograph.'

Anne smiled, obviously pleased, and drew a Brownie camera from her copious bag. She moved back to take

176

the shot; one of Glenda sitting on the bench, her hair prettily windswept, her nose sprinkled with freckles from the sun, smiling down at her beautiful baby daughter.

It was Wednesday evening and Harry had managed to get hold of a bottle of whisky. He avoided the local pubs now, especially the Castle. He'd once been looked up to, his company sought out, but nowadays he was mostly avoided like the plague. He was viewed with scorn; few men were willing to talk to him, and he couldn't really blame them. He'd lost his swagger too, and now walked with his head down, avoiding eye contact with anyone.

His mind was filled with Betty Howard as he walked. Guilt overwhelmed him and he picked up his pace, desperate for a drink. Whisky dulled his mind, and he intended to drink himself into a stupor. He'd drink until he passed out; that way he'd be able to sleep, something that was eluding him at the moment. If he was late for work again, so what – he was already on a warning. The foreman, once a mate, had abruptly told him that unless he pulled his weight, he'd be out of a job. Harry had ignored the warning. There were plenty of building sites around; bricklayers were in demand, and maybe finding work in another borough where nobody knew him would make things a bit easier.

Harry sat in his fireside chair and poured himself a generous measure. He threw the drink back, grimaced, but then poured another and downed it in one. He'd been so swamped with guilt since Betty's death that he hadn't given a thought to Glenda, but suddenly her face filled his mind. He'd been a bastard to her too, he realised that now. Harry carried on drinking, and by the time he drained the last dregs from the bottle, he was so fuddled with alcohol that his mind was numb, thoughts of Glenda disappearing into the fog.

On Friday evening, Maude called over her shoulder to her husband as she left her house, 'I'll see you later, Bob.'

'Yeah, all right,' he called back.

She'd told Bob that she was going to see Phyllis Brown, who lived at the end of the street. Though she rarely went calling on neighbours, she and Phyllis had been friends for many years so her popping out to see her, supposedly to help with a problematic knitting pattern, hadn't caused any suspicion. She'd settled Johnnie down for the night before leaving and Bob was happily listening to the radio.

She gently tapped on Helen's door. Helen checked up and down the street before Maude entered.

'All set, gal?' she asked.

'Yes,' Helen answered, 'but I've got to say, I'm ever so nervous. I'm really not sure that this is a good idea.'

'Have you got a better one?'

'No, but what if something goes wrong and he hurts you? He's a nasty piece of work, Mrs Jenkins, and I'd never forgive myself if anything happened to you.'

'Now you listen to me. I ain't afraid of the likes of Billy Myers. It's him that needs to be afraid of me! There'll be no need for you to worry, and, if you position yourself behind the fence like we said, you might be able to hear everything.'

'All right, but I'm still not sure.'

'I'll be fine. Now get the kettle on and make me a cuppa before I go and see to this little bastard,' Maude said as she rubbed her hands together. She was quite excited and almost looking forward to this confrontation with Billy. It had been a good few years since she had found herself in a fight and, though she was getting on a bit, she still enjoyed a good set-to. The thought of Billy Myers thinking he could get one over on the Jenkinses had her riled up. How dare he? The man had already caused enough problems and was lucky that he still had kneecaps after Harry had sorted him out. If Maude had had things her way, she would have made sure he wasn't walking again.

'I've got a big plank of wood and if he tries to hurt you I'll be ready for him,' said Helen with a bit more spirit as she passed Maude a cup of tea.

'It won't come to that. By the time I've verbally torn strips off him, he'll be ready to crawl back into whatever hole he crawled out of. And I've got another little surprise for him and all – well, two, actually.'

Before long, they both heard the faint chime of the clock in the front room. Eight o'clock. Neither spoke as Helen followed Maude out of the back door and into the dark garden. Helen scuttled into place behind the high fence and Maude nodded at her before slowly opening the back gate. She stuck her head out and looked up and down, but it was so dark she couldn't see anything.

Then suddenly a match flared and Maude saw the shadowy figure of a man opposite her, standing in front of the entrance to the alley. Without hesitation, she steamed towards the shadow.

'Billy bloody Myers,' she screeched and as her eyes focused in the gloom she saw a cigarette fall from Billy's mouth. 'You look surprised to see me. What's wrong, were you expecting someone else?'

'I don't know what you mean. I wasn't expecting anyone,' said Billy as he looked behind him, obviously concerned that Harry or someone was about to sneak up on him.

'You're a liar. We'll add that to your list of desirable traits, shall we? A liar along with a blackmailer.'

'I don't know what you're talking about.'

'Yes, you do. Fancy a little worm like you thinking you can get away with blackmailing a young woman for sex.'

'I haven't blackmailed anyone,' Billy blustered.

'Oh, so you didn't say that you know where your brother is, and threatened to tell my Harry?'

'Yeah, well, I might have, but surely you want to know where he is too.'

'No, I don't, and I don't want my Harry knowing either. We both know what he's capable of and I wouldn't want him to do time or, worse still, swing for the likes of Frank and Glenda. So I'm warning you, if you dare open your mouth and tell him or anyone else where they are, it'll be the last thing you ever do!'

Billy started laughing. 'And what do you think you can do about it? Look at you, you're a bitter old woman. What are you gonna do? Slap my bottom?' he mocked.

Maude's hackles rose. 'I'm not that bloody old. Don't underestimate me. I'm only going to warn you the once. If you think what Harry did to you was bad, then you ain't seen nothing yet.'

Billy turned round, leaned over and chuckled. 'Go on then, *old* woman – as I said, do your worst and smack my bum.'

'Yeah, have your bit of fun, but this not-so-old woman knows people, Billy, the sort of people you wouldn't want to meet in your worst nightmares. Don't worry, I won't have you killed, but I can arrange that by the time my people have finished with you, you'll wish you were dead. So once again, I'm warning you, if my Harry *ever* finds out where Glenda is, I shall hold you personally responsible and you'll regret the day you were born.'

'And why should I believe anything you say?' Billy sneered as he moseyed towards her.

'You don't have to believe her, but you'd better believe me,' a male voice said, stepping from the shadows.

'And me,' said another.

Maude's brother and his grown-up son stood at each side of her, one brandishing a wooden club, the other a knife, though both were muscular enough to intimidate anyone by size alone.

Billy gave a sharp intake of breath and turned to run.

'And stay away from Helen, or else!' Maude shouted after him as he disappeared into the blackness of the alley.

'Thanks, boys,' said Maude, smiling at her family.

'No problem. Shame we didn't get to knock him out, though,' her brother laughed.

'It still did the trick, the little squirt soon scarpered,' Maude answered.

'Give us a shout if you've got any other scumbags who need sorting. Always a pleasure to help out my little sis.'

'I will, Ed. And thanks for all popping round yesterday, it was smashing to have so many of us together again. Reminded me of the good old days.'

'Yeah, it was good, and next time we're round these

parts, you can come to us. It'll do you good, remind you of where you come from. I'll never get the way you can settle down like you have. We all miss you, Maude. It ain't the same on the road without you.'

'Oh, get off with you, you soft sod. Now give us a kiss and bugger off. I know the funfair is off to new grounds tonight so I won't keep you, but I'll see you next time you travel this way. And give my love to that lovely wife of yours. Tell her from me that she deserves a bloody medal for putting up with you!'

Maude went back through Helen's gate and gave the girl a big smile. She didn't see much of some of her family as they travelled the country, but luckily her brother had been in the area. 'I told you there was nothing to worry about,' she said to Helen. 'We were raised to look after our own and we never let each other down. I've other family members I can call on too, so you won't have to worry about Billy Myers any more.'

Chapter 17

Helen was dashing home from work; she was a little bit late and the neighbour who kept an eye on her parents would be waiting to leave. She was also keen to get a letter written to Glenda. With all that had been going on since Betty's funeral, she still hadn't told Glenda that Harry had agreed to let her take Johnnie to see Ted and Elsie.

She debated with herself whether to tell Glenda about Harry seeing Betty Howard, Betty's pregnancy, and then her death. She finally decided that she would. She had never kept secrets from Glenda before and didn't want to start now. The only thing she didn't want to share was the whole Billy Myers incident; he was Frank's brother and it might cause all sorts of problems if it came to light, so least said soonest mended, now that Maude had sorted Billy out.

But best of all, now that Harry knew she would be having Johnnie, she didn't have to worry so much when she went off to meet Glenda in two weeks' time. Helen was really looking forward to the trip to Bromley again; she couldn't wait to see Polly, who from what Glenda had written sounded absolutely adorable. She wondered what Johnnie would make of his little half-sister.

As she ran around the corner she careered into someone and a croaky voice slurred, 'Whoa, watch it.'

Helen's stomach flipped. It was Harry, but he looked awful: he was unshaven and, as he swayed on his feet, she realised he was drunk. 'S–sorry,' she stuttered nervously.

She needn't have worried. Harry's eyes looked unfocused and without saying another word he stumbled past her. Helen frowned, wondering if Maude knew that Harry looked as though he was falling apart, and obviously wasn't at work. Had he lost his job? Maybe she ought to tell Maude. After all, Maude had been quick to help her with Billy Myers and if anyone could sort out Harry, it was his mother. She continued home, made lunch for her parents and, as soon as they took an afternoon nap, she hurried to see Maude.

That evening, Joyce Myers pulled the letter and small photograph from her apron pocket again. For the umpteenth time she peered at the baby in Glenda's arms, wishing it was a larger picture as she could only just make out Polly's face. Polly! Her first grandchild. She would have loved to show it around, to tell her friends and neighbours that she was now a grandmother, but knew she daren't risk it. If it got back to Harry he'd be round like a shot, demanding she tell him where he could find Frank and Glenda. Though she'd put on a brave front when Harry turned up soon after they had done a runner, she'd been shaking inside. The man was a thug; look what had happened to Betty

Howard when she made the mistake of getting mixed up with him.

It saddened Joyce that she couldn't hold her grandchild, and she missed Frank, but there was no way she wanted anything to do with Glenda. She was still married to Harry, and Joyce wanted nothing to do with the Jenkins family ever again. As she stared at the photograph, her stomach rumbled, a pain shooting through her, and she groaned. Her stomach was playing up again as it had done for years; hurriedly she threw the letter down on the table and made a dash for the outside bathroom, only just making it in time.

Billy was sitting at the kitchen table. He had read his aunt's letter and studied the photograph, more interested in looking at Glenda than at the baby in her arms. He could tell she was still a stunner. He sighed heavily, knowing Glenda was now out of his reach. He was still smarting after his run-in with Maude Jenkins, but he was no fool and knew that if he wanted to stay in one piece, he'd better keep his mouth shut. It also meant that Helen was a no-hoper too; his chance of having a woman on hand whenever he fancied a shag was well and truly gone.

Still, there were other women out there, decent ones too, and there was no way he was going to pay for sex. Maybe it was time he started looking for a wife. He'd go to the local dance hall on Friday night to check out the talent.

As he considered this, Billy's mother came in through the back door into the kitchen, paling when she saw that he had arrived home from work. He sat up straight, flourishing the photograph of Glenda and the baby.

'So,' Billy said as he held it up, 'Frank's a father now, is he? I suppose that makes me an uncle.'

Joyce looked panicked. 'Billy, son, please, you've got to keep it to yourself. If Harry finds out, well, what he'd do to both Frank and Glenda doesn't bear thinking about.'

'It's all right, Mum. Calm down. I'm not about to tell Harry about this. I didn't have a lot of time for Betty Howard, but after what Harry did to her I wouldn't give him the time of day.'

Joyce slumped onto a chair with relief, unaware that, in truth, her son was keeping his mouth shut because he feared retribution from Maude Jenkins and her wide-spread family if he didn't.

That evening Maude paced up and down, waiting for her husband to come home. She wanted to sort Harry out, but didn't want to take Johnnie with her. From what Helen had told her about her son, she wasn't sure she'd be able to hold her temper, and it would only upset little Johnnie if he heard her shouting. Maude smiled wryly. She hadn't worried about her sons hearing, or feeling, the brunt of her temper but she was softer with Johnnie, even though he ran her ragged at times.

'About bloody time,' she snapped when Bob walked in.

Bob looked confused. 'I'm not late. I came home straight from work.'

'Yeah, well, your dinner is in the oven and you can keep an eye on Johnnie. I'm off out.'

'Where are you going?'

'I'm going to see Harry. He's turning into a drunk and I'm going to sort him out once and for all. Apparently he's not been in work either. He's got to pull himself together.'

Bob said nothing and Maude could guess why. His attitude spoke a thousand words. He was ashamed of Harry, ashamed of what he'd forced Betty Howard to do, and in all honesty she felt the same way too. Nevertheless, Harry was still their son and she wasn't about to let him end up in the gutter.

It didn't take her long to reach Harry's house. She knocked on the door and was relieved when he opened it straightaway. He looked dreadful, his skin sallow and grimy and his clothes unwashed, but at least he appeared sober. 'Mum, I was just going out.'

'Where were you going? To buy more whisky?'

'What's it to do with you?' he asked belligerently.

'Let me in and I'll tell you,' she said, pushing past him. She was appalled at what she saw. 'Harry, this place looks like a pigsty!'

He shrugged and flopped onto a lumpy-looking fireside chair. 'It suits me.'

'It's not fit for animals to live in, and it's no place for Johnnie.'

'Johnnie? What are you on about? He lives with you.'

'Not for much longer. He's your son, Harry, and your responsibility.'

'Mum, I can't look after him.'

'Now you listen to me. I'm not getting any younger and after raising you and your brothers I'm not prepared to get stuck with raising another child. I've done my bit, helped you out, but now it's time for you to look after Johnnie.'

'But I can't. I'm at work all day.'

'Are you, son? That's not what I've heard.'

Harry looked sheepish. 'Yeah, well, I might have lost my job, but I'll get another one.'

'Harry, listen to me. You've got two choices. You can learn from your mistakes and let them make you a better man, someone for Johnnie to look up to and be proud of. Or you can wallow in self-pity and alcohol and see your son taken into care.'

'Mum, you wouldn't!'

'I will unless there's some changes,' Maude firmly told him, though in truth she had just said that to shake Harry up.

'What sort of changes?'

'Well, son, to start with I want you to stop drinking and find yourself another job. Once you've done that, I'll continue to look after Johnnie during the day, but you can have him after work and every weekend.'

'But . . . but that means I'll be stuck in every night.'

'Like I am, you mean! Bloody hell, you're a selfish bugger. Johnnie is your responsibility, your son, but it's me and your dad who are tied down with looking after him. It ain't right, Harry, and I've had just about enough of it.'

Harry ran both hands over his face and was quiet for a while, but then he looked up at her and said, 'Mum, you're right. I've been wallowing in self-pity and I've been selfish. I haven't given a thought to you or Dad. I've just taken it for granted that you're happy to take care of Johnnie.'

'Yeah, well, it's time for you to pull your socks up and make a fresh start. By the weekend I want to hear that you've found work, and that this house is clean enough for Johnnie to stay in.' She wasn't prepared to back down, not now that Harry had seen the error of his ways. She knew all he had needed was a bloody good talking-to. He might well be a grown man, she thought, but he respected his mother and mostly heeded what she said.

'Mum, I'm sure I can find a job by then, but I'm not sure I can get this place cleaned up that quickly,' he said, looking around the room as if seeing it for the first time. 'I'm not very good at doing housework – can you give me a bit more time?'

Maude was tempted to give him a hand, but feared if she gave him an inch he'd take a yard. 'No, you're going to look after your son this weekend and this place had better be sparkling clean when I bring him round.'

Harry gave her the ghost of a smile. 'All right, Mum, and thanks. You're right, I need to sort myself out but it took you to make me see that. Things are going to be different from now on.'

'Good, I'm glad to hear it. I'd best get back to see to Johnnie, and I'll leave you to start cleaning up this mess. While you're at it, clean yourself up too, ready to go out tomorrow to find a job.'

Harry said he would and Maude left a lot happier than when she'd arrived. She felt that giving Harry a talking-to had done the trick and that he really would make a fresh start.

When the day came to see Glenda, Helen knocked excitedly on Maude's door. The last two weeks had dragged by and she was desperate to see her best friend, though after the episode with Billy Myers she was glad of the lack of any traumatic events in her life. Maude answered the door, but she didn't have Johnnie in his pram ready to go as expected.

'You'd better come in, love,' Maude said and beckoned. 'I need to have a word.'

Helen's heart dropped. This didn't sound good.

'Go through and take a seat,' Maude instructed.

Helen did as she was told and waited for Maude to speak again, but the look on Maude's face told her that this was not going to be good news.

'I know you're off to see Glenda today, but I think this will have to be the last time.'

'Oh, no!'

'Listen, there's good reason. It's still all right for Johnnie to see Ted and Elsie because Harry knows about that, but Johnnie is talking now. Harry has pulled himself together and sees the boy regularly. What if he says something to his dad about going on a train?'

'But it's only baby talk and surely we can explain it away, say he's talking about a toy or something,' Helen said.

'Harry isn't stupid, and I think you're clutching at straws there. Do you really want to risk him finding out that you've been taking Johnnie to see Glenda?'

'No, of course not, but it will break Glenda's heart if she can't see Johnnie.'

'You'll have to tell her that it just isn't safe now that Johnnie can talk. Not only that, I've never liked going behind my son's back and for who, eh? For Glenda, that's who. Let's face it, she's the only one who benefits from this and she wasn't thinking about Johnnie when she ran off with that Frank.'

'She felt she didn't have any choice, Mrs Jenkins.'

Maude's expression softened. 'Yeah, well, that's as may be, and I've no doubt that seeing Johnnie means a lot to Glenda, but it's got to stop. I'm sorry, Helen, you'll have to tell her: no more visits after this. I should never have allowed it in the first place. Now I'll put Johnnie in his pushchair and you can go, but don't be late back.'

Helen slowly nodded her head and stood up to leave. She could see it would be useless to try and argue with Maude, but she dreaded the thought of having to tell Glenda the bad news. She seemed so happy in her letters and looked forward so much to seeing Johnnie, but now Helen knew that her friend's heart was going to be broken all over again.

Glenda scanned the seats for Helen as the train pulled into Bromley station. It had been months since she had last seen Johnnie and her arms were aching to hold him again. A familiar figure cheerily waved at her from the train. Glenda could see little Johnnie balanced on Helen's lap, his hands flapping excitedly.

She ran to help her friend disembark the train as it appeared Helen was struggling with holding Johnnie in one arm and carrying his pushchair in the other hand.

'Helen, I'm so pleased to see you,' said Glenda as she lifted Polly from her pram, 'and this is Polly. Let's swap.'

Helen passed Johnnie over and, after admiring Polly, put her back into her pram to push her to the park. Glenda was surprised at how heavy Johnnie was as he wriggled in her arms to get down. 'He's grown so much,' Glenda gushed, 'and look at him, walking now. I can't believe how much I've missed – his first steps, his first words. Oh, Hel, it simply breaks my heart.'

'Sit down, Glenda,' said Helen, gesturing to a park bench, 'there's something I need to tell you.'

Glenda could tell from the expression on Helen's face that this wasn't going to be good news. It flashed through her mind that her mother or father were ill, but nothing could have prepared her for what Maude said.

'But she can't do that,' Glenda cried after Helen had finished speaking. 'I'm his mother! I have every right to see my son.'

'I know you do, Glenda, but, the way Maude sees it, you gave up those rights when you left. I tried, I really did, but you know how stubborn she is when she's made her mind up. The problem is, with Johnnie talking now, I can't risk coming to meet you behind Maude's back. He's only got to say something about the "choo-choos", or, even worse, he could mention you or Polly, and that'll be it, game over.'

Glenda watched Johnnie toddling on the grass, his little face beaming. She couldn't imagine never seeing him again and for a fleeting moment she thought about just scooping him up and running away, but she knew it was impossible. Harry would go mental, and what he might do to Helen didn't bear thinking about. She'd been stunned when she'd read Helen's letter, shocked to the core to learn that Harry had been seeing Betty Howard, and what had followed, and that he was now being blamed for her death. It showed just what he was capable of. If she took Johnnie, he was sure to resume his search for them.

Glenda picked Johnnie up and hugged him to her.

After what Harry had done, forcing Betty Howard to abort a baby which resulted in her death, he wasn't fit to be a father and she was determined that one day she would get her son away from the man who still had the ability to strike fear into her heart.

Part 2, 1967

Chapter 18

December 1967

'Get a move on, Polly,' Frank Myers shouted up the stairs in the hall, 'we don't want to miss our train!' He walked back to the family kitchen, where Glenda was cutting bacon sandwiches in half.

She handed him one and he took a bite before rolling his eyes. 'Teenage girls!' he said. 'It's not like Polly wears all that gunk and stuff around her eyes like some of them do, so how come she spends so bloody long in the bathroom?'

'Because that's what young women do,' Glenda said, laughing. 'Now calm down before you give yourself a heart attack. We've got plenty of time. The train doesn't leave for ages.'

Frank glanced out of the window at the ice and frost, thinking that their garden looked like a Christmas card. He loved this time of year with all the excitement of the big build-up to Christmas, with just two weeks to wait until they were opening their presents and then sitting round the dining-room table with bellies full of roast turkey. Frank clapped his hands together and gave a whoop, causing Glenda to jump.

'You silly sod, what was that for?'

'I am so looking forward to Christmas.'

'You're like a big kid and you nearly frightened the life out of me,' Glenda said then smiled playfully as she whipped Frank with her gingham tea-towel that matched her red and white curtains.

'Come here, woman,' Frank said, putting his sandwich down to pull Glenda into his arms. 'I can't help myself, and I'm really looking forward to today too. Polly has never been to London. She hasn't seen all the Christmas lights, or been on the tube, or seen a double-decker bus, let alone all the historic buildings. She's going to love it!'

'Yes, I'm sure she will.' Glenda smiled back at Frank. 'But she might find it all a bit overwhelming too. You know yourself, she's only ever worked at that farm and she's never really been outside the village apart from the odd school trip when she was younger. I'm worried today might be a bit of an eye-opener for her, you know, give her ideas.'

'What sort of ideas?' Frank asked, puzzled. He had thought their day trip to London to see the lights and do some shopping had been a great idea. After all, as Glenda had said, their daughter was nineteen years old, but she had never really been outside Ivyfield.

'You know, ideas about fashion and boys and the bright lights of the city. What if she finds it all so exciting that she gets it in her head that she wants to move there? You know what these youngsters are like nowadays . . . all those mods and hippies, they're different to how we were, Frank. We were like our parents, but this lot, well, look at them with their own music and fashions. And they haven't got the morals we had. I mean, just look at the blinking length of their skirts, it's obscene. I blame that bloody birth-control pill, 'cos nowadays young girls haven't got to worry about getting in the family way. I don't know, Frank, it just scares me that our Polly will have her head turned.'

Frank was passionate that Polly's experiences should be expanded and that the girl spread her wings, but he understood the reasons for Glenda being so over-protective of their child. She hid her feelings well, but Frank could see the pain behind Glenda's cheery persona. Though so much time had passed, he would sometimes hold her in the night when she cried silent tears for Johnnie, and this time of year was always the hardest for her. Apart from a pile of letters from Helen and the odd photograph, it had been nearly nineteen years since Glenda had last seen her son, and it was clear to Frank that she would never truly get over leaving him.

He often wondered if, somewhere deep down, she resented him for making her leave Johnnie, but if she did she never showed it. He had done his best to make her happy, working long hours to buy this house, and, though finding the mortgage had been a struggle at the time, it was all paid for now so they were a bit better off. He felt that her fear of losing Polly too was the reason why she wrapped their daughter up in cotton wool. 'I think you're worrying over nothing, love,' he said. 'Polly is sensible, and though she's seen all the fashions on telly and heard the music, you know she's happiest when she's growing things and would rather be wearing a pair of wellies than winkle pickers. There's no way she's going to want to leave her garden behind in exchange for a dirty, loud, smelly city life.'

'I hope you're right, Frank Myers, I really hope you're right . . .'

Polly clipped a pair of small pearl earrings to her lobes and, hearing her mother call from the kitchen, dashed downstairs, taking the stairs two at a time.

'Slow down, Polly. What have I told you about running down the stairs like that? You'll break your neck one of these days!'

'Yeah, sorry, Mum. What's for breakfast?' Polly asked as she pulled her long brown hair into a tight ponytail.

'A bacon sarnie,' Frank boomed as he tickled Polly's ribs, 'but you've taken too long to get ready so it's probably stone-cold.'

Polly hated it when her father tickled her. She was nineteen, not nine, but he was acting like a big kid himself this morning so she giggled along with him. He was always like this at Christmas time and if he had his way, Polly thought, he would still have me believing in Santa Claus.

She ate her sandwich and drank a glass of milk and soon after they were on their way, trudging to the station. By the time they got there her feet were numb and she stood stamping them on the platform while her father bought a newspaper from a stand. She was relieved when the train came in, and sat next to her dad, who soon became engrossed in his early-morning edition of the *Daily Mirror*.

Polly scanned the headline on the front but it looked boring, something to do with a government cabinet crisis between Wilson and Brown, nothing of any interest to her. Instead, she copied her mother and turned her head to look out of the window at the Kent countryside as the train sped through it. She was looking forward to seeing London. Growing up, she had once questioned why her parents spoke differently from other people in the village. Her father had told her it was because they were from working-class stock in South London, but she wasn't sure if they'd be visiting that area. She hoped so.

They passed grazing cattle in fields that stretched further than the eye could see. She helped her dad with his crossword and then they all played I-Spy, until at last the train pulled into St Pancras station. Frank was up and out of his seat first, with his hand on the door handle ready to jump off the train before it had fully stopped at the platform.

'Frank, wait and calm down, will you,' Glenda chastised her husband. She smiled at Polly, who grinned back, happy and excited to finally be in the city.

Polly had never seen her dad so eager but then again, they had never been to London together before. This must be like a homecoming for her father, she thought, looking at the beam on his face. She didn't know much about their young lives, just that they'd met when Glenda was in hospital after an accident with some stairs and that's when her mum had broken her nose. Her mum had told her plenty of war stories and about how they had lost their parents during the Blitz. Apart from her aunty Anne, who was in a home and suffering with dementia, there were no other relatives. Maybe that was why their little family unit was so close, Polly thought. She liked the way Frank referred to them as 'the three musketeers' – it made her feel safe and secure.

Polly had never seen so many people in one place before and suddenly felt a little apprehensive. Though she considered herself a grown woman, she reached out and grabbed her mother's hand, just as a small child would, anxious not to be lost in the throng of people, all busy with their heads down, rushing to their destinations. The crowd seemed to increase as they approached the entrance to the Underground and as they made their way past the ticket booths and onto the escalator, Polly grabbed the moving handrail. Her legs felt a bit shaky as the escalator crept down towards the platforms and she nervously giggled.

'Just mind out at the bottom,' Glenda warned, 'make sure you don't trip.'

Polly looked at the bottom step as it moved under the floor and thoughts flashed through her mind of tripping over, her fingers getting crushed. But just as the horrific thought came, so did a tube train, and a sudden gust of wind took Polly by surprise as it whooshed through the station.

'Quick, run,' her dad shouted as he raced towards the platform where a train was loading with passengers, but they were too late and before they all reached it the doors closed. 'Not to worry, there'll be another one along soon,' he said, and then pointed to a map on the wall with lots of coloured lines and circles connecting them. 'Look, Polly, this is where we are now, and this is where we're going.'

Polly looked at the map and, once her father had explained how it worked, she found it quite straightforward. While they waited for the next train, her mother told her that many of these underground stations had been used as air-raid shelters during the war. Polly was amazed. She tried to picture dozens of families cuddled up under blankets on the cold, paved platform. 'Oh, Mum, it must have been horrible for you, being stuck down here,' she said.

'No, love, we didn't have an underground station where we lived, but our area got bombarded and there were many nights we all crammed under the kitchen table. Your dad wasn't so lucky. His house was flattened, along with two others. It left them with nothing other than the clothes they stood in. In those days, if you lost your home the community did what they could to help, but furniture was rationed so if you got bombed out or were newly-weds, you had to make do with utility furniture. It was basic but it did the job and I remember some homes still having the utility stuff for years after the war. Built to last, that's how things used to be.'

'Enough of all that "during the war" stuff,' her father said. 'Here comes our train and we'll soon be in Oxford Street. If you haven't got a "wow" to say, or if it ain't about Christmas, then the rules are you aren't allowed to say anything.'

'Oh, Dad, you're such a wally sometimes,' Polly said with an affectionate laugh, 'but thanks for today, I'm loving it already. Do I get to pick my Christmas present out if I see something I just have to have?'

'We'll see about that,' he answered with a wink while her mother just shook her head.

The tube train was packed by the time they reached Oxford Street. Feeling like a tinned sardine, Polly was glad to get off. They went up the escalator to the street thronged with shoppers and she found herself more impressed with the extraordinary window displays than the goods on sale. She had never seen so many Christmas trees as at Selfridges, and the lights draping the street mesmerised her. Big red double-decker buses moved slowly up and down the street, and she lost count of the number of black taxi cabs that passed them. The buildings were so huge that Polly felt dwarfed by them. Street vendors were selling hot roasted chestnuts that made her nostrils twitch. Several 'coloureds' walked past her and Polly did her best not to stare. Though she had seen people of other races on the television, she had never seen one in real life before.

Still walking with a tight grip on her mother's hand, Polly felt herself being pulled around a corner and up a narrow side street. 'Before we start shopping, I'm a bit peckish, and I know a lovely little café up here,' said her father, leading the way, 'I haven't visited it for twenty-odd years. I wonder if old Nancy still runs it. She used to go to school with me and ended up marrying some Italian bloke.'

'If she does, will she remember you, Frank?' her mother asked.

Polly wondered why she sounded a bit uneasy, but then her dad replied, 'After all these years, I doubt it, but so what if she does.'

Tucked around another corner, well off the beaten track, they found the small café and Polly heard her mum joyfully announce, 'Oh, Frank, a proper Italian coffee shop. I haven't been to one of these for years.'

'A coffee shop?' asked Polly. 'You've brought us all the way to London to have coffee? And there's me thinking we were going to have something fancy in one of those new arty-type places.'

'Polly, trust your old dad, you're going to love this. This will be the best coffee and ciabatta sandwich you have ever had in your life. Now come on, get inside and prepare yourself for a taste sensation.'

Polly was astounded when she walked into the café to find that it was like stepping back in time. On one side there were long marble-topped tables with wooden benches that reminded her of church pews. The tiled walls were gleaming white and, from what Polly could tell from the customers already eating, the sandwiches were served up in bread that was long and stick-like, not like the square slices she was used to. Still, from what her dad said about it she was prepared to give it a go even though she had no idea what ciabatta was.

She and her mum took a seat on one of the 'pews', which was partitioned off from the one behind it with frosted glass framed in dark oak, while her dad went up to the counter to place their order. 'This vinegar looks a bit funny,' Polly commented as she picked up the bottle.

'It's not vinegar, it's olive oil,' her mother told her. 'It gives the bread a bit of extra flavour.'

'What's that green stuff on that bloke's plate?' Polly asked.

'It's called pesto. I think it's made from basil, garlic and pine nuts.'

'Sounds yummy,' said Polly sarcastically. 'Can't wait to try it.'

They both laughed and then her father returned with mugs of frothy coffee saying, 'They're getting fresh bread out of the oven so it won't be long. Cor, I'm telling you, this place ain't changed a bit. I thought that was old Nancy when I walked in but it turns out it's her daughter, and she's the spit of her mum. I'll be back in a jiffy, just going to nip to the gents.'

'Hang on, Frank, I'll come that way with you and use the ladies. I've had my legs crossed since we got off the train,' Glenda said.

A few moments after her parents walked off, the woman who had been behind the counter walked towards Polly holding two white china plates. She stopped halfway up the aisle, frowned and then turned to call, 'Bella, can you smell gas?'

Polly suddenly became aware of a putrid smell, and as silence fell across the café a faint hissing noise could be heard.

'Oh, my God, there's a friggin' gas leak!' the woman shouted.

Almost in slow motion, Polly watched as the woman turned to go back to the counter, but seconds later there was an enormous force of air pressure followed by an ear-piercing boom. Polly's whole body shook from the vibrations of the explosion and the woman with the plates was blown off her feet, her body flashing past Polly. There was no time to collect her thoughts or to comprehend what was happening as the blast brought down the walls and an intense fireball raged through the café.

Polly found herself instinctively diving under the marble table for cover, but all around her grey dust was falling along with bricks and timbers. She covered her face to protect it from the searing heat, her ears ringing and her head spinning. She tried to breathe, but the dust clogged her lungs and she coughed violently. She was unable to focus through her stinging eyes, but over the sound of the roaring fire she heard a deafening creaking noise: metal twisting and concrete crumbling as the roof of the café, along with the upper two floors, caved in on top of the marble table, rendering Polly unconscious and entombing her in a grave of rubble.

Chapter 19

Polly tried to open her eyes but they felt as though they were full of grit. She tried to wipe them but her arm wouldn't move. Something seemed to be pinning it down. Her mouth was dry and she licked her lips, but they tasted of dirt. Though her head was pounding, Polly tried to think. She was lying in darkness and could feel something heavy on top of her. What had happened? In the distance she could hear the sound of emergency sirens, and faint voices calling out. A man was groaning in pain and a woman was screaming, yet Polly still couldn't comprehend where she was or what was going on around her.

Confused and disorientated, she felt everything go black again as she drifted in and out of consciousness, for how long she didn't know. Gradually, she became vaguely aware of someone holding her hand. She couldn't see who it was; there were bricks and rubble blocking her view, but there was a small glimmer of light shining through the tomb where she lay.

As she came fully conscious again, Polly gasped and immediately began to cough. Oh, my God, she thought as her memory returned and she remembered the explosion in the café. Fear engulfed her injured body as she realised she was trapped under a fallen building. Where were her parents?

'Mum . . . Dad . . .' she called weakly.

She heard a man's voice through the debris, not one she recognised. 'It's all right, love, I've got you,' he said and Polly assumed it was the person who was holding her hand on the other side of the wreckage. 'Over here,' she then heard him call out, 'I've got a live one.'

A live one, thought Polly, did that mean that people had died? Her parents? Were they OK? Were they alive too? Panic shook her, but as she moved her head blackness overcame her and once again Polly sank into it.

Bleep . . . bleep . . . bleep . . . Polly could hear the sound but wasn't sure where it was coming from. Bleep . . . bleep . . . Her eyes were closed but she heard a soft voice, 'Hello, dear. You're back with us then. Try not to speak, you're in the hospital.'

Hospital? thought Polly, wondering why she was in hospital. What on earth was going on?

Ever so slowly her eyes fluttered open, but the bright lights hurt her retinas and she flinched. As she did so, she felt a pain in her leg, her chest and her left arm. In fact, there wasn't much of her body that wasn't hurting.

She managed to turn her head to see a chubby woman in a nurse's uniform standing at the side of her bed and gently patting the back of her hand. 'You're in St Mary's Hospital, dear. Don't worry, you're in the best place and will get the best possible care.'

'Th–thirsty,' she managed to croak.

'Here, you can have a little water, but not too much

at first,' the nurse said, lifting Polly's head. 'We don't want you to be sick.'

Polly gratefully took a sip through a straw, then groaned as the nurse lowered her head again.

'You've some nasty injuries, but nothing that won't fix. Now try and rest. I'll be back to check on you shortly.'

The nurse gave Polly a lovely warm smile and turned to walk away. 'Wait,' Polly managed to call, 'please, can you tell me what happened?'

'You were involved in an accident, but for now no more talking. You must rest, so close your eyes and try to sleep.'

'Please, I can't rest until I know what has happened to my parents. Where are they?' Polly asked, becoming increasingly distressed and trying to sit up in the bed. Her injuries prevented her from getting very far.

'Now, now, calm down,' said the nurse soothingly as she gently pushed back on Polly's shoulders. 'I'll tell you what I can. You were caught up in a gas explosion and were rescued from under a pile of rubble by the fire brigade. From what I know, I think a heavy-topped table saved your life. As for your parents, I'm afraid I can't tell you anything. The ambulances are still bringing people in and not everyone has been identified yet. I'm sure the police will be around to talk to you soon and they will want you and your parents' details. In the meantime, please try to stay calm and rest. You're in good hands here.'

Polly closed her eyes, but how could she rest when she didn't even know where her parents were or whether they were injured? Tears stung her eyes. Everything ached and her throat was sore, but she was so desperate to see them that all she could think about was her mother and father.

An orderly dropped a metal tray of instruments and the loud clatter echoed through the ward. The sudden noise made Polly jump and for a moment she was back in the café, screaming as the explosion ripped through the building.

'It's OK, it's all right,' the nurse soothed. 'You're safe now. It was just someone dropping a tray.'

Polly realised that even with her hoarse throat she had been screaming uncontrollably and abruptly stopped, though she was shaking in panic.

'Take a few deep breaths, in through the nose and out through the mouth, that's it.'

She was glad to listen to the nurse's calming voice and followed her instructions, but once her nerves had settled again, her first thought was for her parents. 'Please, nurse, can you ask a policeman to come and see me now? I need to know where my parents are,' she begged.

'I'll do my best,' the nurse promised.

The minutes ticking by felt like hours, but at last Polly was relieved to see two uniformed officers approaching her bed.

'Good evening, Miss. This is PC Whitton and I'm Sergeant Trent. Can you confirm that you are Polly Myers? We found a library card in a small bag close to where you were rescued.'

The sergeant with his grey hair and broad shoulders looked a lot older than her dad, and he had an air of confidence, unlike the PC who looked almost as young as she did with his baby blond hair and soft blue eyes.

'Yes,' she agreed, 'I'm Polly Myers, but please, can you tell me where my parents are? My mum's name is Glenda and my dad is Frank Myers.'

'Were you visiting Nancy's café with your parents, Miss Myers?'

'Yes, we got the train up from Kent. Mum and Dad had just gone to the toilets when there was an explosion and I haven't seen them since. Please, are they all right?'

Polly noticed a look pass between the two policemen and then the older one said, 'Can you describe to me what your parents were wearing?'

'What they were wearing?' Polly asked confused. She thought that was a strange question but then if they had been knocked out by the blast, maybe they hadn't been identified yet. 'My mum had a long purple coat on with a gold and pearl butterfly brooch on the lapel, and my dad was wearing his work coat – a long black one that he wears when he's on the buses. He's a bus conductor. Oh, and a trilby, he never goes anywhere without his old trilby hat. Do you know where they are? What's happened to them?'

There was a pause. The sergeant's expression was grave. 'I'm very sorry, Miss Myers,' he said, 'but I have some bad news for you.'

Polly felt bile rise in her throat and cried, 'No, please, don't say what I think you're going to say! Don't tell me they're dead.'

'I'm sorry. I'm afraid the bodies of Frank Myers and Glenda Myers have been recovered from the scene of the accident and yes, they are both dead.'

'No,' Polly screamed, 'no, you're wrong, it isn't them.

They can't be dead, they just can't be . . . you've made a mistake, you've got the wrong people. They'll be out there looking for me, they'll be worrying about where I am. I have to let them know I'm all right,' she gabbled, ripping furiously at the IV drip in her arm in her determination to get out of the bed and find her parents.

The sergeant turned to his younger colleague. 'Quickly, get a nurse,' he ordered as he tried to stop Polly from removing her IV. 'Miss, please, stop this. You can't go anywhere. Look, your leg is in bandages and I doubt you can walk.'

The plump dark-haired nurse was back at Polly's bedside and in a kind but commanding manner she instructed Polly to calm down.

'He said my parents are dead! Please, nurse, tell him he's made a mistake . . . please, tell him . . .' Sobs racked Polly's body as she bawled her heart out. 'They're not dead, they can't be. Please . . .'

Chapter 20

Jackie Benton drained the last dregs of her tea and sighed heavily before leaving the staff room to resume her night shift on the ward. It had been a long night and she had two more hours to go before she could go home. There she would find her daughter, Katy, probably singing happily in the bathroom, and her son, Ross, moaning that Katy was taking too long and he would be late for work.

Oh, the joys of family life! But then the thought of that poor girl in bed number nine crossed her mind. Polly Myers had no family. She had been in hospital now for over two weeks and not a single visitor had been to see her. It was no wonder Jackie's feet were throbbing: she had been up and down most of the night comforting Polly, who was suffering from nightmares and pining for her parents.

No, thought Jackie, even though no doubt there'd be a sink full of washing-up waiting for her, she wouldn't moan. She was grateful for her family and, having seen so much death on the wards, she knew there were people far worse off than her. She had to admit, though, it was hard work being a full-time nurse with two grown children still at home. But what choice did she have? Not a lot; her husband had run off with his much younger secretary and now contributed precisely nothing to the household.

Jackie passed a long window and checked her reflection. Her uniform was pristine but it clung to her rather large curves, pulling across her heavy bosom. Her dark-brown hair was short with tight curls that her husband once said reminded him of a poodle. She also had bingo wings that wobbled when she walked, so maybe she shouldn't have been surprised that her husband's head had turned. With two children to raise and countless foster kids from troubled backgrounds, it was little wonder that she hadn't found time for herself.

Dismissing her thoughts, Jackie marched onto the ward and was immediately drawn to Polly's bed. The girl was hiding under her sheets and from the little movements Jackie guessed she was sobbing again. The tea trolley was making its way round so the thoughtful nurse took a cup and went over to Polly.

'Good morning, dear, I've got a nice cuppa here for you. Are you awake under there?'

She heard Polly sniff.

'Come on, Polly, all this upset won't do. I know you can hear me so pull them covers back, sit up and drink this tea.'

Polly slowly emerged from under the sheets; her red-rimmed eyes were swollen and her nose all snotty.

'Here you are.' Jackie offered Polly a tissue. 'Blow your nose. I know you miss your mum and dad but, as harsh as it sounds, you can't bring them back and they wouldn't want to see you like this now, would they?'

Polly shook her head.

'So come on, then, I know it must have been awful for you spending Christmas in hospital, but you may be allowed to go home soon.'

'No, no, I can't face going home to that empty house. I've no family now, or any real friends. It was always just me, Mum and Dad. And I'm so scared. I mean, I haven't got the first clue of how to run a home, you know, pay bills and stuff. My parents did all that. Oh, nurse, what can I do?'

Polly began sobbing again and Jackie held her tight to her soft chest. It broke her own heart to see this young woman in so much pain and anguish. She was about the same age as her Katy and she wondered if her daughter would cope if she too was in Polly's position. No doubt Katy would struggle, but at least she had her own friends and an extended family, which was a lot more than Polly had. The poor girl had no one.

That's when Jackie's mind was made up. She had been thinking about it for a few days and could see no reason why she couldn't do it. She had fostered before and though she had stopped a few years back when her husband left, there was nothing to prevent her offering Polly a home. The girl was in such a bad state and, though she was too old to be fostered, Jackie could suggest that she moved in with her and her family.

'You'll be out of here in a few days, so what do you think?' Jackie Benton said, beaming.

Polly's mind was blank after Jackie had finished telling her about the idea of moving in. She just looked back at the kind nurse and thought that with her big, rosy cheeks, fuller figure and nurse's uniform, Jackie looked just like

Hattie Jacques from *Carry on Nurse*. For the first time since losing her parents, she began to laugh, and the more surprised Jackie looked, the more it made Polly giggle. 'I'm sorry, Nurse Benton, it's just you remind me of a very funny film that I watched with my dad.'

'Oh, do I now? And what film was that?' asked Jackie.

Polly didn't want to be rude or insult the nurse and thought that maybe a comparison to Hattie Jacques would upset her. 'I can't remember the name of it, but it was really funny,' Polly lied.

'Well, I'm surprised you didn't say it was a *Carry On* film. It's what I usually get told. If I had a penny for every person who said that I look like Hattie Jacques, I would be a very wealthy woman!'

'Yes, that's the one!' Polly spluttered. 'But of course, you're much better looking.'

'Flattery won't get you anywhere with me,' Jackie said, smiling. 'Anyway, you haven't answered my question. What do you think?'

Polly was quite taken aback by Jackie's generous offer and she had to admit, it did sound very appealing. She felt so alone, and she had dreaded going home to an empty house.

So she said, 'If you're really sure, then yes, please, I'd love to come and stay with you.'

'That's settled then,' Jackie said, looking chuffed that Polly had accepted her invitation. 'I'll get your room ready. I'm afraid it's a bit small, but I'm sure you'll find it comfortable enough. And just wait 'til you meet my Katy. I think the pair of you will get on like a house on fire.'

Polly was really looking forward to meeting Katy; Jackie

had told her that she worked as a hairdresser and loved to dance. She'd never had a real girlfriend of her own age, and Jackie had said that there might be a job going in the salon where Katy worked. It wouldn't be much, just washing hair and sweeping up, menial things, but at least it would mean that she could offer to pay Jackie for her keep. It would be very different from the sort of work she did at Oak Farm. She loved being outside in the fresh air, mucking out stables, feeding cattle and milking cows, but it was a tough job, especially in the winter. Maybe a change would be good, she thought, looking forward to the experience.

It still pained her to think of her parents' house, but it was safe and sound, locked up for now, and Jackie said she would help her arrange for the bills to be paid using the savings that her parents had left. Luckily, Mrs Stewart next door had a spare set of keys to the house so Polly decided she would write to her, explaining where she was and what had happened, and ask if she would be kind enough to throw out any food and keep an eye on the place until Polly felt strong enough to return. She was sure Mrs Stewart would oblige as she was a bit of a nosy old bag and it would give her the opportunity to have a mooch around the house. With no idea when she'd be going back to the village, Polly knew she'd have to write to Oak Farm too to tell them that she wouldn't be returning to work.

At first Polly had thought that maybe she should go back to collect some clothes, but she couldn't face it yet – couldn't walk into the home that would hold so many memories. Jackie had been understanding and suggested that she use a little more of the savings to buy new clothes for now.

It was thanks to Jackie that Polly slept better that night, feeling less alone in the world. What the kind woman had said played over in her mind: the last thing her parents would want was to see her grieving. Her heart still ached, though, but she held her pain in and tried to concentrate on the new life she was about to embark on.

Chapter 21

As they approached the chapel Polly knew she would be forever grateful to the wonderfully kind nurse. Jackie had done so much for her, helping her to claim the life insurance policy, which had been more than enough to cover the expense of the funeral. The service had been delayed until she was able to attend, and was such a sad affair: a cremation with just Jackie by her side. To Polly's surprise Jackie had a car, and had driven them to the small chapel.

Polly hadn't expected to see anyone else there. Her parents had always been a close unit and seemed to enjoy each other's company. They had a few friends in the village but no one they were particularly close to. It was clear to Polly that she was very much alone now, so she was all the more grateful for Jackie's offer. She had sobbed while Jackie held her, and now that it was over they stood outside the white front door of Jackie's three-bedroom semi-detached house just outside Croydon.

'Here you go, Polly, the front-door key to your new home. Go on then, open the door,' Jackie said as she handed Polly the key.

Polly took a deep breath and did as instructed. It had already been a traumatic day and she was feeling a little anxious about meeting Katy and Ross, but her fears subsided as a vivacious, auburn-haired young woman in a black and white minidress bounded towards her and gave her a massive hug.

'You must be Polly,' Katy said, beaming. 'I'm so glad to meet you and even more pleased that you're coming to stay with us. Mum has told me all about you. My best friend Isobel has just emigrated to Australia so I've been feeling ever so lonesome, but now you're here we can do so much together! Do you prefer the Beatles or the Rolling Stones? I've got an LP player in my room, we can listen to records and I'll show you how to do the latest dances, like the mashed potato and as I've got some colours from the salon, how about we do your hair?'

'Slow down, Katy,' Jackie admonished, laughing, 'let the girl get through the door. Where's your brother, up in his room again? Run up and get him, tell him Polly's here.'

'I did already, Mum. I saw you coming down the street so I told him to come down but he won't, you know what he's like.'

'Yes, I do, and I didn't bring him up to be so rude.' Jackie walked to the bottom of the stairs. 'Ross,' she shouted up, 'where are your manners? Come down here please, NOW!'

Polly smiled awkwardly at Katy. Jackie had a good pair of lungs on her and though she had shown nothing but compassion towards her, Polly could imagine that she was quite a woman to come up against.

Ross trudged down the stairs and offered a reluctant greeting to Polly. She was surprised at how lean he was, with a mop of unruly ginger hair that flopped over one lens of his black-rimmed National Health glasses. Katy was fashionable, attractive and bubbly, but Ross appeared to be very different from his sister. She seemed to remember Jackie telling her that he worked in an accounts office and the first thing that came into Polly's mind was that he might be a bit of a nerd. She inwardly reprimanded herself, thinking how uncharitable she was being, especially as the Bentons had opened their home up to her.

'Nice to meet you, Ross,' Polly said as she held out her hand to shake his, but Ross ignored the offer and sloped off to the kitchen.

'Please excuse my son,' Jackie groaned in a whisper, 'he acts like a teenager even though he's twenty-two. Trouble is, he's too much like his father. Katy, I'll leave you to show Polly to her room and give her the guided tour of the house.'

Polly liked her room. The wallpaper had a white background with pretty pink roses and there was a lilac bedspread, along with lace doilies on the dressing table. When she looked down on the garden from the window, she was disappointed to see it was all concreted. She would miss handling plants and growing things, but still, she reasoned, with working in the salon and Katy already talking about what bands they would be going to see, she guessed there wouldn't be much time left for gardening.

She laid her head back on her pillow and tried to dismiss the images floating in her mind of her mum and dad. Her heart ached. Would she always miss them this much? Would it always hurt whenever she pictured them? Jackie had said that time was a great healer and that eventually the pain would lessen, but right now it still felt all-consuming. Turning to face the wall, Polly gently began to cry.

There was a soft tapping on the door and soon afterwards Polly felt Katy climb onto the bed beside her and gently stroke her hair.

'You must miss your parents terribly,' Katy said. 'It must be awful being an orphan. I can't imagine losing my mum, she's like my best friend. I miss my dad, and he doesn't keep in touch, but at least I know he's alive.'

Polly sniffed and tried to stem her tears, but found it impossible. 'I–I'm sorry, I can't seem to stop crying. I hadn't thought of myself as an orphan, but yes, I suppose I am now.'

'Oh, me and my big mouth, putting my foot in it again and now I've made things worse. I'm so sorry.'

'No, it's all right,' Polly said as she took a juddering breath.

'I know it's little consolation now, but I promise you that things will get better. When you're feeling up to it we'll go out and about, have some fun together.'

'I–I'd like that.'

'Good, now can I get you anything?'

Polly wiped away the last of her tears. 'Not right now, but tomorrow, could you show me where the shops are? I really need some new clothes. I haven't been able to face going home, so literally all I have is the clothes I came in and these nightclothes your mum gave me.'

'Of course! It's my Saturday off tomorrow so we can make a day of it. Mum said I'm to make sure you take it easy so tomorrow night, instead of going dancing, something I love to do, I thought we could go to the cinema. *The Graduate* is still showing and I hear it's ever so naughty,' giggled Katy.

Polly brightened a little. 'That sounds perfect. There isn't one in my village so I've never been to the cinema.'

'Never been to the cinema?' Katy sounded shocked. 'My goodness, from your accent you sound a bit like a Londoner but you're a proper country girl.'

'My parents came from London,' Polly told her sadly.

'That explains it then. Well, I've got a feeling that you're going to be doing lots of things you've never done before here – not just the cinema!'

'Such as?'

'Dancing for one, ice skating – I'm looking forward to seeing you on skates for the first time,' Katy said, chuckling.

Katy's laughter was infectious and Polly found her mood lifting. She had instantly liked Katy and now it was firmly cemented. But, she thought to herself, she still had a lot to learn about Ross, who wasn't quite as friendly as his sister.

When Polly had first arrived, she'd been quiet, tearful and withdrawn, but Katy had worked miracles in the three months she'd been living with them and now Ross was sick to the back teeth of hearing the two silly girls giggling together, their awful taste in music blaring. It had already been bad enough with Katy and her 'singing into her hairbrush' antics but now he had another girl to put up with too.

There was a knock on the front door and it was a welcome relief for Ross to find Toby on his doorstep.

'Am I glad to see you,' Ross moaned at his best friend

before Toby had even had a chance to step over the threshold. 'These bloody girls are driving me mad!'

'From what you told me, you're a bit outnumbered with females. Three to one and even your cat is female so that makes it four, but, to be honest most blokes would be happy with that. Let's face it, you get all your washing, cleaning, cooking and ironing done, unlike me in my little bachelor pad. I have to do it all myself,' Toby pointed out.

'Yes, but you get plenty of peace and quiet and don't have to put up with all the hormones, not to mention the undergarments hanging up in the bathroom.'

'Do you know how to make a hormone?' Toby asked with a deadpan face.

'Oh, no, not your chemistry stuff again. No, I don't know how to make a hormone,' Ross answered.

'Don't pay her,' said Toby and laughed.

Ross groaned. 'As much as you are my very good mate, your jokes stink! Now, I must be mad giving up Saturday afternoon to help you put shelves up in your shop, and I suppose we should get a move on, but do you want a quick coffee first?'

'Yes, please, and a bit of toast – I've run out of milk and bread at home,' Toby answered with a cheeky grin.

'Come on through, Toby,' Jackie shouted from the living room, 'I'll put the kettle on and what do you want on your toast?'

Ross was pleased his mum was so accommodating to his friend, as he'd witnessed Toby on the receiving end of many an unpleasant jibe on account of his black skin. Toby didn't call round that often as Ross usually went to meet him at his flat, glad to get out of the house and away from his mother's fussing, but when Toby did call round she never batted an eyelid. Ross assumed it was because she had fostered all sorts in the past: Jamaican, Irish and even a Chinese baby girl once. But he didn't like it that she was so accommodating to this new waif and stray, Polly bloody Myers. He'd thought those days of taking in 'problem' kids were behind them, so he was none too pleased when she came home from work one evening and announced that Polly was moving in with them. It wasn't as if she was a child either. Polly was nineteen years old and surely capable of looking after herself, but there'd been no discussions, no opinions asked, his mother just telling them it was going to happen. He had to put up with it, tolerate having Polly here, but it didn't mean he had to be nice to her.

'Thanks, Mrs Benton, jam, please,' Toby answered, already licking his lips.

Katy and Polly ran down the stairs, both of them wearing knee-high white patent boots and short mini-dresses with a psychedelic swirl pattern. Ross surreptitiously looked at Polly and thought how different she looked now. When she'd first arrived, she had been quite mousy, but now her brown hair was bleached blonde and she had applied heavy black eye make-up and pale-pink lipstick. He hadn't noticed before, but she really was quite pretty. But he still didn't like her living there with *his* family.

'Hello, Katy, and you must be Polly. Nice to meet you. I'm Toby,' Toby said.

Polly seemed nervous, yet she smiled nicely at Toby and shook his hand before the two girls went giggling back up to the bedroom. Ross watched Toby as his eyes followed Polly up the stairs. Oh, no, he thought as he rolled his blue eyes, please don't say he fancies her!

'I've never touched a coloured person before,' Polly whispered to Katy. 'His skin felt so . . . normal.'

'Of course it did. What did you expect?'

'I'm not sure, just different, I suppose. So where is Toby from?'

'His parents came to England when he was just a baby so he's lived round here all his life, but I think his mum and dad are from the West Indies, wherever that is. He has a little shop off the high street selling model cars and planes and stuff. Just a big boy's toy shop if you ask me, though he swears it's specialised. His dad died a few years back and his mum went to live with her sister up north somewhere and you know what my mum's like, she sort of took Toby under her wing. He hasn't been round for a while and Ross said he's been busy refitting his shop, though if the way he was looking at you is anything to go by, we might see him more of him.'

'Don't be daft,' said Polly, her cheeks reddening. 'I'm not the sort of girl that fellas like.'

'Oh, yes, you are. Take a good look at yourself.' Katy turned the mirror towards Polly.

As Polly looked at her reflection, a small tear leaked from the corner of her eye, leaving a black smudge running down her cheek.

'Whatever is the matter, Polly?'

'Nothing really,' said Polly as she wiped her cheek. 'It's just that in such a short time, so much has changed, including me! My mum wouldn't recognise me if she saw me now and she'd probably be mortified at this dress.

And my dad wouldn't be too happy with me wearing all this make-up.'

'But, Polly, you look fantastic and I'm sure they would both be very proud of you. Come on, cheer up, there's a local band playing in my old school hall tonight – how about we go and check them out?'

Polly didn't want to seem ungrateful for everything that Katy had done for her, so reluctantly nodded, but really all she wanted to do was snuggle up with a good book.

'Good. Let's go to my room and try on some outfits for later then,' said Katy, oblivious to Polly's real thoughts.

'Thank you, Mrs Benton, that was lovely toast and, may I say, perfectly prepared,' Toby said to Jackie, affecting a haughty manner.

'Go on with you,' she said, smiling. 'Anyone can make toast.'

'Not as good as yours,' Toby insisted, back to his normal persona as he rose to his feet. 'Come on, Ross, we'd best get going, though I think we're going to have to take the long route. Those Purvis brothers were hanging about on the corner.'

'We're not at school now, Toby. They can't bully us any more. We're grown men so why are we still worrying about those two idiots?'

Little did Ross know that Alan Purvis and his backward brother Kenny were frequent visitors to Toby's shop and they still had the power to bully him.

'At least at school we could hide in the toilets or behind a teacher but we can't run away from them now – and yeah, we might have grown up but I don't think they have, especially that Kenny. Though he's backward, he's as nasty as his brother,' Toby said with gusto.

'Are you talking about the Purvis brothers?' asked Jackie as she came back into the room from the kitchen.

'Yes, Mrs Benton. You remember what a hard time they used to give me and Ross at school?'

'Yes, I do. The trouble is their parents were just not interested in them, or their education. I know the headmaster sent letters home on many occasions but no one ever saw hide nor hair of either the mother or the father. In fact, the only time I ever saw their dad was when he was at the shop buying alcohol. Such a shame, you've got to feel sorry for them really. I think I heard that they were moved here from a very poor area in London and I don't know how they managed to slip through Social Services after that, but they did.'

'Feel sorry for them? Are you having a laugh, Mum? Have you forgotten how many pairs of my glasses were broken when I would get my head shoved down the toilet, or my nose punched? Then there were the many times my trousers got ripped when they would trip me up. They're a pair of thugs and they haven't improved with age. They're just bigger and nastier now.'

'I know, son, but look at the home life they've had. They were dragged up, not brought up, and let's face it, they're never going to amount to anything. Not like you two, doing something with your lives and working hard. I know they were bullies, but I still can't help but feel sorry for them.'

'Huh, they won't be getting any sympathy from me,' Ross said. 'Come on, Toby, let's go, and I'll be buggered if I'm going out of my way to avoid the likes of them.'

As they went to leave, Ross noticed Toby give a glance up the stairs, probably looking out for Polly. A tight knot formed in his stomach and he felt irritated. I won't have it, he thought, I don't want my best mate to have anything to do with that sorry case my mother took in.

As they turned the corner at the end of the street, Ross and Toby came face to face with the Purvis brothers and, although Ross had been defiant at home, Toby could see the blood drain from his friend's face and recognised his nervous expression.

'Well, look who it is,' said a very thickset Alan, 'it's Carrot-top and Sooty.'

Alan and Kenny stood side by side, taking up nearly all of the space on the pavement to prevent Ross and Toby from passing.

Toby could feel sweat breaking out on his brow and though he hated being referred to as sooty, wanting to retaliate by calling them honkies, he kept quiet in fear of what the bullying brothers might do during their visits to his shop. For two months, Alan and Kenny Purvis had been intimidating him, demanding protection money which he'd been reluctantly paying.

'Excuse me,' Ross said but Toby could hear his voice was shaking.

'Why, what ya done?' Alan laughed and dug his brother in his ribs which made Kenny laugh too.

'Come on, Toby,' said Ross as he went to step off the pavement to pass the brothers.

Alan quickly stepped in front of him. 'Hang on, not so fast, you four-eyed ginger nut. We see your mate here regularly, but we ain't clapped eyes on you for a while.'

Ross shot a puzzled look at Toby before asking, 'What do you want, Alan?'

'Well, now, the thing is, me and Kenny have gone into a new line of business. I'm sure your mate here can tell you all about it, 'cos he's one of our best customers.'

Toby knew that Ross was looking at him, but he kept his eyes focused on the ground as he realised the embarrassing truth was about to be revealed.

'What's he on about, Toby?'

Toby said nothing and it was Alan who answered, 'We've gone into the protection business, ain't we, Kenny? See, our customers, including Sambo here, pay us to protect them, and as long as they keep up the regular instalments, nothing bad is going to happen to them.'

'That sounds like extortion to me,' said Ross.

'Call it what you want,' Alan sneered, 'but it works. Toby is taken care of, and we're happy that we're getting paid. Now we want to expand, build the business, so I think it's about time you signed up and start to pay up – let's say five quid a week. That should offer you enough protection.'

'Protection from what?' Ross asked indignantly.

'From anyone who might want to give you a hiding.'

'That would only be you two, so are you threatening that if I don't give you money you'll beat me up? I'll go to the police. You won't get away with it!'

Suddenly, Alan pushed Ross against a lamppost whilst Kenny stood intimidatingly in front of Toby.

'No, you won't,' Alan growled into Ross's face. 'You won't go to the gavvers 'cos I know where you live, along with your fat old cow of a mother and tarty sister. You wouldn't want a fire to break out in your house in the middle of the night now, would you? Or your glasses smashed into your eyes?'

When Ross didn't answer, Alan continued, 'No, I didn't think so, and anyway, if you go to the Old Bill you can't prove anything. It would be your word against mine so best you keep your mouth shut and just pay us. If you don't, you'll be fucking sorry. Ain't that right, Sooty?'

When Ross looked at him, Toby only nodded, and then Alan said, 'See, Sambo can tell you that I ain't messing about. When he tried to skip a payment, we had to show him that we meant business so we trashed his shop. Serves him right and it's ended up costing him twice as much to repair the damage. Love the sign in the window by the way – "closed for refurbishment", ha, that's one way of putting it.'

Kenny sniggered and pushed Toby slightly. 'Yeah,' he said, 'that was a right laugh when we smashed up your shop.'

Toby looked at Ross again to see him shaking his head in disbelief. So, his secret was out, he was being black-mailed by the Purvis brothers and that was why the shop was being refitted. But Alan had demanded a lot more than five pounds a week from him, and since the non-payment the weekly amount had increased to twenty pounds, which was far more than he could afford to lose. In order to keep the brothers happy he had forfeited his rent for the last week and feared that, if it continued, it wouldn't be long before he would be evicted.

'So, have we got a deal or what?' Alan asked Ross.

Toby watched as his friend reluctantly pulled his wallet from his denim jacket pocket and handed Alan a five-pound note.

'Good decision,' Alan said, smiling. 'I'll meet you every Saturday at noon outside the Plough. Pleasure doing business with you.'

Toby saw Ross's shoulders slump as Alan and Kenny sauntered off, both obviously revelling in their newly found wealth.

'Why didn't you tell me what was going on?' Ross asked Toby.

'I wanted to, but I was too ashamed,' Toby admitted.

'They can't be allowed to get away with this. There must be something we can do.'

'Like what? Just as Alan said, the police won't do anything without proof and, to be honest, do you really want to risk giving them an excuse to come after us?'

'I suppose not, but I resent giving them five pounds out of my wages. Christ, that's more than I pay my mother and it's going to leave me nearly broke,' Ross complained.

If only Ross knew the rest of it, thought Toby. Five pounds was nothing compared to what he was shelling out each week and he inwardly cursed the Purvis brothers, wishing that he never had to set eyes on them again.

Chapter 22

'Easy money,' Alan Purvis said to his younger brother. 'Told you them two would be pushovers. Let's go and get some Double Diamond and sit in the park. I don't fancy going home with this money in my pocket.'

Kenny nodded, as Alan knew he would. His brother always agreed with anything that he said, and if for some reason he didn't, Alan would hit him until he did.

As they sat in the park swigging from the recently purchased bottles of beer, Alan could see happy families around him enjoying the sunshine. A father was kicking a ball around with his two young boys and Alan looked on with a touch of envy. He questioned why his own father had never done anything like that with him and Kenny, but rather than take them to the park, David Purvis would get drunk and then beat them. Alan took another glug of beer and scoffed; it wasn't as if his mother was any better. She was more of a drunk than his father and had always made it quite clear that both her children were mistakes she deeply regretted.

'Al, I'm hungry, can we go and get some chips?' Kenny timidly asked.

'Yeah, in a bit,' Alan answered, though he was disinclined to leave the bench.

'Can we take some home for Mum and Dad too?'

'Sod them!' said Alan angrily. 'Why should we?'

'I don't know, Alan. I just thought it might be a nice thing to do 'cos I don't think they've got anything to eat.'

Alan looked at his younger brother's sad face. He might be a big grown man, he thought, but he will always have the mind of a child. He gave in. 'Yeah, all right, if it makes you happy, but they don't bloody deserve it.'

'Thanks, Alan. It might make Mum happy though. She's always sad or angry, and I know when I'm sad a bag of chips makes me happy.'

Alan knew it would take more than that to make his mum happy, but it wouldn't hurt to take some grub home for her. After all, she was so painfully thin that a bag of greasy chips might put a bit of meat on her bones.

The lift filled with the aroma of chips smothered in salt and vinegar as it slowly rose to the seventh floor.

'Remember what I told you, Kenny. Don't lean against the walls 'cos you never know who's been pissing up them.'

'Oh, yeah, sorry, Alan.'

The doors opened and the brothers walked down the corridor until they came to their own scruffy front door, the one that had been repaired with odd bits of wood on numerous occasions when their dad had smashed it. Alan hesitated before putting his key in the lock, but then as quietly as possible he opened the door, his ears cocked, thankful that he couldn't hear any shouting. All seemed calm, and he saw that Kenny looked excited to be carrying the chips along the uncarpeted hallway.

They walked into the sparsely furnished front room and Alan saw that the curtains were still drawn, his mother semi-conscious on the brown mock-leather sofa. She had a dirty blanket half covering her tatty nightdress and her hair looked like it hadn't been washed or brushed for weeks. No change there then, he thought cynically. There were several cider bottles strewn around on the bare floor amongst cigarette ends and mouldy glasses. The sight wasn't something that shocked them as they were used to seeing both the room and their mother in this state; she would quite often have vomit down her and it wasn't unusual for her to have a black eye or two.

Alan sat himself at a wobbly wooden table as Kenny gently shook his mother. 'Mum, Mum . . . look, we've brought you some nice hot chips with loads of salt and vinegar.'

'Ugh, get them away from me, the smell is making me feel sick,' she grunted, pushing the newspaper-wrapped food away and knocking it out of Kenny's hands. It fell to the floor and the chips spilled out as David Purvis appeared in the doorway.

'I go for a slash,' he slurred, 'and come back to find chips everywhere. What's going on?'

'We brought you both some chips. Do you want some?' Kenny asked, cowering slightly from his father.

'Where did you get the money for chips?'

'We . . . we've been doing a bit of business,' Kenny stuttered.

Alan cringed; trust Kenny to open his mouth. He'd warned him not to say anything, but his brother had the memory of a bloody goldfish.

'What sort of business?'

'We look after people, Dad, and they pay us for doing it.'

Alan was inwardly willing his brother to shut up but it was too late. He had said too much and now the cat was out of the bag.

'I see,' said their father thoughtfully, 'sounds to me like a protection racket, and I bet this was your brother's idea. Is that right?'

It seemed the penny finally dropped with Kenny and he looked towards Alan, eyes wide with fear.

'Yeah, Dad,' said Alan, 'we've got a couple of knobs who we squeeze a bit of cash out of, nothing major league, just a few bob a week.'

'And you bring us home bags of lousy chips,' his father shouted. 'I ask you, Eileen, are you listening to this? Your sodding sons have been earning money and instead of buying us a bottle of something, they bring us chips. Useless! The pair of them are fucking useless!'

Their mother didn't answer. She looked out of it, her eyes glazed, but their father suddenly lurched across the room and whacked Kenny hard around his head. As he raised his fist again, Kenny dropped to the floor with his arms wrapped over his head protectively.

Alan got to his feet and, seeing the movement, his father turned towards him.

'How much have you got left?'

'Not much, Dad, only a pound or two,' Alan answered meekly.

'Hand it over, and from now on I want half the money you collect. It's about time you earned your keep, and I'm warning you, don't try to pull a fast one by pocketing extra for yourself.'

Alan was gutted. He knew the money would just feed his parents' drinking, and to him that was like pouring cash down a drain. What a bloody waste, he thought to himself as the mental picture of the shiny motorbike he'd been dreaming about began to vanish. If he had to hand over half of what they made to his dad, give Kenny a bit and still feed them both, it wouldn't leave much for himself – definitely not enough to purchase a bike. In fact, he might just about save enough to buy a leather jacket, but what good would that be without the mean machine he had his heart set on?

Alan dug into his pockets and grudgingly handed over two quid to his father.

'You miserable sod. I've put a roof over your head all your life and look at the fucking face on it. Do you see this, Eileen? The tight bastard resents having to give us our share.'

Alan hated his father, but dared not answer him back for fear of getting a good hiding. As far back as he could remember he'd taken slaps, punches and kicks from his dad, beatings which had left him badly battered and bruised. Kenny hadn't been spared his wrath either, but Alan always seemed to come off far worse than his brother.

He watched as his father stuffed the notes into his trouser pocket, then without another word he grabbed his coat and left, slamming the front door behind him. Alan knew his father would be going to buy a bottle of spirits, probably whisky as booze was the only thing he spent his money on. The cupboards were always bare, and he couldn't remember the last time his mother had cooked them anything. Considering the lack of food, it was ironic really that he and Kenny were so big, and when they were children school dinners had been a godsend. They'd become bullies, taking sweets or anything else the other kids had, and stealing from local shops and market stalls.

'You bloody idiot!' Alan barked at Kenny, who was still cowering on the floor. 'I told you to keep your big mouth shut. Now look what you've gone and done.'

Alan gave his brother a swift kick in his back with his size-ten boots. Kenny winced and yelped in pain, but incensed, Alan felt no sympathy.

'I'm sorry, Al. I'm sorry,' Kenny cried.

Alan took a deep breath. Was it any wonder his brother had been born stupid, he thought, as he looked at the state of his mother. She had told them both that she drank heavily during her pregnancy to try to get rid of her unborn child, but instead of killing it she had given birth to an idiot. Alan hated her for calling Kenny that, but counted himself lucky that he wasn't born the same way. He'd been forced into looking after Kenny and sometimes resented it, showing his feelings by giving him the odd slap.

Eileen stirred from her drunken stupor. 'Where's your dad?' she slurred.

'He went out,' Alan snapped.

He didn't know if his words had registered as she drifted off again, and he looked at her with disgust, hating her as much as he did his father. He wanted to scream at her, to ask how she could call herself a mother and question why she never protected him, fed him or loved him, but he knew it would be pointless. He doubted she even knew what day it was; she'd hardly be coherent enough to give him any satisfactory answers.

'Kenny, get yourself off to bed now. You don't want to be up when Dad gets back home,' Alan said.

Kenny was still sniffling. 'But I ain't tired and it's still light outside.'

'Don't make me tell you twice,' Alan warned. 'You've let me down today with your big gob so just do as you're told. Anyhow, once Dad comes home he'll be boozing again and you know what he's like. Go on, off to bed, you don't want another hiding from him.'

Kenny sloped off out of the room and Alan sighed heavily. He didn't want to go back out wandering the streets, but couldn't face going to bed in the room he shared with Kenny. Though he did his best to keep on top of things, Kenny wet the bed and the room stank of urine. His mother never bothered to do any washing, so when he had the money it meant trips to the launderette, where he cringed with embarrassment as he stuffed the stinking sheets into the machine. It wasn't a nightly occurrence nowadays, but after getting a slap from their dad today, and a kick from him which he now regretted, Alan was pretty sure Kenny would have one of his 'accidents' tonight as he always did when he got nervous.

Alan tried to hold his patience because he'd been a bed-wetter too, but had grown out of it when he hit puberty. He shuddered as he recalled the other boys in school circling him, calling him names and jibing him about smelling of wee. But it had toughened him up, and once puberty had set in, along with testosterone, Alan had resolved to never be bullied again. Instead he became the tough kid, and with Kenny copying him, they had become a pair you didn't mess with.

His thoughts turned to his father again and Alan scowled. Now that their father was demanding a share of their protection money they would have to find another victim to menace by saying they'd look after them. A soft touch this time – maybe a woman.

Kenny lay in bed, tossing and turning as the bright evening sun shone through the tattered bit of material that was nailed to the window frame. He didn't think it was fair that he had to go to bed and with no pyjamas and only a thin blanket on the bare, lumpy mattress it wasn't warm or comfortable.

Bored and restless, he felt under his pillow for his favourite toy – a green plastic dinosaur that he'd had since he was seven years old. To get it, he'd punched a kid in his class in the mouth and wrestled it from him. He imagined the dinosaur roaring so loud that it blew his dad over and woke his mum up. Chuckling to himself, he thought what a good day it had been with the park and the chips. He liked the park, but didn't like it that Alan wouldn't let him play on the swings. Alan said he had to behave like a man now, and men didn't play silly games, they sat and drank beer. Kenny scowled. He didn't like beer; he liked chips and swings and slides, but he had to do what his brother said. If he didn't he would get into trouble again and get smacked. He didn't like it when Alan smacked him, but it was even worse when his dad did it.

Kenny turned on his side, still clutching his toy. His brother was clever and knew everything about everything, and only smacked him when he was naughty. Not like his dad who smacked him even when he was being good.

He'd smacked him earlier even though he'd brought him chips.

The door opened and Alan came in and sat on the edge of his bed. 'Do you want to play with my dinosaur?' Kenny asked, thinking that Alan looked sad.

'No, thanks, mate. You play with it. Just keep the noise down 'cos Dad will be back any minute now and I'm going to read my comic.'

'OK, Al, I will. But you've read that comic loads of times and you've read it to me millions and trillions of times. Ain't you fed up with it yet?'

Alan slowly nodded his head. 'A bit,' he answered, 'but it's all about men with superhuman powers who beat the baddies. I like it when the baddies get beaten.'

'Yeah, me too,' said Kenny, 'our dad is a baddie and one day I'm gonna have superpowers and I won't be scared of him no more.'

'That's right, Kenny, one day.'

Kenny rolled over to face the wall and pictured himself with the strength of the Hulk riding on his big green dinosaur. His dad would be scared of him when he saw him on his dinosaur and he wouldn't hit him again. No, he'd run away, Kenny thought, smiling at the image of his dad running and screaming.

One day, Alan had said, one day, and on that thought Kenny drifted off to sleep.

Chapter 23

Katy and Polly were on their way home from the Saturday market when they bumped into Ross and Toby, who were standing outside the Plough pub.

'What are you two doing here?' asked Katy. She knew they weren't the sort to frequent pubs and they both looked a bit shifty, like they were up to no good.

'None of your business,' Ross abruptly answered.

'All right, keep your hair on, I was only asking,' Katy responded with a sarcastic tone.

'Hello,' said Toby shyly, smiling at Polly. 'How have you been? You look fantastic.'

'Hi, Toby, I'm fine, thanks, and thank you. Katy helped me with my hair and outfit. We're going to see a band tonight at the Star Hotel.'

'Really, what band are you seeing?'

'Jethro Tull.'

'I don't think I've heard of them. What are they like?'

'To be honest, neither have I but Katy said they're a pretty cool rock band. We're not really into rock but there's not much going on this weekend so we thought we would give it a go.'

'Well, have fun,' said Toby.

Polly flushed. Toby was staring at her intently and it made her feel a little uncomfortable.

'Haven't you two got somewhere else to go?' Ross said abruptly.

'Yes, we have,' Katy answered. 'We've got better things to do than hang around pubs with you, loser!'

'Just get lost,' Ross snapped.

Katy turned and flounced off, saying, 'Come on, Polly.'

'See you, Polly,' Toby called.

Katy grabbed Polly's arm. 'Don't look back or answer him,' she said quickly. 'My brother is out of order and that Toby might be a nice bloke but he shouldn't let Ross talk to us like that. Just ignore him.'

Polly didn't want to offend her friend so did as she was instructed, but though she found Ross quite difficult, she didn't agree with Katy about Toby. He wasn't responsible for Ross's offhand manner.

'And it's so obvious that Toby fancies you,' Katy continued, 'God, you can spot it a mile off! But please, tell me it's not mutual. Or is it?'

Polly liked Toby and was intrigued by his exotic dark skin, but with the death of her parents still raw, she wasn't ready to think about a boy in that way. 'He's nice, but I don't want any complications at the moment,' she said. 'It's been hard, you know, moving to Croydon and everything and you've been amazing, Katy. A boyfriend just isn't on the agenda for me for a while.'

'I understand,' Katy sympathised, 'and you know, you've done so well. I mean, look how far you've come and the fun times we've had. Eventually you're going to be up for dating, but for now, today is rock chick day! I know we've got hours to go but let's get home and back-comb my hair.'

'You've got a thing for her, haven't you?' Ross asked Toby, annoyed that his best mate could have any feelings for the girl who had disrupted his home life.

'Yes, I think she's really nice. Katy's your sister and she's all right, so I don't understand why you're so short with them both.'

'No, you wouldn't, but do me a favour. If you're thinking of asking Polly out, forget it.'

'Why?' Toby asked, confused.

'I have my reasons, and as your friend I would appre-ciate a bit of loyalty.'

'You sound so pompous,' Toby said, and as a thought crossed his mind he added, 'Hang on, don't tell me you like her too?'

'No, I don't, I can't stand her, and I don't see why she can't go home to her own bloody house instead of living in mine! Oh bugger it, here they come.'

Alan and Kenny Purvis approached them in their usual tough manner, both looking scruffy and smoking roll-ups.

'Look, Kenny, it's rusty nuts and his jungle bunny.'

Ross inwardly fumed. He wanted to show them up, to tell them that they were just ignorant louts who didn't even know their geography – Toby didn't come from the jungle – but in truth he was too scared of them to open his mouth.

'Right,' Alan continued, 'we ain't here for social reasons. Hand over the readies and we'll be off. And by the way, glad to see that you're here on time. We wouldn't want to hang around waiting for you, 'cos if we did you'd have to pay interest on your payments, say sixpence for every minute you're late. Remember that for next time.'

Ross could feel his blood boiling and silently seethed as he resentfully handed five pounds to Alan.

'Nice one,' he said with a grin of triumph. 'See you next week, tosser, same time, same place, and Sambo, we'll see you in your shop on Monday. Pleasure doing business with you,' he said before moseying off with Kenny.

There was a pause, and then, after sighing heavily, Ross said, 'Come on, Toby, let's get out of here. We'll go to your shop to finish off the last of the refit, then after dinner tonight – and you're invited to ours – do you know what I fancy?'

'No, mate.'

'A bloody good drink!'

'Ross, I've never known you wanting to drink,' Toby said looking surprised.

'Maybe not, but then you've never known me to be blackmailed before either. Let's go out tonight and get drunk!'

Polly and Katy only had small portions of Jackie's mince and mash as they'd decided they didn't want to show bloated tummies in the outfits they were wearing for the rock concert. They were in Katy's bedroom adding the finishing touches to their make-up and doing last-minute outfit changes, both excited at the prospect of seeing the rock band.

'Did you think Ross seemed a bit moody over dinner?' Polly asked.

'No more than usual,' Katy replied. 'You know what he's like, the miserable so-and-so. Don't worry about him. But I was right about Toby, he definitely fancies you. Even my mum noticed.'

Polly was mortified. 'Oh, no, what did she say?'

'The same as me, that it's obvious Toby likes what he sees.' Katy lowered her voice to a whisper. 'Do you know, I've never known either of them to have girlfriends so they must be virgins.'

'So are we,' Polly pointed out.

'Yes, I know, but they're older than us and most chaps who are over twenty-one have done it by then, or at least make out they have. But those two, I don't know, they just seem different from the rest of the young men around here.'

'Well,' said Polly, 'I think it's nice that they're saving themselves for the right girls and don't go round boasting about their sexual prowess.'

Katy laughed, 'Nice, you reckon? More like they can't get girlfriends!'

That evening when the girls went to the Star Hotel, they were surprised to find there were no queues to get in. A poster outside was advertising the Jethro Tull event.

'Oh, no, Katy, look . . .'

'What am I looking at?'

Polly pointed to the poster. 'We've got the wrong date! The band isn't on until next week.'

Instead of being disappointed, Katy burst out laughing. 'Trust us, all that effort to look this good, wasted . . . or maybe not. We're here now, let's go in for a drink.'

Polly wasn't sure that this was a good idea. She'd never

been in a pub bar before unless she was there to see a band, but Katy seemed so confident that after just a moment's hesitation she followed her friend in.

'I'll have a gin and tonic. What about you, Polly?' Katy asked as they stood at the bar.

'Oh, just a Coca-Cola for me, thanks.'

'Don't be such a party pooper, Polly. We haven't got work tomorrow so we can let our hair down a bit. Come on, have a vodka in that Coke at least.'

Polly half-heartedly agreed, not convinced that she would like the taste of vodka, but, as it transpired, she found it quite pleasant.

After another two drinks, Katy suggested that they went up the road to a more modern bar that she knew had a jukebox.

'I feel a bit dizzy,' said Polly as they walked outside and the fresh night air hit her lungs.

'That'll be the vodka. I feel the same, but I like it,' Katy said as she skipped a little then twirled around a lamp-post. 'Isn't this fun!' she squealed.

Polly didn't think it was fun. She felt a little queasy as they walked along, glad when she saw the pub in sight. When they walked inside she was surprised to see Ross and Toby sitting in a corner supping on pints. Polly's nausea passed and the caffeine from the Coca-Cola kicked in, giving her a bit of a boost and making her feel quite lively. Katy went to the bar and ordered their drinks whilst Polly, who was feeling unusually brave, went to join the lads.

'Wotcha, Toby, Ross. This is a nice surprise,' she said, slightly slurring her words.

'Wish I could say the same,' Ross snapped back.

'Oh, Ross, you're always like a bear with a sore head.

245

You should take a leaf out of your sister's book and lighten up a bit,' Polly told him.

'Who do you think you are, coming into my home, acting like you own the place and then having the audacity to tell me how to behave?'

'Whoops.' Polly looked at Toby and giggled like a naughty schoolgirl, unaware that she was more outspoken than normal, the vodka lowering her inhibitions. 'Seems I've upset him.'

Katy arrived at the table with a drink in each hand. 'Well, I never,' she exclaimed, 'Ross and Toby drinking in a pub!'

'Sod off,' Ross snapped.

'Yeah, we will,' said Katy. 'Come on, Polly, we don't want to hang around with these two boring old farts.'

*　*　*

Quickly finishing her drink, Polly staggered a little as she got up to leave. 'Where are we going?' she asked, feeling fuddled and confused.

'We're going back to the Star. There might not be any music but at least I won't have to look at my brother's miserable face.'

Polly followed Katy out of the pub, but her legs didn't seem to want to go where she wanted them to and she staggered and held on to the wall for balance. With Katy's help she managed to stand up straight, and they made their way back to the Star. Once back inside and sipping another drink, she giggled, 'Oh, Katy, the room seems to be spinning. Tell it to stop.'

Katy didn't answer and a befuddled Polly turned to

see her friend making eyes at a very tall and slender mod who was leaning against the bar. He was eyeing Katy back, but Polly felt her stomach lurch. 'Katy . . . I–I think I'm going to be sick,' she gasped and as quickly as her wobbly legs would let her she headed outside.

The door Polly took led out onto a dimly lit carpark and she stumbled to a dark corner as vomit rose in her throat. She thought she saw two figures on the opposite side of the carpark, or was it three or four? Her vision was out of focus, but at least she still had the sense to pull back her hair as she leaned forward to throw up.

Polly heaved over and over again, and once she had emptied the contents of her stomach she fished around in her handbag for a handkerchief to wipe her mouth. As she turned back around she realised the two figures were no longer on the other side of the carpark and were now standing right in front of her. They were burly-looking young men who appeared menacing rather than friendly. She tensed, and though she was drunk, she could tell from their stance that they weren't there to see if she was all right.

Rain was beginning to fall and all Polly wanted was to get back inside to the safety of the pub, but the two men were blocking her way.

'E–ex–excuse me, please,' she stammered, suddenly feeling more sober.

The larger and obviously older of the two men stepped forward so he was now standing just inches from her.

'What's a pretty girl like you doing out here on your own?' he asked.

'I–I . . . didn't feel well. If you could let me pass, please, my friend will be worrying about me.'

The man was standing so close to her that she could smell his bad breath, laced with stale beer.

'There's no rush, is there? I think you and my brother here should get a bit more acquainted . . . you know, have a bit of fun,' he said and he reached out his arm around her to grope her backside.

Polly screamed, suddenly very frightened. 'Get off me!'

'Shut your mouth and stop screaming or I'll shut it for you.'

The smaller of the men moved in closer, and, terrified, Polly waved her arms in the air as she screamed even louder. Something hit her on the side of her head and she felt herself falling to the wet and muddy ground. Everything was hazy.

'Go on, Kenny, get her knickers off! Don't just stand there. It's about time you became a real man.'

'I can't, Al,' another voice said.

Polly could hear what the man said, but his voice sounded distant.

'Just fucking do it, get her drawers off and get on top of her. I ain't gonna tell you again!'

Polly felt hands on her, the sensation of her underwear being yanked down, but her head was swimming and she thought she might be sick again. Oh, Dad, Dad, her mind screamed. She wanted him to be there now, to rescue her, to save her from the two men who were now savagely abusing her.

Her dad couldn't come. He was dead, and now Polly wished she was dead too. It was then that something shut down in her mind, and as rain poured down, she fell into a black pit where nothing could touch her any more.

*   *   *

Alan Purvis hadn't expected to bump into a tasty piece in the carpark. He and Kenny were there to rob cars. It was a good spot, dark and isolated from the main road, out of sight of anyone unless they left the pub by the back door, and they could keep an eye out for that happening.

After taking the five quid from Ross they'd bought some fags, had a decent meal in a café and played for ages on the fruit machine, losing a packet. After that they'd been drinking most of the day, and, without much cash left to give their father, they were too scared to go home. Alan had had a lot more to drink than Kenny, but it'd still been his idea to see if they could break into a few cars to find stuff – stuff their dad could pawn or sell to keep him happy. It was always him who had to come up with ways to make a few bob and Alan had just been thinking that it was about time his brother grew up a bit when he'd spotted the young woman across the carpark. The thought occurred to him that if Kenny had his way with her, it might just do the trick. Maybe if he became a real man, he wouldn't be so stupid and, best of all, he'd stop wetting the bed.

It was a stroke of luck that the girl was drunk and once he had whacked her she didn't put up much of a struggle. In fact, looking at her now, he thought she was out cold. 'Go on, Kenny, get in there,' he urged again.

'But I don't know how to.'

'Look, get yourself ready like this,' Alan said, undoing his flies to demonstrate, but with the amount of beer he'd been drinking, he wasn't able to make much headway.

Fortunately, when Kenny copied him he rose to the occasion.

'Right, you're ready now,' Alan told him. 'Go on, stick it in her.'

'But what if she doesn't want me to?'

'Don't you worry about her, they all say no but they don't mean it. Anyway, she ain't in any fit state to object.'

Alan stood watching as Kenny at last managed to get it in and began to writhe on top of the girl. He might have been unwilling at first, but Alan grinned widely as he saw that his brother was really getting into it now, pounding hard on the girl beneath him. 'That's right, Kenny, go on, give it to her good and proper.'

Suddenly, Alan heard a female voice shouting from the other side of the carpark but through the sound of the thundering rain, he couldn't make out what she was shouting. 'Quick, Kenny, get on with it,' he warned, not wanting to be caught in the act.

The voice got closer, but before Alan had a chance to react a dark-haired girl holding a thin stiletto-heeled shoe in her hand was leaning over Kenny and he watched in horror as she brought the shoe down hard on Kenny's head. The sound it made as it hit Kenny's skull was sickening, and Alan was sure he heard bone shattering.

'Get off of her, you filthy bastard,' the girl screamed.

But Kenny couldn't move. He was lying motionless on top of the unconscious girl on the floor.

No doubt due to drink, Alan's reactions were slow as he went to grab the one-shoed girl, who was still shouting and screaming. He stared down at his brother. Kenny wasn't moving. 'Kenny, Ken . . . get up, mate,' he urged.

It was then that Alan saw it. The long thin heel was sticking out of the back of Kenny's head, embedded in his skull, and a trickle of blood was running from the wound onto the wet ground. He couldn't take it in, couldn't accept what he was seeing. 'Kenny, come on, get up, stop mucking about,' he said desperately, but Kenny was still motionless.

'Oh, God, what have I done?'

Alan looked at the one-shoed girl who was standing transfixed to the spot, staring at the two bodies on the floor and shaking uncontrollably.

'You fucking bitch,' he spat as the truth hit him. 'You've killed him. You've murdered my brother!'

The girl slowly turned her head to look at him. 'He . . . he was raping my best friend. I–I had to stop him.'

Alan's legs abruptly turned to jelly and he collapsed to his knees. All he could hear was the sound of the rain belting down, and it suddenly dawned on him that it was his fault that his brother was dead. He had made Kenny do it, made him *rape* the girl. He hadn't thought of it as rape, just as a bit of fun – he'd only wanted Kenny to get the feel of a real woman.

But Kenny hadn't wanted to do it and he had made him, forced him, and now his brother was dead. 'I'm sorry, Kenny,' Alan cried out, 'this is all my fault. Oh, fuck, I'm sorry . . .'

Polly felt the sting of rain on her face and opened her eyes. Her head was thumping and something felt heavy on top of her. She could hear a man crying, and for a moment she was back under the table in Nancy's café, but as she reached up with her arms she felt that the weight pinning her to the ground was a man's body. It was then that she remembered where she was, and the two men in the carpark.

251

They had attacked her, were going to rape her! Her body felt bruised and she feared the worst as she felt something warm drip onto her cheek. She reached up to touch a sticky substance and then looked at her fingers, sure, even in the dim light, that it was blood. But it wasn't her blood! It was dripping from the man on top of her.

Still dazed, Polly tried to push the man off her, but either he was too heavy or she was too weak. 'Help me,' she managed to call with a hoarse voice. 'Please, help me . . .'

'Polly, oh, Polly, thank goodness you're all right.'

Sure it was her friend's voice, she begged, 'Katy? Help! Get him off me!'

'Don't you touch him, you murdering fucking cow. Don't you dare lay a finger on my brother!' Another man's voice cut through the darkness.

'I didn't mean to kill him!'

Polly was barely aware of their words, but she somehow instinctively knew that they were talking about the man on top of her. The horror of it slowly began to sink in. He was dead, but his blood was still dripping onto her. She didn't know how he'd died, nor did she care. She was lying under a dead body and her only thought was to get him off of her. She began to hyperventilate. 'Get him off me! Get him off! Get him off!' she hysterically screamed.

'All right, all right, shut up!' the other man said.

Through the dim light, Polly recognised the man's face as he leaned over her. 'Don't touch me!'

'I ain't gonna touch you,' the man gasped as she felt the body being lifted away. 'Oh, Kenny . . . Kenny.'

'I didn't mean to kill him,' Katy howled again. 'Polly,

he was raping you! I had to stop him but I didn't mean to kill him.'

Polly managed to sit up and looked to one side to see a man lying on the ground with another man sobbing over his body. She knew it was them, the ones who had raped her. She saw blood on the floor mixing with the rainwater spreading out around her, while her best friend, sobbing and obviously in shock, looked to be drenched too. They all seemed to be frozen in shock, but as Polly felt mental exhaustion washing over her she managed to say, 'We need to call the police.'

Still nobody moved, but her screams must have raised the alert and a crowd was beginning to gather around them. She could hear sirens getting closer and wanted to stand up, but found she didn't have the strength.

It was like a horrific dream, an unbelievable nightmare that unbeknownst to Polly was about to get worse.

Chapter 24

Jackie opened the front door and guided Polly through. The poor girl was traumatised and though Jackie felt deep empathy for her, she was more concerned for Katy, who was locked up in a police cell and would possibly be charged with murder.

Those hateful Purvis brothers, she thought, and to think that just last week she'd said she felt sorry for them. Well, one of them was dead now, and from what Jackie had been told he was a rapist, and the surviving one an accessory.

'Ross, thank goodness you're still up. Please, put the kettle on. We could do with a cuppa,' Jackie said as she gently eased Polly into an armchair.

'Are you serious, Mum? You're still going to let her stay here after what's happened? My sister is in prison because of *her*! I knew she was bad news the minute she set foot in this house. Get her out, Mum, I'm telling you, she's nothing but trouble.'

Unable to believe what she was hearing, Jackie turned to her son and said angrily, 'Don't be so silly. Firstly, your sister is not in prison, she's in a police cell at the station, and secondly it was not Polly's fault. The Purvis brothers attacked her and Katy did what anyone would do if they saw their friend being raped. Now stop being so melodramatic and go and put that kettle on.'

Ross jumped up from the sofa, saying before he stormed out of the room, 'Do it yourself. I'm going upstairs. I'm having nothing to do with Polly and God help her if my sister goes down for murder, which she probably will.'

Jackie hoped that Ross was wrong; just the thought of her precious daughter being locked up in jail for years on end caused her to break out in a cold sweat. Katy wouldn't be able to handle it, Jackie was positive of that. But surely they couldn't send her down for murder? She'd tried to protect her friend. She wasn't a cold-blooded killer. Jackie only hoped the police believed Katy. And to think that the other disgusting Purvis brother was under the same roof as her beautiful daughter. It's a shame she didn't kill them both, she thought angrily, but then quickly pulled herself up for having such wicked thoughts.

'I'll go and make us a cup of tea, love. Why don't you go and put your pyjamas on,' Jackie spoke softly to Polly, who looked as white as a sheet.

'Can . . . can I have a bath? Now that the police doctor has collected all the evidence I just want to scrub myself clean, to get that monster off of my skin. I feel so . . . so dirty.' She shuddered. 'Dirty and violated.'

'Of course you can. I'll bring you a cup of tea, and listen, take no notice of anything Ross says. What happened is not your fault. Katy won't get charged with murder and she won't be going to prison.'

'Oh, I hope not,' Polly whispered.

Jackie inwardly prayed she could believe her own words

as she went to the kitchen. She put the kettle on the gas to boil and decided on a coffee for herself. It usually prevented her from sleeping, but it wouldn't matter this time as she was probably going to be up all night worrying about her daughter, who, instead of being in her own bed, would have to sleep in an uncomfortable police cell.

Polly stood looking down at the steaming bathwater. Her head was aching and her body felt bruised and sore, but she had no regard for her physical pain as her mind kept going back to the carpark and to the moment of coming round to find a dead man on top of her. She felt uncomfortable down below and knew she'd been raped, but had no proper memory of it.

She slowly peeled off her torn, muddied clothes, letting them drop to the floor, then kicked them into the corner of the room in disgust. As she turned back to the bath, she caught sight of her reflection in the bathroom mirror. Her face was swollen on one side, but what caused her the most pain was the thought of her lost virginity and the way it had been taken in such a violent manner. Turning away from her reflection, she carefully stepped into the hot water and submerged herself, wanting to wash away the feeling that was making her skin crawl. With her head under the water she closed her eyes and held her breath, wishing that she didn't have to breathe ever again.

With her lungs bursting for air Polly surged up, drawing her knees to her chest. She longed for her parents, longed to be held in their arms. Life had once been good to her; she'd had a blessed childhood, protected from the evils of the world, but the last few months had been a whirlwind of pain. She'd had to grow up fast, and had found a measure of happiness when Jackie had taken her in, but now everything was shattered again.

Polly hugged her knees tightly and at last gave in to the tears that came from deep inside, releasing the shock, anger and agony of the night's events. Oh, Katy, she sobbed as guilt overwhelmed her. If she hadn't drunk so much and gone outside to be sick, Katy wouldn't have come looking for her. It was her fault that Katy had been arrested, and Ross was right, she had caused this family nothing but trouble. She was the one who deserved to be locked up, not Katy.

There was a knock on the bathroom door and through her tears Polly saw Jackie coming in, a cup of tea in her hand. She placed it top of the laundry bin and then sat down on the edge of the bath, saying soothingly, 'That's it, have a good cry, but I hope you're crying for the right reasons. I won't have any tears over Katy, she did the right thing. If it had been me who had found you in that situation, I swear I would have done exactly the same.'

'I'm so stupid,' Polly sobbed. 'It's because of me that Katy is in trouble.'

'Of course it isn't and you're not stupid, just young, and a little naïve. Neither of you should have been drinking, especially spirits, but that doesn't mean that either of you deserved this.'

'I–I thought you'd blame me.'

'No, Polly. All the guilt lies with that Alan Purvis and I hope to God that he rots in hell!' Jackie insisted as she reached for the sponge to soap it and softly wash Polly's grazed and bruised back. 'Don't let them win. Don't let what they did to you ruin the rest of your life. You will get over this. You're a strong young woman, stronger than you think. Just look how you've come to terms with losing your parents and being so badly injured yourself. If you can get through that, then you can overcome anything that life throws at you, and we *will* have Katy home soon.'

As Jackie continued to gently wash her, Polly found that some of her words sank in and at last her tears subsided. 'I never thought of myself as strong but you're right, I won't let those sickos bring me down. They may have taken my virginity, but that's all they'll take.'

'Good girl,' Jackie said. 'Now, I'll leave you to wash all that mud out of your hair.'

Polly watched her leave, and then quickly washed her hair before climbing out of the bath. She dried herself and then put on her pyjamas before going back downstairs. Though Jackie offered her food, she didn't feel like eating, and soon, mentally and physically exhausted, she said she was going to bed.

'Yes, do that, love, and try to stop worrying. As I said before, Katy will be home soon,' Jackie reassured her.

It had been a long night and as Polly rested her weary head on her pillow, she imagined what Katy would say right now if she were there. It would probably be something from their favourite film, *Gone with the Wind*. Yes, she decided, that's exactly what Katy would say and so that's what she herself would do, stop worrying about things for now and sleep. I'll think about that tomorrow, she thought. After all, tomorrow is another day.

Chapter 25

The cell walls were made of grey cement, etched with the names and scrawlings of many detainees before him. There was a wooden slatted bench along one wall with a thin, itchy blanket and a plastic-covered mattress which Alan sat on, rocking himself back and forth.

He'd been allowed one telephone call but had declined. What was the point? He had no one to call. His parents wouldn't care where he was and he doubted they'd be bothered that Kenny was dead. They had seen his brother as nothing but a burden, and, as for him, they would probably quite happily see him rot in jail. The duty solicitor would be in to see him soon, since the police would have called him, but he wasn't bothered about seeing him either. As far as Alan was concerned, he deserved everything he got.

What had he been thinking, making Kenny rape that girl? Admittedly, he didn't rate women much, especially as his mother was such a fine example of a rotten one, but he had never hurt one before. Yes, he'd been violent, had given a good few blokes a bruising and had knocked Kenny about when he needed teaching a lesson, but he had never hit a woman – not once, and he hated it if he saw his dad hitting his mum.

All of a sudden, Alan realised that now he was just like his father, an aggressive, controlling thug of a man who had made his life a living hell. Alan had sworn to himself that he would never grow up like him, and the appalling truth hit him like a ton of bricks. He had done just that. He was a carbon copy. He had even started drinking copious amounts of booze just like his father.

Poor Kenny. What sort of life had he had? A short one filled with contempt from his own mother, violence from his father and bullying from his older brother. Alan felt the cell walls begin to close in on him as he thought of Kenny and his naïve innocence. They say that ignorance is bliss and in Kenny's case it had been. He had looked up to Alan, admired him, and what had he shown him in return? Nothing! Nothing but the same example his father had shown him.

He shuffled along the bench until he was sat side on to the wall and then smashed his head brutally against it, yet felt no relief from his internal torture. He slammed it into the wall again, then again, over and over as blood began to ooze from his skull.

He paused for a moment and touched his head, and bizarrely the sight of the blood made him feel better, so once again he slammed his head onto the bricks. Blood gushed now and Alan knew he deserved this, deserved to be punished for causing his brother's death. The more he hit his head, the better he felt and soon there was no more pain, just numbness in its place.

Drool dripped from Alan's mouth and bright-red blood splattered on the cell wall, but still he continued to smash his head, crying for the loss of Kenny, the one person who had ever truly loved him.

It'll be over soon, he thought to himself. I'll be dead, just like Kenny.

Chapter 26

It was May and it could still be months before Katy's trial. In the meantime she was on remand, and with bail set at such a high figure Jackie had no choice but to leave her daughter behind bars. It had broken Jackie's heart and she was still on sick leave from her nursing job at the hospital, but at least it gave Polly the opportunity to return some of the kindness that Jackie had shown her. She had been cooking her meals and keeping up with the household chores, and though Polly felt it wasn't much, it was better than nothing.

Ross did nothing to help, and made life at the Bentons' house almost intolerable for Polly. Most of the time he simply ignored her, never once thanking her for the hearty dinners she served up night after night. But Polly preferred it that way, because when he did speak it was only to make a nasty jibe, and some of the comments were so cutting that they really hurt her feelings.

One afternoon when Polly was in the kitchen the doorbell rang. She rushed to answer it and found Toby standing on the doorstep. It had been some time since he had been to see them, and Polly assumed it was because he was giving them some space to deal with all that had happened.

'Toby, hello, come in,' she said, smiling.

'Thanks. Hello, Mrs Benton, how are you?' Toby greeted Jackie as he walked into the living room.

'As well as can be expected, I suppose, what with my Katy being locked up in that awful prison.'

'I know, I'm sorry. How is she coping?'

'Better than me, I think, but I think she puts on a brave face so that she doesn't upset me. At least we've been able to apply for legal aid to cover the cost of lawyers, so that's something, I suppose.'

Ross came running down the stairs. 'Toby, I thought I heard your voice. Come on, let's go for a walk.'

'Aren't you going to stay for a cup of tea?' Jackie asked.

Ross fixed accusing eyes on Polly, saying, 'No, he won't want to stay, not when there's such a rotten smell in here.'

Polly could feel her cheeks flame red and looked at Toby, who appeared to be taken aback by Ross's comment.

'Ross,' Jackie cried, 'this has to stop. You're causing such a bad atmosphere, and I can't take it any more. Things are bad enough and it's not fair on me, or on Polly!'

'Well, if Polly doesn't like it, she knows where she can go. It's not like she's homeless. There's a perfectly good house with her name on it sitting down in Kent and I think it's about time she went back to it.'

Polly couldn't take any more either and fled from the house, barely aware that she only had slippers on. Just before she turned the corner, she heard Toby calling out to her. His voice halted her and she stopped, but as soon as he drew level she carried on, walking now instead of running.

'I know I haven't been round for a while,' Toby began, 'but I can't believe the way Ross is behaving. I hoped he'd have come to his senses by now, but he's just as bad. He's my best mate but I don't like the way he talks to you, or to his mother. It isn't right.'

'He's upset about Katy and he's got every right to be. Since I moved into their home I've caused them nothing but trouble,' Polly said.

'Come on, let's go and sit in the park for a bit and we can talk,' Toby suggested.

Polly saw the warmth in his eyes and nodded her head, unable to speak for fear of bursting out crying.

It was a sunny Saturday afternoon and there were quite a few people about, meandering around or walking their dogs, but despite the balmy weather Polly shivered. Toby removed his jacket as they sat on a bench and placed it around her shoulders, then asked, 'Does Ross always talk to you like that?'

'Yes, but if you remember he wasn't any different before.' Polly paused. 'You know, before everything happened.'

'You're right. I remember having a conversation with him and he told me to stay well clear of you.'

'What do you mean? Why would he say that?'

Toby looked suddenly shy and lowered his eyes. 'I told him that I liked you, and still do.'

'Oh,' Polly said, at a loss for words.

'Please, don't go back to Kent. I should have found the nerve to ask you out ages ago, and I should have had a word with Ross about the way he treated you and Katy. I can't help but blame myself for what happened that night. If I had spoken to Ross, maybe you and Katy would have stayed in the pub with us instead of going back to the Star, and then none of that dreadful business would have happened.'

'Toby, you can't blame yourself. You didn't do anything wrong. If anyone's to blame, it's me,' Polly told him, deliberately ignoring the bit that Toby had said about liking her and hoping he wouldn't mention it again.

'No, you're not, but perhaps we all have regrets about what happened that night,' Toby said soberly. 'I want to be here for you, Polly, and as I said I've always liked you. I'm sorry if you think I've let you down in any way, but if you'll let me I'll prove to you that I'll never let anyone hurt you again.'

Polly bit her bottom lip and thought for a moment. She did like Toby, and she found him attractive, but the thought of being physically close to a man turned her stomach.

'I'm sorry, Toby, but after what the Purvis brothers did to me, I'm not ready for any sort of relationship and I don't think I will be for a very long time. I hope you understand. Can . . . can we just be friends?'

Toby looked disappointed but said softly, 'Yes, I understand, and we will always be friends. Who knows, though? Maybe one day, when you're ready, we can be more than that?'

'Maybe,' Polly answered, but she doubted it. With Ross being so cruel and wanting to be rid of her, she had made up her mind to return to her parents' house, and the sooner she could leave the better.

With Jackie still traumatised, it was June before Polly felt that she could leave. She had waited four weeks and was now more determined than ever to make a go of it back in Ivyfield. When they got to the station, Jackie threw her arms around Polly and gave her the tightest squeeze before releasing her and pulling a suitcase from the boot of her car.

'Go on, Polly, hurry up or you'll miss your train. I know you want to leave, but if you ever want to come back you'll always have a home with me, and . . . and please stay in touch,' she said with tears in her eyes.

'I will, I promise, and I'll be back soon for Katy's trial. I don't know what to say, Jackie – "thank you" just doesn't seem enough. When I lost my parents, I didn't think I'd be able to carry on, and I don't think I'd have got through any of it without you.'

'Yes, you would have. I've told you before, you're stronger than you think. Anyway, enough of all this, I hate goodbyes, so let's just say "see you later" instead.'

Polly smiled at the dear woman who had been her rock for the past six months and then turned to walk away. 'All right, see you later,' she called over her shoulder. She didn't look back even though she wanted to, as she knew Jackie would be in floods of tears, and that was something she couldn't bear to see.

When her train arrived Polly climbed on board, but as she took a seat her mind was flooded with memories of the last time she had been on a train. It was with her parents, on that fateful Christmas trip, that happy journey that had ended in tragedy. She was filled with sadness. It would be hard to return to her old home for the first time since the death of her parents. She knew it would be filled with memories, but at least they would be happy ones.

As the train chugged along Polly looked out of the window, eventually seeing the beautiful Kent countryside. Unexpectedly, it lifted her spirits.

And then came the moment when she found herself

standing outside her old home. It felt wonderful to be there; she hadn't realised how much she had missed the place. With all that had happened in London, this quaint stone cottage offered her a safe haven, a place of tranquillity where she could hide away from the world and heal her emotional wounds.

The garden looked overgrown, with weeds sprouting up everywhere, and the windows needed cleaning, but everything else looked just as it had the last time she was there. Except she was alone. Polly suddenly felt very melancholy and fought to dismiss her sadness. She had worked hard to prepare herself for this moment and was determined not to let depression overtake her.

With trepidation she entered the house and immediately noticed the silence. In the past the radio would have been on, and her mum would have been singing along, but the absolute stillness made her feel very alone. Dust had settled on every surface, something her mother would have hated. The lift she'd felt on the train was rapidly replaced with grief. Though she had cried many tears for her parents, being back at the home they had loved brought the pain of their loss surging back.

Polly fought back tears, trying to push her sadness to one side by making herself busy with things that needed to be done. She saw the pile of letters that her neighbour, Mrs Stewart, had left on the hall table, most probably addressed to her parents, but as there might be some for her containing condolences she couldn't face looking at them yet. Instead she dusted and vacuumed upstairs and down, but, knowing the sight and smell of her parents' clothing and personal belongings would make her break down again, she left their bedroom untouched for now.

With the housework done, but unable to sit, Polly poured herself a glass of water and then looked in the kitchen cupboards. She would have to do some shopping, but the savings her parents had left were rapidly diminishing. Polly stiffened her shoulders. It was time to stand on her own two feet, to really grow up, and as her job on the farm was sure to have been filled by now, she would have to find another job to support herself. She turned up the radio and at last sat down, but most of the music being played reminded her of the good times she'd had with Katy. Another memory surfaced so she began to sing along to one of the songs, loudly – refusing to let the Purvis brothers infiltrate her thoughts.

After all, Polly told herself, it wasn't as if they could ever hurt her again. Not now. They were both dead.

Chapter 27

In London, Helen was late arriving at the church, but the service for Maude's funeral hadn't started and, as there was standing room only, she took a place at the back. She looked to the front and could see Maude's sons and their partners, and Harry sitting next to Johnnie.

My goodness, she thought, Johnnie looked so grown up now, and was a good-looking young man. Glenda would have been so proud of her son and it was such a shame she'd missed out on him growing up. Helen recalled the many hours she had spent with Johnnie, but it had been years since he was a small child and she had taken him out. As he grew, Johnnie had often popped up to see her in her eleventh-floor flat and it warmed her heart when he still called her Aunty Helen.

She had heard recently, though, that he'd been in a bit of bother with the police. Apparently he'd been caught riding in a stolen car, but as he wasn't the driver he'd managed to get off without any charges. It disappointed Helen to think of him getting in with a bad crowd, especially as he'd always been such a good boy and done well at school when he was younger. He hadn't made it all the way to grammar school so had followed in his father's footsteps as a bricklayer, and before Maude had died she'd told Helen that the lad was a grafter, worked hard and spent his money wisely.

The service began and Helen couldn't help but shed a tear for the sometimes ferocious old woman who lay in the coffin. During the time when she had gone to pick Johnnie up every fortnight, she'd built quite a bond with Maude, especially after Maude had been unexpectedly widowed when Bob had died of a heart attack. How odd, thought Helen, that it was 1968 and Maude had been sixty-eight when she'd died. It was as though she had lived along with the century; the woman had survived two World Wars and was a tough old bird. Who would have thought that a common cold would have led to this? But she was a stubborn woman and had refused to see the doctor, pneumonia finally finishing her off.

Helen hated funerals. There had been far too many of them and each one reminded her of how life changed for those left behind. Her own mother had died peacefully in her sleep, and her dad had soon followed her; the heart had gone out of him after the death of his wife. With the area scheduled for demolition, Helen had been rehoused in a one-bedroom flat in one of the new tower blocks on the Winstanley estate. She didn't like living there. It made her feel very isolated and she'd become lonely, her nieces and nephews rarely visiting. There had been some compensations, such as a fabulous view over Clapham Junction, and a modern kitchen and an inside bathroom with constant hot water. She had her little budgerigar for a bit of company too, and for amusement she had taught him how to say a few simple words.

As the service ended, Helen wiped her eyes and made

her way outside to view some of the beautiful wreaths that had been laid on the ground. She noticed Harry leaning against a wall smoking a cigarette with Johnnie standing a little way off from him, kicking the ground and scuffing his highly polished black shoes. She wanted to chastise him, but he wasn't a child any more so instead she walked over to offer her condolences.

'Thanks, Aunt Helen,' Johnnie said, 'I know you meant a lot to my gran.'

'As she did to me,' Helen replied. 'I will miss her, but at least she had a good innings and didn't suffer any horrible illness. Anyway, young man, it's been a while since you've been up to see me. Why don't you pop up for a meal after work tomorrow?'

'Yeah, sorry, I've just been a bit busy and that, you know how it is, but thanks, I'd love to,' he replied with a genuine warm smile.

Helen didn't want to speak to Harry. Despite all the years that had passed, she would never forgive him for the way he'd treated Glenda. Maude had told her that Harry had become a bit of a recluse and rarely went out socialising, even to the local pub. It had all begun years back when Betty Howard died. It had affected Harry badly and he'd never been the same since, yet she couldn't feel any sympathy for him. She turned her back to him and said to Johnnie before leaving the old churchyard, 'I'll see you tomorrow then, love.'

He waved a goodbye and as Helen walked along a path close to the Thames, she pondered what treat she could cook up for Johnnie tomorrow. Once her mind was made up on sausages and mash with fried onions, she began to consider giving him a good talking-to about his antics with the stolen car. With Harry seemingly indifferent and Maude no longer around to give him any motherly advice, Helen felt it was down to her and she knew it was what Glenda would want.

Thinking of Glenda, she realised she hadn't heard from her in a while, at least six months in fact. She frowned, worried that something was wrong with her friend, and hoped that she hadn't fallen ill or anything. The last correspondence Helen had received was a Christmas card, and Glenda hadn't replied to her last letter, which she'd sent to her back in February.

Maybe Glenda had been busy or her letter had been lost in the post. She would wait until after Johnnie's visit tomorrow and then write again with an update, but maybe it would be best not to mention that her son had been involved with the police. It would only worry Glenda and Helen didn't want that.

The small bunch of flowers that Johnnie had for Helen were wilting slightly, but he knew she would still be chuffed with them. Anyway, once she put them in some water, they might perk up a bit.

The lift opened and he walked across the landing to knock on her door. The sound echoed loudly off the windowless walls. As the door opened, Johnnie got a waft of onions and Helen looked really pleased to see him.

'Johnnie, I'm so glad you came. Oh, and you've brought me flowers, how lovely! I can't remember the last time anyone gave me a bunch of flowers. Thank you. Your meal is almost ready, and if I remember it's your favourite.'

'Sausages,' he said, grinning as he walked into the living room and sat on the sofa.

'Spot on, and I'm just going to mash the spuds. I won't be long,' Helen said as she bustled to the kitchen.

Johnnie smiled. Helen had been a part of his life for as long as he could remember, and he now berated himself for not visiting her more often over the past couple of years. She had aged, and he resolved to call in at least once a month from now on. Helen's home was warm and friendly, albeit very old-fashioned; it felt like a reflection of her. The sofa was plump with a caramel floral design and she'd hung orange curtains. The fitted carpet was flowery too, but olive and red so nothing really matched. Even so it felt cosy, and he'd noticed that Helen was dressed in an outfit that reminded him of one of his old spinster schoolteachers. With her large bust, round stomach and greying hair worn in a bun, Helen was a funny little woman, but Johnnie was deeply fond of her. Apart from Maude, she was the closest person he had to a mother.

'Grub up,' Helen called from the kitchen.

Johnnie walked into the room and took his place opposite her at the small kitchen table, salivating at the large plate of sausages, mash and onions, covered in rich, thick gravy. Maude's culinary skills hadn't been the greatest, though he would never have complained, but he did miss a good home-cooked meal like this and relished the thought of getting stuck in.

'So how have you been, Johnnie?' Helen asked as they ate. 'I expect you're missing your gran. Any ideas about where you're going to live now that she's passed on?'

'I'm not sure yet. I did think about moving in with my dad, but he's a bit of a funny bugger. Whoops, excuse my French.'

'You can speak French as much as you like. You know me, it's nothing I ain't heard a million times before.' Helen laughed. 'So if not with your dad, where then?'

'I've got a mate who's offered me a room in his gaff and for pretty cheap rent too. I'm thinking about it but it's down on the Surrey Lane estate, quite a way from the station.'

'And this mate of yours, does he work?'

'Yeah,' Johnnie answered, 'but that's a funny sort of question.'

'I'm just a bit worried about the company you've been keeping of late. I've heard about you and that stolen car. What on earth were you thinking?'

Johnnie hadn't intended to tell Helen about his run-in with the law, but he should have realised that with all the local gossips she'd have heard about it. 'It was just a bit of a laugh, nothing serious,' he said, trying to defend his actions.

'But it was serious! You could have been charged and ended up in prison, or what if the car had crashed? Either way you could have lost your job. Come on, Johnnie, you know better than to be mixing with the likes who go around nicking cars. How would you feel if you had a car that you worked hard to buy and then some hooligans stole it? Think about that. I'm a firm believer in karma. What goes around comes around, remember that too.'

Johnnie hung his head in shame. He knew that Helen was right, and didn't intend to get into trouble with the law again, but the talk of karma made him feel angry. '"What goes around comes around," you say, but what about me losing my mum to cancer when I was just a

274

baby? I hadn't done anything bad so why did she die? I don't remember her, nothing about her. I ain't even got a photo and my gran would never talk about her much. She told me not to mention her in front of my dad in case it upset him. But what about me? Don't you think it upset me, not knowing anything about my own mother? It's not fair. Life ain't fair, so I don't believe in all that hippie karma rubbish. My mum's dead, my gran is dead, and my dad's pretty much brain-bloody-dead so who have I got left? No one, that's who, so I'll be looking out for number one from now on, regardless of bloody karma!'

Helen looked taken aback and Johnnie instantly regretted his outburst.

'I'm sorry, I didn't mean to lose my rag,' he said. 'You were just trying to put me straight, and you're right, I'm an idiot for getting involved with that crowd of layabouts. They're not my real friends, just some old mates from school.'

'It's all right, Johnnie, you have every right to feel angry, and I understand that you feel cheated, but you're not alone. You've got me and your dad. OK, I know he keeps himself to himself these days but he's still there for you.'

'You don't get it, Aunt Helen. Yeah, I love him, but we don't have much to do with each other. I wouldn't really know how to have a conversation with him. He's . . . well . . . weird. Yesterday was the first time I'd seen him in months and he hardly said more than two words to me.'

'He's just lost his mum, he was probably too upset to talk.'

'Yeah, maybe,' Johnnie said, but he didn't look convinced.

'He'll come round, and in the meantime, as I said, you've got me.'

'I know you'll always be there for me, but no offence, you ain't proper family.'

'I–I know, but I'm very fond of you, Johnnie.'

'I'm fond of you too and forget what I said. I'm just being maudlin 'cos of my gran. She was like a mother to me,' he said sadly.

There was a long silence and Johnnie worried that he'd upset Helen, but then she spoke. 'Johnnie, if I tell you something, you've got to promise me not to go off your head.'

Johnnie nodded his head, intrigued.

'I don't know where to start and please don't hate me, or anyone else, but I think there's something you should know.'

'You're worrying me now. What is it?'

'It's about your mum. You see . . . er . . . well . . . there's no easy way to say this – she isn't dead.'

Johnnie dropped his cutlery onto his plate and looked at Helen in complete astonishment. His head whirled. 'What do you mean, she's not dead? I don't understand.'

'I know this is hard for you to take in, but your mum is alive and living in Kent.'

'I don't believe this. Kent . . . how –'

'She had to leave London,' Helen interrupted. 'You see, when you were a baby your dad was, well, difficult, and things happened that forced her to run away. Oh, Johnnie, she didn't want to leave you and trust me, it was the hardest thing for her to do.'

It was too much for Johnnie to take in and questions were flying through his mind. He left the table and looked out of the window, but hardly noticed any of Clapham Junction as his thoughts raced. Helen said his mother was alive, but was it true or was she losing her marbles? He had a mate whose gran had gone a bit funny in her old age. Was that happening to Helen? She wasn't even an old woman yet. He spun around.

'Why did everyone tell me she was dead? Why did she leave? Aunt Helen, you've got some explaining to do, none of this makes sense!'

'I know, and I'm sorry to drop it on you like this, but there have been so many lies and secrets for too long. Your mother loves you, she always has, and I think she'll be thrilled to bits that you finally know the truth.'

'But she left me and let me think she's been dead all these years. What sort of mother does that? And you reckon she loves me, but that don't sound much like love to me!'

'Johnnie, you've got to understand, she had no choice.'

'Then make me understand, tell me what happened, everything.'

'Well, back then your dad could be a violent man, and to be honest your mum was petrified of him. It wasn't unusual for her to be covered in bruises. One time he put her in hospital and the beating was so bad that she had her nose broken and a couple of teeth knocked out. That's where she met Frank Myers. He showed your mum a bit of kindness and I swear your mum tried to fight it, but she fell in love with him. Trouble was, your dad found out about it and he was on a mission to kill them. In those days he was more than capable of it, and though I don't like to speak badly of your dad, that's how it was. So your mum only had one option, and that was to run away. Once she and Frank went into hiding, you went to live with your gran and the way your father was, your mum could never come back for you, not safely anyway.'

'I just can't take this all in,' Johnnie murmured. 'Why wasn't I told? Why?'

'Your dad and gran decided to concoct the story about your mum being dead, but I've been secretly writing to her over the years, sending her the odd photo of you, and Johnnie, she's missed you so much. But you must see, there was nothing else she could do.'

Johnnie sat back on the kitchen chair, reeling with shock. He was speechless, confused as he tried to digest it all, and didn't know if he should feel anger, bitterness, relief or joy.

'I don't know what to say. My dad wanted to kill my mum, then 'cos of him she left, and he's lied to me all these years? And my gran knew too, but so did you?'

'I wanted to tell you, Johnnie, I really did, but your dad was . . . scary. I don't know, maybe I've been a coward and should have told you before now. Your mum was my best friend and I missed her badly when she left. I was never really one of Maude's friends – well, not at first. I promised your mother that I would look out for you and you became like one of my own nephews. It's a shame you don't remember your other nan and grandad, but Ted and Elsie died years ago when you was just a toddler. They thought the world of you. It tore your mum to bits, but she was too scared to attend either of their funerals. She knew your dad would watch for her and she was right. He turned up expecting to find your mother – thank Gawd she had stayed away! I hated your dad for what he did, but I've got to say, the years do seem to have mellowed him. As for your mum, she's made a life for herself in Kent, but I know she has never stopped wanting you, or loving you.'

Johnnie had no reason to disbelieve Helen, and he did have vague recollections of angry outbursts from his dad, though he couldn't imagine him capable of killing anyone. 'Can I see her?' he asked, not entirely sure if he wanted to – but if Helen was telling the story as it really happened, then his mother wasn't to blame.

'Yes, of course, but Johnnie, you have to swear *never* to tell your father. He might appear to be a mild, quiet man now, but I don't believe a leopard changes its spots. If he gets wind of you seeing your mother, I shudder to think what might happen.'

Johnnie could see that Helen was serious and obviously very worried. 'As I said, I hardly see him, and if I do, I promise I won't say a word about this.'

Helen nodded, 'All right. I'll give you your mum's address. She calls herself Glenda Myers now, though rather than just turning up on her doorstep, it might be best if you write to her first.'

He thought about it for a moment before answering. 'No, too much time has passed already. I'm not doing any overtime this weekend so I'll go to see her tomorrow, and if she misses me as much as you say, then she won't mind me just turning up.'

Helen gave Johnnie the address but he could see she was still worried, no doubt frightened of what his father would do to her if he found out she'd told him the truth. 'Don't worry, I'd never put you in any danger, and my dad will *never* find out about this. Thank you, Aunt

Helen, thank you for telling me about my mum. If you hadn't, I might never have known that she's alive.'

The worried expression left Helen's face and she smiled. 'When you see your mum and she gives you a hug, give her a bloody big one from me too. I haven't seen her for donkey's years, must be at least ten or so. I suppose we're more sort of pen-friends nowadays, but tell her I'm coming for a summer holiday. Johnnie, you'll love it down there, she's got a sweet little place.' Helen pulled something from her pocket and handed it to Johnnie. 'I thought you might like to see this photo of her. It's a bit old but it's a good one.'

Johnnie studied the black and white image of a woman he didn't recognise. The picture was a bit grainy but he could tell she was pretty. If fact, she was quite a stunner and Johnnie felt unexpectedly proud. The good-looking woman was *his* mother and he couldn't wait to meet her.

Chapter 28

On Saturday, as the taxi drove into Ivyfield village, Johnnie's heart was beating thirteen to the dozen. He clutched the piece of paper with his mother's address in his clammy hand, nervously sucking in deep breaths in anticipation now that he was just minutes away from her house.

When the taxi pulled up he couldn't tell if anyone was home, but he paid his fare and went to knock on the front door. He tried to recall the well-rehearsed introduction that he planned to say, but his mind went blank. Nobody came to the door so he knocked again, this time a little louder. There was still no answer, but an elderly woman came down her garden path from the house next door.

'Can I help you, young man?' she asked.

Johnnie thought she was probably just being nosy, but decided to see if the old dear could help. 'Er, yes. I'm looking for Gl–Glenda,' he said, finding it strange to be using his mother's first name. 'Glenda Myers. I'm an old family friend and was hoping to surprise her.'

'Oh, goodness, haven't you heard what happened?' the old lady asked, aghast.

'No, I've been overseas, working. Why, what's happened then?'

'Shocking it was, absolutely shocking!' The old woman twisted her apron in her hands and shook her head. 'I don't know if I should be the one to tell you, but I'm sorry, young man, you're about seven months too late to surprise her. She's passed away. She was killed in an accident.'

'An . . . ac–accident?' Johnnie stammered.

'Yes, it was some sort of explosion, gas I think, and it killed her and Frank. Awful business, they were such a nice couple, what a waste. I'm so sorry to be the bearer of bad news.'

'Right, thanks,' Johnnie managed to say but he felt sick inside as he walked up the small street where his mother had lived. If only Helen had told him the truth earlier. Now it was too late and he would never meet his mother. He felt sad, but then questioned his feelings, wondering why he was so upset about losing someone he had never met. It was the thought of having a mother – a mother's love, something he had never known.

He wasn't looking forward to telling Helen, who would probably be devastated. His mind was in a whirl of conflicting emotions and he couldn't face going straight back home to London, not without a couple of stiff drinks first to calm his fractured nerves.

He wandered aimlessly through the small village, hoping that he would come across a pub or at least an off-licence. He could have kicked himself for not questioning the old woman further but the shock of the news of his mother's death had been enough to take in. He wondered where she was buried or if he had any other long-lost relatives that had attended her funeral. He would never know and supposed it was water under the bridge now, but it didn't stop him pondering the possibilities.

He turned a corner and spotted on the other side of the road a whitewashed building with a thatched roof. A hanging sign read 'The Oak and Ivy'. Relieved to have found a watering hole, Johnnie darted across the quiet street, eager to get a brandy down his neck.

Just as he stepped off the pavement, he heard a shrill scream and turned in the nick of time to see a young woman on a push bike hurtling towards him. With only seconds to spare before she would collide with him, the woman sharply swerved her bike to the left, narrowly missing Johnnie. He watched in dismay as the back wheel of the bike skidded around to the front, causing the woman to unceremoniously lose her balance and tumble to the ground, leaving the bike lying a couple of feet away from her.

Johnnie dashed over to check if the woman had been injured but she was already getting to her feet.

'You stupid idiot!' she exclaimed as she brushed her trousers down. 'You walked out in front of me without looking to see if the road was clear. Don't you know how to cross a road?'

'I'm really sorry,' Johnnie replied. 'I should join The Tufty Club,' he added with a smile, hoping that a bit of humour would soften her annoyance at him.

'Yes, you should. A five-year-old would have more road sense than you.' She took a couple of deep breaths, seeming to relax a little as she looked at him. 'Oh, well, no harm done,' she said at last. 'Just look where you're going in future.'

Johnnie was pleased that the woman appeared to have

calmed down and was unhurt. Her strikingly pretty looks hadn't gone unnoticed by him and he wondered if he could use the situation to his advantage. As he helped her lift her bike from the ground, he decided to chance his luck.

'I really am sorry for being so careless. I was on my way to that pub over there. Would you join me and let me buy you a drink to say sorry?'

The woman hesitated before answering, 'That's very kind of you but I'm just on my lunch break and was actually popping home for a bite to eat. Thanks all the same.'

'Well, I'm guessing they do food in the pub so will you allow me to buy you lunch?' Johnnie asked, undeterred.

'Thanks, but there's really no need to.'

'But I'd like to,' Johnnie answered quickly.

There was a short pause, then she said, 'Thanks, I'd like that, but we'll go halves.'

'No way, a gent always picks up the tab,' he insisted.

'Oh, so you're a gentleman, are you?'

'Too right I am,' Johnnie said, taking her arm as they crossed the road. 'I'm Johnnie, by the way, nice to meet you.'

'Hello, Johnnie, I'm Polly. You're not from round here, are you? I haven't seen you in these parts before.' She was very pleasant and he thought he could detect a slight trace of a London accent, but maybe as this was Kent it was a local dialect.

'No, I came up from London on the train to visit an old friend but they've moved on so I've found myself a bit stranded. Lucky I bumped into you, literally,' Johnnie said with a laugh. Not wanting to go into detail about his mother, he had lied about the 'friend'. Since running into this pretty lady, all thoughts about his mother's death were rapidly fading . . .

Polly was warmly greeted by the pub landlord and the few customers in the bar, but all eyes were on the good-looking stranger who sat with her.

'Ignore them,' Polly said quietly to Johnnie. 'They don't know you so they're just curious.'

'Have you always lived in this village?'

'Yes, all my life until recently. I lived in Croydon for a while, but it didn't work out so I came back here a couple of weeks ago.' Polly hoped that Johnnie wouldn't press her on why it hadn't worked out in Croydon as it was something she would much rather not talk about. It broke her heart to think about Katy, still on remand and awaiting trial, and a part of her dreaded having to appear in court. After what had happened with the Purvis brothers she was still nervous of men and had almost refused Johnnie's offer to join him, but there was something about him that made her feel safe.

'I live in Battersea and Croydon isn't that far away,' Johnnie said, breaking into her thoughts. 'You must find it a lot quieter here – it's such a small village. What do you find to do when you're not at work? And what do you actually do for work?'

'I work in the garden centre just outside the village and when I'm not there I read, watch the telly, and at weekends, weather permitting, I like to look after my own garden. I realise that probably sounds boring to a *sophisticated* Londoner but it suits me just fine. I like a quiet life and the easy pace,' Polly told him. After what she had been through, it was true.

'It doesn't sound boring to me. It sounds idyllic, and I wouldn't mind a bit of peace and quiet. London is all right, but I've never seen a place like this before and it's a bit of an eye-opener . . . I love it!'

Polly liked the twinkle in Johnnie's eye and was surprised to find herself so relaxed in his company. She realised she didn't want their lunch to end.

'I expect you'll be heading back to London soon,' she said, fearing that she might never see him again.

Johnnie glanced up at the big clock on the wall. 'Blimey, is that the time already? I suppose I should, and you'll be needing to get back to work. Time flies when you're having fun. Polly, I would love to see you again. Do you want to meet up when you've finished work? If I can find a bed locally for the night, I can make my way back to London tomorrow.'

Polly hadn't been expecting him to be quite so forthright and felt her cheeks flush. For a fleeting moment she considered offering him a room at hers but then decided against such a reckless idea. She had only just met him and for all she knew he could be another rapist, and she wasn't going to risk being alone with him.

'They do rooms here, with breakfast,' she said, 'so have a word with the landlord. It would be lovely to see you again.'

Johnnie went to the bar, paid for their meal and came back to the table flashing a wide smile. 'That's me sorted for the night, and as it's Sunday tomorrow, do you fancy spending a day in the country with a stranded Londoner?

Or would having to put up with me for dinner tonight and a day of it tomorrow be too much for you?'

Polly had hoped that this meal with Johnnie wouldn't be their last but felt a surge of disappointment as she realised she already had commitments for later.

'I like that idea but I've just remembered that I've promised my boss that I'll work late tonight. We've had a big delivery that needs sorting out and there's loads of repotting to do. I'm so sorry, Johnnie, but tomorrow I'll make us a picnic,' she offered, 'and I know just the place to take you. If you can ride a push bike you can use my dad's.'

'Of course I can, though as I ain't been on a bike since I was a kid I might be a bit rusty. And don't worry about this evening, I understand. I'll waste my time in here tonight, no big deal.'

For the first time in ages, Polly felt a rush of happiness. It would be lovely to spend a day in the countryside with this good-looking man, and somehow she felt that she could almost trust him.

With plans for the next day finalised, Johnnie walked Polly to her bike, which she'd left leaning against a wall outside. As she mounted it, Polly turned to look up at him and found that he reminded her of someone, though she couldn't quite put her finger on who it was. Her eyes lingered on his mouth and, unexpectedly, she found herself hoping that he would kiss her goodbye, even though she had only just met him.

'So, I'll see you tomorrow then,' she said as an awkward silence fell between them.

'Yeah, and thanks, Polly. I had a really good time.'

'Yes, me too.'

'Well . . . see you soon then,' Johnnie said but made no attempt to leave.

'I–I'll see you tomorrow. Goodbye,' she said, still looking up into his face, and wishing she was brave enough to at least kiss him on the cheek.

Johnnie suddenly put his hand around the back of her neck and pulled her towards him for a kiss, but he had misjudged slightly and his lips ended up partly on her chin. Then, just as swiftly as he had reached for her, he let her go and turned to run back into the pub.

Polly had tensed, but instead of fear she found herself thinking that though Johnnie appeared worldly-wise, he'd just shown that he was far from experienced. It made her smile and any doubts about him dissipated. He was a nice young man and nothing like the Purvis brothers.

Polly raised her eyes to the sky as she cycled along the country road. The shining sun always made her think of her parents and as she arrived at work and parked her bike, she wondered what her mum would've said if she was still alive to see the goodbye kiss. She smiled to herself as she imagined the scenario, the unrelenting questions she would have faced. Oh, yes, thought Polly, her mum would've had plenty to say if she had seen her kissing Johnnie!

Helen flicked through the three television channels but wasn't taken by any of the programmes, least of all *Match of the Day*. Saturday nights were normally pretty dull but tonight she was growing increasingly concerned about Johnnie, who had promised to come and see her as soon as he returned from his visit to Glenda. Maybe it went so well that he stayed the night there, she reasoned.

Now that Maude had passed on, it had been such a relief to finally tell Johnnie the truth about his mother, though despite Johnnie's reassurances she was still petrified that Harry would find out. Still, at least Johnnie would get to know his mother now, and better late than never.

She could just imagine Glenda's face when she opened the door to find Johnnie standing there. It would have been a very emotional meeting for them both and she couldn't wait to hear all about it. Helen glanced at the clock, and seeing that it was now past ten she doubted Johnnie would be back tonight. With a sigh she gave up on the television, made herself a cup of Horlicks and climbed under her pale-green candlewick bedspread, intent on finishing her latest historical novel, *Cousin Kate*.

As Helen tried to read, to lose herself in a different world for a while, memories of 1947 kept swimming around in her head and most of them were not good. Harry had been the cause of so much upset in those days and the catalyst for Glenda's departure from Battersea. Not to mention the reason for Betty Howard's death. Although Maude had told her that Harry was a different man now, Helen still despised him and felt no pity for his lonely existence. She wondered what had become of Billy Myers, the man who had tried to blackmail her, and the one who had told Harry about Glenda's affair, something she could never understand, especially as Frank was his own flesh and blood. She had despised Billy Myers too, and though it had all happened so many years ago, the memories remained.

Helen put her book down to switch off the bedside lamp in the hope that she would succumb to sleep and not be plagued all night by Harry Jenkins and Billy Myers, yet no sooner had she closed her eyes than the occupants above her on the twelfth floor began to blare out 'Jumping Jack Flash'. She wouldn't have minded so much if they were playing the Beatles or Tom Jones, but she couldn't stand the Rolling Stones.

The sun shining through the curtains woke Johnnie from his slumber. As he opened his eyes it took him a short while to fathom where he was. He was tired after being awake for much of the night, first thinking about his mother, then fantasising about Polly. He was overwhelmingly attracted to her and her gorgeous figure. He could only hope that she felt the same way too.

Johnnie groaned and threw back the covers. He had kissed her, a fumbled, embarrassing kiss, but a kiss all the same. He'd have to try to do better today.

As he started to get dressed, Johnnie thought about the events of the previous day. His mind was a mess, full of conflicting thoughts and feelings. This wasn't supposed to have happened. On the train from London, he'd imagined his mother opening the front door and instantly recognising him before taking him into her arms and then excitedly introducing him to Frank. Finding out she was dead had been such a shock. It had thrown him off kilter, but then meeting Polly so quickly felt a bit like fate, and she had cheered him up no end. He couldn't wait to see her.

A loud knock on his door made him jump and a voice called, 'Breakfast is ready, Sir.'

'Thanks,' Johnnie called back, 'I'll be down in a tick.'

The thought of breakfast turned his stomach after the amount of ale he'd consumed last night, but the anticipation of seeing Polly, her picnic and those deep-brown irresistible eyes was more than enough to drag him down the stairs.

It was only five past nine and Polly's excitement was already growing even though it would be another two hours before she would go to meet Johnnie.

By eleven the housework was done, the picnic packed, the bikes oiled and leaning against the shed ready for the off. Polly couldn't quite believe that she was so eager to see Johnnie. Since she'd been raped, she hadn't expected to ever want a man to touch her again, but she felt drawn to Johnnie and spent most of the night tossing and turning as she imagined him holding and kissing her.

She'd taken extra care when getting herself ready for their date, but didn't want to look like she'd tried too hard so had chosen pink Capri trousers and an off-the-shoulder white lace top. By the time she had to leave, Polly felt like a headless chicken as she ran around the bedroom, not knowing what she was looking for but flapping about all the same. Pull yourself together, she thought, and drew in a deep breath before checking herself in the mirror for the umpteenth time.

She placed the picnic in a basket on the front of her bicycle and set off for the Oak and Ivy, wheeling both her own bike and her dad's, one on either side of her. She knew she could have let Johnnie come to her house and pick her up, but though she felt drawn to him, she was still being cautious and wanted to hold back from showing him where she lived. It was unlikely that he was a rapist and she knew she was probably worrying over nothing, but she had spent less than an hour with him and reasoned that it was better to be safe than sorry.

With her heartbeat quickening she rounded the corner and was delighted to see Johnnie waiting outside for her. 'Hi, Johnnie, right on time,' she said, hoping that she sounded casual though her heart was now beating so fast that she could hardly catch her breath.

'Hello again, Polly. You look really nice. Thanks for bringing the bike for me.' The sun was behind Johnnie and shining on his thick, black hair which he wore greased back with a small quiff at the front. He was wearing the same jeans and white shirt that he had on yesterday but it looked as though the shirt had been freshly washed.

'This is a great village. Do you live here by yourself?' Johnnie asked, casting his eyes over the stone cottages.

'Yes, it is great and yes, I live alone now but I wish I didn't.'

'Oh, why's that?'

Polly hesitated, but then said, 'My . . . my parents were killed . . . in . . . in an accident.'

'I'm sorry to hear that.'

'Thanks,' Polly said, pushing her sadness to one side. It was a lovely day, the sun was shining and she wanted to try to enjoy life again. 'How are you getting on with my dad's bike?' She tried to stifle a laugh as Johnnie wobbled, obviously out of practice.

'So much for the old saying, "It's like riding a bike,"' Johnnie said, laughing as they rode along the country lane side by side. After a little while, though, he seemed to get the hang of it. Light conversation flowed easily between them until they reached the place Polly had suggested, where there was a small lake with a weeping willow on the banks – the perfect place to lay the picnic blanket.

'I used to ride out here with my mum and dad,' said Polly, recalling the many happy times she had been here before. 'My dad threw me in that lake more than once. It's where I learned to swim.'

Johnnie looked around him and then at Polly before taking her hand in his. 'I can see this is a special place to you, so thanks for sharing it with me.'

She looked up at him and, sensing that he was going to kiss her again, her heart quickened. This time when he dipped his head the kiss was long and tender, very different from the misjudged one of the day before. His tongue explored her mouth and aware of his mounting passion she panicked and pulled away. 'No, don't!'

'I'm sorry, Polly, I didn't mean to scare you. It's just that you're so . . . so special, and different from any other girls I know.'

Polly could see that Johnnie was clearly distressed and reached out to reassure him.

'Don't be sorry,' she said as she touched his arm, 'I wanted you to kiss me. It's just that I had a bad experience, but I know I've got to put it behind me.'

'What sort of bad experience?'

'I don't want to talk about it. It's in the past now and I want to forget it – I want you to help me to forget it,' she said, and brazenly added, 'so why don't you kiss me again?'

The afternoon flew by and though they held each other and kissed, Johnnie managed to hold back from taking things any further. He enjoyed being with Polly and wanted to stay longer, but he had work the next day so regretfully said his goodbyes, though not before making arrangements to visit her the following weekend.

As the late-evening train trundled along the tracks through the Kent countryside, Johnnie reflected on his weekend with Polly. It hadn't been anything like he had planned and though he was gutted he had missed out on meeting Glenda, spending time with Polly had been wonderful. They had so much in common and though they hadn't spoken about it, both had recently experienced the death of their mother and somehow Johnnie felt this brought them closer. He felt warm when he thought of her; she was such a pretty little thing and good company too. He found her very different from the girls he knew in Battersea and couldn't wait to see her again.

First, though, he would have to pop in to see Helen and tell her the awful news. It wasn't a job he was relishing, in fact, he was absolutely dreading it. Still, one small compensation was that at least he wouldn't have to keep any secrets from his dad. Glenda was dead and Johnnie would never know his mother or how much she loved him.

Chapter 29

Jackie really resented being searched as she entered the prison to visit Katy, but it was a necessary evil that she had become accustomed to. It didn't help that Ross was moaning about it and voicing his opinions to the prison officers.

Once through all the security checks, Jackie sat at a small table with Ross beside her annoyingly tapping his leg up and down. 'Can't you just sit still?' Jackie said through gritted teeth.

'I can't help it, it's this place, it always makes me nervous,' Ross replied as he scanned the room for visitors.

'Well, if you're nervous being in here, just think how your poor sister feels!'

'Yes, I know, sorry. But if you hadn't brought that girl into our home, none of this would have happened.'

'Ross, will you give it a rest and change the record. Now put a smile on your face before Katy comes in!' Jackie told him, sick to the back teeth with his whingeing. His constant griping was getting to her, especially as he was supposed to be the man of the house, but instead he acted like a spoilt child.

'Here she is! Over here, Katy.' Jackie waved as her

daughter entered the room with a dozen other remand prisoners.

'Oh, Mum, it's so good to see you, and you too, Ross!'

'And you, my love. How have you been? Are they treating you OK?'

'It's not that bad, and, as I said on your last visit, I'm on a wing with all the remand prisoners which I'm told isn't quite as tough as being in the real prison.'

Jackie's heart was breaking as she looked at her beautiful daughter, who seemed to have lost quite a bit of weight since her last visit. 'Don't you worry, love. I spoke to your lawyer yesterday and he reckons we've a good chance of getting you off. It's just a matter of waiting for a court date and this bloody legal system doesn't rush itself. I'm afraid he reckons it could be months yet.'

'Yes, I know. He came to see me last week and said pretty much the same thing. I just miss you so much. Time goes so slowly in here – it's only been a few months but it feels like I've been locked up for years.'

Jackie could see that her daughter was trying to hold back tears and admired how strong and brave she was being. 'We miss you too, and it won't be for too much longer.'

'Polly came to see me last week. She seems to have settled in Kent. I'm pleased for her. She's got a boyfriend too, a chap from London.'

Jackie was surprised and said, 'Oh, has she indeed? She's been back in Kent about a month now and when she rang me there was no mention of a boyfriend. Still, I'm pleased for her.'

'And how are you, Ross?' Katy turned her attention to her brother.

'All right, same as usual, but I don't get why you two are so bloody nice about Polly. It's her fault you're in here!'

Jackie quickly intervened. 'I've told you, ENOUGH! This is the last time I'm going to say this! It is *not* Polly's fault any more than it's your sister's. Dead or not, the blame lies with those Purvis brothers and it's about time you got that into your thick head.'

Ross lowered his eyes, saying nothing, and Jackie turned back to her daughter. 'Now then, Katy, are you getting enough to eat? Plenty of sleep?' Jackie knew she sounded like a typical mother but she was worried about Katy, who not only appeared thinner but looked pale too, with dark circles under her puffy eyes.

'Mum, stop worrying, I'm fine. The food isn't anything like your cooking, but it's edible and though I manage to sleep it isn't easy. There are so many noises in the night – you know, women crying and shouting out. It echoes in here but that's to be expected. Honestly, I'm doing OK.'

'So why do your eyes look like piss-holes in the snow?' Ross asked.

'Ross!' Jackie said, shocked. 'Where on earth have you heard such an awful expression?'

'Probably from one of the waifs and strays you've taken in, or maybe Polly.'

'Polly would never say something like that and I don't want to hear it said again.'

Ross just scowled and Jackie turned to her daughter. 'Have you been crying, love?'

'Yes, but it's only because I get a bit homesick. I feel better now I've seen you.'

'You're not being mistreated?'

'No, Mum, I'm not. I've made a couple of really good friends and even some of the screws are nice, sorry, I mean the prison officers. The thing that gets to you in here is boredom, and having nothing to do gives you time to think. I've been doing a lot of that and, brace yourself, Mum, but when I get out of here I'm thinking about going to Australia to live with Isobel. Just imagine it, sunshine, sandy beaches, blue seas, oh, Mum, it'll be fabulous. Isobel has always been on at me to come and join her, especially with me being a hairdresser. I'd have no problem finding work so I'm going to be a ten-pound pom! I know this must come as a bit of a shock to you, and I don't know, maybe it's just a fantasy, but it is something nice to think about when I'm bored in here.'

Jackie didn't have the heart to tell her daughter that if she was convicted and served her time, with a criminal record she wouldn't be let into Australia. Anyway, she knew Katy would never leave Blighty. The girl had said so on many occasions when Isobel had left. It was only one of Katy's fanciful pipedreams and Jackie refused to get upset about it unless it really happened. 'One thing at a time, eh. Let's get you out of here first then worry about the rest of it.'

As visiting time came to an end, Ross, who had hardly spoken a word, was up and out of his seat quicker than a Jack-in-the-box, but Jackie found it difficult to pull herself away. She hated leaving Katy behind in here. 'Take care of yourself, stay out of trouble and I'll be back to see you as soon as I can. I love you, Katy.'

'I love you too, Mum,' croaked Katy.

'See ya, sis, take it easy,' Ross said. He looked for a

moment like he wanted to grab his sister and give her a hug, but Jackie could see he was uncomfortable with the whole situation and he couldn't wait to get out of there.

Jackie had seen a lot of heartache in her time as a nurse, but nothing had prepared her for this. Somehow she managed to hold herself together, yet knew that her pillow would be wet with tears again that night.

The stack of unopened letters on the corner table was rapidly increasing as Toby added another to the pile. He knew it was probably another bill, more demands for money that he couldn't pay, so, he reasoned to himself, what was the point of looking at them and worrying? It was easier to stick his head in the sand and just ignore them in the futile hope that they would go away. Only something was niggling Toby about this letter and he had the distinct feeling that whilst his head was buried, something nasty was going to come up and bite him on his bum. In spite of this, he still ignored the unpleasant fact that the bills needed paying. It was Monday morning and he had a shop to open, so once again Toby disregarded his concerns and set off towards the town.

The shop had a sign in the window that stated the opening time: nine o'clock. Toby checked his watch and saw it was already gone a quarter past. Still, he didn't bother to rush. What was the point? he thought to himself. It wasn't as if he ever got any customers.

Business had been very slow for the past few months, which was making Toby consider if he should diversify his lines of products. It seemed that there wasn't much interest in model cars in Croydon and, though it was a passion of Toby's, he wasn't selling enough to even cover the rent on the shop. He had thought about stocking records, or even children's toys and games, but there was a major problem with changing his stock. He had no funds to purchase anything. The Purvis brothers had been milking him dry for quite a time, which resulted in him taking out a bank loan and a Provident loan and pawning just about everything he owned. That left him with just the stock he held on the shelves, a few Green Shield stamps and the pile of bills at home. He rented his flat and the landlord had knocked on the front door on several occasions, but he'd avoided answering, just as he did when the Provident agent called for payment.

He was sorry that Katy was in prison, but he wasn't sorry that the Purvis brothers were dead, and if that made him a sick bastard Toby was past caring. Because of the Purvis brothers it had come to this. He had once been a proud man, but was now reduced to hiding behind the sofa when someone called for money. His only hope was that either business would pick up or he'd have a win on the football pools.

Ross would be calling in later. He'd taken the day off work to go and visit Katy and would pop in on his way home. Poor Katy, Toby thought, but whenever Katy came into his mind, so did Polly. He still couldn't shake away the feelings he had for her and he could have kicked himself for not telling her how he felt before the rape had happened. He wondered how she was getting on in Kent. He knew that Jackie kept in touch with her, but he daren't ask Ross as he would go into one of his sulks.

Toby stared blankly out of the shopfront window and noticed a young boy looking in awe at the model cars on display, but the lad was soon yanked along by his mother. There goes another potential customer, he thought, his mood sinking even lower.

By four o'clock, Toby had almost given up on having so much as an enquiry in the shop when Ross walked in with his usual sullen face.

'Hello, mate, how was Katy?' Toby asked enthusiastically, glad to at last have some human interaction.

'She was all right, I suppose, pretty much as I expected, but I was glad to get out of there. It's a horrible place. I feel sorry for my sister. If only that bloody Polly Myers hadn't come to live with us. I blame her for all of this. I knew she was no good the moment I set eyes on her.'

'Well, hopefully Katy won't be in there for much longer,' Toby said, trying to placate his friend.

'Yes, hopefully. Mum said to ask you round for tea tonight. She's done a stew that just needs warming up, so it's ready when you are.'

Toby licked his lips and felt his stomach groan. He loved Jackie's stews, and in any case he hadn't eaten a proper meal in days. He had nothing at home other than a couple of slices of stale bread and a bit of mouldy cheese in the fridge. He just about had enough change in his trouser pocket for a bag of chips but the stew sounded much more appealing. 'Sounds good to me. Come on, I might as well shut up shop early. I haven't had a single customer today.'

Just as Jackie dished up the beef stew, the green plastic telephone rang, making everyone jump.

'I'll answer that. Get stuck in, don't wait for me. It's probably Polly ringing as she knows I've been up to see Katy today,' said Jackie as she went to answer the phone.

'Hello, Jacqueline Benton speaking.'

Toby tried not to laugh at Jackie who was doing a very good unintentional impersonation of the Queen.

There was a pause, which Toby assumed was the coins in the pay phone dropping, before Jackie spoke again. As he tucked into his plate of stew, he listened intently.

'Hello, love, I thought it might be you. Yes, she's fine, seems happy in herself. Yes, we're all good, thanks, and what about yourself? Oh, good . . . really . . . yes . . . Toby is here having his tea . . . yes, I'll tell him . . . and what's all this that Katy tells me about you having a boyfriend? What? . . . the pips are going . . . no more change . . . all right, love, speak soon.'

Jackie replaced the receiver and said unnecessarily as she sat at the table again, 'She's gone. That was Polly.'

'We would never have guessed,' Ross said sarcastically.

'She said to say hello to you, Toby, and hopes you're well.'

Toby smiled at Jackie, though inside he was reeling. In May, Polly had rebuffed him, but now, just two months later, she had a boyfriend. After what she had said, he hadn't expected her to get over the attack that quickly. He suddenly lost his appetite and though Jackie and Ross were chattering over their dinner plates, all Toby could hear was a buzz in the background as his thoughts were firmly fixed on Polly. He wondered who the boyfriend was, what he was like, and felt envious and let down. Still, despite this, he also cared enough about Polly to hope that she was happy.

What a horrible day: more bills, no customers and now he had lost Polly to a man he knew nothing about. Could things get any worse? Knowing his luck, probably!

Chapter 30

Polly's heart was hammering. Johnnie was due any minute now. This was the third Friday night in a row he'd travelled to Ivyfield to stay for the weekend, but this time, rather than pay out for an expensive bed and breakfast, she had suggested that he stay with her, though he'd have to sleep on the sofa.

She knew Mrs Stewart next door would be quick to spread the gossip around the village, but as long as her conscience was clear, Polly didn't care. She wouldn't be doing anything untoward that would've embarrassed her parents, so she could hold her head high. Let them talk, she thought defiantly, sticks and stones and all that.

There was a knock on the door and Polly answered it to find a very nervous-looking Johnnie with a black holdall in hand.

'What are you looking so worried about? Come in, you silly sausage, I don't bite!' she said, laughing.

Johnnie hovered in the hallway, still appearing quite uncomfortable.

'I don't know about this, Polly.' He looked distinctly worried.

Polly smiled at him. He was obviously nervous about staying the night.

'It's fine,' she said, 'as long as you're happy with the sofa. I know there's my parents' room, but I haven't touched it yet and it wouldn't feel right to let you or anyone else sleep in it. Maybe one day, but just not yet.'

'The sofa's fine with me,' Johnnie said abruptly. He wasn't quite meeting her gaze.

Polly got the distinct impression that something wasn't sitting quite right with him. She led him into the front room where she had prepared some snacks. She'd also lit some candles, and with music playing softly in the background she hoped it looked suitably romantic.

'This is nice,' said Johnnie, 'but I could really do with a drink. Let's get out of here and go to the pub.'

'Oh, I thought that after a hard day's work and a long train ride here you might appreciate a bit of time to relax. We can go out tomorrow night. I think they're doing some sort of new Saturday-night quiz in the pub, which should be fun,' Polly said.

She noticed Johnnie's eyes flitting around the room then coming to rest on a photograph of her parents that was placed on the sideboard. He stared intently at the picture and blinked hard.

'Are you OK?' she asked, wondering suddenly if it had been such a good idea to invite him into her home when he was behaving strangely.

'Y–yeah, I'm fine. Are they your parents?'

'Yes, it's a lovely photo of them. I really miss them.'

Johnnie looked at Polly then back at the photo, his face pale. His horrified expression began to unnerve Polly even more.

'What's the matter, Johnnie? You look like you've seen a ghost!'

'Nothing,' he snapped, 'nothing at all. Sorry, it's just that you look so much like your mum.'

'I hope that's not a bad thing?' Polly asked as she sauntered towards him.

'No, of course not. Your mother was a beautiful lady, and so are you.'

Polly relaxed again, glad to see the smile back on Johnnie's face.

'I'm happy to stay in tonight and this is perfect,' said Johnnie, but he made no attempt to kiss her, instead flopping down onto the sofa.

Polly leant over him and reached her arms around his neck. 'I'm so glad you're here, Johnnie,' she said, kissing him hungrily.

Johnnie responded immediately. Polly felt a shiver down her spine. Thanks to Johnnie she had lost her fear of intimacy, and she had missed him so much. She didn't want to stop kissing him, and moved herself so that she was kneeling across him. She felt his excitement pushing against her as they fell back along the sofa together and her own excitement mounted as she ground herself against him.

'Polly –' Johnnie pulled away, breathless '– you're driving me crazy. We have to stop or soon I won't be able to.'

She pulled him back to her and kissed him again, her voice husky as she said, 'Don't stop. I want you.'

As Johnnie took her, the last of Polly's fear melted away as she gave herself up to the joy of his lovemaking.

* * *

It was some time later, and their naked bodies lay entwined on the front-room floor, both glowing with satisfaction. Polly leaned across Johnnie to take a puff on his cigarette, and then said, 'That was amazing. I never dreamed that making love could be so wonderful.'

'Do you mind if I ask you something really personal?'

'I don't know. It depends on the question.'

'You're not a virgin. It doesn't bother me, but as you were so nervous of me even kissing you when we first met, I just assumed you would be.'

Polly took a moment to answer and suddenly felt very exposed. She reached around for the throw on the sofa to cover her nakedness then sat up cross-legged on the floor. She hadn't intended to tell Johnnie about the rape, not yet, but as he'd asked, it forced the issue.

'Do you remember that I told you I lived in Croydon for a while, that it hadn't worked out there for me and that's why I came back here?'

'Yes,' Johnnie answered, 'but listen, you don't have to explain anything to me.'

'I know, but I should tell you. You see, what happened isn't over yet.'

'What do you mean by that? Have you got a boyfriend or husband or something?'

'No, nothing like that, but I do have a court case coming up. I'm a key witness to a murder.'

'Murder! Blimey. What happened?'

'My best friend, Katy, was trying to defend me when she saw a man raping me. She took off her shoe and hit him over the head with it, but . . . but she hit him so hard that it killed him.' Polly found herself crying, suddenly overwhelmed at reliving the memory of what had happened. In Johnnie's arms she'd managed to block it from her mind, but now it had resurfaced.

'Polly, oh, sweetheart,' Johnnie said, holding her as tears fell onto his chest. 'I'm so sorry that you had to go through that, but it's a good job your friend killed the bastard, 'cos if she hadn't, I bloody well would have!'

They stayed under the throw on the front-room floor all night, and made love again to the sound of birdsong as the sun rose in the morning. Polly felt a peace that had been missing since the loss of her parents and for the first time she felt truly safe and protected in the arms of the man she was falling in love with.

Later that morning, as Polly cooked breakfast, saucepans clattering, china clanging, Johnnie sat back on the sofa listing to her singing 'Yellow Submarine' at the top of her voice. He smiled. She was so amazing and it blew him away, but every so often the awful thought would come into his head that had been festering in his mind ever since he'd looked at the photo of her parents: she was his half-sister. His stomach turned.

He lit another cigarette as he tried desperately to dismiss the thought, but it kept rearing its ugly head. Not only had Polly lost her parents, she'd been raped, so no wonder she'd been so nervous of him at first. She had been skittish when he'd tried to kiss her, but last night and this morning she had put her trust in him, given herself to him – so how would she react to finding out that she had been duped into having sex with her half-brother? No, he couldn't tell her.

He'd hardly been able to believe it when he had arrived at her house, only to find that it was the same door he had knocked on a few weeks previously when he had been searching for his mother. It was such a coincidence and at first he hadn't put two and two together. He had just assumed that Polly must have moved in after Glenda and Frank had died.

To his horror, it had become abundantly clear when he had seen the photo of his mother on the sideboard. It had taken him a few minutes to work it out but, once he had, all he wanted to do was run from the house in utter revulsion. Yet something stopped him. Polly.

He'd tried so hard to quash his attraction towards her, but somehow, when she had kissed him, the urge to hold her, to feel her body close to his, had overridden his sensibility and now he had to wrestle with his conscience.

He questioned whether his feelings for her were really so wrong. After all, he told himself, it wasn't as if they had grown up together as siblings. When he thought about their kisses, the feel of her body against his, his excitement rose and he shifted uncomfortably on the sofa. There was a word for what they were doing, he thought. Incest. He sighed, trying to dismiss those negative thoughts. What they were doing felt natural and good, so how could something that felt so right be so wrong? And anyway, he thought, who says it's wrong? The law? The Bible? Johnnie decided he didn't know and didn't care. He wasn't going to live by someone else's rules, not if it meant he would have to give up Polly.

'Johnnie, breakfast is ready,' Polly called from the kitchen. 'Come and get it.'

When he walked into the room, Polly looked so happy when she smiled at him that he couldn't stand the thought of causing her any more pain. He looked at the eggs, bacon, beans and fried bread and, though his stomach was churning, he knew he had to eat it. 'That looks great,' he said, taking a seat at the small kitchen table.

'What do you fancy doing today? We could cycle to the lake again if you like.'

'Sounds perfect to me,' he told her, forcing a smile. He thought he was in love with Polly, knew he wanted to be with her, yet deep in his heart Johnnie knew it was wrong and felt sickened at what he was doing.

He didn't want to hurt her and couldn't bear to see a woman cry. He had never once seen his gran shed a tear, so was unprepared for the sobbing when he had told Helen about Glenda being killed. Though he knew Helen would be upset, he hadn't expected her to burst out weeping. It had made him feel uncomfortable and he hadn't known how to react. So how could he tell Polly the dreadful truth now? Oh, God, she'd be disgusted with him and that was the last thing he wanted. Maybe it would be better if he didn't tell her the truth, not just yet anyway.

In London, the sun was beating down on Harry's bare back, turning his olive skin a deep brown, which gave him a Mediterranean look. He hated working on a Saturday but the job was behind schedule and his foreman had practically begged him, promising him a new labourer as the last one was about as much use as a chocolate teapot.

He had to give it to the lad, this one was like a whippet, which pleased Harry, but he cursed under his breath as Liam just wouldn't shut up chatting.

'I'm right chuffed to be working with you, Harry. I've

heard all about you. It's said that you're the fastest brickie in Battersea. That suits me, see, 'cos I'm a quick worker too. I like to get the job done. Yeah, can't be doing with all that hanging about and stopping for a fag,' said Liam, hardly pausing for breath. Sweat was dripping from his brow but he was mixing cement and collecting bricks quicker than Harry could lay them.

Harry grunted; he really couldn't be bothered to engage in conversation.

'I've been working with your son Johnnie. Nice bloke he is. Mind you, his head don't seem to be on the job any more, not since he's been seeing that bird down in Kent.'

Harry's ears pricked. He didn't know that Johnnie had been seeing a girl, but then he hadn't seen him since Maude's funeral.

'From what Johnnie told me, she sounds like a bit of all right. I reckon he's landed on his feet there, 'cos she's got her own house and all! What's her name, I can't think, but it'll come to me. Proper soppy about her he is, and he doesn't stop bloody talking about her. He even knocks off early on Fridays to rush down to see her. You watch, you'll be digging your best bib and tucker out soon, wedding bells will be in the air!' Liam laughed as he marched up and down holding on to pretend braces with his thumbs as he sang, 'I'm getting married in the morning.'

So, the boy has a woman – good on him, thought Harry. It was about time he settled down and started a family of his own. But Kent was a long way to go. He wondered if Johnnie would move down that way or if his new lady friend would come up to London.

'Polly, that's her name!' Liam shouted. 'I knew it

would come to me eventually. Polly Myers – but I bet that soon changes to Polly Jenkins, eh, what do you reckon, Harry?'

Harry clenched his trowel until his knuckles turned white. Myers! Surely it had to be a coincidence! Surely she wasn't related to Frank Myers, a man he still hated and always would. 'How did he meet this Polly?' he said carefully.

'I ain't sure,' Liam replied, 'but one Saturday, a while back, I asked him if he fancied going to the dogs. He said he couldn't 'cos he was going to Kent to meet someone he hadn't seen in years. He was excited about it, but a bit cagey and wouldn't say who it was. The next thing I know he comes back harping on about this Polly.'

'I'm off,' Harry growled as he threw his trowel down, and without further explanation he put on his shirt before almost running from the site.

There was only one person he could think of who could tell him what was going on. Someone he knew his son saw regularly. Helen. She was sure to know something and Harry was determined that, one way or another, he would get it out of her.

Helen was just filling up the budgie's food pot when a heavy banging on her front door made her jump so violently that she dropped the seed over the bottom of the cage.

'All right, all right, where's the fire?' she called as she walked towards the door, but when she opened it her good humour was soon extinguished when she saw Harry Jenkins standing there.

'I need a word,' he said, and without invitation he pushed past her before she could close the door in his face.

Helen felt sick. Since she had told Johnnie about his mother's whereabouts, she had been dreading this. Johnnie had promised he wouldn't say anything, but somehow Harry must have found out. Well, he was in her home now, so she reluctantly led him to the kitchen and stammered, 'W—would you like a cup of tea, Harry?'

'No, thanks.'

Helen decided that with the cat out of the bag, the only way to handle this was with a direct approach. 'I–I think I know why you're here, Harry.'

'Oh, yeah? So what is it you think you know then?'

'You're here because I told Johnnie where he could find his mother.'

'You what?' Harry looked confused.

'You mean you're not here about that?' Helen gasped, kicking herself as she realised that Harry didn't appear to know anything about it and she had just dropped herself right in it.

'You're telling me you told Johnnie where to find Glenda?'

Helen decided that she wasn't going to cower before this man. She'd had enough of being afraid of him, and anyway, what did it matter now? 'Yes, I did. The boy had a right to know about his mother, especially after your mum died. I kept your secret for years because I was scared of you, but it was wrong, Harry. It wasn't fair on Johnnie, or Glenda, but now it's too late and my only regret is that I didn't tell him sooner.'

312

'What the fuck are you going on about, woman? I don't give a toss about all that secrets bollocks. It's all in the past and I just wanna know about now. So, Johnnie's been seeing his mum, has he? Good luck to him.'

'What? No, he hasn't been seeing Glenda, Harry – she's dead! Before I told him, Glenda and Frank died in a gas explosion so he never got to see her. I couldn't believe it when Johnnie told me . . . it broke my heart.'

Helen was surprised by Harry's reaction. He had turned ashen and looked a bit wobbly. After all the pain he had caused she would never like the man, but she had enough compassion to offer him a chair.

'Here, sit down,' she spoke softly as she pulled one out from the table. 'I'm sorry, Harry, it must have been a shock to hear it like that. Glenda and Frank died just before Christmas last year. I had no idea until Johnnie told me, the poor love. He was so excited about going to see his mum only to get there and find that it was too late. Are you all right? Do you want that cuppa now?'

Harry slowly shook his head. 'Dead . . . I can't believe it. All these years . . . I never stopped loving her, you know.'

Helen said nothing, and whether Harry wanted one or not she busied herself with making a pot of tea, whilst thinking that if he had loved Glenda surely he would never have hurt her the way he had.

Harry regained his composure. 'So who is Polly Myers? She's the one I've come to ask you about.'

'Polly – she's Glenda and Frank's daughter. Johnnie's half-sister.'

Harry lifted his head and the look that Helen saw in

his eyes made her blood run cold. Did he want to take out his revenge on Frank's daughter?

'What? That can't be right. Johnnie's mate has just told me that Johnnie's got a new girlfriend – Polly Myers!'

'No, Harry, he must have got it wrong. Are you sure that's what he said?'

'As sure as I am that a rag doll has got cloth tits! He said Johnnie has been going down there every weekend and waxing lyrical about his new bird.'

'Maybe . . . maybe he's just been saying that. You know what young lads are like, and maybe he's been bigging himself up to his mates while he's really just been getting to know his sister.'

'Yeah, his sister, so I hope you're fucking right! He's down there now so you'd better tell me where I can find him.'

Helen was reluctant to give him the address. 'I'm not sure that's a good idea, Harry. What are you going to do, go down there banging on the door and causing a scene over some silly rumour you've heard?'

'Helen, it might not be a silly rumour, so just tell me where he is. I ain't gonna cause a scene. I just wanna make sure they ain't doing things that they shouldn't.'

'But that would be . . . be . . .'

'Incest!' Harry finished for her. 'It ain't unheard of.'

'But Johnnie would never do anything like that. I'm sure it's all perfectly innocent.'

'Perhaps, but if it isn't I need to put a stop to it and quickly. Now come on, give me this Polly's address.'

Helen reluctantly gave it to him. If any of it was true, she just hoped that Harry would handle the situation with diplomacy and sensitivity. They were two young and vulnerable people who had suffered losses, and though it was wrong they might have been drawn to each other for comfort. The last thing they needed was Harry Jenkins and his great size-ten boots stepping on their feelings.

Chapter 31

Harry didn't arrive in Ivyfield until early evening, but he soon found Polly's house. He didn't notice the pretty garden with its colourful array of marigolds and roses, or the white net curtains hanging at the window. There was only one thing on his mind.

Before knocking on the door he took a deep breath and collected himself. He hoped against all odds that his suspicions were unfounded. Although he had been thinking it over on the train, he still was at a loss as to what he was going to say.

A pretty young woman answered the door and at once Harry was taken aback at how much she resembled her mother. Memories of Glenda flooded his mind, but somehow he managed to push them aside, his voice almost cracking as he said, 'You must be Polly. I'm Harry Jenkins, Johnnie's dad.'

Polly welcomed him with a huge smile. 'Oh, goodness, Johnnie didn't say you were coming today. Sorry, where are my manners? Do come in.'

'Thanks,' Harry replied, following her into a living room.

'Johnnie, look who's here.'

Johnnie jumped up from the sofa when he saw his father walk in, and the colour drained from his face. 'Dad, what are you doing here?'

'It wasn't easy to find you, but Helen finally gave me this address. I think we need to talk, son,' Harry said, trying to keep his tone light.

Polly looked a little puzzled, but asked, 'Can I get you anything, Mr Jenkins? Tea? Coffee?'

'Tea, please, love.'

As soon as the girl left the room, Johnnie asked again, 'What are you doing here, Dad?'

'I told you, we need to talk,' Harry told him, unable to bring himself to ask the question that sounded so despicable in his head.

'Is this about my mum? Because if it is, there's a few things I want to talk to you about too. How could you have lied to me my whole life? You told me she was dead!'

'This has nothing to do with your mother, God rest her soul. This is about you and her – your *sister*.'

Johnnie looked down at the floor and Harry could tell from the look on his face that what he'd dreaded had already happened. He felt sick to his stomach. He'd told himself not to lose his temper, to stay calm, but the thought of what his son was doing made his blood boil. 'How could you, you fucking little pervert! She's your flesh and blood. My God, and she's just as bad.'

'No, Dad, it's not like that. I love her, I can't help it, and Polly doesn't know. I haven't told her we're related. Dad, please, don't say anything, you can't.'

'What you're doing is disgusting. It's unnatural, and if you don't bloody well tell her, I will!'

'All right, but not while you're here. I'll tell her when you leave. Please, Dad,' Johnnie begged.

Polly came back into the room carrying a tray with a china teapot, cups and saucers, but she stopped dead in her tracks when she saw the expression on Johnnie's face. 'What's going on?'

'Er . . . Dad just had a bit of bad news for me, that's all. Ain't that right, Dad?'

Harry nodded absently, still floundering. It was one thing to think that Johnnie and Polly might be committing incest, but to actually know for sure had shaken Harry badly.

'Oh, I'm sorry, Johnnie. What's happened?'

'Er . . . an old aunt has passed away.'

'Oh, dear, were you close?' Polly asked as she poured cups of tea.

'No, not really.'

Harry took the cup of tea Polly handed him, but as she gave one to Johnnie, she quickly kissed him. He felt his stomach turn and then, when she sat down next to Johnnie on the sofa, she rested her hand on his thigh. It looked so intimate and, feeling bile rise in his throat, Harry surged to his feet. 'No! I can't be doing with this, it ain't right!' he bellowed.

'Dad, no . . . don't say anything!'

'It's revolting, that's what it is, absolutely fucking vile, and I can't allow it! Either you tell her, right now, or I will!' he yelled. He could see that his outburst had frightened Polly, and memories flooded back of the times he had seen Glenda looking at him like that.

Polly must have been made of stronger stuff, though, because she seemed to quickly recover. 'Tell me what?

What's going on?' she asked, looking at Johnnie, who refused to meet her gaze.

Johnnie only hung his head, shaking it, so Harry said, 'I'm sorry, Polly, but there's something you need to know. You see –'

Johnnie interrupted, 'Dad, no – wait – you can't do this.'

'I have to. Apart from anything else, what you're doing is illegal. It's wrong, and you know it is. It's got to stop. Now let me get this over with and finish what I was saying.'

'Dad!'

'Shut up, Johnnie. Now then, Polly, the thing is, I was married to your mother, Glenda.'

Polly screwed her face up quizzically. 'I don't understand,' she said.

Harry knew he wasn't very good at explaining things, but he did his best. 'Me and your mum, we had Johnnie, but she left me when he was a baby. She took off with your father and left Johnnie behind.'

'But . . . but . . . I don't understand.'

Harry could see from the blank expression on Polly's face that the penny still hadn't dropped and knew he would have to spell it out for her. He felt awful telling her like this. It should have come from Johnnie, but not only was his son a pervert, he was spineless too. 'Look, love, the thing is, Johnnie is your half-brother.'

For a moment there was no reaction from the girl, just a stunned silence, but as comprehension dawned she suddenly leaped from the sofa. 'Get out! Get out, the pair of you! Go on, get out, get out, get out!' she screamed, waving her arms, almost pushing Johnnie and Harry out of the lounge and down the hallway.

'Polly, let me explain,' Johnnie begged, but his voice was hardly heard over her shrieks.

'I don't want to hear another word from you – ever! Just go, get out!'

Harry pulled Johnnie outside, but he stood on the doorstep, still trying to plead with Polly until the door slammed in his face. Johnnie banged repeatedly on it and called out Polly's name.

'Come on, Johnnie. Leave the girl in peace. You've done enough damage,' Harry bluntly told his son.

Only then did Johnnie turn to walk away.

Johnnie hardly listened to his father's recrimination on the train journey back to London. He hated him for spoiling it all for him and Polly. What they'd had was so special, but his dad had made it seem dirty.

He knew Polly would never see him again, yet there had been such an attraction between them from the beginning that had he told her the truth, he felt that it might have happened just the same. He had been unable to resist her, and he was sure she had felt the same about him.

His dad said it was unnatural, but it hadn't felt unnatural to him. He mused on it all the way to London, his thoughts spiralling, and as the train neared the city, Johnnie came to realise that his dad was probably right. That didn't stop it hurting, though, and the thought of never seeing Polly again cut him to the core.

God, he'd been such an idiot. Such a fool. Not only had he lost the best thing that had ever happened to him, he had also blown any chance of having a sister in his life.

When Johnnie thought of Polly as his sister, he felt like filth and realised what a mess he had made of everything. A horrible, sordid mess.

Chapter 32

Katy's court case came up at last. It was mid-August and she had been on remand for four months, but now she would find out what her future would be. Either she would soon be a free woman or she'd be facing many years locked up in prison. She had such conflicting emotions: part of her was excited and hopeful about the prospect of going home, but another, larger part was dreading the trial and the thought of imprisonment. At least the charge had been reduced from murder to voluntary manslaughter. She desperately hoped her defence of provocation would be believed and the judge and jury would be sympathetic and return a verdict of not guilty. They would be the best words she would ever hear.

Katy was relieved when the officer removed her handcuffs. They were so uncomfortable and hurt her wrists, but it meant it was nearly time to leave the holding cell to be taken up to the court. Her heart was thumping in her chest as she was led up the small staircase to the courtroom. She could see that the viewing gallery above had already filled with lawyers, jurors and press.

The room was ornately decorated with lots of gilt and highly varnished dark wood. She was placed at a table with an officer overseeing her, and two assistants from her lawyer's office. She was very impressed with her barrister, who was wearing one of those funny white wigs and a dark gown. His opponent, though dressed the same, looked somehow more intimidating and Katy suddenly realised that spending her future locked up was a very real possibility.

She looked behind her and saw a few familiar faces in the upper seating area. Her mum was there, waving profusely, alongside Ross, who looked as unhappy as ever, and Toby was there too. It gave her a warm feeling inside to see she had support in the room and she hoped that it wouldn't be long before she could give her mum the biggest cuddle ever.

'All rise,' the court usher announced as a very stern-looking judge entered the court. Katy stood up but felt quite faint and rested her fingers on the table to steady herself. Fear gripped her and she did her best to fight back tears.

The formalities were read aloud and then one person after another took it in turns to take the stand and swear the oath of promising to tell the truth. Soon she was feeling bruised and dazed as the prosecution attempted to slur her reputation, suggesting that she was a 'good-time girl' who drank profusely and was reckless, even intimating that she was a loose woman of questionable morals and standards. It didn't bode well either when the landlord of the pub commented on how drunk she had been on the night in question and said she'd been seen openly flirting with several men.

Katy felt sick inside, but then some very reliable character witnesses were called, including her boss, who fought hard to convince the jury that she was an honest, hard-working young woman who on occasion would innocently enjoy herself but had never shown any signs of violence. Also in her favour, the arresting officer openly apologised to her and spoke about the Purvis brothers with nothing but contempt.

The court adjourned for lunch and Katy was taken back down to the holding cell, where she sat, still dazed, but knowing that the key part of the trial was to come. She would be called to give evidence and of course Polly would take the stand.

Kate offered up a silent prayer to a God she wasn't sure existed, but if He did she needed all the help she could get. Please Lord, she prayed inwardly, please, I've never asked you for anything before, but if you're there, and if you can hear me, I just want to go home. You know I never meant to kill him, so please let them find me innocent.

The thought of returning to the prison and being on B Wing with the most violent women in society absolutely petrified Katy and she wasn't sure if she could survive in that sort of environment. Once again she turned her thoughts to God. If she was found guilty and sent back to prison, she decided there and then that she would be meeting her Maker a long time before she was due to.

There was absolute silence as Polly entered the courtroom and took the stand. The first thing Toby noticed was that her bleached blonde hair had been toned down and was now light brown, and she wasn't wearing heavy make-up around her eyes – eyes that now looked like a rabbit's caught in headlights. Polly was very different from the last time he'd seen her. She looked so fresh and pretty, and he wished he could take her away from all this. He knew that the horror of reliving what had happened would be very difficult for her, especially so publicly in a crowded courtroom.

Toby's heart went out to her as the judge ordered her to speak up when she placed her hand on the Bible, swearing to tell the truth. She was like a nervous little mouse whom he could just about hear.

The defence were brilliant and Toby almost clapped and cheered when they had finished questioning Polly, but he was dreading the next part, knowing that the prosecution would rip her apart. But Toby realised that he needn't have worried. Polly was doing so well. She held herself together and told the court clearly and articulately exactly what had happened without faltering, even when the prosecution attempted to trip her up with their clever questions. She remained calm, even though Toby felt she was being bullied – the way the prosecution behaved, you would think Polly was on trial, instead of a lovely young woman who had been brutally raped. Toby studied the jurors' faces and was sure he could see that most of them looked sympathetic to her.

Polly looked relieved when after nearly an hour of gruelling questioning she was finally able to leave the stand. Toby excused himself past the other onlookers and went through to the corridors to look for her. He found her sitting on a bench wiping her eyes.

'Hello, Polly,' he said.

'Oh, hello, Toby. I'm sorry you found me bawling my eyes out, but I found that tougher than I thought it was going to be. I just hope I said all the right things to help Katy.'

'You did brilliantly. I don't think I would have been quite so calm and collected if it had been me up there. I think it's going well and I can't believe they'll send Katy down.'

'But what if they do?'

'They won't. No jury could possibly find Katy guilty, not after all they've heard, and remember Katy is to take the stand soon too.'

'I'm not allowed to be in there, so will you go back and let me know how it's all going, please?'

'There's no need. Jackie will keep us updated and in the meantime, after that experience, I think you need a strong coffee. Come on, let's get some fresh air. There's a café close by.'

Toby was keen to know if Polly was still dating but didn't quite have the courage to ask. If she was still seeing someone then he'd have to accept that, but if she wasn't he didn't intend to let her go so easily this time.

Jackie spotted Polly and Toby walking along the marbled corridor and ran towards them as fast as her large frame would allow.

'She's been acquitted! She's free! She's coming home!'

Polly and Toby stopped dead in their tracks and looked open-mouthed at Jackie, who was crying tears of relief.

'Did you hear what I said? Katy is free!' Jackie squealed again.

'Yes, we heard you – and it's wonderful.'

'When Katy took the stand, the prosecution were hard on her, but her barrister was brilliant in her defence. He was so insistent that Katy was only trying to defend you, Polly, and that it was an accidental death. The jury went to deliberate and they were back in under half an hour. They found her not guilty and the judge said she's free to go. She's just talking to her solicitor and signing a few papers and then she'll be here.'

Polly threw her arms around Jackie. 'Thank God it's over, Jackie. I can't believe it – Katy's free.'

It was a deeply emotional moment for both women and tears of joy were flowing freely. Toby gave Ross a quick hug before enthusiastically shaking his hand. 'Nice one, your sister's coming home and about time too.'

Security guards gathered at the entrance of the courthouse and the press were there too, but Jackie ignored their shouts. She wouldn't talk to them. All she wanted was to hold her daughter in her arms and take her home to where she belonged.

'Here she is,' Toby announced as Katy walked towards them with a huge smile on her face.

'Come here, darling,' said Jackie as she reached for Katy, 'let's get you home and put this whole affair behind us. Well done, love, I knew you could do it.'

'Yes, home,' Katy said. 'That sounds good to me. I hope you're coming too, Polly?'

'Yes. I didn't think the trial would be over this quickly so I arranged with your mum to stay over.'

'Come on, let's get out of here before those reporters start hounding us,' Jackie said, and together they all made a dash for it.

Polly was glad to be back with her best friend and she loved being amidst the family atmosphere even though

Ross was being his usual sulky self. It helped her to push thoughts of Johnnie to one side, but she knew as soon as she went to bed and closed her eyes, what had happened would all come flooding back.

Katy was pleased to be home, but a little subdued. After what she'd been through it wasn't surprising, but Jackie seemed determined to cheer her daughter up. Despite the hot weather, she cooked them a meal and brought out a bottle of Blue Nun wine, saying as they sat down to eat, 'We're having a drink to celebrate.'

Polly found she liked the taste of the white wine, and when the bottle was emptied she was surprised when Jackie got out another one.

'It's been in the sideboard for ages,' Jackie explained, 'and I'd all but forgotten about it.'

'Mum, mind it doesn't go to your head,' Katy warned.

'It's nice to see that you've perked up, love, and don't worry. I know I'm not one for drinking so I'll only have the one glass.'

Polly was enjoying the meal and the wine. After several glasses, she could feel it going to her head, and was beginning to feel a bit dizzy when Katy said, 'I'm glad you're staying, Polly, but won't your boyfriend miss you?'

'We . . . we broke up. It didn't work out,' she blurted and then to avoid any more questions she stood up. 'I feel a bit woozy so I'm just going outside for a bit of air.'

'I'll come with you,' Katy offered.

'No, no, you stay there. I won't be long,' she insisted, but no sooner had she gone outside than Toby was standing next to her.

'I thought I'd join you. I could do with a bit of air

too. I'm sorry to hear that you broke up with your boyfriend. What went wrong?'

'I–I don't want to talk about it.'

'I hope he didn't hurt you, Polly.'

Yes, she thought. Johnnie had hurt her. It disgusted her that she had slept with her own brother, sickened her, and when left alone to brood the need to confide in someone was strong. Maybe the wine had loosened her tongue too because she found herself blurting it all out.

'I don't know what to say, Polly,' said Toby, looking shocked.

'I know, it's revolting and I can't believe that he did that to me. I'll never forgive him. Never!'

'He doesn't deserve forgiveness.'

'I'm still shocked that my mum had a whole other life that I knew nothing about. I might have other relatives, people I know nothing about, even grandparents. When I go home I'm going to see if I can find anything, papers or photographs. If there were any she might have hidden them, probably in the loft, but I'm not looking forward to going up there.'

'If you like, I'll help you. I could come down one weekend and we could do it together,' Toby offered.

Polly wasn't sure if it was the wine going to her head or the thought of Toby visiting her for the weekend, but she felt strangely lost in his dark eyes. 'Yes . . . yes, all right.'

'Next weekend then, it's a date,' he said, but then frowned. 'On reflection, there might be a bit of a problem with that.'

'Don't worry then, Toby. I don't want to put you out,' she said, slightly disappointed.

'No, it's not putting me out or anything. To be honest, I've had a few problems of my own lately and things are a bit hard. Truth is, I've had to shut the business, close the shop down, and as of next week I'll be officially homeless.'

'Oh, Toby, I'm really sorry to hear that. What happened? I thought with your own business you were doing well.'

'The bloody Purvises – they were blackmailing me for money, more money than I could afford to pay, so I ended up taking out a loan, then another, then I got behind with the payments and my rent. It's a slippery slope, Polly, and once the debts start, they just spiral out of control. Now I've lost everything, only please don't say anything to Jackie or anyone else, especially tonight.'

'But what will you do? Where will you live?'

'I'm not sure. The only thing I can think of is to move in with my mother and her sister. They live in the north of the country and haven't much room, so it isn't ideal. Still, a sofa is better than nothing.'

'I'm sure Jackie would take you in.'

'Yes, I'm sure she would, but until I find my feet I can't give her any money and I refuse to impose on her.'

Polly reacted quickly without thinking it through. 'You could come and stay with me. I've got plenty of room and, to be honest, I could do with the company. I'm sure you'll be able to find work locally, but until you do you can pay your way by doing some things around the house, maintenance, things that need repairing but are beyond me.'

Toby's eyes lit up and he immediately accepted her offer, but Polly was already regretting her impulsiveness. She had already had one man staying in her house – one who had broken her heart. She couldn't take her offer back, but she could lay some ground rules. 'Toby, there's one thing, though – something we need to be clear on from the start. We're just friends, and I don't want more than that.'

Toby looked down at her intently, but then said, 'Friends it is, Polly. That's fine with me.'

Chapter 33

Drip . . . drip . . . drip . . . the water slowly leaking from the tap over the sink was driving Johnnie mad. All he wanted to do was close his eyes, block out his thoughts and the world and go to sleep. At night he had been plagued by nightmares of being chased by a putrid-smelling monster dripping with green slime, but no matter how fast he ran, the monster always caught him and ripped his flesh before gradually crushing his bones. And during the day, in his waking hours, he was tormented by memories of Polly and the sadistic way he had hurt her. Johnnie knew the monster represented his conscience that he couldn't run away from, but he just needed a few hours' respite from dealing with the shame of what he had done.

The state of the bedsit he was renting was reflected in the price he was paying for it. The walls were damp, wallpaper hung off where mould was growing and the carpet was stained and threadbare. The bed was comfortable enough, though Johnnie was sure he was being eaten alive by bedbugs. But as he hadn't returned to work, this was all he could afford.

He threw off the thin cover and went to the sink to wash his face. He caught sight of his reflection in the small mirror. A scraggy beard had grown over his once clean-shaven face and his unkempt hair was greasy, obviously in need of a good wash. He wondered what had become of him, the good-looking, confident young man who now looked like a tramp and smelled like one too. He hated what he saw and punched the mirror, which shattered into smithereens and left him with a cut knuckle. It was a relief to finally let out some of his anger and he hit out at the wall where the mirror had been, again and again, until he couldn't take any more pain. As his blood dripped into the washbasin, Johnnie felt a sense of satisfaction. His hand smarted. Good, he thought, he deserved to be hurt.

After running his hand under the tap and splashing cold water over his face, Johnnie sat on the edge of his bed and rolled himself a cigarette from the dog-ends that were left in the overflowing ashtray. This had to stop, he had to pull himself together and get back out there. After all, apart from himself, what was he hiding from? His dad was the only one who knew what he'd done, and he was pretty sure he wouldn't tell anyone.

Johnnie cursed himself for what he had done, and now cursed the day he had met Polly too. He'd been doing all right until Helen had told him about his mother and his search for her had sent him to Kent. He had worked hard, but played hard too, enjoying himself, before Polly had come into his life. Now it was all falling apart.

Come on, Johnnie told himself, there's no going back. It was over now and he had to try to be his old self. Yet he knew he would never be the same again. Happiness would evade him and be replaced with fury. His mind was unravelling and becoming twisted. But he would hide his contorted thoughts of self-loathing and he would never let feelings for a woman touch him again. He'd never let another woman come into his heart and destroy it the way Polly had.

Harry checked his watch. It wouldn't be long until knocking-off time and today he was really looking forward to going home to some peace and quiet. Liam had been going on all day about the mystery of Johnnie's whereabouts. It seems he hadn't shown up for work and there was no sign of him at Maude's house. He hadn't been seen in the pub, so now everyone was assuming that he had shacked up with his bird in Kent.

'Give it a rest, will you!' Harry barked at Liam. 'What's the matter with ya, are you in love with Johnnie or something? You ain't stopped talking about him all day and you're giving my arse a headache!'

'Sorry, mate, but I thought you could shed some light on where he is, that's all,' Liam replied.

'I told you, more than once, that I don't know where he is and I don't give a shit. He could be in Timbuktu for all I care so just shut it.'

The one thing Harry did know was that Johnnie wasn't in Kent with his 'bird', but it was no surprise to him that his son had disappeared off the face of the earth. As far as Harry was concerned his son was a sick pervert, a coward who should be hiding his face away. He didn't care if Johnnie never showed up again. He didn't have a son now, not one he could be proud of. Johnnie was dead to him.

Harry cleaned his tools as his thoughts continued to turn. It had been difficult telling Helen what he had discovered going on in Kent, and he was glad his mother hadn't been alive to find out that her precious grandson was a nasty, manipulative sex abuser. Yes, that's what Harry considered his son to be, a sex case who deserved to be locked up with all the other perverts.

Yet for all that Johnnie was and wasn't, Harry would never grass him up to the Old Bill, he thought. He'd keep quiet, but if the truth ever did get out, he'd let justice take its course rather than defend his son.

Helen was thinking that it had been a month or so since Harry had called in to tell her the unbelievable news about Johnnie and Polly. She was on her way home from her little cleaning job when she passed the bookmakers, only to nearly bump into Johnnie as he was walking out.

She panicked, not wanting to talk to him, but he mistook her expression and said, 'Wotcha, Aunt Helen. Yeah, I know, it's a mug's game but someone's got to win and I think my luck is about due for a change.'

Helen saw that he was done up to the nines and wondered how he could act so blasé after what he'd done. 'I ain't saying a word, it's up to you what you do,' she offered curtly and started to go on her way.

'Hey, hold up, what's your problem? Oh, let me guess – my dad told you about me and Polly. Well, think what you want, but we were in love and it didn't seem wrong. Still, it's over now so you can get that look off your face. As my gran would have said, what's done is done and it's no good crying over spilt milk.'

Helen couldn't believe that this was the Johnnie she knew talking. Anger rose within her and she couldn't help but speak out.

'Don't give me that. Maude raised you to know right from wrong, and don't tell me you didn't know that what you were doing was wrong. I'm not only ashamed of you, I'm disappointed and disgusted with you too. From now on, I want nothing more to do with you.'

Johnnie didn't try to defend himself. He just looked at her for a moment and then turned to march off. Helen felt like crying. Johnnie had been the closest thing she had to a son, and it broke her heart to see him seemingly so uncaring of what he had done.

Johnnie tried not to let what Helen said get to him. He didn't need lecturing. He'd beaten himself up enough over Polly and he was sick of it. He was doing his best to put it in the past, and to make sure that it was onwards and upwards from now on, or at least that was what he would make the world believe. He was due to start work tomorrow on a new site in Clapham. Mary Seacole House was a big project, a large new office block on the high street, and he was the lead bricklayer. It would mean a few bob extra in his pay packet each week which he intended to spend frivolously. So today he planned on taking it easy and having a few pints. Like a peacock, he was intent on showing off his flash plumage.

He knew that Liam would be in their local at lunchtime and was looking forward to catching up with his mate. Liam had been working with his dad so meeting up with him would be a bit risky, but though Harry had told Helen, Johnnie felt that he wouldn't tell anyone else.

'Hello, mate!' Liam said as he walked into the pub and spotted Johnnie at the bar. 'Long time no see. Where have you been? I was asking your dad about you but he was none the wiser than the rest of us.'

Johnnie was relieved to hear that. It confirmed that his dad hadn't said anything about the affair with Polly. 'You know how it is, Liam, top secret and all that. I couldn't possibly divulge my whereabouts . . . if I told you, I'd have to kill you.'

'Stop playing silly buggers,' Liam said, laughing. 'Come on, tell us where you've been. Having a good time with that bird down in Kent, eh?'

'I was there for a bit, but it got right bloody boring out in the sticks so I went up to the West End and met a bit of posh totty who was keeping me in the lifestyle I could quite easily become accustomed to, but then her old man came back from his business trip so I had to scarper.'

'A posh tart – nice one, mate. Did she give out?'

'Like you wouldn't believe! She was a bit older than me and I'll tell you what, older birds know what they're doing!' Johnnie was enjoying his lies and the impressed expression on his friend's face.

'Did she have a nice pad and a car?'

'Mate, she had the penthouse suite in an exclusive gaff in Mayfair. I ain't never seen anything like it! Lap of bleedin' luxury it was. And her car, she only had one of them brand-new Triumphs.'

'Not the TR5? Convertible?' Liam asked as his eyes nearly popped out of his head.

'That's the one. She drove me all round London and took me to top-class restaurants where she paid for everything; cocktails, champagne, steaks, the lot! And check out my new clobber – straight out of the best shop on the King's Road, this is.' Johnnie's electric-blue mohair suit had cost him more than he earned in a week, but he had afforded it by pawning Maude's brooch that had belonged to her grandmother.

'Blimey, mate, sounds like you landed on your feet. I could do with a bit of that. Has she got any friends?'

'Ha, you're having a laugh, those uptown ladies wouldn't give you a second look. That's more your type,' said Johnnie, indicating two young women sitting at a table in the corner. Both had blonde, bouffant hair and were showing off their long legs, one wearing polka-dot shorts and the other a red miniskirt.

'Don't knock them, mate, they ain't bad,' Liam said. 'I'd take the one in the shorts and you could have her mate.'

'Go on then,' encouraged Johnnie, 'give it a go. Ask them if they want a drink.'

'Don't be daft. I'm in my working gear and they don't look that interested in us.'

'Do you want a bet? I lay five bob on me pulling them, how about it?'

'You're on, my five bob says they give you a blank.'

Johnnie supped the last of his drink. 'Watch and learn,' he winked before mooching over to them.

A few minutes later and Johnnie was sitting at their table, calling Liam to join them.

'Liam, this is Rose and Linda. They work at the South London Hospital, but they've got the day off so I said I'd take them boating in the park. It's a shame you've gotta go back to work.'

'Hello, Rose, Linda, nice to meet you. Johnnie's right, I can't come to the park, but I could knock off early and meet you later.'

'That would be nice,' said Rose, the one wearing the polka-dot shorts.

'Right then,' Johnnie said, 'let's have one more drink here and then we're off.'

Liam went with him to the bar and asked, 'Where shall we meet up?'

'I dunno. You think of somewhere.'

'When I knock off I'll need to shoot home to wash and change. How about the café in the park?'

'Yeah, all right, but don't take too long or I might keep both of them to myself,' Johnnie said, grinning.

'You wouldn't do that to a mate, would you?'

'I might if you don't cough up the five bob you owe me,' Johnnie said, and as he collected his winnings he was thinking that picking up the girls had been easy. All it had taken was smart clobber and a bit of chatting up and they had been like putty in his hands. All right, they weren't tarts and he doubted it'd be so easy to get one of them into bed, but it would still help him to forget about Polly.

A summer shower had Johnnie, Rose and Linda running for shelter in the café. Liam was expected in less than an hour but Johnnie was reluctant to spend any more money on the two women.

They seemed to be quite worldly wise, and Johnnie thought he was in with Linda but he got the impression that Rose was flirting with him too. The thought crossed his mind that maybe he was in with a chance of fulfilling a fantasy.

'Ladies, how about we go back to my place and we can have a drink to celebrate this special occasion?'

'What special occasion?' Linda asked.

'Meeting you two lovelies, of course,' Johnnie answered, convinced that after so easily chatting them up he could charm the birds from the trees. He winked at them both and added, 'I think we need to get out of these wet clothes too.'

'I don't know, what do you think, Rose?' Linda asked. 'Shouldn't we wait for Liam?'

'Nah,' said Johnnie, 'I reckon we could have much more fun if it's just the three of us.'

'Cheeky,' Linda giggled, 'but you could be right. You up for it, Rose?'

'I might be,' Rose purred, 'but I want a few glasses of something nice to drink first.'

'Let's go, and I'll buy us a bottle of something en route,' said Johnnie and he linked arms with the women and led them towards the one-bedroom flat he was renting near Battersea Park train station.

'What happened to you?' Liam asked Johnnie when he saw him in the pub a couple of days later.

'Yeah, sorry about that, mate. It started raining and the girls got a bit wet so I took them back to mine to dry off,' said Johnnie, giving Liam one of 'those' winks.

'Well, thanks for nothing! I bloody well knocked off early and your dad was none too pleased, especially when I told him I had a double date with you and them two lovelies.'

'Like I said, mate, sorry. I would have waited, but the girls wanted to get out of their soaked outfits.'

'Hang on, are you telling me they both took their clothes off?'

'Yep, every bloody stitch! Naked as the day they were born, the pair of them. And I'll tell you what, that Linda didn't half have a lovely pair of tits on her.'

'You didn't do what I think you did?' Liam asked enviously.

'It had to be done, mate, they were practically begging for it. But it's hard work pleasing two women at the same time. I think I'll stick to one at a time from now on,' Johnnie replied.

'You lucky bugger,' said Liam, 'I don't know how you manage it.'

'Stick with me, mate, and you'll have birds hanging off of ya,' said Johnnie. He hadn't given a thought to Polly; he'd enjoyed himself too much and there was no stopping him now. He'd fulfilled his fantasy of two women at the same time but next he was planning something a bit more risqué, maybe that bondage that he'd read about in a dirty magazine. Anything to stop him from thinking about what he'd lost.

Chapter 34

Ross was at work, attending a monthly departmental meeting, but found it difficult to concentrate on what his boss was saying. He hated presentations and meetings at the best of times and after having spent a boring weekend cooped up in his bedroom, giving him plenty of time to think and stew, this was all he needed right now.

When Toby had left Croydon, it had hit him hard. They had grown up together and done almost everything as if they were joined at the hip, but now his best friend had moved away. To make matters worse, Toby had moved in with Polly!

Ross scowled. It wasn't as if Toby had no other choice. After all, Ross had offered him a spare room – Polly's old room, in fact – but Toby had refused. Instead he'd gone to live at Polly's rent free in exchange for some handiwork.

Yeah, I bet, thought Ross, handiwork my eye! Toby had always fancied Polly and it was obvious that he'd rather live with her. It hurt that Toby had chosen Polly over him and Ross felt betrayed. The way he saw it, Toby was prepared to throw away a lifelong friendship in exchange for a girl he had only known for two minutes.

He'll be sorry, thought Ross. Polly was bad news and he was sure that Toby would find out soon enough and come crawling back with his tail between his legs. Ross just hoped it would be sooner rather than later as he missed his friend and wanted him back. He wanted everything to return to normal, to how things were before that bloody girl came into their lives and turned everything upside down.

'Good evening,' one of the locals greeted Toby as he walked through the village on his way home from work. When he had first moved in with Polly, most of the locals had stared at him or had given him a wide berth and he realised they had probably never seen a black man before. They appeared either fascinated by him or scared of him.

Polly's neighbour remained a bit off with her, obviously judging her because she'd first had a man to stay at weekends and now had another staying permanently. However, it was now late into October and he'd become a familiar figure in Ivyfield, securing a job in the village post office. The locals had become friendlier, and a few of them that hadn't travelled loved to hear tales of what life was like in the Big Smoke.

'Hello,' Toby called as he opened the front door, 'I'm home.'

'I'm up here, in the loft again,' Toby heard Polly shout.

Toby dashed up the stairs to join her. 'You should have waited for me.'

'I just wanted to have another look, but if you want to help, go and put some old clothes on. It's really dusty here at the back, but I found a big metal tin tucked away and it's full of stuff.'

Toby quickly threw on some old jeans and a T-shirt before climbing the ladder into the roof space. He stooped and made his way across the loft to find Polly looking very serious as she sat cross-legged in front of an old trunk.

'You won't believe what's in here,' she said. 'I'm beginning to wonder if I ever really knew my mum and dad. The whole secret life I knew nothing about is all in here, look . . .' Polly pointed to a pile of letters and photographs. 'This stack is mail from a lady called Helen, who from what I've read lived in Battersea next door to my grandparents. Some of the stuff she's written about is very interesting. My grandparents were alive when I was born, but of course I never got to meet them. It seems they were too poorly to come here and my mother was too scared to take me to see them because Harry, her husband, whom she had to run away from, would probably have killed her. They died years ago. That must have been hard for my mum, especially as she couldn't attend their funerals.'

'He sounds like a nasty piece of work,' Toby said.

'Yes, he does, and when he came here I had no idea that he used to beat my mother. If I had found this stuff earlier I would never have invited him into my house!'

'Maybe it's just as well you did, otherwise you might never have known the truth about Johnnie.'

'But I would have. Helen writes about him in all of her letters, and look, it's all here, photos of Johnnie as a boy and even a copy of his birth certificate. I don't know how my mum got hold of it, but perhaps Helen sent her a copy. There's so much information here, and a mention of my dad's mother, who passed away two years ago, and of him having a brother called Bill. That means I've an uncle. I wonder if he's still living in London.'

'He could be,' Toby said as he flicked through some of the photos.

'My dad always told me that his family were killed during the Blitz. He must have lied to me to cover up the fact that him and Mum ran away together. It must have been so hard for them, to have left their parents behind, and it must have broken my mother's heart to leave Johnnie. Harry must have been a nasty piece of work.'

'Well, if you think about Johnnie, it seems the apple didn't fall far from the tree.'

'Yes, I know.'

Toby took a letter from the top of the pile and began to read it. The date was from last year so the letters from Helen to Glenda had been sent for at least twenty years, and every time Polly's mum received one she must have squirrelled it away up in the loft. Polly was right, it was all very interesting but Toby feared that if she began to search for any long-lost relatives, she would be opening up a can of worms.

'You must have been up here for ages if you've read through that lot,' said Toby. 'Why don't you pack this up for now and I'll go and make a start on our dinner?'

'OK, just give me ten more minutes. I want to find the Christmas decorations and then I'll be down.'

It was some time away, but Toby was glad to hear Polly talk about Christmas. This would be her first since leaving hospital after her parents had been killed and he'd been worried that it would bring back painful memories for her.

He looked at her with adoration, admiring her strength and resilience, but noticed that she had gone very pale and her hands were shaking as she read one of the letters.

'Polly, is everything all right?'

She looked up, but it was as though she was looking straight through him as she murmured, 'Yes . . . I told you, I'll be down shortly.'

Toby thought her mood had rapidly changed and she was a bit offhand, but he put it down to the thoughts of Christmas. He left her to it and a while later, when she came downstairs, she looked pale but resolute as she said, 'Right, that's it. No more digging up the past.'

'Why? What did you find?'

'Nothing I want to talk about.'

'Is this to do with Christmas? I'll understand if you don't feel much like celebrating this year – you know, with all that's happened.'

Polly ran over to hug him tightly. 'You're so thoughtful. I must admit I didn't think I would either. It's been such a year, enough to drive anyone crazy, and I'm lucky not to be in a loonie bin, but as you've brought me so much happiness I feel we should really push the boat out. Honestly, Toby, after I lost Mum and Dad, I didn't think life could get any worse, but then there was the attack and Katy in jail and then all that nasty business with Johnnie.'

'Yes, you've certainly been through the mill,' Toby murmured as he held Polly to him.

'I never thought I'd be happy again, but then you came to stay with me and though it happened rather quickly, I'm so glad that our friendship has blossomed into love.'

Yes, thought Toby, they had drawn so close in just a

346

couple of months, and a week ago they had started to share a bed. He'd been so nervous the first night, fumbling and scared of hurting her, yet it had still been wonderful. He held Polly closer, saying, 'I'm glad I make you happy.'

'You do, and though I expect I'll be sad at Christmas when I think of Mum, and especially my dad as he loved Christmas so much, I'm determined to put this year behind me.'

Toby kissed the top of her head. 'I'm so proud of you. Most people would have been broken by what you've been through, but not you. You've dealt with it all far better than I could have. Do you know something, Polly?'

'No, what?' she asked, pulling back to look up into his eyes.

He saw the love in hers and his heart swelled. 'You really are an amazing woman and I'm lucky you're mine.'

Chapter 35

A few days passed and, thinking about what Toby had said, Polly felt a bit of a fraud. She didn't really believe she was amazing – if anything, she thought she was weak. Toby had no idea of the pain she carried inside, the big feeling of emptiness that followed her wherever she went and the fear that never left her.

She felt scared of everything, but most of all she was scared of being alone. She wondered if that was why she'd so readily fallen for Johnnie, out of that fear of loneliness. He'd been so keen to look after her and she had quickly accepted it, enjoying the feeling of safety and security he had given her. Was it the same with Toby? she wondered, but she quickly dismissed her doubts, reasoning that she had felt attracted to him a long time before it had blossomed into love.

The oven timer pinged and Polly took out the pie she had just baked in preparation for Katy and Jackie's visit. She was so excited about seeing them both and had spent days getting everything ready. The house was spotless, the autumn garden was blooming with chrysanthemums, and the three-course lunch she had prepared was filling the house with delicious aromas.

Polly felt a wave of nausea again, something she'd been troubled with lately, and wondered if she should see the doctor. It was then that a sickening thought struck her and she quickly did a mental calculation. Her periods had never been regular and with all that had happened she hadn't realised that she had missed not one but two and was about three weeks late for this one.

Her head began to swim and she hurriedly sat down. Oh, God, no, she was nearly three months pregnant, and that could only mean one thing: the baby was Johnnie's.

Jackie pulled over into a lay-by and reached behind her for the flask of tea that Polly had kindly filled for them. It was a long drive back home from Kent and though she had enjoyed spending the day with Polly and Toby, she was tired and in need of a break.

'You've been quiet, love. Are you OK?' Jackie asked her daughter, who had been silently looking out of the window during the journey.

'Yes, I'm fine, thanks, Mum. I've just been thinking about Polly and Toby.'

'Yes, I have too and I can't say I'm entirely happy about the situation. I think they've jumped into a relationship far too quickly and it will make things awkward if anything goes wrong,' Jackie said as she poured two teas from the flask and added some milk from a little jar. 'I can't say I'm surprised, though. Toby has liked Polly since he first set eyes on her. I had no idea she felt that way about him, though, did you?'

Katy took the cup of tea her mum offered and slowly sipped the warm liquid, but her eyes were still vacantly looking out of the window.

'I said, did you know Polly liked Toby in that way? Earth to Katy, hello . . .'

'Er . . . sorry, Mum, I was miles away. I'm not really sure how she felt about him.'

'The girl deserves a bit of happiness. I just hope it works out for them,' said Jackie as she started the car again.

'Mum, Polly told me something. It's not good and I don't know what effect it will have on her and Toby, but she's pregnant.'

'Really, so soon? Still, it's lovely, but hold on –' she paused, frowning '– what do you mean by saying it's not good?'

'The – the baby . . . it's not Toby's.'

'Don't be ridiculous, who else's could it be?'

Katy watched in silence as the shocking truth suddenly dawned on Jackie.

'Please, it can't be,' Jackie said. 'Don't tell me she's carrying her brother's child!'

It was eleven o'clock at night and the Battersea pubs were spilling out, but Johnnie and Liam hadn't been as lucky with the ladies as they'd hoped. They lingered at the bar, joining the other after-hours drinkers until the landlord turfed them out just after midnight. 'Oh, well, Johnnie boy, you can't win 'em all,' Liam said, almost incoherent with drink.

Johnnie looked at his friend, barely able to focus. He slurred a goodbye. 'Yeah, well, I'll see you.'

'Yesh, and shoon,' Liam called as he staggered off up the street towards where he lived in one of the housing association flats with his mother and two sisters.

Johnnie drunkenly thought that he wasn't sorry to see the back of him. He felt Liam held him back when it came to chatting up girls. Liam didn't dress as smartly as he did, and his conversation could be uncouth at times, which didn't do much to impress the ladies. In future, he decided, he was better off alone when it came to pulling a bird, especially the type he was looking for. He wanted them a bit older than him, which meant more experienced and able to take his mind off Polly.

As Johnnie reeled along and approached his flat he saw a young couple standing at the bus stop on the other side of the road. In the light of a streetlamp he recognised Sandra, a young woman he knew who did a bit of modelling and lived over Wandsworth way. It looked like she was crying, and as Johnnie knew the last bus would have gone he called out, 'Are you all right, love?'

Sandra was wearing a short fur jacket with a miniskirt and bright-green tights. Holding a tissue to her nose she called back, 'Yeah, I'm fine, thanks, Johnnie.'

The young bloke she was with began to cross the road towards Johnnie, his chest puffed out aggressively as he demanded, 'What's it got to do with you?'

Johnnie was a bit taken aback. After all, he'd only asked Sandra if she was all right, and he replied irritably, 'I ain't in the mood for this, mate. Just piss off and see to your bird.'

Yet the man kept coming towards him and Johnnie could see a menacing expression on his face as he spat, 'Who do ya think you're talking to?'

That was enough to fuel Johnnie's drunken irritation. 'So you want some, do you?' he growled as he faced him head on and, before the man could answer, Johnnie swung a punch that caught the man square on the jaw.

When he didn't go down Johnnie lashed out again, punching the man over and over as all his pent-up anger was unleashed. A black mist seemed to descend over Johnnie's eyes and he became lost in it, hardly aware of what he was doing. When the young man fell to the pavement, Johnnie flicked his hands in the air, shaking off the blood. He looked down at the unconscious man lying broken on the cracked, dirty pavement and felt a sense of satisfaction. It had felt good to hit him, to feel the man's bones crack under the force of his fist, to vent all his anger and frustration.

Sandra came screeching across the street. 'What have you done?' she screamed as she knelt down beside her boyfriend.

But Johnnie felt no remorse. 'He asked for it.'

'You bastard,' Sandra cried, and she jumped back to her feet and charged at Johnnie with her arms stretched out in front of her, going for his eyes with her long nails.

Johnnie swung another punch, this time hitting Sandra on the side of the head, knocking her to the ground. Stumbling slightly, she got back up again, looking dazed and confused. Johnnie wasn't going to wait for her to come at him again so he hit her hard on the nose, sending her reeling backwards as blood exploded from her face. This time she didn't get back up and Johnnie grinned as he stood over her. She was writhing on the floor, holding her face and quietly moaning. She looked up at him with terror in her eyes and removed her bloodied hands to speak. 'You animal! How could you do this to us, Johnnie?' she groaned.

Johnnie didn't care that the woman was scared and hurt. He had enjoyed the short-lived moment of punching her, and in a blind fit of anger he lifted his foot and brought it down on Sandra's face, rendering her unconscious alongside her boyfriend. It was as though all the anguish he had felt over Polly was pouring out of him in rage, leading to an almost uncontrollable desire to lash out.

He momentarily scanned the scene of carnage before him, breathing heavily, then made his way back to his flat to nurse his bruised knuckles before he could think too hard about what he'd just done.

In Kent, Polly pulled the bedclothes up to her chin and rolled over, her back towards Toby. She was unable to sleep and her thoughts drifted. It had been a long but lovely day and she'd been sad to see Jackie and Katy drive off back to Croydon. When they realised that Toby was more than a lodger now, they didn't seem surprised, though Jackie did look a little disapproving.

Thankfully it didn't spoil their visit, and she had managed to get Katy alone when the two of them had gone for a walk around the village, leaving Jackie and Toby to wash up the dinner dishes. It gave Polly the opportunity she had wanted to confide in her friend about the baby.

Lying in bed now, with Toby lightly snoring behind her, Polly thought about Katy's advice. She'd said that as the baby would be born white, she'd never be able to pass it off as Toby's, and would have to tell him the truth. She knew Katy was right, but dreaded telling Toby that she was going to have her brother's child. Would he still want to be with her? No, of course he wouldn't. She would lose him and the thought of that was more than she could bear. There was another fear too, one that was tormenting her; the fear that the baby would be born with something wrong with it because she and its father shared the same blood.

'Hey, darling, what's up, can't you sleep?' Toby quietly asked.

Polly realised her fidgeting must have woken him. 'No, sorry to have disturbed you. I'm OK, though, so go back to sleep.'

Toby put his arm over her and she flinched. She quickly jumped out of bed in a panic that he might feel a bump where the baby was growing in her belly.

Toby switched on the bedside light and sat up. 'What's up, love? I can tell something's bothering you.'

Polly desperately wanted to tell him but couldn't find the words so just stood, her eyes lowered.

'Come on, spit it out, there's obviously something on your mind,' he coaxed.

She sat on the edge of the bed, telling herself to just do it, to come straight out with it. Yet she couldn't just blurt out that she was pregnant or Toby would automatically assume he was the father. She took in a deep breath, unable to look at him as she said, 'You're right, there is something on my mind and it's a really difficult thing to tell you but . . . but I'm having Johnnie's baby. I'm three months pregnant which means it's impossible for this baby to be yours.'

There was silence as Toby digested what Polly had told him, but then she felt the bed move and heard Toby getting dressed. She turned to see him pulling a jumper over his head; he already had his trousers on. 'What are you doing?' she asked in desperation. This was not the reaction she had wanted, but the one she had feared.

'I can't handle this, Polly.'

'So what are you doing? Are you leaving me?'

'Polly, this is too much to take in. Johnnie's your half-brother, you're carrying his child, and I can't help it, but the thought of that repulses me. I've got to get out of here. I need a bit of fresh air.'

Polly was stunned, hated what he said, and as Toby left the bedroom she shouted after him, 'So, the thought of what happened with my brother repulses you, does it? Huh, it didn't bloody repulse you when you was having sex with me, did it!'

When the front door slammed shut, Polly curled up on the bed and cried. From Toby's reaction she doubted he'd stay with her now, and the fear of being alone raised its ugly head. She sobbed into her pillow, praying that Toby would come back home and tell her that everything would be all right.

Chapter 36

Sandra was vaguely aware of blue lights flashing and the sound of sirens blaring but couldn't work out what was going on. She felt cold and her head was throbbing. Two men were lifting her from the pavement and then she realised she was being stretchered into the back of an ambulance.

She groaned and a voice said, 'Don't worry, love. We're taking you to casualty.'

'Dan– Is Daniel OK?' she murmured to the ambulance man, recalling how the last time she had seen him he was lying flat out on the ground and she didn't know if he had been breathing or not.

'Don't worry, Miss. Your boyfriend is fine. He's sat up over there and talking to the police.'

The ambulance man's face was looking over her so appeared to be upside down but Sandra focused on him. 'It was Johnnie Jenkins. He did this to me and Dan. You have to tell the police.'

'Don't worry, they know and he's already been arrested. Someone in those flats saw you being attacked from their window and called the police.'

Safe in the knowledge that Dan was all right and

Johnnie was no longer a threat, Sandra closed her eyes as a wave of dizziness and nausea washed over her. She didn't know Johnnie well. They had met a few times through mutual friends but she hadn't realised he had such a violent temper on him. She'd heard his father used to have a reputation for being handy with his fists, and now realised that Johnnie must take after him.

'Can I have a mirror please? I–I want to see what he's done to me.'

The ambulance man paused before gently answering, 'It's best you don't look just yet. Wait until the doctors have seen to you.'

Sandra could tell from the man's voice that it was bad. She could see the pity in his eyes too and knew that Johnnie had seriously damaged her face. Strangely she couldn't feel any pain. She just felt numb. She raised a shaking hand and went to feel her cheek but was quickly stopped by the ambulance man.

'Please, Miss, just lie still and don't try to touch anything.'

Sandra feared she would never model again; her life would change for ever. But she was a determined woman and would make sure that Johnnie Jenkins paid for doing this to her and to Dan. She'd see that he was locked up for a very, very long time.

The sofa wasn't the most comfortable place to sleep and Toby rubbed his back, glad that it was Sunday and he didn't have to go to work. He couldn't hear any movement from Polly upstairs, but as he'd heard her crying into the early hours, she was probably still asleep.

The crisp autumn atmosphere didn't do anything to

change his feelings and Toby was resolute that he would be leaving today. Just the thought of that thing in her stomach turned his guts. As much as he loved Polly, he couldn't stand by and watch her give birth to her brother's baby, and if he was honest with himself, her brother or not, he didn't want to bring up another man's child.

He'd intended to surprise Polly with a proposal soon, but there was no way he was going to marry her now. As soon as she left the bedroom and came downstairs, he'd go up there to pack his things. He'd go back to his original plan and travel north to move in with his mother and aunt until he found his feet.

Toby's mouth was dry and he went to the kitchen and poured himself a glass of water. It was going to be hard to leave, and he knew it would hurt her, but he just couldn't stay. Moments later he heard Polly coming downstairs.

'You're going to leave me, aren't you?' she said as she walked into the room, her eyes red and swollen.

'This isn't easy for me, Polly, but yes, I'm leaving.'

'No, Toby, don't go. I can't do this by myself and I need you now more than ever.'

'Polly, I love you, but I'm sorry, I can't stay to see your belly swelling with . . . with that thing.'

'*Thing!*' Sudden anger darkened Polly's eyes. 'Is that what you think you can call my baby, a *thing*? How dare you! Yes, it's Johnnie's baby, but it's mine too, a part of me, and my baby is NOT a thing! Go on then, if you're going, go! There's no point hanging around.'

Her anger gave Toby the impetus to move and he hurried upstairs and shoved his clothes into a rucksack. As he did so, Polly walked into the room, contrite.

'Toby, I'm sorry I lost my temper. Of course you're upset, and that's why you said those things, but we love each other and surely we can find a way to make this work. Can't we?'

'How, Polly? Even if I wanted to, which I don't, that baby is going to be born white so, like you said, there's no way we could pass it off as mine,' he said coldly, brushing past her to go to the bathroom to grab his shaving kit and toothbrush. He stuffed them into a pocket in the rucksack and, closing his ears to Polly's sobs, hurried back downstairs and threw his keys onto the hall table.

He heard Polly cry out to him, but walked out of the front door and quickly closed it behind him. He was leaving the woman he loved, but knew he was making the right decision, the only decision that he could live with. He hoped Polly would be all right, but her unborn child was not his responsibility, nor one that he wished to take on.

Unsure of how he would get there with only a Sunday train service, Toby tried to put all thoughts of Polly out of his head and concentrate on new beginnings in Manchester, but it proved to be harder than he thought.

A light tap on the front door woke Harry from his afternoon doze. Feeling irritated, he went to see who had disturbed him and was surprised to find PC Redman on his doorstep. The policeman and Harry had been at school together and, though Micky Redman had felt Harry's collar a few times in their younger days, they had always had a quiet mutual respect.

'Micky, what brings you here? I haven't seen you for

ages. You ain't here to nick me for that bank job last week up the Junction, are you?' Harry said with a laugh.

'Hello, Harry. It's been a while. No, we've already got the blokes who did that job, but I do need to have a word with you.'

'You'd better come in then. Got time for a cuppa?'

'Yeah, that would be nice, thanks.'

Micky removed his helmet and sat on the sofa while Harry went to make the tea.

'Them bloody helmets you wear,' Harry said when he came back with the brew, 'every time I see one of you lot wearing them, I think to myself that it looks like you've got a bloody great tit on your head.'

Micky chuckled, 'Well, believe it or not, Harry, it's written in law that a pregnant woman can request to urinate in my helmet!'

'Well, I'll be buggered,' said Harry. 'You wouldn't want to be wearing your helmet after that!'

Micky sipped his tea. 'Harry, I shouldn't be telling you this, but we go back a long way and you have a right to know. It's your Johnnie, he's down the nick. I'm sorry to say that it's not looking too good for him. He could be facing a bit of a stretch.'

'What's he done? It ain't like Johnnie to be getting into trouble with you lot, not since that incident with riding in a stolen car.'

'I'm afraid this is a bit more serious than that. He's been charged with GBH with intent.'

Harry sat back in the armchair, flabbergasted. 'My Johnnie! Never!'

'Sorry, but a young woman has been seriously injured and there's a witness to prove he did it.'

Harry was sickened. First Johnnie had taken up with Polly, his half-sister, and now he'd beaten up a girl. Well, there was no doubt in his mind now. His son was a pervert and a coward, and as far as Harry was concerned the sick bastard could go to hell and rot in jail.

It had been a few days since Toby had left, and Polly was pining. She felt so alone, and very afraid of the future. The house felt so empty, just as it had when she first returned to Kent. On Wednesday, on her way home from work, she went to use the village telephone box to call Jackie, wanting to hear a reassuring voice telling her it would all be all right.

'Why don't you come and stay here for the weekend?' Jackie offered sympathetically. 'You know Katy would love to see you, we both would.'

'I don't know, Jackie. It's really nice of you to offer, but you know how Ross is with me and I'm not sure I can take it at the moment.'

'Don't you worry, I'll deal with him. You just get yourself on a train this weekend. Tell me what time it arrives and I'll meet you at the station. I won't take no for an answer.'

'All right then, and thanks,' she said, reassured. She needed to talk to someone and with Jackie being a nurse she would also have the opportunity to ask questions about childbirth, which she knew nothing about.

Back at home, Polly settled down in front of the telly and put her feet up on the sofa but her mind kept drifting to Johnnie and she wondered if she should tell him about the baby. It was such a mess. He was the baby's father and, if nothing else, when she had to give up work she would need some financial support. She sighed. She hated the thought of seeing him again.

She looked down at her belly, sure that it was bulging, and pretty soon there would be no hiding her pregnancy. It would cause a lot of gossip in the village, worse than when Toby had moved in, and as an unmarried mother she'd probably be pilloried.

Polly's thoughts continued to turn as she worried about her future. Not that she wanted one now, but no man would take on an unmarried mother and she would have to spend the rest of her life bringing this baby up alone. Once again she wondered how she was going to manage for money when she had to stop working. She didn't want her baby to go without, and it was then that Polly came to a decision. She would have to face seeing Johnnie again to tell him that he would have to share the financial burden.

On Thursday, Helen was just savouring the last mouthful of a thickly buttered toasted teacake when she picked up the local newspaper. She would normally flick straight to the horoscopes and then to the crossword but the headline on the front page caught her attention. The story was about a man charged with attacking a local model, and as Helen read on she almost spat out the last of her teacake when she saw Johnnie's name in print.

It was there, as bold as brass in black and white. Johnnie Jenkins had been arrested after violently assaulting a young couple. Helen's hands began to shake. She couldn't believe it, not of Johnnie, but then again he had proved that he wasn't the young man she'd thought he was. But to beat a woman! Surely he wasn't capable of that.

Helen quickly pulled on her coat and wrapped her head in a scarf before heading up to Northcote Lane, where she knew Harry was working. She passed the market stalls where the costermongers were shouting out their bargains, but hardly heard a word as her mind was focused on the appalling story in the local paper. Just off the main road Helen came to the site and soon spotted Harry, grafting hard even though the wind was blowing a gale.

She called out his name but her voice got lost on the wind so she called again, more loudly this time. Harry didn't hear but one of the builders did and caught Harry's attention. He clambered over the construction area and came to speak to her. 'I can guess what you're doing here.'

'I've seen it in the paper. Tell me it isn't true,' said Helen, hoping against all odds that Harry would say there had been a terrible mistake.

'What can I say? I wish it wasn't, but it is.'

'But, Harry, Johnnie wouldn't hit a girl. What he did with Polly was very wrong but this! Surely not!'

'The evidence proves he did it and I've washed my hands of him. There's nothing I can do for him and quite frankly I don't wanna know him no more. I don't hold with hitting women and by all accounts he did a right job on her, even stamped on her head.'

Helen could hardly believe her ears. Harry had obviously chosen to forget what he had done in the past. He had not only hit her, he'd hospitalised his wife. 'Harry, if you think back, I took a hiding from you and look what you did to Glenda! Maybe that's where Johnnie gets it from. He's turning out to be just like you. It seems it took a while for it to come out in Johnnie, but it's bad blood. You've both got bad blood and I'm just glad your mother didn't live to see how Johnnie has turned out.'

There was a time when Helen wouldn't have dared to talk to Harry like that, but he was a different man now and she was no longer afraid of him. She spun on her heel and marched back up the Northcote Road, saddened by what Johnnie had become, but pleased with herself for finally telling Harry a few home truths.

Harry went back to work, though as he laid bricks Helen's words still stung, and what she had said made him think. He'd only hit Glenda because she wound him up so much, and all right, he'd once lost his rag with Helen, but what Johnnie had done was totally different.

It wasn't as if Johnnie was a little boy any more. He was a grown man and responsible for his own actions and though Harry did feel a pang of guilt when he thought about Glenda, it wasn't enough to change his mind about his son. The boy was still a pervert and now it appeared he beat women for fun. Harry wanted nothing to do with him.

The afternoon dragged on but eventually it was knocking-off time and Harry could at last get the beer that he found himself craving. He hadn't been much of a drinker for years, but on this occasion he had a real thirst for a pint.

When Harry walked into the public bar at the Castle he found it hadn't altered much since the last time he'd been in, over ten years ago, though there was a new landlord behind the bar. He ordered his drink and stood quietly supping his pint. The liquid felt good as it went down his throat and Harry was already looking forward to his next pint. He didn't recognise any of the faces around him, but then the door opened and Harry frowned when he saw a familiar one. The man walked towards the bar.

'Evening, Pete, a pint of your finest, please.'

'Hello, Billy, how are you?' asked the landlord.

'All good, can't complain.'

'And the wife and kids?'

'They're all good. The missus has taken them up the Grand to see that *Chitty Chitty Bang Bang* film.'

'I know the one,' the landlord said, 'with that flying car. Mind you, I wouldn't fancy going to the Grand. It might sound posh but it's a blinking fleapit!'

'They ain't fussy,' Billy said with a laugh.

'Well, she can't be,' the landlord quipped, 'she married you!'

Harry put his pint down and turned towards Billy, saying, 'Well now, fancy seeing you here.'

After a moment's recognition, Billy Myers suddenly turned pale. 'Harry Jenkins, well, I never,' he said nervously and reached out to shake his hand.

Harry didn't take it, and still looking nervous Billy drew the landlord in, saying, 'This is Harry Jenkins. He used to be a regular in here but we ain't seen him for bloody years.'

'Is that right?'

When he didn't answer, Billy filled the silence. 'Well, Harry, it's good to have you back. Can I get you a drink?'

Harry could tell that the Castle wasn't the only thing that hadn't changed. Billy was still his creepy little self and he still had no time for the man. 'No, I'll buy my own pint.'

'Come on, let me get you a drink for old times' sake.'

Typical of the man, thought Harry, he never knew when to stop. 'I said no, Billy.'

'What's the matter with you? We used to be good mates. Go on, have a drink with me.'

Harry's irritation was rising but he bit his tongue. 'Don't kid yourself, Bill. We were never good mates.'

'I see, like that, is it?' said Billy and added with a sneer on his face, 'I'd have thought that with your Johnnie being banged up you could do with a mate, but suit yourself.'

That was it. Billy had gone too far and he shouted, 'You little shit! Who the fuck do you think you are to mention my son to me?'

'Calm down or I shall ask you to leave,' the landlord said quietly over the bar.

'No, it's all right, it's my fault,' Billy said placatingly. 'Sorry, Harry, I didn't mean anything by it.'

'Billy, I never liked you all those years ago,' Harry snarled, 'and I don't like you now, so get the fuck out of my face, you mug!'

'I'm no mug, Harry. I've still got my wife and kids, what about you?' Billy sneered, appearing to suddenly grow a spine. 'Oh, yeah, that's right, your wife left you, she ran off with my brother. Your mother's dead, your brothers don't have any time for you and your son is just like you, a nasty piece of work. Oh, and by the way, I've known for years where Glenda and Frank have been living so if anyone's a mug, you wanna be looking closer to home.'

Harry's eyebrows rose. For once the little squirt was standing up to him, but he couldn't let him get away with it. The trouble was, what Billy had said about Johnnie had deflated him, his words hitting home. He wouldn't let Billy see it, though.

'I admire your spunk, Billy, you ain't as much of a wanker as I thought, but that will be the first and only time you talk to me like that. Watch your back from now on,' Harry said menacingly. He picked up his glass, downed the last of his pint and snarled as he walked out, 'One more thing, Billy – your brother Frank – he's dead. Thought you might like to know.'

Billy's hands were shaking as he picked up his drink. He couldn't believe Harry hadn't hit him, but he would've been ready for him if he had. A long time ago he'd joined a boxing gym and had learned how to look after himself, so much so that it had given him the confidence to speak up to Harry.

Yet even so, Harry had still got the last words in, and they had left him stunned. He said Frank was dead, but how did he know? Had he found him? Billy's blood suddenly ran cold. The only way that Harry could know that Frank was dead was if he'd killed him.

He shook even more now knowing that he'd just fronted out a man who'd probably murdered his brother. He couldn't acknowledge feeling any grief at Frank's loss, but he did fear Harry's threat. 'Watch your back,' Harry had warned. Did that mean that the man was coming for him next?

Billy ordered a whisky, tossed it back and then straightened his shoulders. Let him come, he thought, knowing that Harry would never find him. He only had to work out the rest of the week then he and his family would be hundreds of miles away – living in Wales on his wife's parents' sheep farm.

Chapter 37

Polly followed Katy up the stairs and into her bedroom. She was glad that her best friend had chosen to stay at home and had forgotten all her dreams of moving to Australia. The smell of freshly baked scones wafted through the house, which made Polly feel even more welcome. She loved being back with Katy in Jackie's house and in some ways she wished she still lived there.

'I'm so sorry to hear that Toby left you,' Katy said, her eyes soft with sympathy.

'I miss him, but I've had time to think now, and I don't think he really loved me. If he did, he wouldn't have left me so easily.'

'How are you coping?'

'All right, I suppose, but I'm not sure how I'll manage financially. I think I might have to tell Johnnie about the baby and see if he'll help.'

Polly waited for Katy's response. She half expected her to say that Polly should never go near him again, but she nodded. 'At the end of the day he's the father and of course you'll need help. It won't be easy raising this child by yourself. You know how people can be about single mothers.'

'You're saying exactly what I've been thinking,' Polly told her.

Katy paused in thought and then said, 'Here's an idea. If Johnnie agrees, you could tell people that he's the baby's uncle and that way he could still be involved in the baby's life. It could work but it would be better than a scandal.'

'No, when the baby's born it would mean I would have to see him regularly and I don't want that. I just want his financial support.'

'All right, I can understand that, but do you know where he lives in London?'

'Only that it's in Battersea, but do you remember I told you about all those letters in the loft from my mum's friend Helen?'

'Yes,' Katy answered.

'Well, her address is written on them so I thought I'd go to see her. She should be able to tell me where to find Johnnie.'

'Would you like me to come with you?'

'Oh, Katy, it's lovely of you to offer, but I think this is something I need to do by myself, especially seeing Johnnie.'

'So when are you going?'

'I thought I'd go after having lunch here tomorrow. It's not that far from here so it'll save me travelling all the way from Kent.'

Jackie called from downstairs, shouting that a meal was on the table, so Katy and Polly joined her and Ross for a feast of toad in the hole. So far, whatever Jackie had said to Ross appeared to have worked: he ignored her, but he hadn't yet said anything derogatory.

'Have you had any prenatal care for the baby yet?' asked Jackie.

'Do we really have to discuss that spawn of the devil over our lunch?' Ross snarled without looking up from his plate.

A silence fell across the table, then Jackie very calmly placed her knife and fork on her plate. 'I've had enough of your attitude, Ross, and I've warned you about this sort of behaviour. You're supposed to be a man, the man of the house, but all you do is act like an insolent child and I've had it to the back teeth with you. This is my house and you will live under my rules. If you don't like it, then I suggest you pack your things and move in with your father.'

'I am not a child and you can't tell me where I'm going to live. I don't want to move in with my father.'

'Have you got any money saved?'

'No,' he said shortly.

'Well, then, you must know that if you want to move into a place of your own, you'll need to pay a deposit and rent in advance.'

'Fine, until I can raise the money I'll move in with Dad.'

'Good, I'll call him and tell him to expect you,' Jackie told him and with that she went to the telephone.

Polly felt very uncomfortable and didn't know where to look, but Katy reached out and placed a reassuring hand over Polly's as they sat in silence listening to the one-sided phone call.

'Yes, it's me,' Jackie said. 'I need you to come and collect Ross. Yes, he's moving in with you,' Jackie said down the telephone. 'Yes, that's right, he's coming to you . . . Well

I'm sorry if it interferes with your precious lifestyle, but he's your son too and it's about time you took some responsibility for him. Good, see you in an hour.' Jackie put the receiver down and turned to Ross. 'I'm sure you heard all that, so I suggest you go and pack your things.'

'This is ridiculous. I can't believe you're throwing me out.'

'You can hardly call it that. You've had more than enough chances to change your behaviour, but you chose not to. Anyway, it might do you some good to spend some time with your father. He might be able to do something about your attitude because I certainly can't.'

'All right, I'll go. I can see you'll be glad to be rid of me.'

There was an awkward silence and Polly glanced at Jackie who had hung her head and was slowly shaking it. She knew the woman well, and guessed that Jackie was about to offer an olive branch to her son. It just wasn't in Jackie's nature to reject anyone – she was the most caring person Polly knew – and the hurt expression on her face revealed how difficult she was finding this.

'Look, Ross, I'm angry with you now but I'm still your mum and always will be. I'll always love you but this is for the best for now. You can come back to see us when-ever you like.'

Ross threw his chair back. 'If that's how you want it, so be it, but don't expect me to visit you, not if her and that freak in her stomach are going to be here!' He stormed up the stairs.

Polly could feel tears beginning to prick at her eyes but tried to hold them back. That's what people were going to think of her baby, a freak or, like Toby had called it, a thing. Yet as she cupped her stomach she knew that she had already fallen in love with her precious cargo and felt protective towards her unborn child.

The rubber shower attachment sprang off the cold tap over the bath again, causing the hot water to almost scald Helen's head. Annoyed, she wrapped her hair in a towel and vowed never to wash her hair using that useless contraption again.

Her irritation was interrupted by a quiet knock on the front door and, still annoyed, she bustled along the hall to answer it, only to find a nervous-looking young woman standing there. As Helen took in the woman's features she nearly screamed, because for a split second she thought it was Glenda. Of course, that was impossible, Glenda was dead, but the penny dropped even before the young woman spoke.

'Hello, are you Helen?'

'Yes, and I've no need to ask who you are! You're Polly and, my goodness, you look just like your mother. Come in. It's so lovely to meet you though I did have the pleasure of meeting you a few times before.'

'Really? I don't remember.'

'Of course you don't. You were just a baby,' Helen said, showing Polly through to the living room and leaving her to admire the view from the eleventh floor whilst she went to make some tea. Waiting for the kettle to boil she rubbed her hair with the towel, then combed it through. Putting her curlers in would have to wait.

'It's amazing,' said Polly as Helen came back into the room with two cups, 'I've never been so high up before. You can see for miles!'

'Yes, it's quite spectacular. Anyhow, what brings you here and how did you know where to find me?'

'I found all the letters you sent to Mum, and it's funny really, but from reading them I feel like I know you. But I do have some very sad news about Mum –'

'It's all right,' Helen interrupted. 'I already know and I'm so sorry, love. It must have been horrendous for you and I'm really sorry about Johnnie too. As I was the one that sent him down to Kent, I feel responsible for what he did. Of course, at the time I had no idea that Glenda and Frank had been killed but even so, what he did to you was unforgivable.'

'It's not your fault. You did what you thought was right but it is Johnnie I've come to see you about.'

Helen's guard automatically went up. Surely the girl wasn't still harbouring feelings for Johnnie? If she was, Helen would have to talk some sense into her. There was no way she could encourage such a wicked relationship. 'What is it that you want to know about Johnnie?'

'Do you know where he lives?'

'I do, but even if it was possible, I don't think it would be a good idea for you to see him, not after what's happened. It wouldn't be right, Polly.'

'But I have to see him. It's really important,' Polly pleaded.

'Listen, love, I know you ain't got your mum around to talk to, but I know she would never have encouraged you to see Johnnie. Whatever you feel about him, you have to remember that he's your brother and that's all he can ever be to you.'

'You don't understand – I'm not in love with him, if that's what you think.'

374

'Good, I'm glad to hear it.'

'Helen, I need to see Johnnie because I'm pregnant and he's the father. He needs to know.'

'Oh, good Lord above! No, this is terrible. Blimey, I can understand why you need to see him now, but there's a bit of a problem. Johnnie has been arrested for . . . for . . . attacking a young woman and it looks like he's going to be doing time – quite a bit, I should think.'

Polly looked shocked at first, but then her eyes filled with tears. Helen reached for a box of tissues and handed her one, saying, 'I'm sorry, love, but it's probably for the best in the long run.'

'For the best! How can it be for the best?'

'I hate to say it, but Johnnie has turned out to be a bad lad, and he'd be an unfit father. Come on, dry those tears, things have a way of working out and I'm sure they will for you too.'

'But how? How's it going to all work out? I'm an unmarried mother and for all I know my baby may be born with all sorts of problems. You hear about it, don't you, when parents have the same blood. Oh, what am I going to do? I can't do this by myself!'

'How far along are you?'

'Over three months, and so . . . so I can't have . . . yet even if I could . . . I don't want an abortion.'

Helen thought that Polly was bordering on hysteria, and really, who could blame the girl? It was bad enough that she'd been intimate with her brother, but now the unthinkable had happened and Helen felt totally out of her depth to deal with this.

'Of course you don't, and you're not alone,' she offered. 'I'll be here for you and there's always Harry. He's the baby's grandfather and I'm sure he'd want to help out.'

'Harry – no way! I know what he did to my mum and he wanted to kill my dad. That man is mad and he's having nothing to do with my baby!'

'Listen, he's mellowed and he's so disgusted with Johnnie that he's disowned him. Nevertheless, the baby is his grandchild and I reckon he'd want to help you.'

'I don't think so. He came to my house and lost his temper with Johnnie.'

'Yes, with Johnnie, not you, and can you blame him?'

'Well . . . no . . . I suppose not, but if I let him into my baby's life, it would mean I would have to forgive him for what he did to my mum.'

'It was a long time ago, pet, and I really think that given the circumstances your mum would forgive him now. It's all water under the bridge, and remember – your mum wasn't totally blameless. Yes, Harry was a violent husband, but your mum did have an affair and, credit where credit's due, Harry was a good dad to Johnnie. Think on it for a while, Polly, but I believe your baby will be better off having its grandad in its life.'

Polly was quiet, obviously thinking, while Helen had to admit to herself that she wasn't overly convinced she'd given the girl the best advice. She just hoped that if Polly chose to go to see Harry, he'd be kind to her.

As they walked along the street together, Polly realised how much she enjoyed being in Helen's company. 'Have we got far to go?' she asked.

'No, love, and the house where Harry lives is the same

house he shared with your mum when they were married. It's hardly changed.'

'I'm beginning to doubt that this is a good idea.'

'What's the worst he can do, slam the door in our faces?' Helen answered. 'It'll be fine and, let's face it, apart from anything else you'll need some financial support, so there's no harm in giving it a go.'

'Just as long as you're sure that he won't get nasty.'

'Harry's fighting days are long behind him,' Helen said and soon she stopped outside a house. 'Right then, this is it. Are you ready for this?'

'Not . . . not really.'

'Deep breath,' said Helen and she knocked loudly three times on Harry's front door.

The inmate in the bunk above Johnnie was chuckling out loud, finding amusement in whatever book he was reading, but Johnnie didn't feel like laughing. He doubted he would ever laugh again.

If there was one thing prison did, it gave you time to think and that's what Johnnie had been doing . . . thinking long and hard. And now the reality of who he was had sunk in, leaving him feeling utterly disgusted with himself and ashamed of the man he'd become.

He had been pretty drunk when he had attacked Dan and Sandra, yet even through the haze of his blurred memories the image of Sandra's cheek hanging from her face was clear in his mind and he almost retched as he recalled the pleasure the sight had given him at the time.

It wasn't just reckless behaviour; it was sickening, monstrous, and he hated himself for revelling in the violence. Johnnie knew from what he'd read in the papers that he'd ruined Sandra's life. She would never work again as a model.

Johnnie rolled over in his narrow bunk, his mind still turning. He knew his rage and fury stemmed from his treatment of Polly, another innocent life he had ruined, yet somehow his guilt had become twisted into resentment. He didn't know if he had been furious with her for not wanting to be with him, with Harry for splitting them up, or with himself for committing incest and deliberately enticing Polly under false pretences. He just knew he had a burning rage within him that seemed to subside a little when he lashed out at Dan and Sandra.

But now his selfish ways and need for self-gratification had led to him being sentenced to nine years in this nick, which was no more than he deserved. He wondered if any of his family or friends would ever forgive him or talk to him again. He wouldn't blame them if they didn't. He couldn't forgive himself, so why should his father or Helen even try to?

He was locked away with some of the most sinister and evil minds in the country – with men who had carried out atrocious criminal acts, the worst kind of crimes. As Johnnie lay there, it slowly dawned on him. He was one of those men.

Harry had just finished hanging out his washing when he heard someone knocking on the front door. He wasn't in the mood for company so sneaked a look out of the front-room window to check who it was. If he didn't want to see them they could bugger off. He frowned when he saw it was Helen and Polly, and, wondering what they wanted, he went to open the door.

'Hello, Harry. I bet you're surprised to see us here,' said Helen, sounding falsely cheery.

'You could say that,' Harry answered.

'We don't want nosy neighbours eavesdropping on our conversation, so can we come in?'

'Yeah, all right,' he said, wondering why Polly looked so nervous.

They followed Harry through to the front room and he asked, 'So what's this all about?'

Neither answered, and then Helen said to Polly, 'Do you want me to tell him, love?'

'Ye–yes, please.'

Harry looked at Polly's frightened face and thought again that she reminded him so much of Glenda. She had her mother's eyes and nose and the same small frame. 'Look, why don't we all sit down,' he suggested.

Once seated, Helen said, 'Right, Harry, I'm not going to beat about the bush. I'll come straight out with it, but prepare yourself for a shock. Polly's in the family way and Johnnie's the father.'

Harry sat in stunned silence. He felt a wave of anger, but seeing that Polly looked petrified he forced it down. She'd been an innocent in all this, deceived by his son's lies. 'I'm sorry to hear that,' he said as softly as he could.

'Harry, this baby is your own flesh and blood, your grandchild,' said Helen.

'Yes, I think I've worked that out,' Harry told her.

'Polly came to see me, looking for Johnnie, but of course I had to tell her that he's been locked up.'

'What do you wanna see him for?'

When Polly looked at her helplessly, Helen once again spoke for her. 'Ain't it obvious, Harry? She's a young woman on her own with no family, and though she doesn't want anything to do with Johnnie, she was hoping he'd give her a bit of financial support.'

'There's no chance of him forking anything out. He'll be in prison doing a long stretch.'

'We were wondering if *you* could help her out, Harry. After all, it's your son that got her into this mess, and as she's more than three months gone it's too late to even think about an abortion.'

Helen's words hit Harry with a jolt and what he'd done to Betty came flooding back. She'd been having his baby and had died at the hands of a back-street abortionist, something he'd never forgiven himself for. God, he'd been a bastard to Betty. Was this his chance to redeem himself – to make up for what he had done?

'Harry, I hope your silence doesn't mean you're going to refuse to help.'

Helen had become a right feisty little woman lately, he thought, never too scared to tell him exactly what she thought of him. He remembered the time when he'd struck her to the floor and wished now that he'd been a better man. 'Yeah, all right, I'll offer a bit of money where I can.'

'That's good.' Helen beamed. 'How much are you thinking of?'

This was a step too far for Harry. She had spoken for Polly, said her piece, but Helen wasn't family and his finances were none of her business. 'I'm not being rude, Helen, but when it comes to discussing money, it's between me and Polly and I think you should let the girl speak for herself.'

'Yes, you're right,' she agreed. 'Polly, as long as you're

happy to speak to Harry alone now, I'll make my way home.'

'No, please don't go,' Polly appealed.

'Look, I can see that you're a bit scared of me, but there's no need,' Harry told her. 'This is family business and we've got a lot to talk about, but when we've sorted everything out I'll walk you back to Helen's place.'

'You'll be fine,' Helen told her. 'I'll see you later.'

Polly nodded reluctantly and Harry could tell she wasn't comfortable. He saw Helen out and then offered to make Polly a cup of tea, thinking that talking about Glenda might put her at ease.

'Polly,' he said, 'I've still got some stuff of your mother's, a bit of jewellery and her compact. While I'm brewing the tea, if you go upstairs to the first room on the left you'll find them in the dressing-table drawer. I'm sure she would have wanted you to have them.'

When Polly left the room, Harry walked through to the kitchen. Sending Polly upstairs served another purpose. He needed time to think about how much money he could afford to offer the girl. She might have inherited the house in Kent, and also have a job, so she wasn't exactly on her uppers, but when the baby was born she wouldn't be able to work for a while. Babies weren't cheap to run and at that thought Harry chastised himself. 'Cheap to run.' Huh, the baby wasn't a car.

No, it was his grandchild. He just hoped that it would be all right and not born deformed or funny, but if it was, well, they'd have to face that problem. He wondered if it would be a boy or a girl. He hoped for a girl, a perfect, pretty little thing, just like her mother and grandmother. What a shame Glenda was going to miss out on this, but then again, at least she'd been saved from the shame and hurt of how the child had been conceived.

Polly came back downstairs, walked into the front room and nearly took Harry's breath away. She was wearing Glenda's pearls. 'Polly, you're the absolute spit of your mother and she loved that necklace. It suits you, too,' Harry told her gruffly, his emotions all over the place.

'You . . . you used to hit her,' Polly said, at last finding her voice.

'Yeah, I know, and I won't blame you for hating me. I was a rotten bastard to your mother and if I had caught up with your dad, well, let's just say it was a good job I didn't. Look, love, I'm trying to say I'm sorry, but I'm not making a very good job of it. Your mother was a good woman and deserved better than me. I hope your dad treated her well and gave her a good life.'

'He did and they were very happy together. I didn't know until after they died that they weren't married! All those years and they were living in sin. It's funny really, I'm a bastard and now . . . now I'm carrying another one.'

'Now then, don't you go saying things like that, and anyway, what does it matter? Your mother was with your dad for donkey's years, far longer than she was married to me, and as far as I'm concerned that makes her as good as his wife. When I look back now, I can see that I drove her off. I just wish I'd got the chance to tell her that I'm sorry.'

'It sounds like you really did love her.'

'Yes, I did, and I never stopped,' he told her, glad to see that her fear of him seemed to have gone. He'd seen that same fear in Glenda's eyes and he didn't want to see it in her daughter's. 'Come on now, sit down. I've made the tea so let's get down to business.'

Polly sat at the table, fingering the pearls, and then said, 'I'm not sure about this. None of this Johnnie business is your fault so I don't think I can take money from you.'

She's a lovely girl, thought Harry, Glenda would've been so proud of her. Unlike some women she wasn't out for what she could get, she was just a very scared and vulnerable young woman facing an uncertain future, with no parents or husband to help her through it. An idea began to form and he asked, 'Is this the first time you've been to Battersea?'

'Yes, though it isn't far from friends of mine in Croydon.'

'Battersea ain't a bad place, and not far from here there's a lovely park with a funfair, a boating lake, a zoo and fountains.'

'That sounds nice.'

Harry pressed on. 'It's not a bad place to raise kids and I've been doing a bit of thinking. I know I've done a lot of bad things in my life, I've hurt people, and it's time I made up for it. I don't think you should be left to cope alone, so what I'm offering you and that grandchild of mine is a home here with me. I'm not filthy rich or anything, but I've been on my own for a long time with nothing much to spend my wages on, so I've got a fair few bob tucked away. It means I can look after you both when it comes to money and I'll treat you like the daughter I never had. I think it's what your mum would have wanted from me and, after what my son has done, it's the least I can do.'

'But what about your friends and neighbours? I won't be able to hide that I'm pregnant.'

'It's none of their business, but no doubt when they see I've taken you in and your belly swelling, they'll assume it's Johnnie's. There's no need for them to know that he's your half-brother, and Helen won't open her mouth.'

Polly began to cry, which Harry hadn't seen coming. He jumped up and fumbled around for a hanky to give her. She took it, wiped her eyes, sniffed, and then sat looking down at the table. Harry hoped she was thinking it over. He gave her a couple of minutes and then said, 'It's up to you, love. I won't be offended if you turn my offer down.'

To Harry's surprise Polly suddenly jumped up and kissed him on the cheek, saying emotionally, 'I don't care about the money. I was just dreading being left on my own. After listening to all you've said, who better to live with than my baby's grandfather?'

Harry found that he was dead chuffed at the thought of Polly moving in with him. His house had never been a home since the day Glenda had left, and it was funny how things worked out, almost turning a full circle.

'That's all sorted then,' he said with relief, 'and I don't know how you feel about this idea, but if you own that house in Kent you could rent it out. It would give you a bit of independence, your own money, but of course it's up to you,' Harry said, not wanting to sound controlling.

'I think that's a brilliant idea,' Polly said, smiling and looking so much brighter than when she'd arrived.

Another thought crossed Harry's mind. 'There's just one more thing . . . about Johnnie. Do you still want to tell him about the baby?'

'I don't know. What do you think?'

'Well, love, if he doesn't hear it from you, there's a chance he might hear it from someone else, but after what he's done I don't suppose you'll want him involved in the child's life.'

'No, I don't think I do,' Polly said.

'There's no need to worry about that now. It's going to be many years before he's released so we'll cross that bridge when we come to it. Come on, get that frown off your face. When the time comes, trust me, I'll take care of Johnnie.'

'Yes, I really do think I can trust you,' she said, 'and because I realise that now, there's something else. I think you should see this . . . I found it in my loft. It . . . it's a letter my mother wrote to Helen, but never posted. She . . . she says that . . . that she's going to have a baby, but she doesn't know who the father is.'

Harry frowned as he read the letter, the paper yellow with age, dated at the top *December 1947*. It hit him like a tonne of bricks and he reeled in shock. 'This . . . this means you could be mine! My daughter!'

'Yes, I could be, though in my mind Frank will always be my dad.'

'Yes, well, he's the one who brought you up so I can understand that,' Harry said.

'I haven't told anyone else about this.'

'Yeah, well, maybe it's for the best that we keep it just between ourselves, and though I may never know for sure if you're my daughter or not, this settles it, my girl. When are you moving in?'

Polly smiled. 'I'll have to go back to Kent to hand my notice in at work and to sort out tenants for the house, but once that's done I'll be back.'

'I'll be looking forward to it, and in the meantime I'll get the spare room decorated. After that I'll see about getting a cot, and a pram.'

'There's no need to buy them yet. The baby isn't due for six months.'

'Well, I can still look around, check them out. After all, I only want the best for the nipper and for my girl!'

Polly grinned and, patting her stomach, she said, 'Did you hear that in there? I think you're going to have the best grandad in Battersea!'

Q&A with Kitty Neale

1. Where do you get your writing inspiration from?

My stories are mostly set in and around the area of London where I grew up, and my working class roots are reflected in the lives of my characters. My books tell of the hardships and challenges faced by many families in the post-war era. Inspiration will begin when a character and a realistic situation pops into my head. From there, a story will form, though I often find myself writing something completely different from what I originally planned.

2. How do you get inside your character's heads as you write?

I often feel like an actor but one with many roles all in the same film! I literally imagine I am the character I am writing about, and in my head I even have different voices for them. I place myself in the scene, and look at my surroundings, but I have to switch quickly from one character to another which is where it is useful to have the different voices.

3. What tips would you give to those who want to try their hand at writing?

Just do it! I wish I had started years before I actually did. I found there was a lot to learn about setting out a book with regard to things like punctuation, past and present tense, viewpoints etc., but don't get too hung-up on the technicalities. Write your book, learn as you go along and if you're lucky enough to get published, listen to the advice of your editor.

4. What is your own favourite literary character and why?

It has to be Bridget Jones. I think she has many aspects to her character and most women will find something about her they can relate to. She's intelligent and funny, yet often awkward and goofy. It's refreshing to have a heroine who isn't drop-dead gorgeous. In fact, she's a bit overweight but still very sexy.

5. How long does it take you to write your books?

How long is a piece of string? It can vary, depending if I'm 'flowing' or not. On average, I would say four to six months, but that's not writing all day, every day. The trick is to resist the urge to keep going back and adding or changing what has already been done.

You can never leave a bad man behind . . .

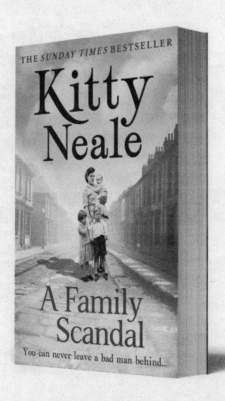

A gritty and emotional family drama from the *Sunday Times* bestseller.

A Family Scandal is your next must-read!

How far would you go to find happiness?

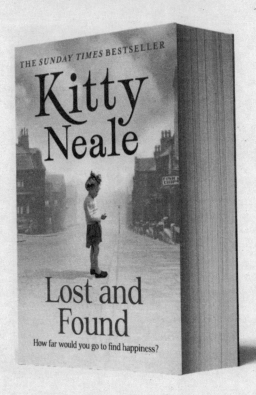

Bullied by everyone around her for years, has Mavis Jackson finally found happiness?

Or has she jumped straight from the frying pan into the fire?

A mother must fight for all she holds dear . . .

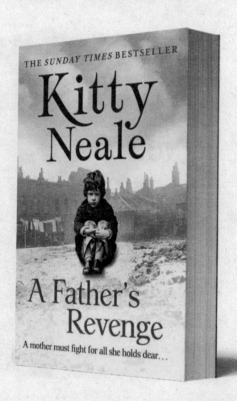

THE *SUNDAY TIMES* BESTSELLER

Kitty Neale

A Father's Revenge

A mother must fight for all she holds dear…

In this tale of revenge and family feuds,
a mother must put her life on hold
in order to save her son from
her abusive ex-husband.

Abandoned and alone, you'll do anything to survive . . .

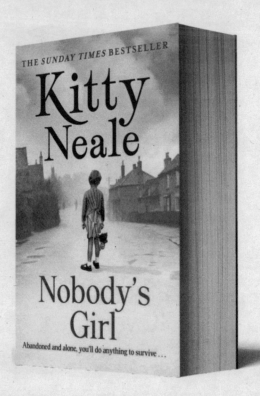

Left on the cold stone steps of an orphanage,
only a few hours old and clutching
the object which was to give her name,
Pearl Button had a hard start to life.

But will adulthood be any better . . . ?

The past *always* comes back to haunt you . . .

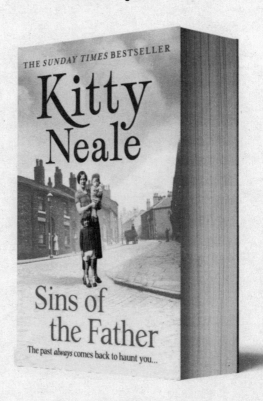

Desperate. Degraded. In danger . . .

Emma Chambers has a way out of the poverty-stricken life she lives – but it might just destroy her to take it . . .